A MILLION
D$LLAR BOY

WITH A BILLION-DOLLAR DREAM

SHARRIEFF ALI MCGEE

This is a work of fiction. All of the characters, names, incidents, organizations, and dialogue in this novel are either the products of the author's imagination or are used fictitiously.

Archway Publishing books may be ordered through booksellers or by contacting:

Archway Publishing
1663 Liberty Drive
Bloomington, IN 47403
www.archwaypublishing.com
844-669-3957

ISBN: 978-1-4808-9740-3 (sc)
ISBN: 978-1-4808-9741-0 (e)

Library of Congress Control Number: 2020919636

Print information available on the last page.

Archway Publishing rev. date: 10/14/2020

PROLOGUE

P Double was fucking the shit out of Sweetness. He had bagged the bitch about six months earlier, when he went on the run, down in Kinston, North Carolina. Sweetness was the baddest bitch in the whole damn town. On some real shit, she had the body of Ki Toy with the face of Alicia Keys. The only thing sour about the broad was she had one of the nastiest attitudes known to man, and she was a world-class stripper.

"P, fuck this pussy, uhh, yes, P, yes!" she said with the hunger for more.

P had her chocolate ass spread-eagled on their imperial-size mattress, facing the mirror. He was drunk off of Hennessy, so he had been giving the pussy a black eye for forty-five minutes now. Plus, you really had to fuck Sweetness long and hard to shut her the fuck up. His phone had been ringing off the hook for the whole forty-five minutes when he just burst all up in her.

"Oh, P, I'm nutting too, daddy! Oh shit!" She quivered. Then her pussy started to gush like a hot spring. She fell facedown, said, "Thank you, daddy," and fell asleep. P grabbed a towel and his phones and headed for the shower. He liked his bathroom with the solid gold tub and faucets. The tub was also a Jacuzzi with a deluxe whirlpool and built-in TVs with his PlayStation. Even his sink and toilet were made of gold, while the floor and walls where made up of the finest marble. Just when P was about to hop into the shower, his phone rang.

"What's good, Moe?" he answered.

"Shit, why the fuck you ain't been answering your phones, my nigga?" Moe said. Moe was a nigga from his block back in Springfield, Massachusetts.

P was a don, and Moe was his student. Basically, Moe was the Jay-Z of the field, because to that day, he hadn't done time. But still, P Double didn't answer to anyone.

"Who the fuck you think you screaming at, lil nigga?" P said.

Moe responded with, "Just shut up and listen, God. Fatback just died," with hurt in his tone.

"You can't be serious!" P screamed. "If Tanto or one of them Ave niggas ... I swear—"

Moe cut him off real quick. "I said shut the fuck up and listen, my nigga. He got in a motorcycle accident on Maynard Street. He just won a quarter million dollars off the Dreads on Dunmoreland Street. He was going to pick up Brandy and stash the funds when someone backed out their driveway, and he smacked into them."

P said, "No, it can't be, Moe, but how?" with no strength left in his voice. He let the phone drop into the shower water he had running. P just started thinking about how Money made his clique what it was in the first place and how the Bristol Street crew grew up to be what it was.

CHAPTER 1

GROWING UP FAST

Presley Williams was young and athletic at an early age. He was sixteen and already living in the fast lane. He was five feet ten and light-skinned and looked exactly like a young Nick Van Exel. He was a member of the Marlborough Street Posse, or MSP. They had their side of Springfield on smash.

P had just finished his pack when he went to go see Eddie Haul. Ed was a ghetto legend around his way. All the younger cats P's age looked up to him because he had money, power, bitches, and the utmost respect. As P walked up to the duplex on Bristol Street, he saw the brand-new 535 BMW Coup outside of Ed's crib. It was powder blue with chrome rims and the darkest tint P had ever seen.

"Damn, one day, I'm gonna be that nigga," he said to himself.

As he was about to ring the doorbell, the door flew open with grace, and the sweetest perfume the young thug had smelled in a long time came through the air. Mama came into view, and my, was she a sight to see. She had the fattest ass in the world—no doubt she was the new-wave Rosie Perez, with her high-maintenance ass. I mean, the bitch had on this black Gucci catsuit with the matching pumps, and she was Spanish. P loved the way she purred his name when she spoke.

"P Double, come on in, baby boy," she purred. "Ed's been expecting you. He's in the kitchen."

"Thanks, Mama," the young boy shot back on his way to the lab in the basement.

Ed called his lab "the kitchen" because he was a master chef when it came to that crack cocaine. On his way to the lab, P had to stop and look at the fish tank. Every time he came, he looked at the big 250-gallon tank with exotic fish. Ed had five fatulla sharks that just ate goldfish all day long. It was 1990, and back then, Ed's crib was what you would call *laced*. His favorite team was the North Carolina Tar Heels, so his whole living room was baby blue and white. The carpet was two inches thick, and it was baby blue, while the leather furniture was baby blue and white. Even the nigga's TV was baby blue.

Nobody knew what Ed's bedroom looked like. He told P one day when he first started fucking with him that if a nigga knew what your bedroom looked like, either he was fucking your bitch or trying to steal from you, so you gotta kill that nigga, no questions asked.

As P descended the stairs, he announced himself, "Yo, Ed, it's P," he said.

Ed said, "Come on down, lil nigga; it's almost ready."

The whole basement smelled like straight fish scale, which is pure cocaine. The lab was serious; Ed had the same setup downstairs as he had in his living room, except his stereo system was bigger. At the time, he had Brand Nubian banging out the speakers. "Slow Down" was that shit. Ed had a gas stove down there that he was slaving over. He was cooking a kilo, and he had another one on the table ready for rock.

"What's up, lil nigga? How the streets been treating your crazy lil ass?" Ed said.

"Bad. If you don't hurry up with this batch, my pager is blowing up right now," the young god quoted.

"Damn, young blood, you look stressed. Sit down, and take the load off your feet," Ed said as he whipped the caine over the fire. "What's wrong this trip, P? You short or something?"

"Nah, Ed, it's nothing like that. I got your grand right here, and I got two of my own. It's just them Ave niggas again. Man, you know they deep as fuck; last night, they caught Bates up around their way, and they fucked him up bad. I mean, he was black and blue. You know that nigga is a redbone. As soon as I got word, Fatback and I stole a car and shot Stymie's mother's crib up on Quincy Street. I just hate them niggas," P said with a grimace.

Ed splashed a little cold water into the pot and said, "I know what you mean, but you're wrong, P. You never bring war to another man's doorstep unless you want it at yours. You already know how you feel about your grandmother; why would you put her at risk?"

"Come on, Ed. You already know I had the black hoodie on low. Man, nobody saw shit. But you're right though," P said.

"I know I'm right, P. Remember this, if you don't remember shit else."

"And what's that, Ed?" P asked.

"You can't get money and beef at the same time, lil nigga," Ed said just as he dumped the caine out of the pot onto some paper towels. Then he looked at P and started to break the giant rock in half so it could dry quicker. "I didn't get to where I'm at from beefing and look."

"I feel you, but I'm doing just fine—plus, I'll be damned if niggas run all over me," P snarled with a sour expression on his face.

Just then, Ed pulled out a MAC-10 from under the table and pointed it at P.

P jumped back and said, "What gives?" with a quizzical look.

"What are you trying to say, P? That I'm a bitch nigga because I love my money and my bitches? I been put in my work, boy; remember that," Ed said with an angry look.

"Naw, dog, I din't mean nothing by what I said, Ed. If it sounded wrong, that's my fault; I didn't mean shit by it. You know you got my respect."

Ed was nineteen, but as far P was concerned, he was an OG that you could learn a lot from. Ed put the gun down and turned the fan on to dry the caine. He then went to the minibar downstairs and grabbed a green Garcia y Vega and told P to roll up while he poured a double shot of Hennessy. He washed his hands, poured them both shots, and said, "You know what? I like your little ass, so I'm gonna treat you like my son and show you how to get that real money, lil nigga. The real money is in what you just seen me doing, and that's cooking this shit. I'll show you when you can stack ten grand," Ed said.

P said, "Thanks, Ed; that's what's up. But I really gotta get moving right now."

"Are you trying to rush me, boy?" Ed asked.

P said, "No, but how am I gonna stack ten grand sitting here talking to you?"

"That's what I like about your hardheaded ass." Ed smiled. "Give me that three grand and take these nine ounces. Bring me back four grand."

P looked happy as all hell and said, "Thanks, Ed. I swear I won't let you down—I promise."

Ed said, "Here. Be safe; holla back when you're done, and make sure you tell Fatback and them niggas to holla too."

As P walked away, he said, "All right, peace."

Ed said, "One more thing, P."

P got scared and thought Ed was gonna take the 250 grams back.

"Tell Mama to lock the door behind you and get her fine ass down here at once."

As P was coming out of the basement, he saw the fine-ass Mama on the couch with her legs up watching *Yo! MTV Raps*. He told her what Ed said, and she shouted, "Damn, that nigga just want his dick sucked."

P left and ran down the block to where he had his illy Acura Legend parked. He pulled it earlier in the day, so he figured he'd be at least safe until tomorrow. All he had to do was man over the whip a couple blocks over so he could bag up the caine at his grandmother's house. When he got there, he kissed his grandmother on the cheek, and she said, "Tinco, what was that for?"

He stepped back and said, "I just love you more and more each day; that's all."

After that, P ran to his room and locked the door. He threw the .380 automatic on the bed with the nine O's and bagged up a half ounce. Then he stashed the rest. Just then, he looked at his pager and saw that while he was talking to Ed, he'd gotten ten new pages. Six of them were sales—he told them he was on his way—two of them were from bitches he would fuck later on that night, and the other two were from his men Fatback and Lil Kev, his road dogs.

Fatback was a little, fat, hardheaded motherfucker who was always ready to beef at the drop of a dime, or for anything really. He must've gotten that shit from his mother, because she was even crazier than he was. He told P she beat two bitches with a hammer the other day. Mrs. Back was a beast in her own right.

His man Kev was a money-getting-ass nigga. He always had the latest kicks on no matter what, and he had mad bitches.

P hit Kev up first. "What up, B?" P said.

Kev said, "What's popping tonight, besides Moist Monica?" Monica was this Malado bitch all the cliques used to run trains on. At the age of sixteen, she was the only bitch giving head in her age bracket.

"Fuck that bitch," P said. "I got some bitches in Colonial Estates that are ready when we are."

"So it's a date," Kev said. "I'll hit you up later—right now, I got to go see Ed."

P said, "Ain't nothing wrong with that; I just came from over there. I wanna fuck Mama bad, Kev."

Kev said, "You?" with ferociousness in his voice.

"I'll fuck the shit out of that bitch. Ed's a lucky dude," P said.

Kev hollered, "Not really; we will have a shot at the title one day. Be cool, my nigga. Until later, peace."

As soon as P hung up the phone, he called Fatback and told him he was on his way. But first he needed to make a couple bucks, so he had to make a couple plays first. He had made five of them already, but he couldn't wait to make it to the sixth one's crib, because Mimi was a fly-ass basehead. The bitch kept herself up because she worked at MassMutual Insurance Company. P came up when he met this bitch because she was one of his mother's friends, but she started smoking on the low. She was good for at least three hundred dollars a week. Mimi had a one-family house on Fenwick Street that she owned by herself. P couldn't figure out why she wasn't married. He thought she was a dyke because the bitch was a mirror image of Toni Braxton with no man. P parked the Legend in front of her crib and looked in the mirror in the car. A nigga always had to look his best fucking with Mimi. He lit a Newport and stepped out of the Legend on his dean. Young P stayed fly; he had on a red Champion hoodie, red-and-white Francis Girbaud jeans, and matching Champion sneakers, which were red-and-white suede, on his feet.

P dusted his shoulder off and walked up her steps with the confidence of a grown man ahead of his time. She had the door open, but the screen door was locked. So he knocked lightly to make his presence known. Mimi came to the door with some pink Puma tights on and a Puma top to match. She gave that award-winning smile and told him to come in.

Then she said, "P, you sure are growing up, nigga. You stay in the latest getup."

The god shrugged it off and replied, "I try to do what I do, Madame Mimi."

She blushed and said, "Nigga, don't call me that; you make me feel old."

P got kinda nervous and said, "I'm sorry, love, but what is it you need, Mimi?"

She sat down and told P to sit down for a minute. He was smooth, calm, and collected when he sat. She suddenly jumped up and said, "Damn, what kind of woman am I not to offer you a drink, young man? What are you drinking, P?"

He sat back, put his arm on the armrest of Mimi's couch, and said, "Hennessy on the rocks, if you don't mind."

She said, "Boy, that's a man's drink."

That was when P shot her a look that could kill and said, "Are you questioning my manhood, Mimi? Because this cat right here has always been the coolest man in two shoes, baby doll. Now be a good girl and fetch my medicine before things get ugly."

She looked at P with that *you-go-boy* look and went and got his drink. When she left the living room, P wiped the sweat off of his forehead and said, "Bitches. Can't live with them; can't live without them." For a minute, he sat back and looked at Madame Mimi's pad, which was decorated with the finest taste possible. I mean, she had the big sixty-inch TV with a Pioneer sound system that had two eighteens with the crazy wood grain. Her living room was decked out in gray and black. She had two lamps on her end tables that looked like they came from China somewhere. Even the grandfather clock she had in the living room was gray and black.

P got off the all-black leather recliner and looked at the shelf of books she had. On the shelf she had *Roots*, Machiavelli's *The Prince*, all of Sidney Sheldon's novels, and a book called *The Art of War*. The rest were money management and self-help books. He picked up *The Art of War* just when she swaggered in the room with them pink-ass tights on. She handed him the drink, swigged a sip from her own glass, and licked her lips as she spoke.

"So I see you picked up *The Art of War*."

P said, "Yeah, I can always learn some new shit to add on to my gangsta."

She looked him up and down and said, "P, is that all y'all young cats think about? Is being a gangsta?"

He looked her up and down and said, "No, not really, but do you really wanna know what I'm thinking about?"

She said, "Shit. Shoot, daddy."

P took a sip of his drink for this one and hollered, "What's on my mind right now, Mimi, is—damn, how can I say this …" He paused for a second. "You're wearing the fuck out of those tights." And he smacked her on the ass after he said it.

She answered back, saying, "You couldn't handle this sweet pussy if you were old enough." And she smacked him back on his ass.

P just laughed and threw fifteen joints on the counter. "Here you go, ma. You owe me three hundred." She kissed P on the cheek and said, "Thank you."

P said, "No problem, ma," and walked out the door and down the steps. His first move was to look up and down the street. You always had to be on point fucking with the Ave niggas. The coast was clear, so he hopped in the Legend and started her up. His pager went off immediately, letting him know he had ten unanswered pages. He put the seat back and cracked a Vega. Young P still had some ty stick from last night. He scanned his pager; seven feins needed servicing, and Fatback had paged him twice. The other page came from Little Lee. Lee was the kind of nigga who would always talk shit when they were deep, but if he got caught with his pants down on the wrong side of town, you best believe he was a world-renowned track star.

P Double roasted his el and turned his radio on. Chubb Rock filled the airwaves with, well, coming back. In 1990, Chubb jumped on the scene with a lean and a hard-core dream. P relaxed with that first choke of ty stick and drove down the street to Cumberland Farms, where he called all his plays and Little Lee back. "What up, Lee? I'm on my way to grab back right now."

Lee said, "Okay, come and snatch me up too."

P took another choke of that good and said, "Done. Give me a lil minute." And then he hung up. He made a quick seven off the half and then went and picked Fatback up.

Back hopped in screaming, "What took you so long, my nigga? Damn, you know my mother is crazy as hell. I gotta stash my money before I walk in the house or get taxed every time."

P just yawned and passed him the el. Back took a couple chokes and mellowed out while P drove to Lee's crib. On the way there, Back pulled out a big forty-four Magnum revolver. That shit had to be the Dirty Harry edition.

When P saw that shit, he said, "Damn, Fatback, where you get that shit from?"

Fatback laughed. "I won this shit in a card game from crazy-ass Jim Brown."

Jim Brown was a crazy-ass MSP veteran who would stand on the block with a shoulder holster on like he had a gun license or something.

Lee was already sitting on the porch when they pulled up. Lee hopped in and said, "You didn't have to do it like that, P, car matching with what you got on!"

The outside was cherry red, and the inside had the plush leather white seats you just sank into. Back got mad and said, "That's all you do is dick ride, nigga. When are you gonna be your own man, little nigga?"

Lee rolled his eyes and said, "Little nigga, I get more money and pussy than your fat ass could ever get, bitch nigga!"

"Bitch nigga!" Back snarled. "Hold up. I'll show you how bitch I am, punk!" and he reached for the door handle. P grabbed Back's arm because even though they were all boys, Back didn't play that, the calling him out of his name shit.

Double spoke in a calm manner. "Both you cats cut the bullshit, or I'm leaving y'all right the fuck here."

They both said, "My bag," at the same time and showed each other love, but Fatback still had to have the last word.

"Lee, you already know I'll smack the fuck out of you still, chump."

Lee laughed, said, "Whatever," and threw a Garcia Vega on Fatback's lap. "Make yourself useful, fat boy, and roll up."

"I got your fat boy nigga word." P started laughing and pulled off.

Fatback said, "What's up with some drink? First round is on me."

P and Lee looked at each other and said, "That's what's up." And he banged a right off West Ford Circle and onto Dunmoreland Street, heading to J&J's package store. P was whipping the Acura with precision as he pulled into the full parking lot. There were mad junkies and winos in the lot.

Fatback rolled down the window and called over this crackhead dyke bitch named Weenie, "Yo get the fuck over here, bitch. Where's my fucking money?"

As he stepped from the Acura all in one quick motion, P and Lee shook their heads because they already knew what Back was about. She looked at him like he was a lil nigga and rolled her yellow eyes. She squeaked, "I know your fat ass ain't acting up over twenty bucks." That was it. Back just cuffed her with three vicious smacks that split her lip and busted her nose.

As she fell to her knees, she pleaded, "Please, Mr. Fatback, no more," in a scared voice. Little did she know that just enticed the boy, because he pulled out the big forty-four Magnum and grabbed the fein by her hair. Then he really went to work pistol whipping the bitch ferociously. P and Lee hopped out of the Acura and grabbed Back because he was out of control.

"Bitch, you think you a man? I'll beat you like a grown-ass man."

The dyke bitch got up and ran her fastest mile ever. P and Lee had Fatback contained for a sec.

P looked at back and said, "Damn, you almost killed her nigga."

Back was breathing heavily when he gasped, "What the fuck you think I was trying to do? Now get off me."

As they let him go, he brushed himself off and tucked the forty-four back into his waist. He called this other basehead named Westbrook over. Westbrook was a skinny giant of a man, with rotten teeth and dirty clothes. The man's hair was almost dreaded by its looks, and his feet were coming out of his British Knights. The giant approached the boys on shaky legs and in a cracked voice, squealed, "Please, Mr. Fatback, I swear I don't owe you nothing, and I didn't see nothing." He went on.

Fatback looked at him with a nasty aftertaste. Truthfully, the giant's breath smelled like a dirty diaper. So he answered by saying, "Shut the fuck up, bitch nigga. Say another word, and I'll push your shit straight back. Now nod your bitch-ass head if you understand."

The fein nodded, scared for his life. Back then pulled out thirty bucks and told the chump, "I'll get two green Garcia Vegas and a fifth of Hennessy."

The giant walked off and came back with the package minutes later. Back gave the man two ones and made him promise to buy two packs of Big Red gum. The fein walked away and nodded his head when Back shouted, "Nobody wanna smell your nasty ass and your breath at the same time."

Just then, Five O rolled by, so they walked the other way to Bird's New York boutique. They went inside, where there were a bunch of older cats from around the way playing blackjack for high stakes. This was big-boy night for real. Mike Tuitt was there with this used black-and-white suit that had to at least cost four hundred. He had the illest gold fronts with a giant herringbone chain controlling the deal. He had way more bucks than Ed, but he didn't believe in fucking with little niggas, period. Lan and Dave were there as well. The nigga Lan had all the block money fucked up. He was like Fabio, a pretty-ass nigga who had a 740 BMW and the bitches to ride in it. He also had mad guns for sale. He had the most beef because he stayed fucking the next nigga's bitch. Dave was a chocolate Mack like his boy, but Lan had the brains. Anybody could see that. Jim Brown's crazy ass was there, as was Ed. Bird had his daughter Miss Bee running the store. She was a fine piece of pussy, but you already know Lan had that little pussy wrapped around his finger.

Lee said, "Shit, at least they got some new clothes in here."

Back said, "Fuck the clothes. What's bank?"

Mike just skunked the board and was raking in a large amount of cash when he looked up with a smirk and was like, "Y'all little candy store money don't mean shit here, chumps."

Fatback looked mad. He pulled out two grand and said, "Let's get it."

Bank was three grand, and Back asked if he was taking bank stoppers. He looked at Back and said, "Match it, you fat fuck."

Fatback looked at P. P gave him seven hundred. Lee was kind of scary about the three he put up, but he knew Fatback was good for it. Fatback slapped the money down there and said, "Run that shit."

Mike laughed and said, "Yeah, cut the cards, fat fuck."

Back was angry and said, "I'm not gonna be too many more fat muthafuckers' word."

"Man, shut the fuck up and cut the deck, boy," Tuitt said with authority in his voice.

Back took the middle of the deck and put it on top; then he cut low and left it there.

"That cut ain't shit," Mike said.

Lan and the rest of the crew laughed.

"If that little nigga bust your ass, Mike, you gonna be hotter than fish grease." Lan snickered.

Mike said, "I'll be damned if this little fat fuck can beat me at anything or anyone of these little chumps."

Finally, the cards were dealt. Back had a deuce showing, while Mike had a brick. He told Back, "Hit till you bust, nigga."

The young thug looked at his cards and had a four under there.

"Give me a hit up and then down," he said, and he turned Mike up without looking at his cards all the way.

Mike had a king and queen of spades showing and buried his cards. The thug shuffled his cards and pinched them slowly. Tuitt got angry with the young street punk and snatched the money. "You know you lost, fat fuck."

Then Back smacked up a five of diamond with the four. "You lose, nigga, twenty-one! Now who's the bitch, bitch?"

The whole joint started to laugh, which pissed Mike off, so he slapped the shit out of Fatback and pulled out a chrome thirty-eight special. "I'll kill your fat ass, boy. Now, say you're sorry, bitch!" Mike shouted.

Back said, "Nigga, you better just kill me now because we're gonna straighten this shit sooner or later."

That was when Lan stepped in and said, "You lost fair and square, Mike. Just pay the little nigga."

Mike threw the money on the ground and spit on it. "Man, fuck y'all niggas!" and he stormed out.

Fatback looked at P Double and said, "I'm gonna make that faggot feel it. Watch me."

Lee said, "Let's get the fuck out of here and tend to this fifth of sauce we got."

The three gave everyone dap and walked out of the store and back down the street toward the Acura. Lee's pager went off, so he went inside J&J's and used the pay phone while Fatback and P waited for him in the whip. While they were waiting, Fatback cracked a Vega and started rolling up. You could see the anger and stress in his eyes as he rolled the el. "Yo, P."

"What up, Back?"

"I can't believe that nigga put his hands on me, yo. I swear I'm never gonna let this shit ride, word up," he stammered.

P said, "Yeah, don't worry. We'll catch that chilly chump slipping one day. Then we're gonna take his ass for everything, and that's my word."

The two thugs slapped palms and said, "Fuck MSP. We're Bristol Street, nigga."

Lee walked out of the store smiling and jumped in the back of the whip when Fatback started roasting the el. They passed the bottle around, and each one of them tapped it. P cracked it and took the first swig, which burned his throat mannishly. He beat his chest and passed the bottle back as he pulled out of the parking lot. It was dark, so P hit the lights. Lee started complaining, saying he wanted to get dropped off on Worthington Street, so he could go fuck this bitch.

P said, "Man, fuck that. What, nigga, you want us to go to jail or some shit?"

Fatback followed his man's lead and said, "Are you dumb or what, nigga?"

Lee said, "I got three bad bitches over there right now, y'all, word. And I swear they all fucking."

P Double never turned down pussy, so they were on their way. When they got down there, they saw trouble already. B-Black was out there on the stoop. Kid thought he was the king of worthy. He was an ugly gorilla nigga, but the kid was always ready to put in that work.

Black said, "What the fuck y'all stopping over here for? Bristol Street is back that way. Y'all better take y'all assess back to Tully's or some shit."

Lee rolled down his window quickly and said, "Suck my dick, Black. You already know I'll go wherever the fuck I choose."

"So get your bitch ass out and talk that shit," Black said, taking off his jean jacket.

Lee got out and swung on Black. Black took the punch on the cheek to see if Lee had any punching power. Satisfied that he didn't have that one hitter quitter, Black hit Lee with a three-piece combination that dropped him. As soon as Lee dropped, Black started stomping the nigga. Lee was rolling around with his hands over his face. That was when Fatback and P hopped out of the Acura. Fatback put Black in the yoke, trying to put him to sleep while P was giving him rib shots. Black was grunting with pain every time P delivered.

Lee got up and said, "Yeah, bitch nigga." He grabbed the half-full Hennessy bottle out of the car and told Back to let him go. Back let go of the hold and then pushed him toward Lee as P side-stepped and tripped him. While Black was falling, Lee cracked the bottle over his head. That split Black's forehead wide open. Black got up and ran. The three thugs gave chase, not knowing that Black now brandished a gun from up under his shirt, and he shot without looking back.

Lee said, "Oh shit!" and put on his track shoes, while P pulled out a .380 automatic from his Champion hoodie. P let off two quick shots while Fatback pulled out the massive forty-four Magnum from his waist and clapped thunder.

Black cut into an alley and disappeared. They were on his home turf, which meant he knew every escape route. The two thugs stopped. Back swore under his breath, "Shit." He was out of breath.

P said, "Let's get the whip and get the fuck out of here."

They turned around, jogged back to the whip, and drove off.

Back said, "See, you should have let me fuck Lee up from the jump."

But as he said this, all they could see was flashing lights behind them, and P hit the gas immediately.

He screamed, "Fuck, man! I knew I didn't wanna come down here for a reason."

P turned the radio up, "You gots to chill," by EPMD. They were driving up Federal Street doing seventy and then eighty, hoping to catch the green light on State Street. P was handling the Acura like he was Jeff Gordon in a NASCAR race, when all of a sudden, the tire blew and made the car go out of control. P Double tried to straighten it out, but he couldn't. They jumped the curb and crashed into the Rialto skating ring. P Double was knocked out on impact, while Fatback's head hit the windshield. He was stunned for a split second. Then he looked over at his boy. P was slung over the steering wheel. Back just hoped he wasn't dead. That was when he heard the sirens getting closer and closer. He didn't wanna leave his boy fucked up, but he had no choice. His door wouldn't open so he climbed out the front windshield. Just as they pulled up, Fatback was out the back door. He hit the fence and ran through the graveyard. As soon as he made sure nobody was following him, he stopped at a big tomb and gathered his breath. He felt his forehead. Blood was running down his face slightly. It wasn't as bad as it looked though. All that was on his mind was whether P Double was breathing. As the ambulance came and gathered his man, he started a light jog through the graveyard.

CHAPTER 2

COMING OF AGE

aystate Medical Center was buzzing with all kinds of activity. P-Double was in a single room with IVs and monitors attached to his body. The young man's injuries were so brutal that two different doctors performed surgery on him. They had him lying on his stomach because they found an extra bone in his back that had cracked and lightly damaged his spinal column. Also, he suffered from a lot of head trauma, being that his head went through the windshield. His right arm was broken as well. The near-fatal accident had happened seven days earlier, and young P was still in a coma. P Double's grandma was by his side from day one, praying for her grandbaby to get strong and healthy and rise up out of that unconscious state he was in. Every day, she would tell him how much she loved him and how much his little sister and family needed him.

All of a sudden, she heard a grunt come from her grandson as she was saying one of her daily prayers. She called for the nurse and doctor at once as young Presley began to stir. "Don't worry. I'm here, baby. I always knew you were strong," she said with tears streaming down her cheeks. "Thank the Lord Jesus for saving my baby!" she screamed over and over again.

The doctor prescribed some Percs to the young boy to help with the pain. Nurse Johnson ran to the hospital's pharmacy to fill the order while the doctor stayed and spoke with his grandmother. "Mrs. Williams, I'll need to run a couple more CAT scans on him and make sure that the swelling in his brain is going down. I also need to see if there's any internal bleeding that we haven't discovered yet."

"Yes, Doctor."

"You also better get him a lawyer because as soon as I bring him back in, the police are gonna wanna question him at once."

"Don't worry, Doctor. I'll have his lawyer present in a half hour," she said. "And, Doctor, thank you once again, but can I talk to him alone while you guys are getting prepared?" Mrs. Williams smiled.

"Why, sure," Dr. Zinger said. "I'll leave you two alone right now."

As soon as the doctor walked off quietly, Mrs. Williams moved closer to her grandbaby and said, "Boy, when you fully recover, you know you gotta answer to me, Presley Jr.," she moaned with a shaky voice.

P already knew he was in trouble. Every time his grandmother added the "Junior" on his name, he was seriously in trouble. He tried to turn but was in serious pain.

"Uggh!" he screamed. "Grandma, what's wrong with me?"

She broke everything thing down that the doctor told her. She also told him, "Don't say nothing to these crackers. Your lawyer, Vincent Bongorni, will be here in a second. Now, I gotta go out here and call him, so sit tight."

P said, "Okay," as she strolled out.

Nurse Johnson came in and gave P some pain meds, which he swallowed with a glass of water she had brought him. He looked up to see Nurse Johnson was a thick black chick with mannish features. He quietly thought to himself, *Damn, this is one ugly bitch.* But his stomach started to rumble, so he asked the grotesque-looking nurse what was good with a couple burgers. She smiled and told him they would be there waiting for him when he got back. Right then, they had to wheel him down to get all the necessary tests run.

P nodded his head and said, "Let's do this."

After his CAT scan, Nurse Johnson wheeled him back to his room, where he found his food waiting for him and a Sprite soda. He really wanted to lie on his back, but he had a cast back there, and the doctor told him he would have to lie that way a couple days longer. P had just taken a bite of his cheeseburger when two plainclothes detectives walked into his room and locked the door. P wished his grandmother was with him, but she must have been out there somewhere waiting on his lawyer. One of the detectives was white, and the other was black. The black cop introduced himself as Larry Acres. He said, "My partner's name is Tony Peogi."

P thought, *Oh shit, did I kill somebody?*

Larry Acres continued, "We found a .380 automatic in your possession. We also know you were with someone else, Mr. Williams, or should we call you P Double?"

P didn't answer, so he went on, "Now, we found about eight shell casings that were fired into Thirty-Five Quincy Street the night before you had this accident. Now, if you give us what we need, I can talk to the judge and maybe get you probation. If not, then you are on your own. We also wanna know who was with you that night and the night you crashed." Acres spoke calmly.

P looked at him with the smirk of the century and said, "Word."

Acres said, "Word. Now, give us what we need so we can go."

P looked at Acres and then at the white cop and said, "Well, first of all, y'all can suck my dick—"

Before P could get another word out of his mouth, the white cop snatched his broken arm and twisted it into his back. Then he started hammering on the cast on P's back while P screamed dearly.

Peogi said, "Do you think this is a game, you nigga fuck? I'll kill your black ass right here now." The cop was foaming out his mouth when he said this. He released the grip on P's arm and said, "Now, give us what the fuck we came for."

P screamed, "Okay, okay." It took him a minute to catch his breath. Then he said, "You know what? Suck my dick, and kiss my black ass, you cracker bitch."

The cop went into a rage and started pounding on P's back repeatedly, while screaming, "Talk, nigger, talk!"

P never felt so much pain in his life. It was too much to handle. The boy just fell unconscious as the cop hovered over him in a rage. Then the knock came. "Hey, open up in there! Hey!" the voice went on.

The cops looked at each other and then opened the door. It was the boy's lawyer and grandmother as well as the doctor. His grandmother went crazy. "What did y'all do to my baby?" she said over and over again with tears in her eyes.

The cops lied and said, "We found him asleep already," and they stormed out.

Vinny said, "Don't worry. I'll handle them," and walked out.

$ $ $

Two days later, P woke up with his hand cuffed to a different bed in another strange room. A pretty white lady walked in and said, "Welcome to the real world, Mr. Williams."

This woman had rosy cheeks and an everyday, bullshit-ass smile. She went on saying, "Hi, my name is Nurse Keller, and I'm the head nurse at CHD Juvenile Detention Center for Boys. I'm glad to see you're finally awake."

P said, "Cut the shit, lady. How long is it gonna take me to heal up?" in a barely audible tone.

"About four to six months," she said. "Don't worry; we'll take very good care of you."

He said, "Shit," under his breath.

P never thought he would get locked up, but he had to deal with it. The nurse explained that he had to go to therapy every day to get his natural strength back. She also explained to him that he had to stay in the medical unit until his strength was up to par. P didn't mind because he already knew that most likely he would have to fight every day of the week. So really they were doing him a favor whether they realized it or not.

After a couple months of Nurse Keller's therapy, young P was ready for rock. "Miss Keller, when can I go to population?" he asked anxiously.

"Well, Mr. Williams, you got court tomorrow. Maybe we'll see after that," she said, showing her pearly white, evenly spaced teeth.

"Thank you," he said and fell asleep.

The next day, P showered and changed into his court clothes. His grandmother had brought him what he asked for, which was a pair of low-top black Timberland boots they called Chucks and a gray-and-blue Francis Girbraud button-up with the two-tone jeans to match. He ate scrambled eggs and toast before they transported him to court. Once there, they threw him downstairs in a single cell at the court lockup. His lawyer came down and said all he had to do was four more months and six months' probation.

P said, "Cool, I can handle that."

Just as his lawyer was about to walk away, the two plainclothes cops walked in and stood in front of P's cell. One said, "Are you gonna give us what we want or what? We can help you."

Both the cops looked at P and smiled.

His lawyer said, "Listen, my client isn't about that."

P told him to be quiet. He yelled for the cops to come closer. He said he was ready to play ball. Peogi moved closer and said, "Spit it out," in a gruff voice.

P said, "Okay," and spit a giant lewy in the cop's face. "The answer to your questions are still suck my dick, you fuckin pigs."

Vinny laughed and told the two pigs to beat it. P copped out to six months' and the six months' probation. The judge also committed him until he was eighteen. As they transported him back, they told him to go gather his things at the medical unit because he was going to population. P packed up all his clothes, mail, and sneakers just as his caseworker walked in. He was a black, light-skinned male in his early thirties with a fade. He wore some cheap-ass Stetson cologne and introduced himself. "Hi, my name is Charlie Darwin, and you must be Presley Williams." The caseworker was jolly as all hell.

P looked the stupid man up and down and said, "Yeah, that's me. Now, let's get this process over and done with. I need to run some ball."

He answered harshly, "Okay, okay, you got that, young blood." As the caseworker started walking down the hall, the chump let P know all the rules and dropped him off at C block. The first thing P did was scan the dorm for enemies or some of his team. One of his bitches wrote him and told him that Kev and Bates had gotten caught in an illy, and Lee got bagged on the block with like thirty joints. He scanned the place and didn't really see too much of anybody.

A brolic-ass white boy was mopping the floor. He noticed P looking around and said, "Everybody is at the gym."

P said, "Good," as he still looked around. There were two tiers with fifteen rooms a piece. To the right was a day room with a TV, pool table, and Ping-Pong setup. Also, there were a couple of card tables. In back of him was a big desk with a CO behind it. P walked up, told the cop his name, and got his room. He was in cell twenty-three on the second floor. There were no doors on any of the cells, so he walked by and noticed that everybody was gone. He walked into the room and saw that the furniture consisted of two beds across from each other and a desk, which was in the middle of all that. Under the beds were lockers to keep clothes and food in. P wondered who the fuck his roommate was. He looked at a couple of pictures and saw a couple of beautiful black bitches, but he also saw an ugly-ass old lady who was wearing some loud-ass colors. P threw his shit in the trunk and asked the white boy who was mopping where the gym was. The kid said he would show him in a minute. And then he continued to mop the rest of the tier. They walked out of the unit into the same hall P took to get there. They banged a right and then a left and were at the gym. P once again scanned the place and saw his man Kev in the weight room with Bates. P also noticed a lot of Ave niggas too and was wondering how the fuck everybody could live together. There were a couple of Rockville cats from the Rifle Street crew, a couple of Hilltop niggas, and even some Robinson Garden niggas. Everybody was doing his own thing. Some people played basketball while others lifted weights. P decided to holla at Kev and Bates.

"Oh shit," they both said.

"What's good, P?" Kev said as they slapped palms.

He gave Bates some dap and also said, "Shit, I gotta finish these four more months; that's all."

Kev said, "Bates and I both got six more months left."

The two thugs both had their shirts off. They were buff and heavily sweating as they talked to P. P was looking around until he couldn't hold it in any longer and said, "How the fuck is everyone living together like this?"

Bates said, "Because this spot is sweet. Nobody wanna go to Westfield."

"Why? Who's out there?" P said.

"For one, your boy Fatback," Bates said. "He was shooting at some Worthington Street niggas again and got bagged with the forty-four. Then he came here, chilled for a day, and knocked Kid Quest from Hilltop out."

Kev said, "You already know Back is crazy as all hell."

Then they all looked at each other and laughed, until Kev said, "What dorm you in?"

"C block," P said.

"Oh, me and Bates are in A block, and Lee is in B block."

Just then, they said rec was over, over the loudspeaker.

They all said, "We'll see you at chow," but little did they know that was P's last night there.

P found out that his roommate was this Jamaican cat named Sun Sun from around the way. P didn't mind because he was half Jamaican himself. They shook hands and kicked it for about an hour, and then P went and took a shower. He came back and Sun Sun was on a visit, his next door neighbor said.

P said, "Fuck it," and got in his zone. He started reading *Master of the Game* by Sidney Sheldon when Sun Sun came back into the room, wearing P's all-black used outfit and black Champion sneakers.

Young P jumped up and said, "What the fuck?" angrily.

Sun Sun just laughed and said, "Rude boy, you got some nice tings, no. Me like 'tis suit, so me charge you to live here, boy."

P hit the Jamaican boy with a five-piece and a biscuit. Young P forgot about the cast on his back as the young Jamaican screamed, "Fuckery!" and ran P's back into the wall. P felt the unfamiliar pain again as his back hit. The Jamaican hit him with a couple rib shots. P grunted, snatched the Jamaican up by his legs, and dumped him. Then he acted like a world-class soccer star and kicked the Jamaican in his face, breaking his nose. The CO ran up there, grabbed P by the waist, and dragged him out of the room. The Jamaican got up yelling all types of obscenities, such as "Suck your mother! Me kill ya bum ba Claud star! Boy, me wicked!"

The CO saw Sun Sun charging and put P down just in time for P to scoop him again and get on top of him. P delivered two crushing blows before the CO pulled him off him. By that time, more COs flooded the block, and they grabbed the Jamaican so that he was secured. P already knew he was on his way to the juvenile max, Westfield Detention Center. They shackled P's legs together and brought him to segregation, which was located in the basement.

Nurse Keller came down to check on the young man at once, seeing if he felt pain anywhere. She checked the cast on his arm and back. After P announced that he was okay for the tenth time, she finally left. Mr. Darwin then entered and told P to make sure he was up bright and early because they were transferring him. P already knew he was going to Westfield; it was just a matter of time. An hour later, they slid P's dinner through a trap in the door. It consisted of chicken, white rice, bread, and broccoli. They also gave him chocolate milk and Jell-O for dessert. P bit into the chicken and saw that the inside was pink. "Fuck," he said. The shit was raw, so he just ate the white rice and broccoli. He didn't eat pork, so the Jell-O remained on the tray as well. All the young man could think about was what Ed had told him. The real money was in cooking the coke itself. He slapped the wall not once but three times, thinking to himself that he was just this close to learning the game the way he wanted to learn it. But he had to pick dumbass Lee and crazy-ass Fatback up. There was no use crying over spilled milk, so he lay down, closed his eyes, and dreamed the dream he always dreamed when he went to sleep—and that was the dream of becoming a billionaire.

P woke up quick when he heard three sharp knocks on the door. Then it cracked open. Two guards entered and told him what he already knew, that he was being transferred to maximum security. The pigs' names were Warfield and Murphy. Warfield was a light-skinned brother with a fade. You could tell he thought he was a pretty boy because he was well groomed and he had on a chunky bracelet with the matching chain. But the man also had a fake-ass smile and a conniving way about him. The pig Murphy was ugly as fuck. Now that was the ugliest cracker P had ever seen. Murphy looked like Alfred, the dude on the front of the *MAD* magazine cover. He had pimples all over his face to broaden his ugliness and had an attitude that looked just like his face. Murphy got angry because P took too long to pack his shit, and he flew the coop.

"Hurry the fuck up, or you won't take shit. No, let's fucking go!" he shouted.

P looked the man up and down and told him to kindly suck his dick.

"Suck your little black dick. You probably piss on your balls every time you take a leak, faggot," Murphy shot back. "Now hurry the fuck up!" he screamed.

"You pig-looking, *MAD* magazine in the face, howdy-doody, pimple-face bastard, has anybody ever told you that you have mud in your bones because you're a straight mud bone," P said with a smile.

Warfield started laughing so hard he had tears coming down his cheeks. After P put the last of his shit in the big bag, they were on the move. Warfield looked at Murphy every now and then and started chuckling.

"Cut the shit, Derick. I mean it," Murphy said with a red face, but Warfield just kept on laughing.

They pulled up to some shit that looked like a big-ass mansion and brought P through the front door. They handed P to the biggest white boy P had ever seen in his life. Sergeant Thomas looked like Hulk Hogan, a big six-foot-eight, 350-pound giant. Even his face had muscles. The man's voice was filled with muscle.

"Presley Williams, huh? Well, you're going to D block. Follow me, boy," he said in a deep, muscley voice.

Murphy laughed deeply. P looked at the grotesque man and shook his head while following the big man. When they got in front of D block, Sergeant Thomas buzzed the door so the sally port would open. He walked the kid inside and said, "This is where the CHD people wanted you. This is the craziest block there is. Have fun."

P was ready for rock anyway. The guard at the desk said, "You're in cell seven on the flats."

P looked around. There were three tiers with fifteen cells on each floor. There were big sliding doors with a tiny window you could see out of and a trap on the door. On the wall in the unit was a twenty-seven-inch TV and a bunch of card tables. A Ping-Pong table and a pool table were in the middle of the unit. There were also three showers on each tier with metal doors and a little window to look out of. P walked down to seven and was lucky because it was empty. He unpacked all his shit and placed his pictures on the desk in his cell.

Two hours later, they called rec time and popped the cells. P walked out and stood with his back on the wall, watching what was going on when he saw his road dog Fatback.

"What up, nigga?" the boys both said at the same time as they hugged each other.

Back said, "I missed your ass to death, nigga. I had to terrorize Worthington every day to get some retribution for my dog."

"Yeah, Kev and Bates told me you were acting a fool out there. You ever see that chump Black again?" P said with malice.

"That nigga is crazy. I'm gonna kill his ass," Fatback said with a mean mug. "His bitch ass came through the block letting off a couple times. He didn't hit shit though."

P stepped back and looked at his friend up close for the first time in months. "Damn, Fatback, you're getting kind of big around here!" he hollered.

"Free weights is the new drug of choice around here, P. You know I'm trying to knock a couple cats out when I hit the bricks, like that Mike Tuitt chump."

P laughed and said, "Fuck all that. What's the word on the streets, Back?"

"Man, you already know most of us are in here, so word is there's a lot of new niggas repping right now, and that bitch-ass nigga Mike Tuitt is hitting every last one of them, getting rich off our block," Fatback said.

"Wow!" P grimaced. "You mean all the older cats are going for this shit?"

"Them niggas are still doing them out there, but he's hitting Iran, Tykey, and a couple of other niggas. I swear I'm gonna get that nigga for everything he's got, and we're gonna blow, P, mark my words," Back said. "Let's hit the gym."

"Let's go!" P shouted.

The next couple of months flew by. They took the cast off P's arm on his birthday, and he started playing ball heavy. Fatback always made him work out every day too, because you always had to be ready for combat. P also learned how to play poker there. He became very good. He applied poker rules to real-life shit, because a lot of cats be acting like they're through until you call their bluff. He was that nigga for weeks until this fat-ass nigga named Big Butch fucked the whole game up.

Butch weighed about 270 and had a face like a bulldog. He had a little bit of skill with his hands and a big mouth and heart to go with it. Every day, he would sit at the table with his shirt off looking like a hairy-ass ape, talking shit and eating honey buns. This night, they had been playing for hours, and Butch was down some shit to P. After a while, it came down to Butch and P Double because everyone else had quit.

Butch said, "We're gonna play piles. You can use one card from each pile, and your low in the hole is wild but with a twist." He grinned. "No five of a kind. The best hand is a royal."

P said, "All right. Deal 'em."

Butch dealt out five cards and said, "Let's just put everything I owe you on this hand, double or nothing, before we even look at the cards."

P said, "Fuck it." He was still up all them other niggas' money anyway, so why not?

Butch then laid his cards down and said, "I gotta straight flush to the king," and he put his hand on his chin.

P looked at him, laughed, and said, "You know what? I don't even need the cards down there," and he paid his hand down. He had the ten, the jack, the queen, the king, and the ace of diamonds. "Royal flush, fat boy. Pay up."

The crowd around the table said, "Oh shit." Because that was the first time they had ever seen somebody get a royal flush in their hand.

Butch jumped up, screamed, "Your bitch ass cheated! I ain't paying shit!" and walked to his cell on the second tier. Butch was in a cell in the corner.

P looked at Fatback and said, "You already know what's up."

The young thugs took the stairs two at a time and ran down to Butch's cell.

Butch said, "I already told you—"

He didn't get a chance to finish because P hit him with a flurry of blows at once. Butch shook it off and hit P with a two-piece that made the young boy stagger back. P had to back up out of the cell and fight the nigga on the tier. He already knew if the big brute grabbed him, it was a wrap for him. Butch came charging out, growling like a mad dog and throwing wild punches. You could feel the air from the blows he was throwing. Butch was too busy trying to hit P to notice that Fatback was behind him. Fatback threw the bully in the sleeper. Butch fell off balance at first and then straightened out and leaned forward, flipping Fatback.

Before Butch could recover, P hit the big man in his throat, taking his breath, and then he hit him with twenty body blows. Butch recovered from the body blows and hit P with a massive blow to the chest. P flew back, tripped over Fatback, and fell. Back got up in time to scoop Butch as he came running at him full force. Back had him up in the air and flipped him over the rail. The big brute fell hard and screamed as something broke. The young thugs ran downstairs and continued to work the big guy over. Two COs ran and tackled Fatback. P kicked the CO in the face until Sergeant Thomas came in and earth-slammed him. P was knocked out on impact. He woke up below the jail somewhere in pain. He was happy because they had fucked Big Butch up badly.

The only thing P didn't know was that he wouldn't be going home the next month. The jail had pressed charges because he assaulted Butch, and the CO pressed charges too. One of them wound up with a broken nose. Butch had four broken ribs and a broken leg and nose. The judge gave P another year, while Fatback got six months.

P Double wouldn't hit the streets until he was eighteen, and he still had to give them six months' probation on top of that. All he knew was that the system owed him for taking a year and a half of his life. Somehow, some way, he would wreak havoc on the Springfield streets. He was bound to blow, like Malcom X said, by any means necessary. The streets were his; they just didn't know it yet.

CHAPTER 3

BOUND TO BLOW

The last night of his incarceration, P Double couldn't sleep. All he could think about was making a million bucks. He still had eight and a half ounces at the crib on stash. The only thing fucked up was Fatback went home six months earlier, and he came back two months later with a fresh year. That man was crazy. He got caught shooting at some Cambridge Street nigga. All P could think about was making that ten grand so Eddie Haul could school him.

He was already packed up when his caseworker came and said, "Wrap it up."

P looked at the caseworker and said, "I was born ready. Now let's go."

As they were walking down the hall, the caseworker looked at P and said, "Don't be a fool like your boy and come back, you hear."

"Nigga, I'm going home to live the dream I always wanted to live," the boy said with a glazed expression in his eyes.

"And what's that?" the caseworker said.

"To be that nigga, of course."

$ $ $

P's grandmother was waiting outside with open arms. She kissed him so many times the boy thought he was a Teddy bear. First stop was State

Street. The juvenile courthouse awaited his presence. When he walked into the building, the guard asked him his name and directed him to the third floor, which was the probation department. The front desk was crowded with a lot of people. P waited patiently until the antsy white man asked him his name and told him to wait a minute.

Five minutes later, a woman called his name. "Presley Williams, come over here, please."

For a minute, he was shocked because she was the most beautiful woman he had ever laid eyes on. She was milk chocolate with hazel eyes. Her skin was smooth and rich. The woman had style and class with her. Halle Berry and Nia Long had nothing on this woman whatsoever. Her suit was made out of burgundy leather, and she had on some white and burgundy Prada shoes to match. He walked in and closed the door behind him. When she turned around, she extended one of her well-manicured hands out to greet him.

"Hello, my name is Jaynce Magill, and I'm in charge of your probation, Mr. Williams. Can you please sit down?" She smiled. Her teeth were whiter than piano keys. She was definitely a chocolate Halle Berry. Her office smelled of Lancôme perfume. P thought he had died and gone to heaven. He was thinking about kissing her beautiful lips when he was woken from his daydream.

"Uhummm?" She cleared her throat to get his attention. Then she laid the ground rules down.

The only one P liked was checking in twice a week. As he studied her hands, he didn't notice a ring or any family pictures lying around her office. Bagging this classy dame was another thing he put on his mental checklist.

They shook hands, and he said, "It's a pleasure to meet you, Miss Magill." She smiled and replied, "See you on Friday."

P thought, *Damn, that's four days away.* Miss Magill was definitely the hottest chick in the game, and he wanted that.

His grandmother kept asking him what was on his mind as they drove home. It was kind of hard to tell your grandmother you wanna fuck your PO, so he just shook his head and said, "Nothing, Grandma. I need a home-cooked meal; that's all."

"Tinco, I done cooked so much food. Your friends are waiting at the house to eat it with you."

She laughed. They pulled up and just about his whole young team was there. Lil Kev dapped him and hugged him, along with Lee, Andy Cap, Bates, T Baby, A-Dog, Iran, and Tykey. They all ate and talked about old times. Kev blessed him with a chrome-and-black forty-five automatic and five hundred. The rest of the team gave him a couple hundred and a pager, and T Baby blessed him with a basehead rental from one of his plays.

"P, you're golden for two days, my nigga," Baby said.

P asked him what kind of ride it was.

"Oh, just a money-green 92 ES 300 Lexus coupe, fully loaded!" Baby hollered.

"Take care of my man's shit, P. He's a good custy."

"Man, fuck that nigga. Lee, what's good with one of them pagers, playboy?"

"P, you already know you got that," Lee said, graciously handing him the pager.

"Well, I hate to break this up, fellas, but P Double ain't had no pussy in eighteen months, so I'm up out of here, y'all," P said.

They all dapped him and left. P went upstairs and bagged up a half ounce from the eight and a half ounces. He also changed into a getup to match the car he was in. He hopped into the Lexus and decided to go to all his old plays' houses. He had to let them know he was back and give them his pager number. He would save Mimi for last.

It was almost midnight when he pulled up on Fenwick Street. He checked his face in the mirror and hopped out of the ride. He then walked up the steps and rang the doorbell. She opened the door and had a silk robe on that left little to imagine.

"Come your fine ass in. Damn, you got big as fuck."

Her crib was still laced up as usual, but her body was upgraded.

P palmed her ass and said, "You had me dreaming about this pussy for a year and a half now. I've been dying to beat this shit up, girl."

Mimi said, "I missed your little ass too, but I don't smoke no more, and I gotta man, P. I'm sorry."

"Is the faggot here right now?" the thug said, pulling out the forty-five. She said, "No, but, P, he's crazy."

"I'll kill that nigga if comes down to it, Mimi. You already know."

And he pulled the string from her robe. Mimi moaned in delight as P put one of her chestnut nipples in his mouth and grabbed her ass. She took the robe off and grabbed his dick at once. P pulled his pants down, bent her over the couch, and took it from the back. Mimi still had some good-ass pussy. The young boy was fucking the shit out of Mimi when she started making animal noises.

"P, fuck this pussy, oh shit, uhh fuck!" she screamed in bliss as P jack-hammered the bird. He came about three times before someone rang the doorbell. He pulled his pants up and went to the bathroom. He heard somebody come in and scream at the top of his lungs. Then he heard a loud smack and someone hit the floor. He knew that was Mimi getting her fine ass kicked. He walked out of the bathroom and saw that it was Mike Tuitt standing over the bitch.

"What's good, Mike?" P said.

Tuitt looked at the nigga like he was nobody and said, "Ain't shit good. What the fuck is your bitch ass doing in my spot, punk?"

"My mother told me to come by and give Miss Mimi the new number; that's all."

He said, "Well, get the fuck out before I whip your fucking ass!" he shouted.

P just looked at the man and bounced, but he noticed that Mike had brought a big-ass duffel bag with him as he left. P knew as he hopped in the Lexus that that bag had some shit in it, and he was gonna find out what it was.

P Double came back the next morning because he knew Mimi had to go to work. So first, he called her crib three times from Cumberland Farms. After nobody answered on the third try, he decided to slide though. The front door was too risky, so he went to the back, broke a window, and climbed through it. He started with the closet in the living room and found nothing, so he went upstairs to the second floor. The first door the boy saw he opened. Turned out to be a bedroom, which was decked out in straight pink. He then walked down the hall and found what appeared to be the master bedroom. The first place he looked was under the bed; there was nothing there but dust and cobwebs. Next, he checked all her drawers, throwing everything on the bed. P found a thousand dollars in a pink sock and pocketed it for later use. Now the only place he didn't look was in her closet. When he opened it, he was amazed by the size of it. Mimi had a giant closet with a million garments and shoes in it. P looked on the shelf and found exactly what he was looking for. He tried to snatch the bag lightly and almost dropped it. The shit had some weight to it. He opened it slightly, and his eyes got big. "Bingo!" he shouted and zipped the bag back up.

P ran down the stairs and out the back door in a matter of seconds. All that was on his mind was making it back home. The boy hopped in the Lexus and turned the radio on. Pete Rock and C.L. Smooth blazed the airwaves with "Straighten It Out." P made sure he drove safely. He didn't wanna blow this adventure. He hopped out at his grandmother's house and hit the stairs to his room at once. As soon as he closed his door, he bolted it and dropped the bag on his bed. When he unzipped it, he pulled out a AR-15 assault rifle. It came with two spare clips and boxes of ammo. The young thug threw that to the side and pulled a bunch of money out. He couldn't believe his luck, so he counted that shit again for good measure. In the boy's hands was fifty racks large. P threw that in his little safe at once. Then he dumped out five silver-wrapped packages that had a triangle stamp on them. He opened one slightly, and a pinkish-white powder spilled out. P already knew what it was from watching Ed cook up that day. He had straight fish scale. Right then and there, his life just began because shit just got real. P also found a .357 Magnum with bullets and a Glock 40. P couldn't believe this good fortune came to him on his second day out of the slammer. He had to think for a minute and come up with a plan, because this shit could be gone all in a blink of an eye if he made the wrong move. He decided to wait a week and go to Ed with fourteen stacks. That way, Ed would show him the connect and teach him how to whip that batch to perfection. He called Ed up at the end of the week.

"Yo, Ed, I finished that eight, my nigga. I got your four and the ten. What's good?" P said.

"I'm taking a trip early morning. I'll come scoop you early morning around six. Be ready," Ed said.

P said, "All right, one love," and hung the phone up. P then gave his grandmother ten stacks and told her to do her with it. She questioned him about the money, but he just kissed her on the cheek and ran out of the house. He had a whole night to blow, so he went to the block, mashed a couple of joints, and kicked it with his crew. He had to see what the word on the street was. Andy Cap was on the block clowning Iran and Tykey. Cap was a little baby-face-ass nigga. All he did was suck on pacifiers all day and talk shit.

"Ah ha, y'all faggot ass connect is broke. That's what y'all get for not fucking with Ed," Cap said.

P walked up and said, "What happened, Cap?"

"These bitch-ass niggas were working for Mike Tuitt, and somebody took his ass for all he got!" Cap laughed.

Iran said, "That's all right. We'll get on somehow and get right."

P said, "Hold up! I got some shit for y'all right now, but don't make me kill y'all niggas over my work, because I'm broke out here to."

The two said, "That's what's up, P, good looking on that."

P Double said, "I'll be right back," and he hopped in his rental and went home real quick. He came back and hit Tykey and Iran with an ounce a piece and talked to Cap.

Cap said, "You shouldn't have given them bitch-ass niggas nothing. I would have let they ass starve."

"With that attitude you got, Cap, you'll never get nowhere." P laughed.

Just then, a bad-ass bitch walks by, coming from the store.

P said, "Damn, can I help you with your bags?"

She said, "Me not need no help, rude boy. Me live right there." The girl was Jamaican and exclusive.

"Well, can I at least know your name, baby doll," P spit.

She said her name was Sauna, the Queen of the Pack. He asked her if she had a man, and she said no. P slid her his pager number and watched her switch that fine ass across the street.

Cap said, "Man, I've been trying to bag that bitch for weeks, my nigga."

P said, "Well, you ain't half Jamaican either, lil nigga. I gotta give that pussy a black eye, Cap," he said with lust in his eyes.

"Man, Kev, Bates, A-Dog, and even Lan couldn't bag that little bitch, P. What's really good?" Cap said.

"For one, Cap, I'm not none of y'all niggas, and two, I'm gonna be that nigga very soon around this bitch. You watch and see." P held his head high when he said that. Nothing could stop him but a bad move. He had already played enough chess in the joint to know that a bad move would work you over, so he wasn't into making mistakes.

While talking to Cap, he got two quick pages, so he ran to the pay phone across the street. As P was dialing the number, he heard three quick shots and turned around in time to see Andy Cap drop. He pulled out the forty-five and ran across the street.

Cap was rolling around, holding his leg and screaming in pain dearly.

"Cap, who shot you?" P asked with worry on his face.

"Ah, fuck man, this shit hurt, man! Help me, P." Cap quivered in pain.

P put the gun away and picked Cap up like a baby. The young thug screamed in pain as P cradled him, brought him to the rental, and sat him in the front seat. One of P's baseheads had rented him a Blazer from Enterprise for the week. He pushed the whip to Bay State Medical Center in record time. The he stashed his gun under the seat, along with some coke Andy Cap had on him, and carried him to the front door. There was a wheelchair there, so he wheeled him to the front desk. "This man has been shot! Help!" P shouted in turmoil.

The medics came at once, and P made a quick exit. His pager went off two more times, and he drove to the Getty gas station in the north end to see who it was. The first page was from Kev.

"What up, my nigga?"

"This nigga, Cap, just got shot on the block," P said.

"Who the fuck popped him, P?" Kev shouted through the phone.

"The nigga didn't tell me shit, yo. He was just in pain."

"Damn," Kev said. "Tonight, we gotta ride, P. I'm gonna round up the troops. I'll holla back, peace." He hung up.

P called the other number back. "Yo, somebody paged me?"

"Yes, rude boy, what ya wanna do with a rude girl tonight, boy?" Sauna said with the most seductive voice P had ever heard.

P said, "Oh shit," to himself. This caught him off guard. "Umm, I'm kind of busy at the moment, but—"

She cut him off and said, "What's the matter, Presley? You don't have time to play with the queen? Well, fuck you then." And the beautiful bitch banged on him.

The other two pages were from his grandmother. Word had spread that Cap got shot and he was there. He said he was on his way home, and the conversation ended. As he walked through the door, his grandmother saw all of Cap's blood on him and smothered him with hugs and kisses.

"Tinco, are you okay, baby?" she said, squeezing the boy to death.

"Yes, Grandma, I was across the street when it all went down. I'm okay, I swear. I just need a hot bath to relax and calm my nerves; that's all." P looked exhausted when he said these words.

"Okay, baby, you do that," she said and strolled off.

Young P ran a bubblebath and hopped in the tub. His pager was ringing off the hook, but he already knew who it was. It was his team thirsty for blood and some get-back. They were ready for war, and he was their general. P got dressed and called all his pages back. The clique was gonna meet at eleven in Adams Park to go over the plan. As much as P wanted to bring out the AR-15, he decided it was not the time, not when Tuitt was ready to kill up shit, so he left with the forty-five and dressed in all black.

J&J's package store was just about closed when he sent a fein in for the order. Fred Fred came out with two gallons of Hennessy, two boxes of Garcia Vegas, two two-liter Coke sodas, and a bunch of cups. Young P hit Fred Fred with his number and a joint.

"Good looking, P, anytime," Fred Fred said.

"Man, just call the number and holla!" P shouted out the window of the blazer. He made sure his gun was cocked because he had to go on Chapel Street to grab some weed for the dress in the red house. P pulled up, ran in the back, and slid three twenties under the door. In return, the Dread slid him six dime bags of chocolate. Once he copped the bud, he walked to the end of the driveway and made sure the coast was clear. On them Eastern

Ave niggas' turf, anything could happen. But the coast was clear, so he blew all the way to Adams Park, where his crew was bugging because he was late. Kev was the first one to start talking shit.

"Come on, P. We already told you what time we were coming, man," Kev said.

"Listen, my nigga, I went to the packy and smoke spot. Roll up, and shut the fuck up," Young P said and then went on.

"Is Andy Cap out the hospital yet?" Bates answered.

"Yeah, he came home a hour ago. He said Black came through dumping again."

Bates spit with a sour taste in his mouth. "On some real shit, I'm tired of hearing about this bitch-ass nigga. We should've been laid his ass down to rest a long time ago."

T Baby said with malice, "Matter of fact, let's just air his mother's crib out, his girl's crib, vans, any spot he be at, period. Man, fuck this shit."

Lee screamed, "Y'all hold the fuck up!"

P said, "First, we're gonna crack this Hennessy; then we're gonna plan this shit out because all this unnecessary shooting is stupid. We all know the punk is crazy, so if we shoot his mother's crib up, what makes you think he ain't gonna bring the war to our doorstep?"

His team all shook their heads because they knew he was right.

"Now, roll some weed up while I come up with a plan," P said.

"Matter of fact, let's go to Cap's house and get right with him," Double suggested.

Twenty minutes later, everyone was in Cap's room getting right. Cap was still in pain, but the Hennessy was starting to turn him back into the old Cap.

P said, "I got it. Just let this shit rest for two days, and we'll take care of Black's bitch ass."

Bates screamed on P, "Fuck that! I'm riding tonight. Ain't no nigga on my set gonna get popped, and Ricky Bates don't ride. I'm sorry, Double, but that's not me."

P got angry quick and said, "Y'all niggas handle shit your way then. I'm out of here. Peace."

His boys yelled after him, but P kept it moving. The young don answered to no man, not even his father.

"Who the fuck do Bates think he is?" P shouted in the Jeep. "Broke-ass nigga!"

P pushed the Blazer quickly, making the tires squeal when he hit a turn. Finally, the boy was in front of his crib, where he passed out in the Jeep in a drunken sleep.

CHAPTER 4

BLOWING UP IN THE WORLD

The knocking sound woke P Double up with a fright. "What the fuck?" he said as he jumped in his seat. "Wake yo ass up, nigga. I'm on a time slot," Ed said in a hasty manner. "Fuck my whip. Move over. We taking this shit," Ed said as P moved to the passenger seat.

P Double said, "Wait. I'll be right back."

He ran into the house and grabbed fifteen stacks. Now, the boy was ready for rock. As he slid back into the passenger seat, Ed said, "You ready, young blood?"

P looked at him with dollar signs in his eyes and said, "I was born ready for this shit."

Ed said, "Here we go." He turned the radio up full blast. They wanted effects from Das EFX, cashing checks for some live effects. They came through the factory system. Das EFX was the hottest thing moving on the hip-hop airwaves.

On the way, they stopped at McDonald's to grab a couple of Egg McMuffins and some orange juice. When they got back into the whip, Ed said, "Watch everything, and don't speak unless spoken to. Remember, I'm showing you how to get money, P, because you're a smart young youth. Never bring nobody to the city like I'm showing you. And never teach none of these niggas how to cook, and you'll always be on top. The young bitches and old will be begging you to suck your dick 'cause you'll be that nigga. Do you understand, P?" Ed said.

"Hell yeah, I understand. I just can't wait for you to show me the real deal," the young god said. "I promise to remember everything you show me and grow to my full potential," he added as well.

"Yeah, that's what I like to hear," Ed said as he reached over and turned the radio to Hot 97.

Diamond D came on. "I'm the best-kept secret, to just peep it." The bass was rockin' the Blazer as they entered the city. They hopped on Broadway immediately. The life in New York was fast-paced. Everybody was trying to hustle something one way or another. This was P's style. He loved the atmosphere. Every week, he was gonna be up there, shopping or something. They pulled up at a little Dominican restaurant on Broadway.

"We're here," Ed said. "Just follow my lead, and everything will run smoothly."

They walked into the restaurant, and Ed told P to have a seat. Ed then went to the counter and hugged some old Dominican dude. The dude turned around and started walking P's way. He was short with gray hair and a stocky build. His hands were well manicured, and he had on a couple of expensive chains and bracelets. He also smelled like some expensive aftershave lotion. You could tell he had some bad bitches in his time. He looked to be in his late fifties. He walked up to P and extended his hand. P took it and found out the man's grip was strong.

"My name is Tanto," the old man said.

P's response was "My name is P Double."

The old man said, "Nice to meet you," with a heavy Dominican accent.

"Why do they call you, P Double?" he asked.

"Because my first name begins with a P, and I double everything—my money, my bitches, even the amount of nuts I bust. I even send out double shots when I bust my gun."

The old man laughed, looked at Ed, and said, "I like him already. Please make yourself comfortable, and order some food."

Ed ordered for them and said, "We'll pay in advance." He slid his money, and he kicked P under the table. P did the same, and they waited on their food.

Twenty minutes later, the food was ready. Tanto gave them a couple sodas and told P, "Any friend of Eddie's is a friend of mine. Come back anytime."

P said, "Thank you," and walked out with Ed. Next, they went across the street where Ed copped a quarter pound of chocolate, and they were on their way. P turned the radio down and said, "Ed, where's the caine?"

"Look inside the bag with the food," he said.

P then looked under his tray of food and saw another tray, which he opened. Inside was a bunch of powder.

Young P had just copped seven hundred and fifty grams of raw from the city on his first trip.

Ed said, "I still want my four grand though, little nigga."

"No problem, Ed. No problem at all," P whispered.

The young man was on cloud nine right then. He had met the connect, and now he was about to learn how to whip that batch. They made it back safely and drove straight to Ed's crib. Mama was out shopping somewhere when they got there. They went right to the lab.

"Here, P. Roll up real quick, my nigga," Ed said.

P cracked and rolled the Vega with perfection and lit up, while Ed was setting up shop.

"First, get yourself the best blender money can buy and then always make sure you got fresh baking soda, always. Believe me; it makes a big difference. The way I cook is no less than a half of a brick or a brick at a time. You take the thousand grams and throw it in the blender. Then you weigh out the three hundred grams of baking soda like this, put it all in the blender, and blend it on high for a good minute. You always wanna make sure it's mixed up nicely. Then you add just a little bit of water to this bowl, and you drop the caine in. You wanna make sure the caine is mixed up nicely, and you put it in the microwave for thirty seconds and check it. Then you throw it back in until it looks like this. You got it?"

"Yes, Ed, but I wanna know how to cook my shit over the fire like you did last time when I was here," P said.

Ed said okay and showed him in no time. P turned his seven fifty into eleven fifty and thanked Ed for teaching him the basics, and he walked upstairs. Mama was home now. She was on the couch with her feet up as usual when she saw P. "Damn, nigga, you getting grown around here and cute." she chirped.

"Woman, I been grown and cute. What? You didn't know, love?"

And P blew a kiss at her as he walked out the door. P didn't know it yet, but once he learned how to cook, he just gave off a certain glow. He pushed the Blazer home and thought about how he was gonna take over the field. As soon as P walked into the crib, he got a couple of pages. He called the first back. Tykey and Iran had his two grand. He told the young hoods he would come and scoop them in about fifteen minutes. The second was from Bates.

"Yo, my bag about last night, my nigga. I was drunk as fuck. Let's let bygones be bygones, and take this chump down together," Bates said.

"Yeah, yeah, I'll drop a bug in your ear later on about that. Do you got some work though?" P hollered, hoping he was gonna say no.

Bates said, "I'm kind of low. I was gonna call Ed in a—"

P cut the man off at once. "Man, I got it right here. Matter of fact, I'll be through in a sec."

P's plan was to mash out half of that shit weight and half of that shit on the block. But first, he called the rest of his team and made drops everywhere. That was when Ed paged him and said, "My bag, P. We got a problem, Yo."

"Shit, I'm just fine, Ed. Everything is moving like clockwork," P said.

"Listen, nigga. Everybody is complaining that their customers are talking about the shit smell and taste like gasoline. The whole town got this shit, P. If somebody had some different caine, they'll lock the town down with ease," Ed said sadly. "Anyways, I was just giving you the heads-up, P. I gotta go and bring Cheeks a half bird. Peace out."

P Double was already counting bucks in his brain. It was time to send Grandma on a vacation at once. He went to a travel agency and paid for a trip to Cancun, Mexico, but with a twist. He had them call her and say she had won an all-expense-paid trip to Cancun, and the plane was leaving Logan airport in Boston the following morning at nine. Grandma packed up that night and told P she would be gone for a week.

"Just take care of our home, Tinco, please," she begged him.

"Yes, Grandma, no problem."

He gave her a hug and watched her go. P then drove to the store and bought boxes and boxes of baking soda, a giant Pyrex, and a lot of baggies. He then came home and cooked two bricks, but instead of putting three hundred on each one, he put five hundred on each one. The other three he was gonna break down, and he would take the city by storm. So he just added the regular three hundred to them.

Young P was chopping and bagging up coke all day long and most of the night. P had his pager off. He cut his shit back on, and Little Frank hit him up.

"What's the word, Frank?" P asked him.

Frank was a short, money-hungry-ass nigga. He sold a little bit of bud and some coke here and there. He also messed with the Bristol Street tart Shante. She was a down-ass bitch though. Frank said, "P, everybody got that gas shit, man. Who did you get your work from?"

This was P's chance to let niggas know he had some different coke than all the so-called dons. "Naw, Frank, I got some shit from a new connect I got. Why? What's up?" P Double answered.

"Yo, sell me a couple of ounces, man, please?" Frank begged.

"All right," P said. "But I want fifteen hundred an ounce for this shit."

Little Frank's voice sounded like he was singing opera when he said, "Fifteen hundred, P, are you crazy?"

"No, I'm not crazy," P said. "Fuck it. Buy some more of that bullshit then, nigga."

Frankie was a greedy little nigga, so he already knew P Double was serious. So he finally broke down and said, "You got that, P. I'm sending Shante over with three stacks right now."

Tykey and Iran were also paging him. He told them that he would drop them some shit off in a little while, but prices were up right then, and he hung up. Just then, he heard a sharp knock on the door. P already knew it was Shante at the door. He let her in and locked his door. She counted out the three stacks and handed it to him with a sexy glint in her eye. Shante was about five feet two, light-skinned, and average looking. If you dressed her up the right way, she had the potential to be a bad bitch.

She said, "So you're that nigga out here now, P Double," with a sexy purr to it.

P said, "Bitch, I been that nigga out here. You just now noticed this shit." He poked his chest out to add some effect to it.

She then grabbed his dick and said, "Can I taste it, P?" with this seductive look in her eye again.

P didn't even answer her. He just let his pants drop and pulled his manhood out. Shante dropped to her knees and started swallowing P's dick. P grabbed her by her hair, and he started fucking her face. He was ramming her mouth so hard she started gagging on his dick. So he told the bitch to walk into the living room. Then she stripped while he stripped. She had small breasts with giant nipples and a hairy-ass pussy. P made her lie on her back while he put both her legs on his shoulders, and he just gutted the bitch. He was glad his grandmother had taken that vacation because Shante was a screamer. That just made him fuck the bitch even harder.

"P, wait a minute. Oh shit, uhh uhh fuck!" she screamed.

P just jackhammered the pussy until he reached his sexual peak and bust all in her. His dick was still hard so he fucked her doggy-style until the bitch damn near cried. He let her take a quick shower. That was where he came up with the plan of the century.

She came out of the shower and started getting dressed when he approached her and said, "Yo, I need you to do something for me?"

"Anything for you, daddy," she said with that purr.

"Tomorrow, I want you to go down to Worthington Street and seduce B Black. Rent a room at the Summit, and leave the door open, and hit my pager with the room number. Make sure his pants are down too, so fuck him if you have to. Now, here's the money for the room," P said.

"Yes, Daddy, I said anything."

P said, "So hit me tomorrow."

And he smacked her on her soft ass. P then left the crib and mashed a half a brick with ease. He told his crew the plan, and they were all for it.

$ $ $

The next day, Kev, Bates, and P Double snatched Black's bitch up. They had her in the trunk for an hour when P got the page, Room 303. He then told Cap, Tykey, A-Dog, Iran, J.G., Rubin, and T Baby to meet them at the Summit on State Street. They let Black's girl sit in the car with them as they drove to the motel. She was crying all the way there. "Please, let me go. I swear I won't tell anyone."

Bates punched her and told her to shut the fuck up. They pulled up, and Bates put the snub-nose thirty-eight to her back and said, "Bitch, you run; you die."

P and Kev walked up to the third floor, and they already knew Black was fucking the shit out of Shante, because they could hear it. The door was cracked a little like P told her to. Bates then pushed Shafika through the door. She started going crazy. "You no good son of a bitch, I'll kill you!" she screamed.

Black had one of Shante's legs on his shoulder, working her, when they walked in, guns out. Black turned around like, *What the fuck?* but it was too late. He was hit. Bates hit him with the pistol a couple of times, splitting his shit open. Then they tied him up. Shante got dressed and exited the room. Black was trying to talk tough when Bates hit him with the gun again.

P said, "How do you like this bitch-ass nigga?" and he started ripping Black's girl's clothes off. She tried to fight at first, but Kev gun-butted her, and she fell on the bed. P then stripped her until she was butt-ass naked. Shafika was a good-looking redbone with big tits and a fat ass. Nobody knew why she was fucking with ugly-ass Black. P then stripped and mounted Black's bitch right in front of him. He threw both her legs up and started drilling the pussy.

Black was screaming, "No, please!" but the rope was tight against his hands and feet. All he could do was say how he was gonna kill niggas. So Bates got tired of hearing this and put one of P's socks in Black's mouth and hit him with the pistol again. At first, the bitch was trying to fight P. Then she started moaning and bucking back with pleasure. As P was about to nut, the knock came. Kev answered the door, and it was the rest of the crew. Andy Cap ran over and started on Black at once, while P was busting all up in fine-ass Shafika. P got up and made her suck all her juices off his dick. Then Kev mounted her. P's whole clique fucked her all night long while Black watched and suffered. Cap kept beating him every chance he got over and over again. When the sun came up, P shot Black in both of his knees and elbows. They threw him on the bed and left with his bitch. They took her to Kyle Woods right next to Bristol, and P made her suck his dick again, while Bates and the crew dug her grave. She swallowed all his nut, and he pulled out the forty-five. Her eyes got big when she saw the gun, and she begged for her life. P knew Black was a thoroughbred; he would never tell what happened to the police, but his bitch would. So he put two in her head and dragged her to the grave they had made. From that day forward, P was the head of his clique. He just didn't know Eddie Haul went down, and Bristol Street had a new general. His name was P Double.

CHAPTER 5

BECOMING A DON

P left and drove down the street so he could throw the forty-five in Water Shop's pond. The shit had a body on it; it was no good for him anymore. They say along with murder comes a guilty conscience, well, shit, P didn't feel any worse. As a matter of fact, he felt better. If taking a life was this easy, he would have laid the murder game down. P Double then drove home and took a nice hot shower. He still had a good four and a half days left before his grandmother returned. Even though he loved living at home, he had to find somewhere to cook up at because Grandma wasn't having that shit. Just then, he got a page from Ed, "911."

Damn, P thought, *I wonder what's wrong.* Then his shit sounded again with the same 911. He jumped out of the shower without even drying off, and he ran to his room to make the call.

"Ed, what's the word?" P spoke.

But it wasn't Ed on the other end; it was Mama. "P, Eddie's in jail, baby, and he needs your help," she said.

"What? How, Mama?" P asked, with the utmost concern for his mentor.

"Trevor Cheeks set him up with that half of brick. Ed and Little Mari went to bring it to him. As soon as they pulled up, detectives were all over them. He needs that four grand for now. Can you bring it by?"

"You got that," P said. "I'll bring it right over."

P went over there and gave her four for Ed and a rack for herself.

"Listen, I might need to cook up here, and I might need you to make a couple runs with me, okay?" he said, "But you can't tell nobody, not even Ed."

She said, "P, I'm a grown-ass woman. Why do you think Ed chose me in the first place? I already know loose lips sink ships." She smiled.

P just said, "Damn," to himself, "one of these days."

He snapped out of his daydream and said, "If you ever need anything, Mama, just page me." And he left.

P was moving coke a hundred miles an hour now. Even Lan called him for some caine. But those two keys went quickly, so he said, "Fuck it. This caine is even better than that," and he raised the price to seventeen hundred an ounce. Even that went like hot cakes. A week and a half earlier, P had six keys. Now he was down to his last nine ounces. He knew he had to make a trip to the city, but that gasoline coke was still around everywhere. Only if he could find that shit that had the triangle stamp on it. He thought it out for a minute and knew Mimi was the only one who might be able to lead him in the right direction.

When P went over there, he had no gun on him whatsoever. She was looking down and out when P walked in.

"Mimi, what's wrong, love?" P said in a sad voice.

She looked at him, and tears started streaming down her beautiful face. P wiped her eyes and said, "Talk to me, love," in a smooth, calm, collected voice.

"My whole world is crumbling, P. Mike got robbed for everything, and he blamed me. He said I'm bad luck, and he left me P. He just packed all his shit and moved on." She bawled.

This was the young don's chance to move in and sweep her off her feet. He smelled weakness, so he moved in on his prey. He lifted her head up so he could gaze into her sexy brown eyes and said, "Baby girl, men like Mike are useless. He probably had bitches everywhere anyways. His type don't respect a beautiful working woman of your stature. Mike is the type to give his all to one of those hoodrat weave-wearing bitches. You being independent and all intimidates him completely. He wants his woman to depend on him, not the other way around," the boy told her smoothly.

"But, P, I was willing to help him in any way possible. I would've tried to raise the twenty grand he owes the Jamaican guy in New York. But he said, 'Fuck me, it's over.'" And she cried some more.

P said, "Don't worry, Mimi. I'm here for you always." And he kissed her before she could say another word. This time, she grabbed his hand and led him upstairs. That night, she worked P Double over hard in the sack, until he said, "Mimi, enough." But she still rode his dick until sunup. The next morning, he dicked her down again. The he asked her, "Mimi, did Mike ever bring you where he was copping from?" hoping the nigga at least brought his bitch with him once in a while.

His dreams were answered when she said, "Of course, P, he took me plenty of times. Rudy even tried to fuck me on the low."

P figured that Rudy had to be the Jamaican cat's name. "Mimi, do you think you can introduce me to the dread, love?" he asked, giving his best puppy-dog look.

She said, "But, P, the nigga will kill me. You know Mike owes the man twenty thousand."

"Listen, baby, I'm not Mike. I'll handle everything. Do you trust me?" young P said, staring deeply into her eyes.

"Yes, P, I do," she finally said.

"Well, put your tightest skirt on, and let's move, baby doll. Matter of fact, I'll be right back." P went home and came back an hour later with a duffel bag with two hundred and twenty thousand bucks in it. He left the other hundred and twenty seven thousand in his safe.

P decided to ride in Mimi's Honda because she and Mike used to ride in the same car. She had these red pumps with a tight-ass red Gucci dress to match. When they were halfway there, he turned the radio down and said, "Listen, you're gonna explain to the Jamaican that I'm Mike's nephew and he told me to handle the business end of things. Make sure you tell him that I'm only fifteen, even though I'm eighteen, so they don't try no funny shit. If they ask about Mike, say he had to go see his father in prison, but the business end of shit couldn't wait." He repeated this a couple of times to her and made sure she understood. "Oh yeah, and if he asks why you didn't come by yourself, tell him Mike said women shouldn't meddle in men's affairs."

When they got there, she drove to a Jamaican restaurant on Lennox Ave in Harlem. A bunch of Jamaicans were standing outside chilling when she got out and walked toward a dark-skinned Jamaican with long dreads. He was tall, and he wore a lot of gold. Even his smile was gold.

The plan worked because he walked over and said, "Rude boy, what ya deal wit?"

Young P broke shit down in his Jamaican lingo, and the big Jamaican was impressed how this young Jamaican-American boy was trying to get paid. P told him the money was in the trunk of the Honda. The tall Jamaican signaled for P to pop it, walk into the restaurant, and order what he wanted. Ten minutes later, the food was brought to him and Mimi. When she hopped into the car and started the engine, P hopped in, and she drove off.

P said, "Mimi, where's the coke?"

She told him while they were in the restaurant the Jamaican dropped it in the trunk. P said, "Fuck that. Pull over at that White Castle over there." He hopped out of the whip as she popped the trunk.

She didn't lie. The silver triangle packages were in not one duffel bag but two. The boy let out a breath for the world to hear. Then he hopped back into the Honda, and they headed to Massachusetts. When they got back, she said, "P, are you gonna keep them here?"

Young P looked at the bitch like she was crazy and said, "No, Mimi, I gotta stash house, love, so that way, we can stop niggas from breaking into your crib."

A man knows how to keep things in proper prospective, so being the young man he was, that was the way he explained it to her. In ghetto terms, he really wanted to say, "Fucks no, stupid bitch, so I can be broke like Mike Tuitt? I wouldn't leave a sock or a pair of boxers in this bitch."

P wound up French-kissing the bitch, and he told her to go into the crib and relax. After he handled a little business, he'd be back to fuck her brains out. He then jumped into his rental Pathfinder and skidded out. He had to go to Grandma's and count the dollar signs. He pulled up in front of Granny's and jumped out. He then walked around, snatched the bags out, and headed upstairs to his room at once. His grandmother came back from

Cancun with a little tan and all that. P loved to see his grandmother happy and well. The bolt locked on the door with ease. P Double had a bolt lock put on his door because his grandmother had some shady-ass children. He emptied both bags on the bed and found twenty-six keys. The dread left a note that Mike owed him a hundred and seventy-five grand. P did a quick calculation. Fifteen a key was a crazy flip right now. He snatched up five and called Mama.

"Hello?" she said, sounding sexier than ever.

"Yo, it's P. I'm about to come over and use the lab. Are you all right, love?"

She said, "Not really. Ed didn't leave me with much money, and there's a couple bills that need to be paid."

P wanted to fuck this bitch bad, so he said, "I got everything covered, baby girl. I'll be there in ten minutes and two seconds." And he hung up. P stashed the keys all around his room, and he decided that the next day, he would get his own apartment and make sure no one knew where he lived. Mama was on the porch with a yellow catsuit on when he pulled up. She was looking as gorgeous as ever. She hugged him and told him to come in. P went straight to the lab as she followed him downstairs. First, he threw the bag on the table and took five keys out. Then he gave Mama five thousand he had in his pocket and the keys to the Pathfinder and told her he would be there for a good minute. Mama kissed his cheek and thanked him. She told him to make sure he cleaned up when he was done, and she went shopping. That night, young P cooked up seventy-five hundred grams of crack. The streets of Springfield were gonna find out they had a new general in town, and his name was Presley Williams, a.k.a. P Double.

CHAPTER 6

MORE MONEY MORE PROBLEMS

P Double woke up on his birthday and thanked God for his good fortune. It had been five months since he broke into Mimi's crib and found the five cakes. Shit, as far as P was concerned, things were only getting better. He had his own house with a million and a half stashed in his walk-in safe. The safe was behind a big-ass portrait of himself that ran from the ground to about twenty feet in the air. All of this was located in his personal library and study. He also had a big marble desk with a picture of Tony Montana behind him holding that M-60 machine gun he had in *Scarface* the movie. Fine-ass Mama was just waking up.

"Baby, what's wrong?" she said, looking cute and concerned in the early morning.

P said, "Nothing at all. Today is a good day." He smiled.

She kissed him and said, "Happy birthday, daddy." Right then and there, she pulled the covers back and put P's limp dick in her mouth. P's dick rose for the occasion as usual, as Mama deep-throated the boy's dick in long strokes while looking him in the eyes with that sexy look. P remembered the first day Mama rocked his world.

$ $ $

Young P had finished the twenty-six birds the Jamaican guys had provided him with so he swung through Ed's crib early in the morning and knocked on the door until Mama ran downstairs. "What the fuck, P? Do you know how early it is?" she said, wiping cold out of her eyes.

P thought, *Damn, even in the morning time, this bitch is the shit.* The young don said, "Get dressed. We gotta hit the road right away."

She said, "But where?" in a whinny baby voice.

"Come on, girl, ask me no questions, and I will tell you no lies. Now, let's go." She ran upstairs, washed her face, and brushed her teeth real quick. Then she came down in a Guess suit that said, "Oh shit."

P told her to drive to Burger King so they could grab some breakfast. Then he told her to drive to the city. The whole way there, he was spitting game at her, but she kept saying that P was cute, but he was too young. In his mind, he said, "I'll show this bitch how young my money is then, because it's quite grown." As soon as they hit the city, he told her to drive to the Chanel store. When they entered, he said, "Snatch up what you want, love." And he winked at her.

She said, "You asked for it," and she went and picked out some boots, a mink jacket, and a leather outfit with a matching purse.

P took the items from her and threw them on the counter. An old white lady asked them if it would be cash or credit.

Young P said, "Cash, lady."

The old bitch looked at the tags on the clothing and said, "Young man, all this stuff comes to roughly over thirty thousand dollars."

P kindly smiled at the old bitch and said, "Ring the shit up."

The old bitch snatched the clothes off the counter and called over an older gentleman. He walked over and said, "What seems to be the problem?"

P said, "Nothing, if this old bag would ring up our shit so we could go."

She said, "Well, all this cost thirty thousand dollars."

P pulled out a very healthy stack of hundred-dollar bills, and the man counted it up. The lady was staring at P with malice in her eyes. P saw the look and said, "Excuse me. I don't got all day, you old bag. Now, bag up my girl's shit," he said arrogantly.

The old lady had her mouth wide open in shock when he said this. She just started wrapping the items and said, "Well, I never," muttering to herself. He took Mama by the hand and walked her down the street to Saks and Fifth and copped her a nine-carat tennis bracelet with nine-carat earrings.

He then took her to the best restaurant in Manhattan, where he pledged her his undivided attention. P then copped a ten-thousand-dollar-a-night room at the Waldorf Astoria. He walked her up to the penthouse suite and told her he would be right back. Young P had to handle his real business, and that was going to Lennox Ave. Rudy was happy to see the young boy again. This time, P had a half-million dollars of his own money in the trunk of the whip. Rudy walked him into the restaurant and asked the boy why Mike didn't make the run anymore and how Mike was getting all this good American currency. P made up a bunch of bullshit that the dread ate up quickly. The big Jamaican told P his food was ready, and P drove straight to the Waldorf Astoria.

When he walked into the room, he smelled the sweet scent of fragrance candles burning. He called Mama's name but didn't get a response. The room was decorated with an exquisite touch of high class. There was a large white grand piano in the middle of the room with red carpet on the floor. The carpet was so thick P almost sprained an ankle when his foot sank into its elegance. There was white and red furniture with all types of chandeliers. The fireplace was burning with a gentle crackle from the wood when Mama walked out of the bedroom stark naked. Her long hair ran all the way down to her D-size breasts. She had the earrings in her ears and the tennis bracelet on her wrist. She walked toward P, and the young boy was in a daze because Mama's twenty-two-year-old body was no doubt a work of art. Her ass was gigantic, and it was solid and soft at the same time. There were no dents in this Mercedes-Benz here.

P said, "Well—" She put her hands on his lips and shushed him, and she took all of his clothes off. She then walked P over to the bearskin rug and told him to make love to her. She said little boys fucked; she wanted to be made love to. P then kissed her with more passion than he knew he had in him. He nibbled on her neck, and then he took one of her small pink nipples in his mouth. Her body responded with readiness. She pushed his head down to her womanliness, and P found himself tasting the rainbow for the first time. P thought, *Damn, this ain't half bad.* Nah, Ma tasted like peaches and cream. She then bucked in P's mouth from deep thrills of ecstasy. Mama creamed and shivered wildly. She moaned, "Please, P take me now." P spread her legs and put his dick in Mama's shaved pussy. It was wet, but she was tighter than a virgin. She screamed when P put it all the way in. P fucked her slowly and intensely until they both came in delight. Then he rolled off of her, and she took him in her mouth. His shit stayed rock hard as she swallowed his dick all the way down to his balls. Mama was a master at deep-throating a dick. P thought Mimi was that bitch, but Mama had her beat in every way. Young P got up, picked Mama up, and threw her onto the grand piano. He long dicked her down until her tight-ass pussy couldn't take it no more. Her pussy was the best pussy P had ever had in his life. She orgasmed, and her pussy put the young don's dick in a figure-four leglock. After that, Mama was his bitch, no questions asked. Young P was in love, for the first time.

Lan and all the other older cats couldn't believe it at all. He had to ask P one day, "Yo, ain't that Eddie Haul's girl?"

"Nah, she part of my chain, part of my gang, car getting washed in the rain." And he laughed.

Lan looked at the little nigga and shook his head. "You already know Ed ain't gonna take this shit well, P," he said at last.

"I'm that nigga around here now. Ain't nobody doing shit to this nigga right here, and that's my word. It's not my fault the nigga can't make a half-million-dollar bail, now is it?" the boy asked Lan twice.

Lan shook his head and tried to reason with the snotty youth again. "It's not all about that, P. It's a respect thing, nigga," he said with a challenging glare.

P appeared to be soaking all this in until he responded, "Well, I'm that nigga that's well respected out here. Tell him to respect that. He better be glad I'm the one that's maintaining her and fixing her up and not another mechanic."

Lan just said, "Fuck it," and strolled off.

$ $ $

That night, Ed called his own crib, and instead of Mama answering the phone, P answered it. "Yo, what up?" P said in a tired tone.

Ed went crazy and started yelling, "Who the fuck is this?"

"It's P, nigga. That's who the fuck it is, chump," P said, holding his own.

"I trusted your bitch ass, and this is how you're gonna play me. I'm gonna kill your bitch ass."

P got angry at that comment and said, "Listen to this bitch nigga."

At the time, Mama was lying on the couch with just panties on. P signaled for her to come into the kitchen. He bent her over the counter, pulled her panties to the side, and started fucking the shit out of her from behind.

"Oh fuck, P, yes, yes! Fuck me, papi, iee iee!" she screamed, and he heard nothing but meat smacking as he fucked her to death. They both climaxed at the same time, and then Mama turned around and started sucking his dick. P grabbed the phone and started breathing erratically from the nut he just busted, and he heard Ed denounce his manhood and shed tears over what he just heard.

P said, "I'm the don out here, damn it. And don't ever forget it." He then banged on Ed and continued to get his dick sucked.

Little did P know, Ed wasn't gonna stand for this shit. That night, he called his cousin in New York and asked him how much it would cost to get two people knocked off. His cousin told Ed forty racks. Ed sent the money right away. He might not make that half-a-million-dollar cash bail he had, but he kept money for rainy days like that.

$ $ $

The two hit men were named Specialist and Professional. They were Jamaican brothers from New York. They were feared and wanted in fifteen states already. They got the call and went to meet Ed's contact in the field, which was a young hood named J.G. J.G. was originally part of P Double's crew, but hate was in his blood crazy right then. He used to fuck with Ed heavy when the nigga was home. Now that Ed was locked up, J.G. couldn't stand P Double. He hated him because P was the same age as he was and ran Bristol

Street. J.G. met them at the bus station. They were already paid in advance. All J.G. had to do was show them where Ed lived and show them pictures of P Double and Mama. J.G. gave them two Glocks and the RS 7 basehead rental he was in. The two thugs thought about killing J.G.'s bitch ass but decided to just use him in the future. The two hoods parked down the street and came up with a plan of how they were gonna kill this nigga and bitch combo.

$ $ $

P Double and Mama walked into the crib late that night. They came from the after hour on Dunmoreland Street when they decided to fuck. The two brothers heard P giving it to her and thought this was gonna be an easy job. They drove to the gas station down the street and filled up two gas cans. They then went to the house, poured gas all around it, and set it on fire. P was the first one to smell smoke. He told Mama not to panic as she started screaming. He looked out the second-floor window and saw the two hoods standing across the street. For some reason, he knew Ed sent them. The whole first floor was burning savagely. P and Mama ran to the back of the house and into the bathroom.

P lifted up the window and jumped. He landed on his feet, then rolled forward, and popped back up on his feet. He yelled quietly for Mama to jump. She did and broke her leg on impact. She screamed in pain, but P covered her mouth so he muffled the sound. Just then, they heard a gun erupt in the front of the house and sirens sound down the street. The ambulance and fire department came, along with the police and another ambulance. Apparently, somebody saw the hoods and confronted them, and they killed the poor man execution style and ran off. P hopped into the ambulance with Mama, and they went to the hospital. They put a cast on her leg, and P took a cab to the Holiday Inn until P copped the crib in East Long Meadow they lived in now.

$ $ $

P stopped daydreaming when Mama sucked him dry. Damn, that woman sure could get his attention with a good old-fashioned dick suck any day of the week. P told his bitch to run him some bathwater, and he turned his Motorola cell phone on. P Double moved up in the world with this one. The only thing P hated about the phone was that the shit was big as fuck. He checked his voice mail and found that Kev, Bates, T Baby, and the nigga Raheem from the south end had called him. He loved doing business with Raheem because that nigga had the south end on smash. Mister and the rest of his crew called Raheem for work, which meant that P ate lovely off that plate. P grabbed his phone and started making moves. Already, he sold seven of the fifty cakes he had in his other apartment in town. He had a fireproof safe built into the closet there. That was where he kept all his work and fucked his other bitches. He hopped out of the tub and threw on a turquoise blue and white Karl Kani suit and the matching turquoise blue and white Air Force Ones with the turquoise strap in the back. The Nike sign glittered with turquoise rhinestones. He grabbed his Charlotte Hornets hat and suede Hornets jacket to match it. They both glittered with rhinestones. P threw his two Cuban links on. One had an iced-out Boston Red Sox B on it. But he would tell niggas the B didn't stand for "Boston" quick. He was a Yankees fan. And he had an iced-out Jesus piece for the other Cuban. He threw his gold presidential Rolex on. It was Icy and his iced-out bracelet. Now he was ready for rock. He kissed his girl and left. He had four beautiful whips, but that day, he choose to jump in his all-white Mazda Millenia, with the gold rims and gold tailpipes. Young P was the whole definition of a baller. Shit, he was from the home of the basketball hall of fame, where you ball on and off the court, so why wouldn't he ball? Just then, T Baby hit him up on the jack.

"What up, baby?" P said.

Baby said, "Yo, nigga, turn that shit down real quick."

P had that new Black Moon tape, with buckshot shorty rocking the Millenia.

P said, "I'm on my way, my nigga. I'll be through there in a second. I just gotta make a couple runs first."

Baby said, "I gotta birthday present waiting for you. Come on." And he hung up.

P turned the radio back up. A couple of minutes later, he pulled up on Cliftwood Street in Forest Park, where he kept his caine at. He packed the work in a big duffel bag and made his runs. He got to T Baby's house on Norfolk Street, and T Baby had J.G.'s girl there along with Andy Cap's dame. The young don walked into the crib, blinding everybody with the mix of ice and rhinestones. P took a brick from under his arm in his jacket and threw it on T Baby's lap.

Baby said, "The twenty-five racks is on top of the TV, good-looking."

Cap's girl, Keisha, looked at P like he was magically delicious, as she licked her juicy lips and said, "Damn, nigga, you looking real creamy right now."

P said, "Yo, where Cap and J.G.?"

Quizzically, T Baby said, "Man, who gives a fuck?" He grabbed J.G.'s bitch and said, "I'll be right back."

Baby went into the next room and closed the door.

Keisha then said, "Come here for a second, P."

He walked over and took the load off his feet when he heard T Baby fucking the shit out of J.G.'s girl. Keisha leaned over and said, "Can I suck your dick, P, please? I've been dying to taste that shit."

P thought about it. *It is 1993, and it's my birthday. Plus, Cap would've probably did the same shit to me, so why not?* He unzipped his pants and let her suck. She was making all types of smacking noises, but her head game was straight trash. J.G.'s bitch sounded like she had some good pussy because Baby was killing that shit. That just turned P on. He snatched Cap's girl by the hair and made her stop. He then pushed her skirt up and pulled her panties to the side as he slid his dick into her. She grabbed his ass and screamed, "Uhh," as P rammed his dick in roughly. He then proceeded by palming her ass as he went to work. Keisha's pussy started to gush as P thrust into her. She had some all right bird, but P had had better. P didn't even notice that T Baby and J.G.'s girl had walked in on him jackhammering away. He finally busted in the bitch and got up. He made Keisha suck all the nut off his dick in front of them and zipped his jeans up when he finished.

Baby then said, "P man, I know who burned the crib up, daddy."

P said, "What? Who was it?"

Baby then looked at J.G.'s girl, and she told him everything she knew and made him a believer.

P said, "No problem. Everybody just act regular. I'll handle this shit."

Lately, P had been slipping because he had stopped packing his heat. He now realized this was a major mistake on his part. P grabbed the twenty-five stacks off the TV and said, "I'll see y'all at the Waterfront tonight, peace."

He then went back to the crib in Forest Park and grabbed a Tech 9 and a spare clip. That night was gonna be a hell of a night for sure. He'd make sure J.G. and the brothers got what they deserved. The Waterfront Club was packed. It was the world-famous fish fry as well as P Double's birthday. He made sure the bar was bought out that night. Tuka Gee was controlling the DJ booth and had shit jumping. P went home to change and grab his bitch. He changed and threw on his Bulls leather and suede jacket with the giant bull on the back, rhinestones out. He also had a Michael Jordan Olympic jersey with a pair of fresh blue-and-white striped Girbraud jeans on. On his feet were the Olympic Barcelona Jordans. P also had a Chicago Bulls hat, rhinestones out. He made sure he wore his jewels as well. Nah, Ma had a see-through Coco Chanel dress on, with a matching see-through purse. She also rocked a pink mink coat and was iced out as well. That night, P drove the burgundy V-12 850 BMW. The whole night, P Double was tense because he was scanning the room for J.G. and couldn't find him, but he found his little bitch and told her to meet him at his whip.

When she entered the whip, he asked where the hell J.G. was at, and she said he was on his way. He said, "Fuck it. Might as well have some fun," and he whipped his dick out for J.G.'s pretty bitch to suck. And that she could do. After ten minutes, P exploded in her mouth and told the bitch to signal him when J.G. popped up. She said okay, but she wanted P Double to bust her ass. He told the bitch, "Later, now get out."

The bitch stormed off angry, but so what? P Double then made a guest appearance back in the Waterfront and had a glass of Dom P, to relax his mind. Just then, he saw J.G. walk into the joint. He took off his jewels and handed them to Mama along with his jacket. She said, "Oh God, P. What are you gonna do, baby?" as he stormed through the crowd.

T Baby and the rest of the crew already knew the 411. P approached J.G.

while he was tongue-kissing his bitch and tapped him on his shoulder. J.G. turned around, told P happy birthday, and hugged him.

P said, "It's too loud in here. Let's talk outside for a minute."

As they went outside, he told T Baby and the crew to give them a couple of minutes before they went outside.

J.G. asked P, "What's up?"

Smiling when it was just the two of them, P said, "Yeah, nigga, I heard you don't respect my gangster, nigga?"

J.G. got in defensive mode at once. "Nah, P, you heard wrong."

P said, "The word around town is Ed put a hit on me, and you helped?" P said this with his hands behind his back.

J.G. went on and on saying, "P, you already know I got mad love for you, dog. I'll kill whoever said that shit right now!"

P smiled and said, "Well, kill your bitch then because she just told me this shit while she was sucking my dick ten minutes ago."

J.G. went crazy and said, "You bitch-ass nigga" and tried to take P's head off with a massive blow.

P ducked, power-slammed J.G., and smacked him twice. He backed up, letting the man get to his feet. That was when half the party came out behind T Baby and the crew. J.G. swung again with malice. P sidestepped the blow and hit him with a three-piece stunner. J.G. staggered back. That was when P saw his opening, and he ran up on him and earth-slammed him. P then stomped the man until he was unconscious.

P said, "Yeah, baby, Kev. Get this bitch-ass nigga out of here." The team laughed at J.G. and then picked him up and threw him into the car.

P said, "Yo, baby."

Baby looked back, and P said, "Take his girl with y'all."

Baby grinned and said, "Done."

The young thugs left with J.G. and his bitch as P Double snatched his jewels from Mama and partied hard. P got drunk and drove Mama home. He looked at her and said, "Baby, I'll be back shortly. I gotta handle some business, love."

Mama went nuts and started grabbing at his zipper. P pushed her away and said, "Jahdi, relax."

Mama's real name made her stop. She looked at the young don she had fallen so madly in love with, and tears started streaming down her beautiful face. She said, "P, I love you more than anything I've ever loved in my whole life; I swear it. Please don't leave, daddy. I wanna make tonight special please."

P looked at the beautiful bird and said, "Sweetheart, I swear I'm only gonna be gone a half hour at the most. This shit can't wait. I gotta handle this tonight."

Mama just jumped out of the car pouting and slammed the door hard. She ran into the house crying. P just said, "Fuck it." The bitch would get over it eventually. If not, she could always be replaced. P Double backed the 850 out of his driveway and drove to the Motel 6 in Chicopee, Massachusetts. They had already gotten the room earlier that day, when P Double formed the plan. Room 406 was a double-bed room. The thugs had J.G. butt-ass naked, facedown, ass up, and handcuffed to the bed. They had his girl the same way on the other bed when P knocked on the door and made his powerful presence felt. P walked over and took the gag out of J.G.'s mouth, as Bates, Kev, and T Baby watched, awaiting the plan.

P said, "So you wanted me dead, huh, Jay?"

J.G. looked at the young don, scared to death, and said, "The bitch is lying, I swear."

P put on a pair of brass knuckles he had taken out of his pocket and said, "J.G., just tell me where the two Jamaicans are at, and I'll let both of y'all go. Now where are they?"

J.G. shook his head and said, "Word to everything, she lying." He pleaded.

P said, "All right, wrong answer," and punched him in his nose and mouth. The thugs all heard the crunch as the brass knuckles broke J.G.'s nose and teeth. J.G. screamed in pain, gagging on blood and teeth as he tried to talk.

"Please, P, I swear."

This time, P blackened his eyes. The next time P hit him in the ribs until J.G. couldn't take it anymore. "Okay, okay," he screamed with tears running out his eyes. "They're in West Springfield at the Red Roof Inn room 202 in the back. Please, P, I'm sorry."

P said, "Yeah, I bet you are, but I'm not." He went and got this basehead they called Predator from across the street. He ordered him some food at the fifties diner across the street from Motel 6, and he told him to wait. Predator was the type of basehead who would do anything for crack cocaine. P brought him into the room and flashed a quarter ounce of coke. Predator licked his lips with greed and said, "What do you want me to do?"

P whispered in his ear, and the man got butt-ass naked as they all watched. They all said, "Got damn," as Predator's dick was at least thirteen inches long.

P said, "The girl first." Predator got on top of the bitch and started drilling the bitch from behind. She had a gag in her mouth, but you could still hear the muffled screams as the man fucked the little bitch to death. Soon tears started staining the pillow as he worked her.

P said, "Man, fuck that, fuck her in the ass."

Predator took it out of her, and the bitch started jerking all crazy because she knew what was next. Predator busted her ass wide open because you heard the pop, and it was a bloody sight to see as J.G.'s bitch finally passed out from the pain.

P said, "Now him," with an evil smirk.

Bates even said, "Oh shit," as Predator put his organ in J.G.'s ass. He fucked him until he was bloody and passed out. They gave Predator the quarter and uncuffed the couple. They told predator to wash up and come on.

P was thinking, *Let's see what he gotta say when he wake up with a saucy butt.* They drove to West Springfield, kicked in the two Jamaicans' door, and tied them up. They let Predator do the same thing to them, except this time, they left the handcuffs on them and the door wide open so the cleaning lady could find them. She did because it was all over Channel 40 News how the two murder suspects were found defiled in the Red Roof Inn. P laughed when he saw his latest highlight. Somehow, some way, he was gonna make sure Ed got his manhood taken too. You didn't try and kill P Double and think you were gonna sleep easy at night. The streets were calling him a monster. He liked it though because the late great Machiavelli was right. P would rather be feared than loved any day of the week. If J.G.

feared him in the first place, this would've never happened. The next two weeks went smoothly until P got pulled over and arrested for having over twenty thousand in his pocket. The young eighteen-year-old was angry because in two weeks his probation would be over.

CHAPTER 7

WHAT'S BEEF

They brought P Double to court the next day. His lawyer, Vincent Bonjorni, helped him out by saying, "Mr. Williams was bringing me the twenty thousand dollars as a fee for his uncle, Maurice Williams, Your Honor."

The judge let P Double go home at once, but Jaynce, his probation officer, called him into her office. "Have a seat, Mr. Williams," she said with a fed-up tone in her voice. "Now, I really wanna know what you were doing with over twenty thousand dollars on your person." She looked the boy in his eyes.

"Miss Magill, my lawyer already told you where I—" She cut him off by slamming her beautiful fist on the desktop. She got real ghetto on P real quick. "You don't think I know you're one of the biggest drug dealers in fucking Springfield, Presley, or should I call you P Double?" she said with anger in her voice. "Pull up your sleeve, P Double," she said, shaking her head back and forth. "I know for a fact that's a real Rolex on your wrist."

P got real fed up with this shit and said, "So if you know all of this that you say you so-called know, how come I'm in your face and not in Westfield?"

She said, "For one, because you're smart, and I really can't violate you on a hunch, and two, you really need help, Presley. You're throwing your life away."

P thought she sounded kind of concerned, but why would this beautiful woman care, when he'd been trying to get her attention for five and a half months now? So he asked her, "And why do you care?"

She got up and said, "What? You don't think I know about you sending me flowers, candy, and poetry every other day? I know it's you, and I really wanna help you." She sounded sincere.

"Well, if you wanna help me, you'll have dinner with me tonight," he said. "I'll pick you up at eight tonight. Be ready." The young man spoke as he got up and opened the door.

She said, "Wait. I didn't say yes, and you don't even know where I live."

P looked at her and smiled. "Please, Miss Magill. Yes, I do."

She looked shocked and said, "Tell me how."

He said, "Because my name is P Double, like you said, love. Eight o'clock. Don't be late."

Jaynce found herself wondering about the international man of mystery. She didn't wanna admit it, but she found herself falling for him, slowly but very surely.

$ $ $

Mama was waiting for P when he walked out of the courthouse. She gave him a big hug and planted kisses all over his face. "Baby, I missed you," she said as she hopped in the Millenia with P. He told her to drive him to the barbershop down the street. P went into Smitty's with his head high. Mama sat next to him while he was waiting on Smitty to finish giving this old guy a haircut. His grandmother had been bringing P to Smitty's ever since P was a baby. Smitty asked P how his grandmother was doing as he sprinkled talc on the little brush and cleaned the old man's face off. P then sat in the chair, and Smitty started giving him his weekly number one and line up. P's cell phone went off. Mama answered it, and a voice said, "You and your bitch-ass man is dead, bitch." And the voice hung up.

As soon as she got up to tell P, the barbershop window shattered with gunfire. Everybody hit the floor except the guy who was in the chair in front of P. When the shooting stopped, they found out that the man had taken five shots to the upper body. P heard rapid fire, so he knew someone was firing a machine gun. P called Kev and Bates at once and asked them to pick him up. That was the only way P was leaving Smitty's because he didn't have a piece on him. They came, but they called his phone from a payphone up the street because police were all over the place. P's whip even took a pounding. The whole side was gunned down. He told Mama to catch a cab home and make sure the car got towed. She kissed him and told him to be safe. P ran down the street and jumped in Kev's Honda. They asked him what happened. He broke the facts down to them in a matter of minutes.

Kev said, "Well, it couldn't've been J.G. because word was he had to get eight stitches in his ass. His girl got ten in her ass and five to tighten her pussy. They said Predator also ruptured her uterus. Now she can't even have kids. So he'll be down for the count."

P said, "Damn, I should have killed his bitch ass. Anyways, who do you think shot the barbershop up and my whip?"

Bates said, "I don't know, but we need to find out."

P's phone started buzzing after that. "Who's this?" P yelled into the jack.

"You want war, boy. Me show you fuckery, boy," the voice said. "Jah know you die tonight, bredren." And the voice hung up.

P said, "Some Jamaican just called my jack bugging the fuck out, yo. His voice sounded familiar though. All I know is nobody is gonna disrespect the god and live." Just then, as P was rambling on, his phone sounded again. "Word, we'll be right there, peace," he said and hung up the phone. "Damn, yo," he swore.

Kev said, "What happened?"

"T Baby got popped up bad, and A-Dog took a slug in the ass. We gotta run to the hospital and see what's up with these niggas."

Bay State Medical Center was busy as usual when the trio walked in. They went up to the desk and found out T Baby and A-Dog were being operated on at the time. So they just decided to come back the next day.

$ $ $

Meanwhile, Mike Tuitt was on his way to the Mecca to cop. He rustled up fifty stacks to get back on. His plan was to pay the Jamaicans their twenty racks, spend thirty, and try to get as much consignment as he could. Everything was going according to plan when Rudy ran up in the restaurant with a Mac 10 out.

Mike screamed, "What's wrong?"

The dreads took him to the basement, where they had a bunch of chains hanging on the wall. It stank down there of chicken blood and dead and rotten cow meat. Where they took Mike, there appeared to be a lot of dried blood in that area. Rudy told his two bodyguards to strip the boy down to his boxer shorts and chain his hands in the air. They then hoisted the chains up so that Mike was lifted off his feet. The whole time he was begging and pleading for his life, asking the big Jamaican what was wrong. The pain in his arms was almost unbearable as he hung there and waited for Rudy to state his claim. The Jamaican walked up to him with his hands behind his back and looked Mike in his eyes. He said, "Boy, haven't me treat you good ever since me known your ras Claud boy?"

Tuitt screamed, "Yes, Rudy, please tell me what this is about, please!"

The dread said, "The boy still wanna play like he don't bum ba Claud know, so scream to Jah pussy hole." The Jamaican painted his chest with a chicken foot that was dipped in chicken blood and said, "Me teach you fuckery." Then he signaled for his two goons to give the man the treatment.

As Mike pleaded on and on, the two men came back with a car battery and some jumper cables. One of the goons pulled Mike's boxer shorts down and threw water on his balls while the other applied the jumper cables to them. Mike's whole body shook from the volts that ran through his body. He let out a thunderous scream of sheer agony until the man snatched the cables away. Mike could smell his balls cooking as he cried for God to help him. The dread lifted Mike's head up and said, "Boy, you try to spend fifty, and you owe me two hundred and fifty? What you think this rude boy pussy know?"

Mike said, "But, Rudy, I only owe you twenty, I swear."

The dread applied the cables himself this time, and Mike screamed in what seemed to him like a lifetime's worth of pain. This time, Mike shit and pissed on himself from the pain. The dread said, "Where's your nephew that you always send to buy for you?"

All Tuitt knew was that he was in trouble. "I swear, Dread. This is my first time coming to you in five months," Tuitt said, breathing erratically.

The dread shocked him again and again until Mike passed out. He woke up with the dreads watching him. He didn't know how long he had been in the dungeon or why the dreads were giving him this extreme workover. All he knew was his body was aching all over, and he was dying from his own stench mixed with chicken blood and rotten cow meat. The dread continued his interrogation as soon as he saw his victim awake.

"Boy, where your bitch Mimi at?" the dread said with scorn and crudeness in his voice.

Mike couldn't take another shock so he begged the dread to listen. "Rudy, I stopped fucking her five months ago when I got robbed." Mike continued begging for his life with haste.

The dread said, "So young P Double is no relation to you at all?"

Mike said, "Hell no!" but he knew who had robbed him once the dread spoke those words. The dread continued the interrogation.

"So why did your girl Mimi bring him up here and say that was your nephew then?"

Mike said. "I swear I don't know, Dread, I swear."

Mike was timid and angry at the same time.

Rudy said, "Be quiet, or me send you to Jah. I must think." The dread sat there for a minute while Mike looked at the floor saying a silent prayer. The dread then dialed a bunch of numbers into his phone. He spoke. "When are you gonna come see me, boy?" He grunted to himself for a minute, and then he said, "How is your uncle doing?" He waited another moment and said, "Send him my regards." And he hung up.

Rudy then signaled for his guards to release Mike and cover his order. The dread gave Mike four bricks for fifty and apologized to the man for the torture he inflicted on him. All Mike was thinking about was getting home safely and making somebody pay for his pain.

$ $ $

P Double had Kev and Bates drop him off at his grandmother's house. From there, P took a cab home and fucked Mama well. Then he jumped into the shower to prepare for his date with Jaynce. He wondered why Rudy called him and asked him when he was coming. That was the first time the boss Jamaican had ever questioned when P was coming to see him. Then P began to think that word had gotten back to New York that somebody was trying to kill P. Then his phone buzzed, and his mind became business oriented again. This time, the news made him happy. Raheem had fifty stacks waiting for him. He told the man to give him a half an hour and hung up. Young P dried off and threw on a burgundy Versace suit, with a white and burgundy tie and the hanky to match. He also threw on a pair of burgundy and white gators. As he was spraying on some Polo Sport cologne, Mama flew the coop.

"Where the fuck are you going looking like that, Presley?" she said as her Spanish accent got heavier with her anger.

"I got a business meeting with some very important people tonight," he replied smoothly.

She said, "Well, I'm going too, fuck that." And she opened the closet.

P said, "Baby, I'm sorry. This is a men's affair only. No women are going to be present."

This really drove her mad. "Yeah, right, I bet. You're probably gonna bring one of your other bitches. What you think I ain't heard, Presley? I hear everything. You don't love me. If you did, you wouldn't be fucking half the damn town." And she slapped him. Mama continued to swing viciously when P just scooped her and shit her up with two hard-boiled smacks. Mama's eye swelled up immediately. This was the first time P had ever put his hands on her, and he felt bad. Mama ran to the bathroom and locked herself in.

P banged on the door and said how much he was sorry, and he pledged his love for her and only her. After a minute of not getting a response, he said, "Fuck it," and walked to the garage.

P jumped in the 850 and thought, *I'll make it up to her*, as he drove off. P ran up to his apartment and grabbed for keys. He started to grab the Tech, but he thought about it. His probation officer wouldn't think too kindly of him carrying a firearm so he just walked out without any protection whatsoever. P gave Raheem all four and told the man if he needed anything else to just holla. By the time he made it to Jaynce's house, it was about eight thirty. He figured the roses and candy he stopped for would make up for it. He rang her doorbell and almost passed out when she came to the door, because she was drop-dead gorgeous. Jaynce had on this all-white Donna Karan dress that just hugged her body in all the right places. Her skin gleamed with a luster that made it seem like it was made up of the finest chocolate. P thought, *Now, this is a woman.*

P said, "Here, these are for you."

She took them and said, "Thank you, but you're late."

He apologized to her and said, "It won't never happen again."

She said, "Wait here a minute," and she ran back into the house to put the flowers in water. When Jaynce appeared, P grabbed one of her well-manicured hands and walked her to the 850. P opened the door and shut it behind her. She loved the way her body just melted into the leather and said, "So this is how you charm all the ladies?"

He politely said, "No," and drove to the Chez Josef restaurant.

$ $ $

Meanwhile, Mike Tuitt drove straight home, grabbed his Beretta, and drove to Mimi's house. His body ached so badly, but his mind was running on basic adrenaline. Somebody was gonna pay for the pain he felt, and he meant that with a passion. He hopped out on Fenwick Street and rang the bell twice. Mimi opened the door and was surprised to see him on her porch. As she invited him in, Mike shoved the Beretta under her jaw and told her if she made a sound, she was dead. He told her to have a seat as he locked the door. Then he looked at her and said, "Where the fuck is P Double at, bitch?"

Mike looked like he had aged ten years from the torture he went through.

Mimi said, "Mike, I swear I don't know. Why?" She didn't get a chance to finish before he smacked her with the pistol three times. She screamed in pain as blood oozed out of different parts of her face.

"Now, where the fuck is he, you stupid bitch?" he said with murder written all over his face.

Mimi was spitting teeth out of her mouth when she answered with a muffled, "I don't know."

Mike said, "Wrong answer again." This time, he grabbed her by her hair and hit her three more times.

Mimi hit the floor and blacked out. Mike ran and yanked the phone cord out of the wall and out of the phone. Then he rolled Mimi over and hog-tied her. He walked into the kitchen and ran some water into a bucket. He then walked back into the living room and splashed the water in Mimi's face. He bent down and said, "Bitch, you're not getting out of this shit easy."

As she started to move and groan in pain, Mike started kicking her in the stomach repeatedly as he was screaming, "Where the fuck is he, bitch?"

Mimi started choking on blood and gagging from lack of oxygen. She cried and said weakly, "Please, Mike, I really don't know."

Mike looked at her and said, "Well, I guess I have to find him myself, bitch." He pressed the Beretta to her temple and squeezed twice. Her brain splattered all on his clothes. Tuitt then searched the house and found nothing. As he hopped in his car and drove away, his mind was on where and how to get P Double.

$ $ $

On the other side of town, Black was out of the hospital. He wasn't a hundred percent, but he already knew he couldn't let them Bristol Street niggas get away with the pain they had caused him. For months, he was laid up in the bed, not caring about himself but wondering about his girl Shafika. All he could envision in his mind was all them niggas fucking his girl. He knew they killed her because she had been missing five and a half months now. Every day, his mother and the rest of his kin tried to get him to talk. Even the police wanted him to talk, but Black didn't say a word to anyone. Not even the chiropractor who was treating him got a word out of him. Meanwhile, the streets had ears, and he was listening. Bitch-ass Presley was living like a king while Black had to walk with a cane. Black finally came out of his shell and called his young cousin D Black. D Black was down with the biggest black clique in the city, the Ave, which stood for

"All violators executed." He thought, well, Presley violated, so he wanted him executed. D black was tall and dark skinned and looked like the lead singer from Jodeci. His loyalty to B Black was immense, because he looked up to his older cousin from Worthington Street. Young D Black sat down as his cousin told him the embarrassing tale. His face changed as he switched places with his cousin and felt the pain he was going through.

As the story finished, Black said, "You don't even gotta worry about shit. I got us, doggy." And he stormed out.

$ $ $

Sun Sun had to let P Double know whom he was fucking with. All the while he was in the joint, all he heard was Presley's name. The young Jamaican would spit and swear to Jah. He was gonna take the young don up off of here. P Double put his hands on the wrong Jamaican this time. Sun Sun was a prince, and he was gonna make Presley bow down to him. In his mind, Presley wasn't an official rude boy because he was half American. To him, the boy was a Yankee, and Sun Sun was gonna send him to Jah to repent his sins. Sun Sun couldn't find him, so he went by Bristol Street and hit up a couple of O's boys. He said, "Fuck it." He might as well bring it to all of them. That was when he hopped out and asked T Baby if he knew where P was. Baby said no so Sun Sun said, "Tell him I'm home," and he shot Baby in the chest five times with the little twenty-five-caliber automatic he had.

A-Dog started running, and he shot him in the ass. He told his boys Rocky and Ernie. They saw P Double's girl at the courthouse, so they followed her and waited. Sure enough, P walked out with her, and they followed them to the barbershop, where they let the Mac 10 off like it was the Fourth of July. They made sure they took the car out too. They watched the news together. They all swore when they found out P Double and his bitch had made it out without a scratch on either of them. They got dressed in all black. They decided it was hunting season, and P Double was their prey.

$ $ $

At Chez Josef, P ordered the fettuccine Alfredo and a sirloin, while Jaynce had stuffed peppers and spaghetti with clam sauce. They both ate salads while waiting on the main course. P then asked her if she wanted red or white wine. She said, "White." And he told the waiter to bring them the most expensive vintage brand of white wine. The waiter came back with the manager, and the manager asked for ID. P then flashed him a fake ID, and the manager said, "Okay, but, sir, the best wine we have costs five thousand dollars a bottle."

P said, "That's it. Well, let me get two then, if they're only five a piece." And he pulled out a large wad of bills.

The manager counted the money, turned his lip up, and said, "One moment, sir."

Jaynce said, "Okay, player, I liked the way you handled that. But I could violate you right now for having a fake ID and underage drinking."

P said, "You won't though, because you like my style." He sat back in his seat, and they stared each other down for a minute until Jaynce broke the silence.

"Presley, it's not that at all. I think you need to slow down and think about what you want out of life."

At just that moment, the waiter came back with the wine and the main course. P responded with, "Jaynce, I already got what I want out of life."

"And what's that, Presley?" she asked, looking at him intensely.

"I got money, power, and the utmost respect on the streets. I'm happy with what I got. Thank you," he said as he sipped his wine.

She then went into politics, everyday life, and right and wrong. She tried hard to convince P he was on the wrong route, but P counted every move like he was playing a game of chess. Finally, she said, "It's getting late, Presley, and I really have to get home. I gotta early day ahead of me tomorrow."

Young P said, "You're the boss," and he went to pay the tab. P Double came back, grabbed her hand, and walked her to the car. He once again opened her door and shut it behind her. As she entered the car, she kissed him on the cheek and thanked him for the wonderful night. Young P popped in the Jodeci tape and let his system knock. KC blew the airwaves with "It's been an hour since you've been gone, and that's too long so come back home."

Jaynce said, "I love this song, P," and they both sang the song as they blew back to the field.

$ $ $

Mike Tuitt was stalking every car that came to the Dunmoreland Street after hour. He had been out there two hours when he saw a purple '93 Honda Accord pull up. Mama hopped out in a purple leather catsuit that was ridiculous. He saw her by herself and popped his trunk. He then ran up behind her, put his hand over her mouth, and put the gun to her head.

Mike said, "Yeah, shit is real, bitch. You scream, you can say good night forever." And he yanked her while half dragging her to his car. He told her to jump into the trunk.

She said, "Hell no." That was when he pistol-whipped her repeatedly, picked her up, and threw her in the trunk. Her bag and her cell phone dropped, and he grabbed those and threw them into his car. Mama started kicking and screaming as he drove off, so he pulled over, jumped out, and opened the trunk. Mike then gun-butted the bitch twice. Mama let out a pure scream of sheer pain and terror. Mike said, "You make another sound back there, and you're a dead-ass bitch." He drove her to Fenwick Street and wrestled Mama out of the trunk. He wrestled her into the house and gun-butted her on the back of the head. She hit the ground hard and passed out.

When she woke up, she was stark naked and tied up to a bedpost with her legs tied wide open as well. Mike wished his genitalia didn't hurt so bad because he damn sure would've fucked the shit out of this bitch. Mama was scared to death because the goon was looking at her with lust and hate in his eyes. After a minute, Mike asked her, "Where the fuck is your man, bitch?"

She told him about the dinner plans he had that night. "Well, dinnertime is over now. Where the fuck is he?" Mike said.

She said, "I swear I don't know."

Mike said, "Okay," walked over to Mama's dresser, and grabbed a sock. He then stuffed the sock into her mouth, walked over to her closet, and came back out with a bat. The goon looked at her and said, "Let me show you how real shit is." He raised the bat over his head, brought it down, and crushed Mama's kneecap. Then he hit the other one with the same exact force. Her knees broke with a sick crunching noise that had her screaming in the utmost pain. Two minutes went by, and he said, "Where the fuck is P Double? Matter of fact, where is his stash, bitch?"

Mike snatched the sock out of her mouth so she could respond. She was still crying from the pain when she stuttered, "I don't know. I swear. He don't tell me shit."

That was the wrong answer because Mike shoved the sock back into her mouth and broke a couple of ribs this time. This was the worst night of Mama's life. She was in so much pain she didn't know what to do. She just wished the man would kill her because the pain was unbearable. He asked her again, and the answer was the same as the last two. So he rammed the fat end of the bat in her pussy and rammed it and rammed it until she passed out.

$ $ $

Meanwhile, P Double pulled up at the Getty on Main Street to get some gas. Jaynce was in the car listening to Mary J Blige as P pumped the gas. When he finished, he turned the system up and let Mary speak as he pulled off. He didn't notice the black Camry pull up on the side of them and roll down the window. Sun Sun let the Mac spit. P pulled off, and the chase was on.

Luckily, Jaynce said, "P, who's that?" in time for P to see the Mac, or they would have been goners. Sun Sun was mad because he had the drop on this nigga and only shot the door up. P dipped the V-12 with ease down Main Street, but the Camry was holding its own. As he went past the bus station, the back window of the 850 shattered from the automatic gunfire. Jaynce let out an animal scream as the window erupted.

P said, "Baby, I got this," and banged a right on State Street so he could hit the highway.

He knew the Camry couldn't catch the V-12 on the highway. His car was just taking slug after slug as he was on the craziest chase of his life. P swung a right through a red light and almost smacked into a Bronco that had the green light. He banged another left through a red light as he hit West Springfield Bridge. The Camry pulled up right alongside them as P saw his attackers. Sun Sun let the Mac ring just as P hit the brakes. P then pulled up the emergency brake as he did a doughnut in the middle of the bridge and headed in the other direction. By the time the Jamaicans turned around, they were pissed off. Sun Sun was angry. He had the nigga in the palm of his hand and couldn't crush him. It didn't matter though because P was gonna have to answer for putting his hands on the prince.

$ $ $

P had seen Sun Sun and knew who tried to kill him at the barbershop. *The faggot-ass Jamaican couldn't take an ass-whipping like a man, huh*, P thought.

Jaynce was badly shaken up. P put his hand on her shoulder, and she jumped. "Calm down, Jaynce. Everything is all right." He spoke softly.

She looked at him like he was crazy and said, "No, everything is not all right, Presley. We could've been killed because of the bullshit life you live. You really have to change your life, Mr. Williams, and that's real."

P pulled up in front of Buckingham Street and let her out.

She said, "Think about what I said, and please be careful."

P chirped the 850 home, thinking about how he was gonna kill Sun Sun's ass. When he got home, he saw that the purple Honda was gone, meaning Mama had taken off somewhere. He walked into the crib and went straight to his study. P had to make sure the fifty grand Raheem gave him was accounted for. So he recounted it and hit the secret catch that slid his portrait back. He opened his walk-in safe and deposited the fifty stacks. For a minute, he sat on his money and decided that he and Mama needed a brief vacation. Being a millionaire was no fun unless you seriously enjoyed it. Probation would be over in a week; then he could afford to take a short trip. Right then, his relationship was on the rocks, and he had to mend it at once. What seemed to be five minutes turned into an hour. P looked at his watch and wondered where the fuck his dame was at. He walked out of the safe and shut and locked it. He hit the catch for the portrait to slide back into its rightful place. P then sat on his big marble desk and called Mama's cell phone. The first time he didn't get an answer. The second time, a man answered.

"Who the fuck is this?" P Double said, jumping off his desk, ready to erupt.

The voice said, "Is this that bitch-ass nigga they call Double?"

P got angry and said, "Who the fuck has my girl's phone?"

"Oh, it is your bitch-ass then. It's that nigga you robbed for five bricks and fifty stacks. That's who it is, little nigga. By the way, I got your stank-ass bitch too." He spoke with hate in his voice. "What is the slut bag worth to you?" Mike laughed finally because he knew he had the upper hand on the young don.

P went rogue. He smacked everything off his desk and yelled into his phone, "Mike, if you touch my bitch, I will kill your whole family, nigga."

Mike laughed for a good minute this time. "You're in no position to threaten nobody, punk. Now, what is this little bitch worth to you?" Mike snickered on that note.

P tried to calm down and think rationally. He was only sixteen, but he was always way ahead of his time. He finally said, "Okay, okay. I'll give you your shit back. Just tell me where to meet you at?"

Mike said, "What? How about a half million dollars and thirty birds. Hit me back when it's all packed up and ready. You got an hour, or watch the news." Tuitt hung up abruptly.

P Double hit redial at once, but all he got was Mimi's answering machine. "Fuck!" he swore to himself as he pounded on the marble desk with all his pent-up anger.

Everything was going wrong all at the same time. The Jamaicans were trying to kill him, then his boys got shot up, and just when he thought it could get no worse, Mike Tuitt somehow found out P Double robbed him and snatched his bitch up. He went to his personal bar in his study, grabbed a fifth of Hennessy, and tipped it back while weighing his options, which weren't many. Of course, he had way more than enough to pay the chump.

It would hurt a little bit, but it wouldn't break him in the least. But if he actually paid the nigga, it would be a sign of weakness on his part, and all dudes would have to do would be snatch his bitch to get at him anytime. Damn, the shit would hurt, but P decided he wasn't a bitch-ass nigga like Black or J.G. There was no way in hell P would show weakness over any woman on this earth unless it was his grandmother, the woman P was truly in love with. This was one of the hardest decisions he ever had to make in his life, but he was sure he made the right one. An hour later, young P Double was downing his second fifth of Hennessy when his cell phone chirped its usual ring. "Yo!" he yelled in a drunken drawl.

Mike said, "You got my shit ready, little nigga, or what?"

P said, "Yeah, it's ready, bitch nigga. It's ready for you to suck my dick. I'm not paying you shit, faggot! Your whole family is dead, nigga!" P screamed on and on, but Tuitt hung up the jack.

$ $ $

Mike looked at the bitch and said, "Well, your boyfriend is one tough cookie, so you can say, 'Good night,' baby girl." Her eyes got big as he said this. Tuitt snatched the bat out of her pussy and smashed her in the face with it, rendering her unconscious. He then dragged her from the bed, threw her in the car, and drove to the bridge at Water Shop's Pond. He made sure no cars were coming as he hoisted her up and over the bridge into the water. As he jumped back into his vehicle and hit the gas, he thought about his next move. Mike knew the young boy was gonna go crazy, so he had to think of a way to capitalize on that craziness.

$ $ $

Eddie Haul woke up in Ludlow still trying to figure out how he was gonna beat this case. Shit was easy when he had Mama in his corner. Now that she left, it was hard to make moves. He still had his mistress Italia. She was a Cape Verdean piece of ass with a sick head game. But she wasn't no Mama for sure. Ed was mad that the two Jamaicans he hired couldn't kill P. In fact, the little nigga had made them look stupid coming in the jail. Everybody knew the Jamaicans got run up in by a botty boy, which means "faggot" in Jamaican. Whoever it was fucked them pretty good because their assholes had to be stitched like the nigga J.G.'s and his bitch's. Ed had just decided to worry about getting out when the twelve o'clock news came on. Ray Hershel was talking about finding a woman's body in the Water Shop's Pond. The woman was young and Hispanic. Ed didn't think anything of it until he saw her beautiful face on the front page of the *Springfield Union* news. It said twenty-two-year-old Jahdi Martinez was a victim of foul play in the city's sixth murder of the year so far. Ed flew the coop when somebody said, "Damn, that's a waste of a good piece of ass."

Ed beat the young boy until the COs tackled him. He was still throwing wild punches until they moved him. That night in the box, he knew he was gonna make P Double pay dearly for his loss. Somehow, some way, he knew it had something to do with him. He just had to figure everything out.

$ $ $

For two days straight, the whole world was looking for P Double. His phones were off, and he took the house phones off the hook. His grandmother already knew the deal because she had seen the news. She knew her grandbaby better than anybody in this world. Mrs. Williams knew P had lost some of his backbone and needed to be alone for a while. The whole time P was drinking himself to death, he felt bad about Mama losing her life because of his past sins. But she also had to understand how much hard work went into earning that buck. He finally snapped out of his daze and started making funeral arrangements, so he could kiss his ghetto princess goodbye. He then called his grandmother along with her family and told them that he was fine, and he had made the best funeral arrangements possible. Young P then went to his lawyer's office so the police could question him there.

After a lot of "I don't knows" and a "Please don't leave the country," he was free to go. P snatched up his grandmother and brought her to Ponderosa where they talked about his life. They then talked about his loss and how to cope with the pain of losing that special loved one. As P and his grandmother left the restaurant, his phone rang with some news he couldn't handle. He looked at his grandmother and drove to his house instead of hers. When they arrived, she said, "Tinco, why are we here, baby. I wanna go home. I'm tired."

The young boy said, "Grandma, this is your new home. I'm sorry," with a distraught look on his face.

She said, "Boy, if you don't bring me home right now—"

He cut her off as he shed a tear and said, "Grandma, your house burned down to the ground, and it's all my fault."

She looked at the boy for an odd minute and just embraced him with passion. She told him not to worry about it. "Things will get better. Now, let's take a look at this new house," she said, and they exited the vehicle.

« $ »

CHAPTER 8

PROBLEM CHILD

Henderson Funeral Home was packed with thugs, hustlers, and kin. They all came to pay their respects on this rainy March day. The sky was gray, and it seemed like even God was crying gangster tears over Mama. Inside the funeral home was a sad sight to see because everyone had a sad look or tears in their eyes. Mama's family was going crazy as her mother and sisters cried in front of the closed casket. P was dressed in all white, and all his people were dressed up in all black with sadness in their eyes. As the preacher delivered the sermon, they all bowed their heads in prayer. So they didn't see the two thugs who sneaked in with two Mac 10 machine pistols.

D black said, "Fuck that ho bitch. What about Shafika?" and let his Mac spit instant rage.

His friend fired wildly and shot up the casket along with the preacher and a couple of other people. They then screamed, "Ave!" and ran out of the funeral home to a car that was awaiting them outside. The funeral was a complete disaster. The preacher died instantly along with Mama's mother and one of her sisters. When the boys started firing, they both threw their bodies on top of the casket to protect their loved one from any more harm. Mental Kev also died on the way to the hospital. He was an older cat from P's block. In all, thirty-six people were injured, and there were four casualties. P was going crazy. It seemed like everyplace he went, there were people dying or getting injured around him. Right then, he had too much beef to swallow, but somehow, some way, he was gonna eat it until he was beyond full. The Ave claimed that it stood for "all violators executed." Well, they just violated in a major way, and blood would have to spill. P made sure he and his team left before the police came. He already knew they were gonna get tired of hearing his name in the airwaves.

They all went to Bates's crib and put a plan together that night. But before they could even act up, shit was jumping off. Andy Cap's and Kev's cribs were burning as they spoke. They ran outside realizing that Bates's crib might be next, and sure enough, as they ran out, some niggas in a white Toyota Corolla came through and shot the front of Bates's crib up as they were walking out. He caught two, one in the leg and one in the stomach as he dropped wounded. Then somebody from the car threw a Molotov cocktail through the window that started a serious fire. Kev said, "Man, fuck that!" and ran out shooting his Beretta with ambition. He emptied the whole clip as he heard the passenger grunt with pain as they hightailed it down the street. P called an ambulance for Bates and the fire department immediately as Cap stayed behind to tend to Bates. They were in hot pursuit of the Toyota. Kev was right behind them as they took that right down Wellington Street. The Toyota then sped down Alden Street and over the bridge.

P said, "Man, I'm about to kill these niggas. Pull up on the side of them, Kev."

Kev floored the Honda and pulled up on the side of them as P let the Tech explode with a passion for death. The bullets struck the side of the driver's door, and the glass exploded as P Double's bullets found their mark. One had to have struck the driver as well because the Toyota lost control, jumped the curb, and flew into the woods. The Toyota struck the tree with a sickening crunch that had to finish the two thugs in the car.

Kev kept driving and told P, "Yo, I think you got them, my nigga."

P said, "Yeah, I hit 'em up something awful, but they started something they can't finish because they made me into a problem child."

Just then, his phone rang, and Cap spoke in his ear. "It was Sun Sun that shot T Baby and A-Dog. Bates is in the operating room as we speak. I'm not leaving until I hear something, y'all. What's good?"

P said, "I just took them chumps out. I think you should be seeing them cats come through in a heartbeat."

Cap said, "I'll holla back when I hear something," and he hung up.

P told Kev to drop him off at his whip, and he'd call him later. P just wanted to go to his little apartment hideout and watch the news. Channel 40 News came on, and boy, they had a story to tell, starting with the funeral home and then the burning of all his people's houses. But what he wanted to hear came on next.

"A young man by the name of Lamar Jones was in critical condition today after taking a slug in the arm, chest, and leg and crashing headfirst into a tree near Island Pond Road. There were no other passengers in the vehicle that we know of. In world news—"

P flicked the TV off and lay back to get his mind right. P cut his phone off and grabbed twenty stacks. He hit the highway and drove until he almost crashed from falling asleep. He rented a room at the Holiday Inn down in Philadelphia for a night. The following day, he was gonna drive down to Kinston, North Carolina, where his other grandmother lived. P didn't know if Lamar was dead or not, but he wasn't taking any chances, period. Plus, he needed to get his mind right anyway. When he pulled up in front of the big white two-story stucco house and jumped out, he was in another world. P knocked on the door before he walked in, and his grandmother almost had a heart attack. She hadn't seen the boy in years. Now, all of a sudden, he just popped up on her doorstep. Mrs. Spencer questioned the boy for hours as it seemed to him, and they talked, ate dinner, and talked some more until P got tired and fell asleep.

The next day, P decided to try the town out and see what North Carolina life was really about. He hit up No Jangles restaurant and ordered his favorite, fish and grits, as he watched the scene and tried to blend in as best he could. For some reason or another, Down South folks could smell an out-of-town person from miles and miles away. As he got heavily into his meal, a dark-skinned chocolate beauty walked by him with a mean strut. P wanted to holla, but right then, he was out of his element. She was a couple of tables away when he found himself ear hustling. Her name was Akasha. P found that he was quietly whispering her name to himself. Once in a while, she would catch P staring at her, but she paid the boy no mind. P was thinking, *If she knew I was caked up, I'd bet she would suck my dick right here.* At the time, P was only rocking his Cuban links, which he had tucked inside his shirt. He ate his food, paid his bill, and skated. For a minute, he drove around town with her name in his mind. P also found out the same was a feisty one, which he really liked from the jump, but he hadn't come down there for that; he was down there to chill and clear his mind—that was all. He pulled up at his grandmother's and jumped out of the purple Honda. For some reason, he felt someone staring at him. He looked across the street, and sure enough, it was the chocolate beauty that P had seen earlier that day. The young boy smiled at her and ran into the house. It was Saturday night, and young Presley was bored out of his mind.

His country-ass cousin called up and asked him if he was going to the shindig that night. P had to kindly ask the man what a shindig was. His cousin started telling him about Club Impulse and the late-night waffle joint. Of course, P told his cousin he was all for it, and of course, his cousin said, "Come scoop me in a hour." Damn, he was supposed to be visiting the town, and already, he had to drive. The town was real easy to get familiar with. He had done it that day driving around.

As P was getting out of the shower, his cousin appeared out of nowhere, telling him to hurry up. P got dipped up in his Charlotte Hornets jacket with the giant hornet on the back covered in rhinestones with the matching hat. He then threw on a white and purple Francis Girbaud sweater with the white and purple jeans to match. His purple patent-leather New Balance with the rhinestones in the N polished the outfit off. He brought all his jewels down there too, so he was iced out as usual.

When the door opened, his cousin Tommy said, "Oh shit, you glittering boy. Come on."

Club Impulse was a giant empty warehouse. P parked the purple Honda as close as possible. Tommy and P stepped out and walked to the front of the line. The security guard asked P if they wanted VIP or regular. P said, "Fuck it." He might as well splurge while he was there, and he said, "VIP." He slid the guard two crispy hundred-dollar bills, and the guard clipped two black bracelets on their wrists.

Tommy said, "Damn, little cuz, that's how y'all do up north, huh?"

Tommy was an ugly-ass nigga, but P needed his black ass to show him what was what in this hick town. That was when he spotted her and went crazy. Club Impulse was packed to the tee, and somehow this chocolate beauty stuck out. Impulse had a bar that went around the whole club. There was a stage in the middle with a bunch of strippers on it. The VIP section was located upstairs on the second floor, which also wrapped around the whole club. P gave his cousin three hundred bucks and told him to get two bottles of Moët and a fifth of Hennessy. His cousin asked him where he was off to, and P kindly brushed him off and said, "I'll see you in a minute."

P approached Akasha at the bar and asked her if he could buy her a drink. She politely said no, turned back around, and started her conversation over again with her homegirl. But her girl wasn't really listening to her at all. Her eyes were all over the bangin'-ass nigga standing behind her. She asked Akasha who he was, and Akasha looked at her like "How the hell should I know?" and kept yapping.

Candice moved her friend out of the way and said, "I'm sorry my girl is so rude, but you can buy me a drink," as she winked her eye at him.

P said, "What kind of drink would you like, miss?" as he gave her that "I'm that nigga" look.

She said, "Whatever you're drinking is fine with me."

So he ordered her and himself each a bottle of Moët. As he pulled out a wad of bills to pay the bartender, Candice's eyes got big. He asked her what her and her girl's names were. She told him her name was Candice, but everyone called her Candy and her friend's name was Akasha, but she had just gotten out of a bad relationship with this dude so that was why her attitude was the way it was. P told them his name and invited them up to VIP.

Candice made Akasha come along. As they walked up the stairs, P was thinking, *Damn, Candice is a bad bitch*, but Akasha was the real deal. Candice was five-five with the brownest eyes P had ever seen. She was a redbone with a banging body, but P could already tell by the way she was looking all over him that she was out for one thing, and that was money. Akasha, in contrast, looked like an ebony queen. She was chocolate with a set of deep-dish dimples that a nigga would kill for. P was still trying to figure out how she got that big ole ass in them jeans when they ruined his daydream and asked him where he was sitting. P scanned the floor and found his cousin in the far corner getting bent by himself. P introduced his cousin, but apparently, they already knew who he was. Once again, P tried to holla at Akasha with no luck, when Candice said, "Boy, you sure do talk funny. Where you from, P Double?"

He answered her question and tried to holla at Akasha again. P was throwing more game at this chick than he knew he had, but she still wasn't hooked like he thought she'd be. She finally broke down and asked him if he was some kind of rapper or something. P laughed it off and said, "No, I'm sorry if I disappointed you though. I'm just your average Joe."

As the night went on, they started interacting more and more until the club closed at four in the morning. P asked her if he could bring her home, and she said, "I hope you don't think I'm one of those scallywaggers around here."

P didn't know what it meant, but the word sounded deadly, so he was like, "Of course not. I just know you live across the street. That's all."

He told his cousin to hitch a ride with Candice, and they both sucked their teeth to the sound of that notion. P walked her to the purple Honda, and she said, "Nice rims."

He said, "Thank you," and opened her door first.

As they drove on, she said, "How old are you?"

"I'm sixteen," he answered, "but you can say I'm way ahead of my time."

They rode in silence for the rest of the way home. P pulled up into his driveway and walked her across the street. She kissed him on the cheek and said, "Good night." Then she walked into the house and left P standing there. They went everywhere together for the first two months. Akasha was only eighteen, but she was a very mature eighteen. After awhile, they fell in love, but she wouldn't let P Double fuck her. This was what drove him to fall for this dame even more because she wasn't moved like all the other women P had in his life. P Double was enjoying his vacation a lot, but he really had to get back to the real world and handle his business back up north. He just had to think of a way to tell this woman and hope that she would go back with him. Then he thought about what had happened to Mama and knew he couldn't subject her to his rough and rugged ways.

$ $ $

Back home, the war had gotten crazy to the point where niggas' moms were scared to even go to the supermarket, because they were getting shot at also. Everybody was looking for P Double, but it seemed like he had just dropped off the face of the earth somewhere. Fatback had heard about all the attempted murders on his boy, and he wasn't well. Back got out brolic and ready for rock. He asked everybody where the fuck P Double was, but nobody knew. His grandmother's house had burned down, so Fatback and the crew didn't know where she lived. Back couldn't believe Kev and Bates didn't even know where P Double lived. He called the number they gave him until he finally got through one day.

"Yo, where the fuck you at, nigga?" Back spoke into the phone, happy his nigga finally turned his phone on.

"I know this ain't my nigga Fatback," P said. "I'm in North Carolina. I'll be home tomorrow. Go to my crib in East Long Meadow."

P gave him directions and told him to go by himself.

Back said, "I'll see you then. Peace out." And he hung up. Before Back made a move out there, he had to find him some heat and make the town know that the Back was back.

$ $ $

He couldn't believe his man was home finally. Now, it was gonna be hell on earth. Springfield wasn't ready for the havoc that was about to be caused and the casualties that were about to appear. Young P already decided that when Fatback came home, they were gonna split the cake right down the middle. All the money he stacked up was his. That was hard-earned money. Now somehow, they had to formulate some kind of plan to eliminate all of the enemies he had created since Fatback had been gone. But right then, how was he gonna break the news to Akasha that he was leaving on the next thing smoking. P said, "Fuck it," and called the airline. They had a plane that went to Bradley airport in Connecticut every two hours, so he booked a flight in first class on that. Next, he called his cousin and told him to pick him up in two hours' time. When it was almost time for his cousin to arrive, he called Akasha and told her to come over. He started by telling her to sit down.

"Akasha, I love you very much, but I've kind of worn out my welcome down here, and I must be on my way back home, sweetheart. I'm sorry," he said in a sad tone. As soon as a tear dropped from her eye, he found himself in defensive mode. "Akasha, I swear I'll be back, but there's a lot of things I really need to handle, love," he said.

Akasha said the last thing he wanted to hear. "I'm coming with you, Presley, and that's all there is." This was what he really feared would happen. All he could say was "I'm sorry, but you can't, love. I have too many enemies back home, and I couldn't bear to have your blood on my conscience, Akasha."

"Presley, do you really expect me to believe this bullshit? I'm not the silly little country bumpkin you think I am, bay," she said with tears coming down from her eyes. "You just gotta girlfriend up there; that's all."

That was when he spazzed out and said, "Well, if you don't believe me, then look at this." And he pulled out Mama's obituary and showed it to her. He then broke everything down for her. "Baby, I'll be back in a couple of weeks." In the meantime, he gave her the keys to the Honda and five thousand. He promised to send the title in the mail, and then his cousin walked in. They all said their goodbyes when they dropped him off.

$ $ $

As soon as he got to the airport, he caught a cab to East Long Meadow. Fatback and his grandmother were waiting for him with open arms. The boys embraced each other and hugged for a minute. P broke the silence first by saying, "Damn, nigga, you big as fuck."

Back said, "Yeah but not as big as you are out here. Man, they said you disappeared and coke prices rose like the city's oil prices or some shit."

They both laughed, and P said, "Let's get up out of here and handle some business."

While P was gone, his grandmother had his 850 and his Millenia fixed. They went into the garage, and he asked Back which car he wanted to drive. Of course, Back choose the BMW with ease. As they were leaving East Long Meadow, P told Back to drive to Forest Park. They pulled up on Cliftwood Street, and Fatback said, "Who the fuck lives here, P?"

P jumped out, walked up the stairs, and said, "We do." When they entered the third-floor apartment, Fatback was amazed. There was wall-to-wall carpeting, which was navy blue. The living room consisted of white-leather furniture with exotic tables, lamps, and a big sixty-inch Sony TV. There was also a Pioneer sound system with eighteen-inch speakers. To top everything off, there was a giant picture on the wall of P Double and Fatback on the block. While Back was soaking all this in, P came back into the living room stacking key after key on the table. Fatback had never seen one kilo; now there were twenty in front of him. Then he walked him to the safe in the master bedroom closet and showed him seven hundred and fifty thousand dollars and mad guns.

Fatback said, "What the fuck, my nigga? How in the hell did you ever get this rich?"

P broke it all down from taking the coke from Tuitt and learning to cook from Ed to the gasoline drought. "And you know you're like my brother, so half of this shit is yours."

Fatback couldn't believe all this shit. He hugged P Double so hard he forgot his own strength because he almost squeezed the young don to death.

"By the way, Back, the 850 is yours too, but you might wanna get it painted a different color. You know everybody in the whole town gotta bone to pick with me about something," he said. "We'll plan some shit tonight after we get you a phone so we can communicate with each other, and we gotta lot of money on the streets that I left behind. That nigga Hemy owe us a hundred stacks alone. Matter fact, let me page this nigga right now." P paged the nigga and told Fatback to take twenty racks out of the safe, so they could hit Hartford and do a little shopping. He also took off one of his Cuban links and gave it to his man.

P said, "Here, that's why I bought two."

Raheem called back at once. "What up, P? Where the fuck you been, my nigga?"

"I had to take a brief vacation for a minute, but everything is everything again!" P hollered.

"Yo good looking on that, P. You helped me get right. I got that hundred for you and a hundred of my own," Raheem shot back.

P said, "I'm gonna bring you eight jelly doughnuts, and you owe me a dollar."

Heem was happy with that one. "Good looking, P. I'll holla."

Back snatched up the eight cakes and grabbed the Glock 40 out of the safe. He passed P a Glock 9, and they were on their way. By the time they got back home, it was dark and time to plan things out. Everybody met up at Adams Park and formed a plan for the night. Now, it was time to execute it. Friday night was serious. It was two in the morning, and Pizza King was jampacked with a bunch of Eastern Ave niggas and chicks. D Black was hugged up on his girl Fly Tasha, tonguing her down. G-Money came up, gave the nigga dap, and asked him what was good for the night, when four cars pulled up and started shooting up everything in sight. Women were screaming. Niggas were screaming as well, trying to duck slugs that were taking out everything in their path. P ran out of bullets and popped in a fresh clip. He got out of the car with a mask over his face and emptied the whole clip in Fly Tasha and D Black.

He then said, "MSP," jumped back in the black van, and bounced. Fatback and P wiped the van clean and lit it on fire. They then ran the couple blocks to the 850 and drove home.

They stopped at Dunkin' Donuts and ordered some egg and cheese bagels and went home. The next morning, *Union News* was filled with news of what they were calling the pizza party. Twenty-one people were shot, and there were eight casualties. The Springfield streets were turning into the Gulf War. Everybody was scared to leave their respective homes for fear of catching a stray bullet that was meant for someone else.

Fatback said, "And there's gonna be a hell of a lot more of bodies when it's all said and done."

P said, "Now, I wanna make those faggot-ass Jamaicans feel it too!"

"Nigga, you bagged that bitch-ass nigga's sister. You should've kept dicking her down," Back stated.

P looked at the nigga in shock and said, "Who the fuck is the nigga's sister?"

"That bitch Sauna, the queen of the pack," Fatback said.

P Double jumped up like, "Oh shit! I think I still got that bitch's number from way back, on an old pager or something."

"Well, that's the way to his bitch ass anyways, but fuck that chump for right now. I heard you got the meanest bird game in Springfield, Massachusetts?" Back said, pulling on a Newport.

P said, "I do. Matter of fact, I'm about to call up some bird right now. Madi, what up?" P said into the phone. Yeah, I know it's been a minute. I've been on vacation, ma, but we gotta lot of making up to do at once."

Fatback smiled as his man was working the jack.

"Madi, you got a friend for my man? He just got out the clink ... Aight. I'll scoop y'all in a minute then. Peace," he said and hung up. "Come on, Back. We gotta snatch these dimes up and duck back here real quick."

$ $ $

Across town, Larry Acres and the whole police force were receiving a lot of heat from all of these unsolved murders. Crime in Springfield was so bad that they became ranked twentieth for worst city to live in. The mayor had tried everything so far; he even hired more police, but that wasn't working. So they fired the police chief and hired another one, but that still didn't work.

Larry Acres said, "Fuck, just working homicide. Please, let me run my own gang task force. That way, we can crack down on these drugs and crime. I mean the streets of Springfield are crazier than Boston. Anytime folks are scared to leave their homes, chief, it's a problem." Acres spoke with determination all over his face.

Chief Paula C. Meara was a fat white chick with glasses. She was kind of hit in the looks department, but she made up for it with brains. She was a Harvard graduate with a PhD in criminology, but for some reason, all the tricks she tried to stop crime didn't work at all.

"Okay, Larry, but your ass is on the line. I want all this shit to stop. I wanna see a big difference in two months' time or else."

Acres nodded his head and said, "Thank you, Chief. I won't let you down."

That was the start of the drug task force.

$ $ $

P Double and Madi went into the bedroom and shut the door. Madi was a four-foot-eleven Spanish shorty who was thick to capacity. She had long hair and smooth Indian-looking skin. Madi was also beautiful. P liked her because her mouth game was like fucking a virgin pussy, and her pussy actually squirted when she came. P took everything off but his Joe Boxers and lay on the bed while Madi slowly undressed herself, doing an exotic striptease. When she took her bra off, her double Ds jumped out at P and said, "Please, titty fuck me." She had the fattest nipples P had seen thus far, and he loved milking them with ease. Next, she came out of her thong panties and walked over to the bed. She pulled P's Joe Boxers off.

As she looked him in the eye, she said, "Daddy, can Mommy taste it?" As soon as he nodded at her, she started milking his dick for all it was worth. She brought him to his peak and then stopped and started sucking his balls. P almost jumped from the sensation of her tongue. Then she said, "Daddy, I need it," and hopped on his dick. She rode it until P was about to bust, and then she said, "Not yet, daddy," and decided she wanted to taste her own juices as she sucked his dick with authority. She let him come this time as she deep-throated his dick so he could come down her throat. After all his nut was down Madi's throat, he rolled her over, mounted her, and fucked her with lust and the utmost passion. Madi was nutting all over P's dick and sheets. She screamed in delight as P palmed her ass and long dicked her until her pussy started gushing again like hot fudge. P snatched his dick out, put it between those double Ds, and titty fucked her until he gushed on her chin and chest. He then got up, walked to the bathroom, and washed his dick all the while laughing because he heard Fatback in the other room taking Madi's friend Veronica down, and boy, was she a screamer.

The poor girl was shouting so loud P felt sorry for her. He said to himself, "That's what jail will do to you." All that screaming made his dick hard, so he ran back into the room and worked Madi over again and again until they both fell asleep.

His phone woke him up with a start. As he reached over Madi to get it, she groaned. "Yo, what up?"

He said in a groggy voice, "Man, wake your little ass up."

Lan said, "My uncle called me this morning and said that he's running a new gang task force, so you better stay off the streets, and watch the news."

"Aight, good looking, Lan. Peace." And he hung up, got up, and checked the time. It was 4:45. Sure enough, Channel 40 news was coming on in fifteen minutes.

He woke back up, and they watched together as Fatback rolled a Vega. Lan was telling the truth because Ray Hershel said, "The drug and gang task force swept a couple of sections by storm."

P said, "Damn."

Fifty-one people went to jail from seven o'clock in the morning to four o'clock that afternoon. And the scary shit was that was only the Ave and Worthington Street. The next day, they hit Bristol Street and Cambridge Street. Then they swept the north and south ends. Springfield streets were crazy. The jails were packed with adults and juvenile delinquents.

Fatback said, "Man, fuck them police, P. We need some more coke."

This was what P Double was afraid of. He owed Rudy two hundred and fifty grand. Money wasn't an issue. It was just that he'd been MIA for months now, and he didn't know how the boss dread was really gonna take it. He said, "Fuck it," and called the dread up. "Rudy, what up?"

"P Double, where the fuck you been, boy?"

P just said, "I'm on my way," and hung up. P called his grandmother and told her to go to Budget and rent him a van. She said to give her an hour. The hard part was breaking the news to Fatback that he had to ride alone. At first, his best friend didn't take it too well. Then he understood the concept in the end. Madi and P jumped in the shower together. P liked that because he could pick her little ass up and bounce her on his dick all day long. After an hour of fooling around, they finally toweled off.

"Madi, you and your girl do me a favor, please."

"Yes, daddy, anything you want," she answered.

"Can you please sit in the living room while us grown men talk business, please."

"Of course, baby boy, you know you got that." And she kissed his neck and walked out.

Fatback came in, shut the door, and said, "What's the word, P?"

"We owe the connect two hundred and fifty racks. We got one point two in the safe. Should we spend all or half?" P asked his partner in crime.

Back thought heavy for a minute and said, "Man, with all this shit going on, we gotta save something for a rainy day, God, so I say spend half a mil and get consignment for the rest."

"Yeah, that's the way I've been doing shit. I just wanted to see if we on the same page as usual," P Double said.

They counted the money, and P said, "Fuck that. You and your dame follow us, and we'll do a little shopping too while we there." He smiled.

Back said, "Word," and they dapped each other.

They all rode to his grandmother's crib in the 850. P and Madi took the van and the cash, while Back and Veronica followed. Fatback let badass Veronica drive because he didn't have a license. P threw in *The Chronic* by Dr. Dre and Snoop Dog and started banging, "Bitches Ain't Shit." They got to the Mecca with no problems and were very ahead of their time frame. They decided to stay the night in New York so they could hit some stores and get fly to death. P pulled up to the Jamaican restaurant and walked in with Madi.

Rudy walked inside and told P Double to make the lady wait right there and follow him. They went down into the torture chamber where the Jamaicans made Mike Tuitt feel their wrath. Already, P didn't like it. He almost threw up from the terrible stench down below. They walked into a side office where Rudy had a couple of his infamous bodyguards waiting. Before young P sat down, he already knew he was in trouble.

The dread said, "Me loved you like a son, P Double, but me no like fuckery."

P said, "But I came and brought what I—"

The dread signaled for his goons to grab him before he could finish his sentence. "Strip the rude boy," Rudy ordered at once.

They stripped him at once. Rudy then told the goons to chain him up. The whole time, P was asking the dread what the fuck this shit was about. They chained him up and made the young boy dangle from his arms. P was in so much pain he couldn't think straight.

Rudy said, "The first lie you tell, I send you to meet Jah. Now, why did you say Mike Tuitt was your uncle?"

P broke the whole story down to the dread about how he got on and how Mimi used to be one of his baseheads in all. He told the dread about the gasoline coke that was going around town and all. The dread told the goons to let the young boy down, and he told P to get dressed. When all was said and done, he embraced P Double like he was his son and explained to him that he got on the same way just about. After that, P had a million-dollar credit limit with the dread. P gave him the half a million and asked him for a hundred and fifty birds. He told the dread to have them ready for tomorrow because he wanted to spend the night in New York. Rudy said okay, and P walked out a happy man. P gave Rudy the keys to the van and jumped in the 850 with Fatback and Veronica. First, they hit B-Jay's in Harlem. Then they hit up Macy's and Sneaker King in Brooklyn. That night, they checked into the Sheraton and smoked the finest Branson. In the morning, they hit the Warehouse District in Manhattan and Delancy Street. Then Fatback's phone chirped with some bad news. Iran, A-Dog, Jim Brown, Little Mari, and Frankie got snatched up in the sweep.

The streets of Springfield were on fire. He just hoped everyone could hold his own and not turn state's. The next day, they picked up the van with the work in it and drove home safely.

One day, P was driving the Millenia on the block and saw Sauna. "Get in, baby girl!" he hollered to the pretty Jamaican chick.

She didn't seem to know who he was at first, and then she said, "Oh shit," ran to the car, and got in. She looked P Double over and said, "You're still cute, I see."

P said, "Yeah, you already know ain't shit changed about the god but his finances, sweetheart."

They kicked it for a while, and then P drove her to his crib to watch the new *Menace II Society* movie that just came out. Everybody was going to the movies to see it, but he already had it on bootleg. P blew her mind when she saw the palace as he and Back called it. She took her shoes off and got comfortable on the leather sofa. By the time they killed Cain's cousin in the movie, she was sucking P's dick. Sauna was a beast. The way she was looking P in the eye while servicing the god turned him on. Then she mounted him and did the boggle on his dick. Now he knew why they called her the queen of the pack. P said, "Fuck this," and rolled her over. He was power-fucking the Jamaican beauty, and she was matching him with every stroke. They both fucked each other to oblivion. Fatback walked in while P had both her legs in the air muscling the pussy with long, hard strokes.

As soon as P busted, Fatback put the gun to her head and said, "Bitch, where the fuck is Sun Sun at?"

She told him about Queen's Pizza on State Street and how all the dreads hung there every night and also hung at the Ave store sometimes because Greg was Jamaican and owned it.

Back said, "Fuck all of that, bitch. Where does he live?"

She said he didn't live on Wilberham Road with her and her mother, but he lived on West Ford Ave with Rocky and Ernie. She gave them the house number, and Back said, "Move over, P, my turn." Fatback pulled it out and said, "Bitch, you bite it; you die."

She got on her knees and started sucking Back's dick until his eyes rolled into the back of his head. P took it from the Back. The harder he fucked Sauna, the harder she power-sucked Fatback, until he shot all in her mouth, and then they switched. They fucked the young nympho until sun up. Then Back tied her up and put her inside a sleeping bag. They brought her to Kyle Woods.

P Double dug a grave while Fatback put ice inside a cooler. They unzipped the sleeping bag and fucked the queen once again. After they finished, they tied her to a tree, and Back pulled an ax out of a black bag. The queen knew what was about to happen, and she begged and pleaded with the young thugs. But Fatback got tired of the broad's voice, and he swung the ax with all his might. The queen's head rolled straight off her shoulders. For a second, her eyes were blinking, looking at the thugs while blood squirted from her neck as the queen's body jerked rapidly. P picked her head up and placed it in the cooler as Fatback untied the body. Back threw her in the grave he dug and covered it back up.

P said, "Now, let's go bring Sun Sun a little gift package he'll never forget."

And they packed up the sleeping bag and ax and bounced. They dropped the cooler off on Sun Sun's porch and then shot the house up so he would eventually come outside. P and Back drove up the street, and Sun Sun and his crew emerged a couple of minutes later with all types of guns screaming in Jamaican.

Rocky said, "What rude boy leave this bum ba Claude cooler out here?" He bent down to open it and jumped back like "Oh shit." Sun Sun let out an animal cry that was unheard of. The queen's eyes were open wide, staring at her brother. The young prince couldn't believe this shit. His parents were gonna flip at the notion of his younger sister's death and blame the prince like they always did. There was only one rude boy who was rude enough to disrespect the prince, and his name was P Double. "The Yankee boy must die tonight, ya hear, or I go kill one of you!" Sun Sun screamed at his young band of gunners.

$ $ $

Mike Tuitt was on his grind heavy nowadays. He was angry that the majority of coke on the streets came from P Double and Fatback. If he would've killed them little niggas at birds' jean store, he wouldn't have had to go through this shit. He tried to find out how and when the young don was going to see Rudy, but the big Jamaican was loyal to the little bastard. He thought he had P by the balls when he snatched Mama's pretty ass up, but he didn't count on the young thug being so cold and heartless. Tuitt knew he would get his time, but he just didn't know when. One thing he did know was patience was a virtue he had to rely on. He knew he also had to stay low because those young cats were stone-cold killers, and they had already proven that but, shit, so had he.

$ $ $

J.G. was fucking with the Maynard Street crew heavy. All that Bristol shit was dead in the water. They had violated him to the third degree. Maynard was up and coming. He figured those chumps over there needed leadership, and he would lead them in the right direction. Right then, it was this faggot-ass nigga named Marlon's block. The whole street was selling his coke except for J.G. J.G. knew Marlon was getting hit by this kid named Marv, but Marv wasn't fooling anyone because Jay already knew the caine was coming from Fatback and P Double. The boy hated P Double with a sickening passion. He swore if it could be his last wish on earth, he was gonna kill P Double. Somehow, someway, but right then, he was gonna fuck the shit out of Marlon's sister Brandy.

$ $ $

Big Butch was ready for rock. Mad Dog had his twelve gauge sawed-off ready to rumble. He was equipped with two forty-five automatics with two extra magazines if necessary. On the streets, he was known as the one-man gang. Butch wanted to catch Fatback in the bing so bad. He just wanted to beat the man to death—him and his boy P Double. That night, he had a couple missions to do. First, he was gonna stop by the Getty on State Street and see if he could catch a couple of them Hilltop niggas slipping. Then he was on his way to Bristol Street so he could bring the drama to them hard. The two chumps he wanted to get at wouldn't be out there, but he figured he could still bust a good nut by shooting their strip up. They made him walk with a limp by throwing him off that tier; now, he wanted their whole set to limp like him. He drove down Terrance Street in the big white Impala slowly, and, sure enough, there were a couple of Hill figure cats out there. Butch jumped out and said, "What's good now, Bobby and Rodney?"

They both started running as the big Goliath gave chase. Butch let the sawed-off echo with pain as Rodney fell from the buckshot blast. Mad Dog was at least happy he got one. Now he was on his way to Bristol Street. He rode down there slowly and saw Bates and Andy Cap. As soon as he pulled over, Bates let the Impala hold all sixteen of the nine-millimeter parabellums he had. Butch hit the gas, ran up on the curb like a maniac, and ran Bates over. Cap tried to hop the fence, but Butch caught his leg as he was going over. Just as Butch hit Wilbraham Road, a cruiser was coming, and Butch floored it.

Car 95 gave chase as they radioed in for backup. Butch was moving the big Impala through all types of red lights, trying to stay free. He just hit the streets two weeks earlier, and he wasn't trying to go back. It was too late when he saw the road block. He tried to crash straight through it. That was the last thing he remembered.

$ $ $

Shante called P Double and told him she had five stacks. P Double said, "I can bless you with two hundred and fifty. Meet me at Dunkin' Donuts at the x."

She popped up fifteen minutes later with her sister Roberta in Frankie's CRX. Shante hopped out of the CRX and jumped in the Millenia with P. She set the tone at once. "Long time, no see, playboy. I missed you," she said convincingly.

"Well, y'all had my number. All you had to do was call," P responded.

"And what was I supposed to tell Frankie I wanted the number for? Some good dick? I don't think so, P."

P Double laughed coldheartedly as he set the nine ounces in her lap.

Shante gave P the five stacks and said, "What's business with no leisure time, or you're not the same stud that fucked me to death a while ago?"

"Yeah, that's me, love, but what's up with your sister? Is she game or what? You know I can't have fun without my road dog smashing something."

"No problem. She game," Shante said.

P said, "Aight. Follow me then." He exited Dunkin' Donuts' parking lot, banged that first right, and parked. He got out, walked up the steps, and unlocked the door so they could enter the apartment building. They got out and followed suit. Roberta was a fuckable half-black, half-Spanish bitch like her sister. She wasn't all that in the looks or body department, but she made all that up with some platinum pussy. They went upstairs, and Fatback was watching a rerun of an old Iron Mike Tyson fight when they entered. Fatback passed P the Vega he was smoking on, and P said, "I brought you something else to fight," and Berta and Shante walked in.

"I'll see you in a few, my nigga," P said as he walked to his room to lay his well-oiled pipe game down. Shante stripped herself and P down. She then told P to bend over. P said, "Hold up, bitch. I ain't with all this crazy shit."

Shante laughed and said, "Trust me," so P did it. Shante came up from behind him and started sucking his dick from the back.

"Oh shit," P said. *Damn this bitch is a freak*, he thought to himself, as she swallowed his dick with a practiced stroke. He couldn't take anymore so he picked her up and sat her on his dick. Shante put her arms around P's neck as the young boy bounced her ass with ease. She came with grace and told P to lie down as she sat on his dick backward. P watched her ass bounce up and down as he threw his own strokes up in her every now and then. But P heard his boy Back fucking the shit out of Roberta.

$ $ $

Fatback had Roberta bent up on the couch with both her legs in the air. The myth was true; she did have some platinum pussy. It seemed to him with every stroke her pussy got wetter and wetter. "Oh, Back, stop. It hurts." But Fatback just kept long dicking the bitch, trying to drill new holes in the pussy. He was fucking the poor girl so hard she started crying, but he kept on drilling. All you heard was her screaming through the whole building. This turned Back on so much he started chanting a song as he fucked her. "One, two, three, four, poke that pussy; she wants more. One, two, three, four, poke that pussy till it's sore. Needle dick, needle dick."

P opened the door because the poor girl was screaming in pain and begging for help. All he saw was his man bouncing up and down on her fast and furious, gorilla dicking the young nympho.

Shante said, "Oh my god. P, do something please." P looked at the dame like *How the fuck am I supposed to tell this nigga stop fucking this bitch?* P just snatched up Shante and dragged her back into the room. What he saw just turned him on, so he started gorilla dicking Shante with long, hard strokes. After a minute, she forgot all about the noise that was coming from the living room. Ten minutes later, they heard a heavy knock at the door, and Back stopped and said, "Who the fuck is it?" He opened the door with blood all over his stiff muscle and between his legs and said, "What the fuck do you want? I'm trying to finish fucking my girl before my aunt gets home."

Police looked at the man all embarrassed and said, "Please, just keep the noise down, sir," and they bounced. Fatback went inside the bathroom and washed his dick. Roberta's pussy was so sore that she couldn't move. Back walked into the living room, grabbed her by her hair, and slapped his dick into her mouth. She made him bust, and he picked her up, carried her to the bathroom, and drew a bath for her. Roberta soaked for hours before the young boy toweled her off and helped her out of the tub. She walked to his bedroom and passed out. Shante was passed out in P's bed. P stepped into the living room and burst out laughing as Fatback tried to clean up all the blood that was on the white leather sofa.

Back laughed in return as P said, "You almost killed that bitch the way you were fucking her."

Back said, "Shit, I was trying to kill her. Her pussy was so juicy and tight, man, I lost control."

P then thought about the last time he used Shante, when she set Black up for them. At once, it hit him. He could kill two birds with the same stone—or stones, he should say. "Fatback, listen to this." He explained everything to Back twice, and Fatback agreed that the plan just might work.

CHAPTER 9

THE SETUP

P Double and Fatback decided they needed a new crib. To many bitches knew where the one in Forest Park was, so they also got a rest spot in Chicopee. The new spot they moved all the money and work to, while the old crib was just for fucking. They also decided to sell the whips and get new ones. With 1994 around the corner, why not jump in a new '94? P Double and Fatback both went to the Lexus dealer with P's grandmother just to see what was new. They both were blown back by the new GS 400 and the SC 400s on the lot.

"P, I don't know about you, but this GS got my name written all over it," Back said.

P said, "Fuck it. We might as well get two of them, one for me and one for you."

A week later, P Double jumped out of the Pepsi-blue GS 400 with white and blue soft leather seats. He also had the deep-dish hammers with the Pirelli tires on it. Fatback jumped out right behind his boy with the jet-black 400 with the black and white leather seats and dash. He also had the deep-dish hammers with the Pirrelli tires.

Lan said, "Oh shit, let me drive this shit."

P said, "Go ahead," and he jumped into the passenger seat as Lan took control of the wheel.

"Yo this is it," Lan said.

"Man, I'm about to sell my BMW and get one of these right here."

Lan sure did too. A week later, he had the pearl-white GS 400. Everything was moving like clockwork. The plan was executed one cold winter night.

Two bitches walked in the Ave store one day, and the Jamaicans were all over them. Sun Sun grabbed Shante's ass and said, "Girl, you roll with a prince tonight. Me show you what a rude boy like, no."

Shante laughed and said, "Rude boy, I don't think you got what it takes to handle this package right here."

"Girl, you crazy. Jah know my back strong like bull, yes."

She laughed again at the dread, as Bert was on the other side of the store with a group of dreads fighting for her affection. They all left and went to the crib on Westford Ave, where the Jamaicans were getting smashed off of Guinness stout beers. They were so fucked up that they never noticed that their two female companions never took off their winter coats in a heated house. Shante and Berta started dancing to Shabba Ranks.

One of the girls said, "Oh, we love this song," and they turned the stereo up full blast.

The Jamaicans had their fifteen-inch speakers banging through the whole house. All you heard was ting-a-linga-ling school bell ring. Shabba shouted. Then the girls pulled out two baby macs from their winter coats and let them rip. Little Ernie dived out the window and ran for his life while Sun Sun and Rocky caught the wrath of the girls' fury. They called P Double and told him the job was complete, but ugly-ass Ernie had gotten away from them.

P said, "As long as you got Sun Sun, don't worry about it."

They wiped down everything they touched and got the fuck up and out of dodge. Fatback met them around the corner and snatched up the two macs from the ladies. He told them to head out to Forest Park. P Double had a surprise for them.

$ $ $

P Double was almost happy. It was New Year's Eve. He and Fatback managed to stack some good paper, and they took out some of his enemies.

But the main one who hurt him dearly was still walking the streets, Mike Tuitt. Tuitt was a smart man, in fact, because he took that work and flipped it like he never dipped coke before. Shit, he got tired of hearing Fatback and P Double's name in the streets. There were a lot of pimps and players in the drug trade in Springfield. Don't get it twisted, but they took his work, left him broke, and blew up his shit. Mike couldn't get over that, ever. All that shit them niggas had was due to him, and he wanted it all. Meanwhile, he had gotten back to the status in the hood. They weren't the only ones moving coke a hundred miles an hour. He was too. It was a good year for him too.

$ $ $

Fatback and P Double went to club Mascaras to watch the ball drop. Both boys were icy. The club was packed to capacity with DJ Scope on the wheels of steel. The two young thugs had bitches begging to suck their dicks. Back snatched up a little hot body chick named Tangi and moved to a back table. P Double went and bought the bar out. DJ Scope said, "Big shout out to P Double. He bought the bar out. All drinks are free. Enjoy yourself." Then he played some new shit by this kid named Nas. "Halftime" burned the club down. P snatched up four bottles of Moët and two fifths of Hennessy. Lan came out of nowhere and helped him carry it. Dave ordered a couple more fifths and a couple bottles of Moët. The rest of P's crew came through the door, and the club was going crazy.

P Double walked over to their table and saw Fatback leaning back in the booth. "Yo, where fine-ass Tangi go, Fatback?" P asked.

Back just pointed down. P looked under the table and said, "Wow, now that's the real deal."

Lan had his ghetto princess there. Her name was Pooh. She was one of the baddest bitches in the whole damn town. Her clique was full of bad bitches, but they all hated young P Double because Shafika was a part of their crew. Nothing had been proven, but the streets had been talking, so they knew P Double had something to do with it, but nobody could prove shit. Dave was on floss with Pooh's cousin Nisha. She was another future flavor. P wished they didn't hate him so much, because he wanted to see if Nisha's mouth could really suck a dick. Her lips were perfect, but did she really know how to use them? Kev was chilling with this chick named Nikki. She used to fuck with the other T Baby from the Ave. The night was all right, but P started reminiscing, because everyone was with their bitch but him and, well, Fatback, but Fatback wanted every chick not just one. Scope threw on real love by Mary J Blige. Then the club erupted. All the chicks ran to the dance floor and started dancing. Back finally came. He said, "Oh shit," and his eyes rolled into the back of his head. Then P saw a sight he never thought he would see, and that was Mike Tuitt on the dance floor glittered out, popping with some bitch. P took off all his ice and told Back to watch it. Before Fatback could ask him why, P raced onto the dance floor and tackled Mike like a linebacker. Mike was bigger than P so he rolled him off of him quickly and bounced to his feet. P Double got up too and threw a sharp combo at Tuitt. But the older man ducked under the blows and slammed P Double. He got on top of the young don and struck him with two sharp blows, which busted P Double's nose. But his boy came to the rescue.

Back saw all the commotion and ran to the dance floor. By the time he got there, he saw Mike hit his man twice. Fatback pushed a couple of bitches out of the way and blindsided Tuitt with a monster punch that carried all his weight behind it. Tuitt was on the ground snoring when the ball dropped to announce the New Year. P jumped up and gave him some footwork that woke Tuitt back up. That was when Kev slapped him in the sleeper, and the rest of the crew pounced on Mike. Mike threw Kev off him and ran out of the club. P gave chase, but Mike made it to his car in time to pull out a gun from under his seat. Tuitt let the Taurus rip with five quick shots. One of them caught P Double in the leg, but he kept running after being slowed down a bit. Mike then jumped into the Legend and started his engine just as P got to the car. P kicked the window, and it shattered as Tuitt hit reverse. He then put the car in drive and ran P Double over as he hit Bicentennial Highway and bounced. Fatback saw his man on the ground and went crazy. An ambulance arrived a short time later and put the young don on a stretcher.

P woke up a couple of hours later with his grandmother and Fatback standing over him. They told him he could leave the following day. He just had a broken rib, and his leg and body would most likely be sore. Fatback told him the bullet went straight through his leg, so all the doctors had to do was stop the bleeding. P's grandmother told him police weren't gonna let him leave the hospital until they talked to him first. P told her to call Vinny, which she did on Fatback's cell phone. He announced that he was on his way and hung up. When he got there, Acres and his boy came through. P pled the Fifth, and they stormed out angry.

$ $ $

In the hallway, Tony Peogi punched the wall and said, "I'm tired of that punk. He's moving more cocaine in Springfield than Pablo Escobar. Then to top it off, we know he's in the majority of the shootings on the hill, period. I mean, Larry, every time somebody gets shot or dies, he's linked to it somehow, someway. I might just shoot the fuck myself."

Acres looked at the manic rogue cop and said, "You're right. We know all this, which is very much to our advantage. But we gotta take him down the old-fashioned way, and that's hard-earned policework. Come on, Tony, if we just shoot him, then we're scum just like he is. Now I gotta couple ways we might be able to get at these punks," Acres added with a strong tone in his voice.

Peogi said, "All I know is he got a high-paid lawyer, and he's riding around in a car that cost more than my whole year's salary. Now we gotta take him down and down hard."

They looked at each other and went to Dunkin' Donuts to plan on how to take P Double down.

$ $ $

P Double emerged from the hospital, angry at himself. He was fighting with anger instead of using his head. He always was a smart fighter, but Mike Tuitt had gotten the best of him because he didn't fight with a level head. P already knew they were gonna cross paths again, and this time, he swore he was gonna be the victor. Fatback dropped him off in Chicopee and said he'd be right back. He had a couple drops to make.

"Yo, snatch my man E up and tell him to bring us a half pound of exotic."

E was a black Machiavellian-thinking nigga. He was also the weed man. E only sold exotic smoke though. E's real name was Eric. He was a dark-skinned skinny brother who every set went to see with his problems. E had his own block called Gun Square. He also had mad bitches due to the fact he was smooth with the tongue and of course he was the weed man.

P Double had just hopped out of the shower when Fatback, E, and three bitches walked in.

E said, "What's the word, O?"

P said, "Shit, who are they?" as he stared licking his lips and choosing which one he wanted.

R said, "Asia, Catalina, and Antonette."

Asia was a tall, beautiful Asian and black sister with long legs and rich and creamy skin. She had long black hair, but she had the nasta diagnosis, which was no ass at all. She was hit in that department, and P was an ass man. Antonette was a short chocolate dame. She wasn't that pretty, but she wasn't ugly either. She made up for it by having a banging body and that down-for-whatever attitude. Now, Catalina was a piece of work. She was a red-bone beauty with fangs like Coco from SWV. She was tall and bow-legged and had a well-defined ass. She also had the trace of an accent, which really turned P on. As P hugged E and gave the man dap, his towel fell, exposing his private parts.

The girls gasped and started talking among themselves as P grabbed the towel and scuffled off into the bedroom. One of the girls said, "Nice ass," as he walked off. He went into the room, got laced up in a whole Champion sweatsuit, and threw on a pair of Air Max, with his favorite Red Sox hat with a big B on it, for Bristol Street. For Christmas, P and Fatback upgraded their jewelry as well. P Double had an iced-out bracelet that ran him thirty alone. He also had a giant Cuban with a bigger iced-out B on it. The pinky ring and the iced-out Movado watch made him complete. After seeing the Wu Tang clan with the gold fronts, P went and iced his mouth as well. P Double walked out and blessed E with fifteen hundred for the half pound of Hawaiian skunk the dealer had brought him. All the girls said, "Damn, daddy, don't hurt 'em."

P signaled for Catalina to come and sit next to him. She wiggled over to him with bow legs swaying strongly and sat down. P spit a couple lines at her and knew he had the bitch right where he wanted her.

E said, "Man, what's good with the packy? We need some Hennessy up in here."

Fatback laughed, ran behind the minibar, and put two half-gallons of Hennessy on the counter. "You already know how we rock, E. You didn't even have to go that route." He produced some cups and introduced everyone to Dutch Masters.

"Yo, Back, throw this shit in the radio and bring the cards out," E said.

Fatback said, "Man, what the fuck is this bullshit, with this little-ass kid on it?"

"Man, it's the hottest shit you ever heard in your life, baby boy. Trust the god when he speaks," E shot back at the young thug.

Fatback threw it in the radio and turned it up. P Double broke up the weed while E started rolling up and Fatback poured the drinks.

Then P Double said, "This shit is fire. Back, you listening?"

"The smooth criminal on beat breaks / never put me in your box if your shit eats tapes / the city never sleeps / full of villains and creeps," Nas said in the speaker.

P said, "Damn, everything that nigga saying we going through right now. This shit dope."

"See, I told you. And the whole tape is like this."

P asked, "E, what record store had the shit?"

"P, the shit ain't even out yet, and that's my word!" E shouted over the radio.

"So how you get it, nigga?"

"See now you asking security questions," E joked.

"Nah, nah, I'm just playing though. My cousin from the city slid me this shit. This nigga the hottest thing moving right now."

P said, "I'll give you a hundred bucks for it right now."

"You already know I can't turn that shit down, P."

They all chilled for a minute, and then P said, "Let me holla at you outside."

They both got up and went outside.

"Yo, what's the deal with Mike Tuitt," P shot at him.

"Nothing much really. I heard about the little altercation y'all two had a couple days ago. He just copped a half pound of smoke off me earlier today."

"I'll give you five grand to set that nigga up for me or just let me know when he's coming to cop," P insisted. "Now you already know I got love for both of y'all, so you know you're out of order asking me that. I'm a neutral grounded nigga; that's all. If the shoe was on the other foot, do you think I would've sold you out, P? You already know I wouldn't, so what you just asked me ain't my type of party," E said as he roasted the el.

"My bag, but you can't blame a nigga for trying though. Anyways, what's up with that bitch Catalina?"

"She's a ripe peach, huh?" E said.

"Hell yeah, and I'm gonna pluck her," P Double added.

E said, "Shit, you better. She's got the hots for you. Just don't fall in love, playboy, and you'll be all right."

They went back in, and E said he had some runs to make so he needed Fatback to drop him off at his whip. Catalina stayed with P as the rest of the group retreated. P Double got up and popped in Jodeci as he let KC do the talking through the airwaves. Catalina played with P's dick as she started taking off his sweatshirt. P came up out of it. He had a wife beater on underneath. She started sucking on his chest. She saw the bandage around P's rib cage and whispered, "Don't worry, daddy, I'm the captain of this cruise tonight," as she took his jeans off. Then she drove the young boy crazy with a slow, erotic striptease. P started drooling because Catalina's body was dope as fuck. P lay back on the couch while she squatted in front of him. She put his foot in her mouth. Nobody had ever licked the boy's toes before. Then she took him in her mouth and milked him dry. P's dick was still strong when she got on top of him and rode him to death. She was definitely the captain of this boat, making P bust a nut that was way bigger than the first. Then somehow she tightened up her pussy even more, making the young boy stay erect. She said, "I'm not done with you yet," as she pumped up and down, licking P's ear. No woman had ever fucked P with this much intensity before in all his days. No wonder E told him not to fall in love. This bitch was a beast for real. Her pussy was seriously platinum material.

P said, "Ma, fuck this. Get up." She got up, and he told her to bend over. P cupped her ass cheeks and made them clap as he power stroked. But the bitch was throwing her own back into it. While P was pumping away, she was too. This time, they both came with a holla. Young P had to sit down and gather his breath. She lit a Newport and poured another cup of Hennessy. P was infatuated with this bitch. She had fucked him even when he thought he was fucking her. He knew he had met his match with her. She was just a stone cold freak. Catalina poured some Hennessy on his dick.

P said, "Girl, what the fuck are you doing?"

She started sucking his dick again and then stopped and said, "I'm getting drunk." Then she laughed and said, "Round two fights." She swallowed P's dick with no objections. All the while P was thinking, *What the fuck have I got myself into?*

$ $ $

Meanwhile, Back dropped E off and Asia. He fucked Antonette in the backseat of the Lexus, and then he dropped her off and went for a ride. He knew things were running too smoothly. He was scared to death of the task force though. They didn't know when they were coming, but they knew they were coming. Fatback went to Adams Park and decided to chill. Why did he do that? The task force ran up in the park and hemmed everyone up. It was just his luck that he was by someone's stash of a hundred joints. They took him down quickly, but they didn't bring him to the station right away. Curley and Peck drove him through every block like "Look who we got." Then they brought him out far in the woods and beat the shit out of him. Fatback was half dead when they brought him to the station. He was back in Ludlow before he knew where he was at. Fatback said, "Fuck it. His man's gonna come through anyways. Why sweat it?"

$ $ $

P Double woke up in the morning to Catalina sucking his dick. The boy was physically drained from the nympho. He really didn't wanna admit it, but he was all fucked out. But he wouldn't let this pretty bitch get the best of him, so he let her have her way. After they both showered, P started worrying about his road dawg. He turned his phone on, got dressed, and told Catalina he would pick her up later on that night, but right then, he had some business to deal with. She tried to suck his dick in the car, but enough was enough.

He said, "Tonight, I already told you, woman."

She smiled and said, "I'll be waiting. Don't disappoint me," as she got out of the GS with grace.

P Double was finally able to let out a breath and pull some fresh air in. He lit a port and let Nas rock through his factory speakers. "Represent, Represent" was burning the Lexus down right then. P parked in front of T Baby's house and rolled a fat Dutch of Hawaiian skunk. When he finished, he blazed it, woke T Baby up, and told him to come outside. The baby came down wiping the crust out of his eyes and jumped in the whip. P passed him the el at once.

Then "Life's a Bitch" started rocking, and T Baby said, "Who the fuck is this?"

"This that new Nas shit right here. The tape ain't even out yet."

Baby said, "Speaking of out, did you get Fatback out last night?"

P said, "Out of where?"

"Damn, so you don't even know? Yesterday, he got out and chilled at the park with niggas, and somebody had some shit stashed out there when the task force raided the park. Back just happened to be standing next to the shit," Baby finished. He took a long choke and passed the el back to P.

P said, "That's you. I gotta bounce, man. I gotta cop this nigga a lawyer before they try to play him."

Baby said, "Hold up. I need some shit." Baby ran into the crib and came back out with twenty-five racks.

P said, "It will be a minute though."

"No rush, no rush, I still got packs to move, so take your time."

The boys gave each other dap.

P turned the music up as he made his way down to see his lawyer. When he got there, Vinny told him to holla at his associate Mark Masteronni because it would be a conflict of interest if they ever went down together. Then he could only represent one of them anyway. He assured P that Mark was a great legal mind too and that they would get right on everything at once. P made his way down to the courthouse with both high-powered attorneys. They went down to the bullpen and talked to Back for a minute. Then they went and talked to the district attorney. They told P that his man had to get locked up because his record was very extensive, but they were gonna fight the case to the very end. P walked out of the courtroom angry and bumped into Jaynce. She was looking good and smelling good, as usual.

"Presley, what a surprise. Please tell me you haven't caught a case, boy."

He assured her that he was staying out of trouble, and he wasn't there for himself at all but for his friend. He shot his number to her, and they agreed to talk later on that day. P left the courthouse on a bad note. The young man had just lost his best friend on a hum bug. Fatback was right when he said things were going smoothly. At the moment, his phone chirped, and he cut the music down. He lit a new port and said to himself, "At least that's some good news." His Spanish people had called him. Jujito and Vito were two brothers who controlled the north end. They wanted five birds a piece. P liked those niggas' style because they both took no shit from anybody at all. P drove to the crib and grabbed eleven birds and made the drops. He then drove to his grandmother's and put all his bread in the big safe.

P was sitting down trying to plan his next move when his phone chirped again and again. He had a lot of drops to make. P Double made Veronica and his grandmother go see Fatback the next day. His grandmother said the young boy looked pretty beat up. Fatback told her how they took him out of the city and fucked him up pretty badly. She brought the boy some clothing, sneakers, and a couple of hats. She also brought him a dub of that new Nas album and broke down who her grandson had represent him. She then hugged the boy and got up so Veronica could talk to him for a while.

P Double was back and forth to Mecca every other day just about. Sometimes, he took his whip. At other times, he took his crime partner's whip. His birthday was a couple of days away, and other then get paper, the young boy really didn't know what to do. He was sitting down watching the news when he saw a familiar face pop up. He turned the TV up full blast. Lan, Dave, and Norm were wanted in connection with the murder of Big Doyol. Then, after that, police shot and killed an older cat from the Ave. They thought he had carjacked some basehead's car and killed him in cold blood. Ninety-four was turning out to be a crazy year. Half his team was in the bing, and the other half was on the run. P decided he needed a new nigga to rock with and build up. That was when he found Maurice. He was a little rich kid on the block. He never had to want for shit because his mother owned an insurance company. Nobody really knew what his father did; he was just paid. That's all.

One day, P pushed a little rental Tahoe he had picked up past Adams Park, and he saw Moe making a play. He pulled over and called the boy to the truck.

"Get in," P ordered.

Moe got in, and the don passed the young boy the el. Moe took a choke of the good and started gagging full force from the smoke. P laughed.

"Damn, what the fuck is that?" Moe said, rolling down the window. He spit.

"Some good nigga, that's what it is. Why are you hustling, Moe?" P asked the boy, really wanting to know his reasons.

"Because I want to. I need my own money," Moe answered and added, "and I like it."

P said, "But your family has enough bread already. Moe, you really don't need to be out here."

"Man, didn't I just get through telling you, I need my own bread, yo. Fuck their money! Their money don't mean shit to me!" Moe hollered.

"So who are you hustling for, little nigga?"

"Yo, you're only a couple of years older than me, nigga, and what's up with the twenty questions bullshit? Yo, my pager is ringing."

P passed Moe his phone, and the boy called the number back. "Bring me to Quincy Street real quick," Moe said.

P said, "You're going on them Ave niggas' block to make a sale, little nigga?"

"Why, are you scared or something?" Moe shot at the don.

"Boy, I ain't scared of shit. Not even God, boy. I'll slap the shit out of you if you ever question my manhood, chump," P said with spittle flying everywhere.

He took the young cat to make the sale and said, "I want you to work for me, Moe. I'll show you how to cook, cut, and bag, nigga. But if you bite the hand that feeds you, it's a wrap for you, little nigga."

And that's how their relationship started. Moe was a real quick learner, and now that Lan was on the run, Moe crashed the block after school and half the night. Even P didn't know how the little nigga stayed in school. After P tasted that fast money, he just graduated himself to the streets. Shit, whoever said crime didn't pay was a buster, because P was about nineteen, and he had more money than some of these people had in a lifetime of spending money. P told Moe to pack some shit up; it was his birthday, and they were hitting the road. They drove to the city and copped Moe a fake ID, so they could hit Foxwoods Resort and Casino for the whole weekend. Moe complained about his sale, but P gave the nigga five grand to blow on whatever.

First, they hit up the casino, and P won ten racks playing blackjack. Then P said he had a special treat for them, and they hollered at a couple banging white class dames. They walked to the sporting arena, and it was jampacked. P had front-row seats to the event. When they got there, all the lights went off, and out popped Jodeci. They had the crowd going crazy as they rocked a good five songs. After that, Mary J Blige came out and had the whole place rocking with her electricity. It took her an hour and a half to finish her set. She even sang some of her new songs from her new album. Then Escape came on, but their act was kind of weak. Next was SWV. But the main act was Keith Sweat. Keith lived up to all the hype of being the main attraction because he left all the bitches with their panties soaking wet.

After the show, P Double told the young boy to follow, and they went backstage and chilled with the stars. P's birthday turned out to be a smash hit. They had the time of their lives that weekend. P Double knew that Moe was gonna be a rich dude one day, because he only spent a hundred bucks of the five stacks that P gave him that weekend.

$ $ $

When they got back, they were back on their grind like never before. All P did was stack dough and stack more dough. Fatback's trial was a couple months down the line, so P had to make sure he and his man's foundation was stronger than ever. P had finally convinced Moe to cop a whip. Moe jumped in a Tahoe at the age of fifteen. It was used but shit looked brand new. That summer, P was running through more bitches than he could even handle. But somehow he always found himself fucking crazy-ass Catalina. He really couldn't help it though. He had to admit that no broad had ever sexed him the way she had. In all actuality, if it wasn't for her, than he wouldn't be the stud he was today. P Double mastered the technique of giving women multiple orgasms, and it was all thanks to Catalina. P found himself scooping her up on Friday night. They went to Blockbuster in Forest Park and then went to the apartment around the corner and fucked all night long.

$ $ $

Eddie Haul was fighting his case hard. At first, he went to trial and lost. They worked him over severely by giving him a thirty concord with five mandatory to serve up front. Ed damn near spent every penny he had fighting the case. His lawyer finally got his appeal on the grounds that the judge gave the jury the wrong instructions. So he had a whole new trial coming. While he was upstate, there were cats who did their time by lifting weights. Other cats were into running ball and playing cards. Ed wasn't into any of that shit. All he did was walk the track and think about another shot at the title and getting even with P Double. He made that nigga. How dare he cross the great Ed Haul. Nobody else taught him how to whip that batch. Nobody else schooled him on shit. His time would come, and it would be soon. Italia was holding him down, but he missed Mama to death. He still didn't get word who killed his dame though. He just wanted P to die slowly. Then to top everything off, the bitch nigga robbed his first cousin Mike Tuitt to get on. He was happy to hear Mike beat the shit out of the nigga at Maccaras. Too bad his cousin didn't kill the little bastard. For some reason or another, the chump had nine lives. Ed had to go to trial very soon. P Double better pray he didn't make that guest appearance back into society or it was a wrap for him.

$ $ $

J.G. was doing his thing across town. He managed to stack some good paper to him, but to a nigga like P Double, that was chump change. He had to admit that he fell head over heels for Marlin's sister Brandy. He just couldn't stop fucking though. Everything he thought about how they took his manhood last year, he had to prove to himself that he was a man and stick his dick in anything that was a female. Short, slim, fat, tall, all races, J.G. didn't discriminate. If they were a female, they were getting fucked.

One night last year, he caught the nigga predator searching for crack on the ground late at night. J.G. always carried the fifth on him late at night, because there were a lot of desperate creeps and feins running around. He jumped from behind a bush and peeled predator's wig back with a three round burst. Then he emptied the rest of the clip in the man's groin area. That at least gave him a little closure, but he still wanted the big prize, P Double. One day, they were standing out there, and this kid Snake from Maynard was talking a good one.

"I don't know why everybody is scared of that nigga P Double. His whole style is bitch for real. As soon as I see that chump, I'm testing his chin out, and that's my word."

As soon as he said that, the Pepsi blue GS turned the corner and made its way down Maynard. Snake flagged the man down. He was with Kev and little Lee. They all got out. J.G., Marlin, and T.B. watched as snake started popping shit to the young don.

P said, "What up?"

"You're up, you bitch-ass nigga. That's what's up. Maynard Street's finest is about to represent on your faggot ass." Snake threw a three piece, but P blocked every punch and laughed at the broke nigga. This really made Snake go crazy. He threw a right hook with a lot of velocity behind it. P ducked and hit him with two body shots that buckled him over. P saw his advantage and took it. Snake had a giant Afro from not getting his shit braided up. P snatched up two handfuls of hair and started football kicking Snake in the face.

A car pulled up with a couple of Ave niggas in it to watch the action. Fatkat, Lox, and Turtle jumped out of the Honda and said, "Damn."

Snake was leaking blood that was thicker than spaghetti sauce. After two more monsterous kicks, P let the man go on his own recognizance. Snake wobbled back, knocked out on his feet. He staggered over near Fatkat. P, like a hungry lion, stalking his wounded prey was closing in on him, ready to finish the man off.

"Come on, P. The boy is finished," Fatkat said. "Look at him."

"Well, his bitch ass shouldn't have called me out. That's what happens when you ask for it. And what the fuck are you looking at, J.G. Is your ass still leaking?"

P, Kev, and Lee started laughing as they walked back to the G.S. J.G. hated that nigga even more after that day. P Double would be slipping one day, and he would be there to take advantage of the situation.

$ $ $

Meanwhile, Black was in Ludlow. He got locked up on some bullshit-ass home invasion he didn't do. Every day, he was training his legs, doing squats and leg presses. Right then, he was in the best shape of his life, but his mind wasn't. He sent his little cousin into the jungle and he'd got eaten by some hungry lions. That nigga P Double couldn't be touched, but that was bullshit. Black just wasn't healthy enough to stake his claim to vengeance. Now he was, but he was sidetracked by this bullshit case. One thing he didn't lose was his fight game. Two Puerto Ricans had tried to jump him a couple of weeks ago. Black hit the first one with a two-piece stunner and then a right cross that put the man to sleep. The other gang member had a little something with him but not enough because Black left him snoring too. At first, it was a pack of them on the rec deck surrounding him, but when he made the first goon drop like a log, the rest ran and locked in, except that stupid muthafucker. The kid was a giant up top, but his legs were straight spaghetti sticks, and Black made quick work on the diesel dope fein. After that, Black saw he was ready for rock. If only he could beat this case so he could show P Double life ain't sweet at all.

$ $ $

Mike Tuitt was right for the summer. He was sitting pretty in a brand-new Hummer. He figured he deserved it, all the shit he'd been through. Why not spoil yourself with the finer things in life? He also copped the big Cuban link with the iced-out coffeepot with the spoon on it. This year had been a crazy one so far. At the beginning of summer, somebody killed this kid Greyland. He was hitting off from Rifle Street. Then the Latin King cats were really going crazy because they were killing dudes over prayer beads. Right then, the streets were dangerous because the task force was grabbing dudes from left to right.

One day, he was laying back, getting his dick sucked by Kim, his baby's mother, when his phone chirped. He answered it at once and jumped up, choking Kim with his fast movement. Somebody kidnapped his sister Stacy Tuitt. Not really *somebody*—he already knew who it was already. The one and only P Double.

$ $ $

Kev placed a bug in his ear a whole year ago about that. Stacy Tuitt always wanted to be a late-night scrambler at the Edgewood Street after hour. Well she was gonna dance with the devil in the pale moon light that night. P Double started going to the after-hour a week earlier, and this bitch was always there, looking like her fucking brother. They could be twins. *The chick thinks she's a man anyways. I guess that's what severe ugliness will do to a person.* P Double got fed up seeing this mannish bitch everywhere he went. That night was the night. He told Moe to go into the party, find her, and tell her somebody was in the backyard, trying to buy some smoke.

Moe walked the mannish broad upstairs and to the backyard. She stared spazzing, saying there was nobody back here. "What the fuck is this?" And she snatched Moe up by his shirt. They started tussling when P jumped out of the bushes and gun-butted the dame with a hard knock blow. She fell on Moe, and he held her up.

P said, "We gotta toss this bitch over the fence and carry her to the whip."

They threw her over the fence and carried her to Moe's Tahoe and tied her up in the truck. P drove to Forest Park, where the two lugged her upstairs and tied her to the bed in Fatback's room. P told Moe, "Thanks," and gave him five hundred grams for a job well done.

Moe took the grams and said, "I got school in the a.m."

P said, "It's summertime, nigga. What school?"

"My mother has got me doing this computer class. She said it will help me out in the long run."

P just looked at the boy and shook his head. "Peace, tomorrow then."

And Moe bounced. P went to work stripping and blindfolding her. She woke up that morning bugging. "Where the fuck am I at?"

"Where the fuck is your bitch-ass brother at?"

"How the fuck do I know?" Stacy said, struggling against the handcuffs.

"How about I fuck it out of you, you dike bitch," P stated, fed up with the game playing. He wanted answers, and he wanted them now.

Stacy responded with, "If you stick your nasty-ass dick in this pussy, it will be the last pussy you ever ram it in."

P broke out in a hard laugh. He ran up to her side and smacked her with two well-placed smacks to the face and said, "I'm done beating around the bush with your mannish ass. Now, what the fuck is his number?"

She gave it to him, and he dialed the number. It rang twice before P heard the voice he hated so much with a passion.

P said, "I want thirty birds and a half million dollars. You got until sundown," and he hung up. In the meantime he was gonna have him some dike bush. P Double placed a lifestyle on his muscle. He didn't wanna leave no DNA in this bitch whatsoever. He then tried to shove his dick in her, but she was tight as a virgin. His head wouldn't even fit. P said, "Yeah, bitch, I got some shit for that." P grabbed the KY jelly and lubed his muscle up. Then he poured the rest on her bird and fingered it in there. The boy mounted her this time. He slowly worked his way in. The dike bitch gasped when P managed to fit his whole organ up in her. Then he long dicked her slow and easy. The bitch held her emotions in, but her face gave it all away. Then P just outright fucked her. Stacy started screaming as P bounced up and down on her. Then he slowed it down for a good minute. He felt her tight-ass bird quivering, and he knew she was nutting. P Double fucked her until the sun went down, taking breaks, walking the bitch back and forth to the bathroom and then mounting the dike bitch all over again. From then on, he was gonna try to fuck every dike bitch he could ever get his hands on.

After he finished with her period, he said, "A well-placed dick is way better than licking a pussy any day of the week. Remember that, bitch."

Once again, he found himself dialing faggot-ass Mike Tuitt's number. "You ready for me or what, bitch nigga."

Mike said he was in fact. P told him to send a broad with it to Jim Dandy's and order a large fried clams and fries. She was then to drop both bags on the floor, walk out, and drive off. When everything was all accounted for, Stacy would be released. If the shit was short in any kind of way possible, she'd be on Channel 40 news in the morning."

Mike said, "Okay, okay, you got that. Please don't hurt her."

P Double laughed and said, "You got a half hour."

P then hung up and hit Moe up, telling him to make sure he wasn't followed when he made the pickup. Everything went like clockwork because Moe was there forty five minutes later. He asked Moe if he wanted some of that good bush before he let her go free. Moe worked her for fifteen minutes, and then they dressed the dike bitch up, threw her out in Forest Park, and sped away. P called Mike and said, "She's in Forest Park at the basketball court," and hung up.

P Double blessed Moe with five bricks and twenty stacks for a job well done.

$ $ $

Mike Tuitt was distraught. Everything he worked hard for was gone because of a punk kid. He swore this time he was gonna kill the little bastard on sight. He didn't care anymore. When he got to the basketball court, she was safe and sound. Nobody saw anything, but he already knew what the deal was. It was nobody but P Double. Stacy was angry and wanted to know who held her prisoner all that time. She was acting angry when in fact she enjoyed it a great deal. Her brother told her who it was, and she couldn't believe it. Little Presley's dick was the bomb, and she wanted more. But of course she wasn't gonna let Mike know that, not at all. But whoever the last chump was bouncing up and down on her didn't know how to work it, period. If she ever found out who that was, she decided she was gonna beat him to death with her bare hands. Mike got angry because he kept asking her if the boy did anything to her three times already. She snapped out of her daydream and said, "No," and cussed his ass out for ruining her daydream. Stacy decided to call up one of her female companions. She was in the mood for strapping up and dicking something down.

Mike was furious. This little kid was really making life a bitch, but God forbid the bitch divorce him. He was already planning his next move on the way to drop his pain-in-the-ass sister off. If it wasn't for his brother Rob Tuitt and their father, Stacy's ass would've been P Double's responsibility. He was on the grind day and night for that dollar. Now it seemed like it was all a dream. But it wasn't. This was real life, and it was time to get his duck game in order for real.

CHAPTER 10

GIRL TROUBLE

Shante was going haywire. Everything was going sweet with her and P, and then he just straight up stopped calling her. She tried calling him, but he changed his number once again. She was going crazy. She needed a good dicking down. Frankie was still locked up. He had a month left, but even though her heart belonged to Frankie, her mind and pussy belonged to P Double without a doubt. She was doing okay for herself in the money department, because she maintained Frankie's weed business and his coke business. Shante had two pagers that drove her up a wall sometimes. She decided to throw on her best that night and catch the gaslight in full swing. Maybe she could find some aight dick in the club, but there was no replacing P Double at all. P Double was fucking another chick, but she just didn't know who. All she knew was for some reason or another, he started beating the pussy up for hours, which was all right with her. Her pussy got wet just thinking about it.

Shante threw on a yellow-and-black Coco Chanel catsuit and a pair of yellow-and-black come-fuck-me boots. She knew she had a fat pussy. Her suit was extra tight so it could run through her pussy lips. Shante applied a little lip gloss, and she jumped in the CRX and picked her sister Roberta up. They pulled up at the Gaslight, and the club was jumping out of control. They swaggered to the back of the line and awaited their turn.

$ $ $

Madi was getting dipped. It was Friday night and time to unwind in the right way. She missed P Double. For some strange reason, he hadn't called her in a couple of weeks. She tried calling his phone, but he changed the number and never called her after that. P Double must have gone out of town again or been in trouble because she was positively sure. He would've called her by then. He always told her how great her pussy was, so she knew he couldn't resist it if he was in town. She prided herself on keeping her snatch tight and juicy, and she already knew her head game was like no other. All she did was practice sucking on Blow Pops all day long so she could get that right degree of friction. She still remembered the last time she sucked P Double's dick. That night was special because she brought a can of whipped cream with her and made a sundae out of his dick. It drove her mad tasting whip cream along with her come. It was more than a snack for her. It was a delicacy in its own right. She started rubbing her clit thinking about it. But what fucked her up was his newfound stamina. He was always a bull in the sack, but now he was a matador between the sheets. She didn't think she would ever stop coming. Madi had never come that many times in her life. She just knew he was fucking another bitch, but who? Madi just knew she needed some dick that night, and she was going to the Gaslight to find someone to tame her cat.

$ $ $

Keisha was dolled up, ready for action. Andy Cap had been in the bing a little while now. On some real shit, she didn't wanna be a part of his miserable life any longer. She had class shit. In all actuality, she deserved better than him by far. Keisha deserved P Double. Oh, just saying his name had her pussy soaked. She'd been fucking him ever since he rocked her world on T Baby's couch on his birthday. Of course, Andy Cap was head over heels for her. Who wouldn't b—except for P Double, it seemed? She did everything he asked. He made her suck on Blow Pops all day so she could get her technique going properly. Now, she could suck an orange through a tennis racket at the drop of a dime. Her jaws were well defined now, thanks to this, which made her look more radiant then she already was.

Andy Cap gave her just about everything she ever wanted, except a good, hard-core fucking like P Double gave her. Andy Cap had a little bit of money, but to her, his paper was childish and P's shit was quite grown. Every thug needed a diva, and that was what she considered herself to be—a diva. Shit, she even learned how to make her pussy contract with ease.

Keisha looked in the mirror one last time and licked her pussy lips. "Keisha, you are that bitch," she said to herself. But who was she kidding? P had fucked her a couple of weeks ago and stopped calling her. She needed to see him and find out what she was doing wrong. All he had to do was tell her, and his wish was her command, indeed. Right then, her pussy was thirsty for a dick to wrap around. She would settle for a five-minute Andy Cap special right then. That was why she had to hit the gaslight that night because she needed a piece of wood that could burn all night long.

$ $ $

Catalina was taking a hot bath so she could seduce another gangster. Who the fuck did P Double think he was by not fucking her in a week? She could get dick on demand anytime she wanted it. A million cats were waiting to scratch hers, and she was ready to give it to them. "Catalina, who are you fooling?" she said to herself. She wanted P Double and P Double only. She had to train him to fuck her the way she needed to be fucked, and wow, did he ever? He was the master of the game when it came to making her come without a doubt. Plus, he was young rich, and he had no children. Now where on earth were you gonna find a package like that? Nowhere. Catalina never thought it could happen in her nineteen years, but she had to admit, the love bug had finally bit her right in her big fat ass. She was model material, and she was fucked up over a drug dealer. How could she practice the art of seduction when her pussy just wanted P Double's shaft in it? This was the first time in her life she had ever been head over heels for a nigga, and she didn't like the feeling. Oh well, what could she do but go out, drink her stress away, and try to find another contender worthy of a shot at the title. The gaslight was the night's place to be, and Catalina's fine ass was making a guest appearance, you better believe that.

$ $ $

P Double was on his grind heavy. He decided to give the broads a break for a while. Besides, one of the women he truly loved lived in Kinston, North Carolina, and the other was his former probation officer, Jaynce. She would never fuck with him because of the lifestyle he was living, but he loved his life, and he wasn't changing it for anybody. P loved Akasha, but his business was up there, and he remembered what Mike Tuitt did to Mama on a regular basis. He missed Mama, but she was somebody else's love anyway. Yeah they had been through some shit together, but the only reason she was with him was because Eddie Haul was locked up. All P thought about when he weighed his options was whether it could happen to him. What if he got locked up? Would she run off with a sport coat? Why not? She did it to Ed. So he had to sacrifice her in order to stay on top. All the other chicks he was fucking, he had feelings for them, but he could never fall in love with any of them. They weren't the settling-down-with type. Of course, he loved fucking Catalina's fine ass, but that was all straight lust and nothing else. Fuck it, P decided to jump in the GS and see if he could bag something new at the Gaslight. Half of Springfield's women wanted to suck his dick, so why not let them?

P got up with Kev and Lee. They hit the scene. The Gaslight had a crazy-ass line stretched around the corner. The three hoods just walked to the front like they owned the joint, and Big Brutus, the bouncer, took their money and let them pass. When they walked in, they heard all types of screams and moans outside from what had occurred. The three went straight to the bar and bought a couple of fifths and some champagne. The DJ was rocking some new Naughty by Nature shit, and the dance floor was packed. Little Lee had his eye on a redbone who had all the right moves on the floor. She was bending her body in ways that should be humanly impossible.

"Yo, hold this, Kev. I gotta get this bitch's number or fuck her tonight, either one." And Lee shot to the dance floor.

P and Kev had just walked to the VIP section and copped a squat when P saw this badass bitch about a couple of tables over. They made eye contact, and P Double made his move. "Excuse me. Is this seat taken?" P asked with a smile on his face, showing his iced-out grill.

The cutie said, "No," and P Double took a seat.

"My name is P Double," he shot at her.

"I already know who you are. I heard all about you already." The beautiful woman spoke with a mischievous look on her face.

"Well, since you know about me, and I don't know about you. What is your name?" he asked her.

"Melony, but most people call me Mel for short." And she stuck out one of her gorgeous hands for P to shake.

P Double took her hand and kissed it lightly. He noticed her hands were very soft and well kept, the same as her beautiful smile. To P, she looked like she could be Aaliyah's sister. Melony was seriously a hot shorty. After kicking it with her a while, a banging-ass redbone walked up out of breath, sweating a little bit.

"Yo, Mel, some fake-ass little nigga call hisself trying to holla at me. His game was all wrong." Then she looked at P and said, "Excuse me for being rude. My name is Tamoya, but you can call me Moya. And your name is?"

"P Double," he said as he poured himself a double shot of Hennessy.

Moya glanced at him and said, "You're P Double? Wow. I guess all the hype about you was true 'cause, nigga, you fine."

P wanted to smile but he kept his composure and said, "Weren't you the girl that was dancing with my man Lee?"

"Yeah, that was me. You need to teach your boy about gaming a chick because his shit's down," Tamoya said, rolling her eyes and snapping her fingers.

Then a beautiful chocolate chick walked up to Melony and tongued her down.

P Double said, "What the fuck?" as he was blown back by the openness.

Then Melony spoke. "P, this is my girlfriend, Shawna."

Shawna looked at P and said, "What up?" while sitting on Melony's lap.

P Double said, "Melony, you're a lesbian?"

"No, P Double, I'm not. I'm bisexual, sweetheart. I like dick too if the right nigga can lay pipe the right way."

Just then, Shante spotted P Double from across the dance floor getting his Mack on. She strolled over quietly and said, "Is this the reason you've been dissing me? For a bunch of muff munchers?"

Before P could answer the question, Melony threw her girl off her lap and stood up. "Maybe he don't want no broke-ass bitch, bitch."

Shante said, "I got your bitch right here," and she leaped up, but P Double got in between the chicks and stopped the madness. Everybody saw a little commotion going on and ganged up.

Catalina saw P in the middle of two chicks and said, "P, I know you're not sticking your dick in this dirty bitch right here when you got all this."

Shante said, "Bitch, ain't your pussy dry by now from all the dicks you been servicing?"

All of a sudden, Keisha and Madi came and started arguing. P couldn't control shit, so he did the logical thing and whispered in Melony's ear, "Meet me at IHOP in West Springfield right now. Food's on me." She nodded her head, and he sneaked out just as he heard a bottle break.

$ $ $

Shante hated Catalina. She was always stealing someone's man. Who the fuck did this Amazon bitch think she was? Shante couldn't believe P was fucking this come guzzler. Then two more bitches came trying to stake their claim on her nigga. She wasn't having it tonight. Berta saw all the action and ran up on Catalina.

"Bitch what!" Berta screamed.

As soon as Catalina turned around to talk shit to Roberta, Shante smacked her with the Heineken bottle she was drinking from. That just made the whole club erupt because Madi and Keisha started brawling too. Catalina spit a razor out of her mouth and slashed Berta on her face as Shante was punching the back of Catalina's head. They all fell on the floor, and the bouncers ran over to break the fights up.

One of them wound up getting sliced too because Catalina was swinging the razor like a madwoman. Madi and Keisha each had a handful of each other's hair and were swinging each other back and forth until the bouncers broke them apart. That night, every last one of them went to jail.

$ $ $

P copped a booth at IHOP and waited for Melony and her entourage to show up. Fifteen minutes later, the beautiful trio showed up real giddy. Melony sat next to P as the other two women sat across from them. Melony looked at him and grabbed his dick. P was astonished, but he kept the same unreadable ice grill on as she put her hand in his jeans and stroked him with practiced ease.

Melony said, "You must be a real cock's man because you had four bitches in heat over this toy soldier in these jeans."

All the girls laughed at the same time at Melony's words.

"I just do what I do to make sure the women receive the same pleasure as me; that's all," P shot back.

"Hey, I'm not a selfish lover at all, Miss Melony."

Just then, a phone sounded. P reached for his, but it was Melony's phone that rocked. "How much?" she asked. "Well, I'm busy right now, unless, hold on. Tamoya, can you and Shawna do me a favor and bring Pittems a big for me?"

The girls said okay, and Melony told them where the man was. P Double couldn't believe his luck. He bagged a bitch that got money. This night was getting better and better. They found out that they had a lot in common, and they hit it right off. P found himself drawn to her because he had never met a woman on her level before. Of course, there were women who usually answered their man's phone or pager and made runs for them, but Melony was a hustler's dream because she made her own bread by selling weight. She was independent. She said D Nice had taught her the game when they were fucking around, and she had never looked back since. They were two minutes into the food when the other two women walked in.

Tamoya said, "Is your boy a true cock's man like you?"

P laughed and said, "Sweetheart, I'm the greatest man alive. There's nobody like me you heard." And he dipped a mozzarella stick in some sauce and fed it to Melony. When they finished their food, Melony whispered in Shawna's ear, and they all rose, telling P to come on. Melony paid the bill and said, "The first date's on me, playboy," and she left a big tip as well. Tamoya and Shawna jumped in a red Audi TT while Melony asked P if she could drive his GS. The boy threw her the keys and told her to hop in. She started the Lexus, and Nas ripped the airwaves with "One Love." She hit the highway, dipping the GS with skill and grace for a woman driver.

"Yo, where are you taking me?" P asked the gorgeous female.

"To my pad. I live in Westfield. You know niggas like to hate, so I keep my shit on the low, daddy," P said. "I never met a woman like you before in my life. You're a dream come true."

"No, I'm not. I'm just on top of my game; that's all. I already know what I want out of life. Why should I wait for a man to make me happy when I can do it myself? You just haven't met a woman who is in tune with herself; that's all."

"Yeah, you're right. But you're still a dream come true, and that's a fact."

They pulled up in front of a one-family house that looked freshly built. Mel unlocked the door and punched in her code to cut the alarm off. P was shocked at the inside of her crib. Melony sure did have great taste. Her living room was decked out in purple and black. She had a purple grand piano on the side of the living room. She had a big-screen TV, and a fireplace with solid-gold trimmings. There were a couple of big framed pictures on the wall as well. The dining room was connected to the living room. P saw she had a big table set for twenty people. All the plates and cups were made out of sterling silver. Mel had some serious style with her. She kicked her boots off and turned the TV and VCR on. She inserted juice and let it play while she came back with a bottle of Hennessy.

"Please make yourself comfortable, daddy." And she strolled off somewhere.

Five minutes later, Melony entered the living room wearing nothing but a garter belt. Her body was doper then young P had imagined. She was cut in all the right places and nice and thick in the others. P stripped at once as she threw all the pillows from the couch on the floor in front of the fireplace. P went to work sucking on her rosebud nipples immediately.

Melony moaned in delight and said, "Let's taste each other."

P tasted her as she took him in her mouth. They were both hungry for each other to the point that no one noticed Shawna standing there stripping with lust and envy in her eyes. They both exploded in each other's mouths. Then P mounted her and fucked her with slow, long strokes. Shawna came up behind him and started licking his balls as he was giving her girl the business. This was the young don's first ménage á trois. Shawna put both hands on his ass and pushed down on his cheeks so he could fuck her girl even harder. Melony's pussy squirted with juices at once. That was when P started gutting the bird faster and faster.

Melony dug her nails into his back as he worked her with hard, deep strokes. "Fuck this pussy. Yes, oh, fuck!" she screamed until her body shook.

P got up, and Shawna started tasting the fruits of Melony's watermelon. P got behind the chocolate bombshell and fucked her to death while Melony squirmed on the floor with Shawna's head between her legs. The faster he fucked Shawna, the faster her tongue glided against Melony's clit. P slowed his pace down so he could watch his dick flex in and out of Shawna's tight-ass pussy. Her pink grapefruit was a gusher as she rubbed her clit while P put in work. The young don took his dick out of the chocolate pussy and stood over Melony so she could lick her girl's juices off his muscle. Shawna started licking Melony's asshole out, and then she told P to put it in her ass. P Double was shocked because this was his first experience fucking a woman in the ass period. He threw her legs up on his shoulders, bent Melony's caramel ass like a pretzel, and stuck his dick in her ass. She cried out at once and told him to keep going. P Double busted in her ass as soon as his dick went all the way in. But his manhood stayed hard as a rock because Melony's ass gripped his dick like a pit bull with lockjaw.

While P was taking Melony down, Shawna started licking his ass. This time, P started moaning along with Melony's cries of pleasure. They switched up, and P gave Shawna the same treatment until he was about to bust. He took it out of her, and they both went to work sucking P Double off until he shot off, They both tasted his affection. They all fell asleep on the spot from their lovemaking. P woke up rock hard with Melony riding his dick like she trained horses. Shawna tongued him down and then waited for her girl to finish. She got her rocks off as well. They all took a shower and fucked and sucked themselves clean. Then Shawna made a deluxe breakfast for the trio that they took down quickly. P Double was in love with himself for bagging these classy dames. Some men dreamed about having a ménage á trois all their lives. P actually had one and put in work.

After breakfast, Melony hit him with another treat. She spent forty stacks with him, and he gave her two birds and fronted her two. Melony said, "Welcome to the family, P, but if you give me and Shawna's dick away to any of those bum bitches again, we'll kill your ass." And they both kissed him passionately.

CHAPTER 11

EVERYTHING WAS ALL GOOD JUST A WEEK AGO

Young P was doing big things now. Melony and Moe were moving coke two hundred miles an hour. And the sex was great too. Two dimes were better than one on any given Sunday. Jujito and Vito were also doing their thing as well. They were up to fifteen birds apiece. Every Friday, they all went to the casino to splurge. His credit limit with Rudy was up to $2.5 million. The only thing he was missing was his road dawg Fatback. They kept pushing his trial back further and further. Fatback wasn't even in the juvenile system anymore. He got into a fight with two Hilfiger cats and fucked them up badly, so they moved him to Ludlow County Jail for adults.

P Double missed his team, so he jumped out on Bristol Street one day to show them the new Porsche Carrera he had just copped. Bates, Kev, Lee, and A-Dog were engaged in a heavy blackjack game, so P jumped in. P Double had a quarter brick in his pocket when the task force jumped out on them. P ran to the back but got closelined by Curley. Curley was a cop who hated Bristol Street niggas and Ave niggas. As P was falling, he heard a gunshot, and Curley dropped right next to him. P tried to get up and run, but Curley had a death grip on him as Bates came and pistol-whipped the cop until he released his hold. P got up and jumped the gate, but he heard shots being fired and bullets flying past his head. P Double kept it moving and finally relaxed a couple of streets down and out of breath. He reached into his pocket for his phone and realized he had dropped it and the caine when he made his getaway. He paid a young cat to make a call for him, and Moe came through and snatched his boy up. P dropped the seat all the way back and told Moe to head for the crib in Chicopee.

When they got there, he gave Moe thirty-five bricks that were there and told him to move that shit. He didn't know if police were looking for him or not; he just didn't want any coke around him, period.

"Just bring back seven hundred thousand and me and you are me and you."

Moe packed the shit in the Tahoe at once before P Double threw some keys at him. "Yo, see if my Porsche is still parked over there. If it is, bring it back," P said.

Moe looked at the don and said, "I don't know how to drive stick."

"Well, have Melony drive the whip over here at once. Thank you."

Moe left his mentor on that note to do his bidding. When the young boy left, P called up Vinny to tell him he might be in trouble. His lawyer said he'd make a few calls on his behalf and see what the word was. P went straight to his bar and poured himself a double shot of Hennessy and then another. All the while, he was thinking, *Why did I have to go to the block?*

Ten minutes later, the house phone startled the thug. For some reason, the phone was even screaming at him. P picked it up with dread on his face.

Vinny said, "Jesus Christ, kid. You're in a shitload of trouble. They're saying you are running a million-dollar operation on Bristol Street, and you put a hit on Curley the cop when he tried to apprehend you. You're wanted for attempted murder on a police officer, assault and battery on a police officer, assault and battery on a police officer with a dangerous weapon, trafficking over two hundred and fifty grams, and fleeing the scene of a crime. They got a whole state and citywide manhunt out for you. You're all over the news, Presley. What the fuck?"

All P could say was, "Is there anything you can do for me, Vin, at all?"

"Presley, I'm your lawyer, so I'm gonna try to do all I can for you at once. Just stay by the phone for now," and he hung up.

The phone chirped again as soon as he hung up. This time, it was his grandmother wreaking havoc on the boy. "They ran up in my house and walked through every room to make sure you weren't here, and you're on the news. I told you about hanging with them crazy boys!"

P calmed his grandmother down and told her everything was not true and to calm down. After he said sorry a million times, they finally hung up. P Double didn't know how long he was out, but he woke up to some heavy knocking at his door. He looked through the peephole and saw it was Melony. He opened the door, and she showered him with hugs and kisses. He closed the door and explained the whole story to her. Just then, the phone rang. P answered it, and it was his lawyer on the line.

"Presley, I think we should walk into the police station together and turn yourself in," Vinny said.

P Double flew the coop. "Let me find out you're working for the fucking pigs instead of me, Vinny!" P shouted with strain in his voice.

Vinny shouted, "Calm the fuck down, will ya? If you don't turn yourself in, these assholes are gonna fuck around and kill you on sight, or they're gonna fuck you up so bad that somehow, some way, you're crippled. Now, do you want either one of those things to happen? I think not. Plus, I might be able to get you a reasonable bail."

P sat silent on the phone for second and contemplated all his options. Vinny was right, of course, because he knew if he ever ran into that dickhead cop Peogi, it was a wrap for him. He told his lawyer he'd be at his office in an hour. Then he fucked Melony for a good half hour before he left for his lawyer's office. He walked in, and Vinny broke everything down for him. He told P he would post his bail. He just wanted the money back that day. They walked into the police station together. Vinny immediately threatened the police department with a lawsuit if a nick or a scratch appeared on his client.

P Double was booked and charged the right way. The next day, he was brought into Hamden County District Court in front of Judge Robert E Kumor Jr., where he slapped a half-million-dollar bail on him.

P Double walked out of the courtroom with ease as Vinny posted bail for him. When he got out in the hallway, some strong hands snatched him up and threw him against the wall. Tony Peogi was a beast in a jungle right then. P Double thought if looks could kill, he'd be dead right then. The cop had sweat dripping all over his face when he said, "I'm gonna nail you, you little punk son of a bitch. I mean it."

Vinny walked out of the courtroom and went into hysterics at once, threatening the rogue cop with lawsuits when the cop turned to him and spit in his face. He said, "You're no better than this piece of shit you represent, you high-priced pussy." And he walked away. Vinny went and pressed charges and put a restraining order on the cop for him and his client. Peogi was out of control and needed to be tamed quick, fast, and in a hurry.

CHAPTER 12

DOUBLE TROUBLE

Eddie Haul was a free man. His lawyer, Ed West, finally put in a motion to suppress the evidence on grounds of entrapment. Plus, he also put in a motion based on Agilair and Spinelli saying that the person they were trying to use as a confidential, reliable informant wasn't reliable at all. It was their first time using Cheeks as a snitch so how was he reliable? Ed West went inside the courthouse and put on the performance of a lifetime. If Eddie Haul's life hadn't been on the line, he would've nominated Ed West for an Oscar. Finally, after a couple months' wait, the judge told Ed he was a free man. Eddie was damn near broke, but fuck it. He had his life back—almost, except for his beloved Mama. As soon as he walked out of the courthouse, he called his cousin Mike Tuitt to announce he was home.

Mike scooped him up and blew back some good Hawaiian with him. Then he gave him the whole run down on the field. Ed punched the dashboard when his cousin told him how the young boy had outsmarted him again and gotten him for a half million and thirty birds. "I'm gonna kill that little fuck. I hate that nigga!" Ed spit with enough malice for both of them.

Mike said, "You and me both, but I gotta give it to him. The boy is ruthless as fuck and heartless."

"We'll see about that, big cuz. He ain't fucked with a high-caliber dude like me yet," Ed said.

"By the way, I got twenty stacks, and I need you to front me some shit as well," Mike said.

"No problem, cuz. I thought police did my job for me and took the little punk up off of here, but he bailed out on a half-a-million-dollar bond. The faggot probably used my money for that shit," Ed said.

"Don't worry none. Leave everything to me. I'll handle things from here on in." Mike took him to get the work and then dropped him off at Italia's crib.

When Ed walked in, she dropped to her knees and welcomed him home the right way, with a good old-fashioned dick suck.

$ $ $

Big Butch was watching TV when they were talking about having P Double in custody. That right there brought a smile to Mad Dog's face because that meant he had another shot at killing P Double with his bare hands. He wanted Fatback too, but somehow, they hadn't bumped heads yet in the joint. Then as he watched some more, they showed this nigga walking out of the courthouse. P Double had made a half-million-dollar bond, which really pissed the meaty thug off. Fuck it. He was tired of playing games with these niggas, period. He decided that the first Bristol Street nigga he saw he was setting it on at once. They called Muslim Chapel, and Butch went to the program's building. When he was checking in, he saw Lan and a bunch of Ave cats coming out of the chapel. He asked them why they were hanging with this Bristol Street faggot. Lan laughed at Butch and called him a fat pussy. Big Butch went mad and set it on the Bristol Street veteran with a massive right cross that almost ended it. Lan staggered back to regroup from the hard blow, and he saw the big brute coming at him swinging wildly. He sidestepped Butch and caught the thug on the back of the head with two sharp blows that didn't even faze the big bully. Butch turned around and tried to rush Lan, but Lan backpedaled while throwing ferocious combos at him. He connected with a two-piece that stopped Butch dead in his tracks. Then Lan saw his opening and took full advantage by hitting Butch with a three-piece that dropped the thug down on one knee.

Butch got up and growled with rage as Lan hit him with another combination that dropped Butch down on the other knee. Before Butch could get up, ten COs were on him and Lan stopping the action. LAN's wrist was broken from punching on the big brute. Butch spit in his face when they walked him by, and the COs almost threw the big guy down the stairs. He was angry at them for stopping destiny. Lan wasn't gonna bob and weave too much longer before Butch got his hands on him. Butch said, "Fuck it. There's always a round two," when he got up out of there.

$ $ $

Moe was on top of his game right then. P Double was making him rich right then. His dream was to be bigger than P though, and he was stacking every penny he made to reach his goal. But all work and no play made you a dull boy, so Moe went and picked up this little freak Sandra he was fucking. He parked the Tahoe in front of P Double's apartment in Forest Park. He opened the hallway door for Sandra and wondered why the hallway was so dark. "Damn, the light must be broke," he said to himself on the way upstairs.

All of a sudden, someone grabbed him from behind and put a gun to his head. "Bring me to P, or I'm gonna blow your fucking head off," the feminine voice said.

Sandra said, "Hey, Moe, what's going on?" as she came back to the stairs.

Then two quick shots lit up the hallway, and Sandra yelped as she hit the ground and moaned in pain.

"Now bring me to him, or you can holla like your bitch," the voice said with more meaning this time.

Moe gave in, and the voice backed him out the door and into the Tahoe. When they got into the truck, Shante took off the ski mask and said, "Call him, and make sure he's there, or you can say good night."

Moe called and confirmed that P was at the crib, and he drove straight there. All Moe was thinking was, *Damn, this stupid bitch is crazy.*

$ $ $

P Double was at ease, smoking some good Hawaiian skunk when his young protégé had called him talking stupid. His mind was in another world right then. Melony had brought him a tape by this kid named Biggie Smalls, and that shit was fire. He fucked her long and sweet for that, and then she left to handle some business, which was also his. The only thing he was stressed about was this stupid-ass case he caught fucking with Bates and them. *What the fuck was wrong with Bates anyways?* P thought. *At least get away from police if you're gonna shoot them.*

Bates had gotten caught, and boy, did they beat the shit out of him. P paid for Bates's lawyer as well. The man did help him get away in any event. Kev and A-Dog went down for some coke they had and bailed out. P said, "Let me relax," and he had just popped in some porn and turned the radio back up when he got a knock at the door. He peeped through the peephole and saw it was Moe.

As P opened the door, Moe staggered in from the hard kick Shante delivered to his backside. P said, "What the fuck?"

Shante said, "Yeah, so this is the honeycomb hideout, huh! Well, it's time for me to make my presence felt up in here."

"Shante, what the fuck is wrong with you doing this stupid shit?" P said.

"Moe, get the fuck out, and go tend to your wounded bitch before I shoot you too," Shante said with a wild look in her eyes.

Moe obeyed the order and locked the door behind him. "So this is how you get your kicks, huh? Watching pornos? Well, strip, nigga," she said, waving the gun everywhere.

P said, "Yeah, right."

That was all she needed to hear. Shante shot his lamp up and said, "This ain't a fucking game, P," with tears streaming down her cheeks. P stripped, and she walked up to him and said, "Where's your dyke bitches at?"

As soon as she got close enough, P Double wrestled the gun out of her hands and smacked her so hard she fell on the couch. "Bitch, don't ever try no stupid-ass shit like this again."

P stood over the crying Shante ready to kill her. She grabbed his shaft and started sucking his dick with hunger. P forgot what he was just mad about as Shante went to work. P grabbed her by her hair and started fucking her face with lust. Shante practiced day in and day out sucking on Blow Pops all day still, the way P trained her. She was rewarded when the young thug shot a load down the back of her throat. P let off a cry as Shante milked him for all his worth. P ripped her clothes off violently. When she stood before him naked, he spun her around, pushed her over the couch, and entered her roughly. She let out an animal cry as P ripped her open. "This is what you wanted, right?" he said, thrusting savagely up in her.

"Oh shit! Yes, daddy, yes!" she screamed as her juices started to spice.

P loved the smacking sound their skin was making as he fucked her with raw integrity and determination. He stopped, turned her the other way, and pushed her over the couch, but he held her legs and fucked her even harder than before. Shante's hands were holding her up on the couch as she was screaming for him to beat the pussy. She then fell back in convulsions as her juices squirted all over the young thug. P took his dick out of the nympho and rammed it into her ass. She let out an earth-shattering scream as P worked her virgin asshole to the extreme. Shante never knew so much pain could lead to pleasure as she gushed over and over again from P fucking her ass.

P Double shot a nut deep in her rectum as he came with a shout. They cuddled as they both fell asleep in the comforts of each other's arms. When they woke up, P worked her over again and told her to chill out. Shante was in love, and that was all she knew. She didn't want anybody else, but P Double told her Frankie was her man, and that was the way they had to keep things. She either played by his rules, or there was no ball game at all, and that was that. P finally sent her on her way with another good fucking, and he gave her his new number.

$ $ $

Moe was angry at the bitch for shooting his bird, but what the fuck? Even he had to admit Shante was a soldier he would love in his army any day. Everything was everything until a lone spring day in '95. Moe was on Maynard Street, talking to a brown-skinned shorty named Angela when a gray Golf rolled up. Angela's boyfriend, G-Money, hopped out steaming with fury. G-Money was a tall, brocky nigga from the Ave, so he already knew who Moe was when Angela tried to say that Moe was her cousin. G-Money was with his little brother, D.S., at the time, so that made things worse.

Moe tried to explain, but G-money just hit him with a haymaker that wired his jaw and rendered him unconscious. Little Moe was snoring when the two thugs both stomped him to add to his broken jaw. Moe stayed in the hospital for a month, but he never violated the code of the streets so the police were angry.

P Double was by the young boy's side every day to let him know shit was real. But Moe had to handle this if he wanted to get his stripes. If P handled it for him, niggas would take advantage of him in the future. As soon as he got out of the hospital, Moe said he was ready for rock.

P said, "Okay," and he called Kev and A-Dog up and asked them if they were ready to ride. They said yeah, and the wheels were in motion.

$ $ $

Mr. Fish was popping on Eastern Avenue and Union Street. It was the first of the month, and already, G-Money had made thirty-five hundred, and it wasn't even dark yet. D.S. was complaining because G-Money was smoking the whole el.

"Man, pass the fucking smoke, Gee. You always hogging shit, damn," D.S. said.

"Man, shut the fuck up. I just lit the shit," G-Money established as he smoked on.

Sal walked out, snatched the el from G-Money's hand, and said, "That fucking faggot behind the counter is talking about ain't no more chicken on a bun in this bitch. Man, I'm tired of this shit."

Sal took a couple more tokes on the chronic and passed the el to D.S. The boys were so high they didn't see Moe, P Double, Kev, and Little Lee hop out of the Cherokee Jeep on Union Street. Moe ran into the middle of Eastern Ave and said, "Yeah, what's up with that shit now?" as he let the nine bark in his hand rapidly.

Sal ran into Mr. Fish and jumped over the counter as Moe started firing wildly. D.S. ran straight down Eastern Ave, crying and scared for his life. G-Money tried to pull the forty-five out as he ran into the fish market but took two in the leg. He fell onto the floor.

Moe screamed, "I got his bitch ass!" and the four goons ran for the Jeep and escaped.

Sal was behind the counter for three minutes before he realized the faggot was feeling on him. "Man, what the fuck? Get your gay ass off me, nigga," he said in anger.

The punk looked him up and down and said, "Umm, nice body, baby."

Sal hit the punk with a crazy combo, breaking the faggot's nose and knocking out two teeth. Sal was still working the punk over until he heard his man moan for help on the floor. The thug stopped punching the punk and saw that his man was lying on the floor. He jumped over the counter and said, "Are you all right?"

"Nah, they hit me, Sal. Get me up out of here."

Sal helped the man up as D.S. came out of nowhere and provided another shoulder for his big brother to lean on. "Yo, the car is in the projects on Quincy Street.

They walked him to the car and Sal drove him home. They took his pants off, and you could see the two bullets in the front of his leg. Sal pulled out a saw knife he had and was about to cut G-Money's leg open to extract the bullets when G-Money said, "Man, don't put that nasty-ass knife on my leg, nigga. You cut over fifty muthafuckers with that shit. Hell no!"

Sal laughed and said, "Shit, you right though. D.S., bring me some shit." And they operated on the wounded man.

$ $ $

On the other side of town, Ed was laid up, getting his dick sucked as usual. Italia was a beast with a dick in her mouth. She could suck a dick all night and enjoy it if you let her. She was making more noise than he was. His phone rang as he was about to bust.

"Yooooooo," he said with his eyes rolled into the back of his head.

His cousin said, "Man, what the fuck? I already know you're getting your dick sucked."

Ed blasted off with a sharp scream as his future kids were distributed down Italia's throat. She kept sucking even after his shotgun was empty. Ed asked Mike what the deal was, and Mike broke down the fish market scenario to him. "Yo, I'm tired of P Double and his bitch-ass crew!" Eddie Haul screamed. "I made all them niggas, and all of them faggot muthafuckas sell P Double's coke. They won't even touch my shit. Word to life, I'm gonna kill something tonight, Mike."

"See, Ed, now you're on my level of thinking. Tonight's the night be."

"Meet me tonight at ten at the Waterfront Club. We'll talk business then," Eddie Haul said and hung up.

P Double had to be taken up off there somehow, some way, and Ed knew the way.

$ $ $

While G-Money was suffering from being popped up, P Double and his crew were popping bottles, celebrating Moe's first mission.

"Now, you're an official Bristol Street bad boy," P told the young boy.

Moe grunted and tried to smile. He was still suffering from the broken jaw G-Money had given him.

Kev said, "Man, we ain't been out in a while, daddy. What's up with tonight? The Waterfront rockin. Plus, A-Dog fucks with the bitch at the door, so you already know we can get in with our toy soldiers in our waist."

P Double looked at his crew and said, "It sounds like a plan to me. I'm all for it as long as Matilda can get in with me." That was the name of P Double's forty-four Desert Eagle. Lately, he gave everything a name, even his cars. He named his purple Porsche Violet and his apartment Thong Paradise. Moe said that he wasn't going anywhere with a wired-up jaw so the rest of the crew went to go get dressed.

$ $ $

The Waterfront was packed Tuesday nights. The fish fry was always a serious event to go to every week. Ed and Mike were at the bar, stunting seriously. They were going shot for shot, so they didn't notice P Double and the rest of the Bristol Street bad boys when they made a guest appearance. P noticed them off rip though. This time, he wouldn't rush into anything. Plus, he had Matilda on him in the event that somebody wanted to answer for that fish market shooting. A-Dog, T Baby, Iran, Turkey, Andy Cap, Darris, Kev, and Dave Hill all took seats in the back. DJ Andrew Tees had the Waterfront jumping with "Everyday It Rains" by Mary J Blige.

The new Mary song was a banger. P sent Darris to the bar to buy it out. Then he walked from the bar to the DJ so he could announce it. Andrew Tees said, "Big shout out to P Double and the Bristol Street crew for buying out the bar."

"All drinks are free courtesy of the don."

The whole club rushed the bar to buy drinks. The owner walked over and took P Double and his crew's orders, and he thanked him dearly for the business.

$ $ $

Ed and Mike looked at each other with pure hate when the DJ made the announcement. They scanned the crowded club and saw P Double deep with his young crew of thugs. His whole team sparkled with diamonds of the finest cuts.

Ed said, "Fall back and come with me. I always gotta plan set up."

Ed and Mike both made eye contact with P Double, and the young don smiled at them as they were making their hasty retreat up out of there. When they got outside, Ed placed a call and waited for whoever Ed called in Mike's Hummer. Mike was going crazy. "What the hell are you waiting for, Eddie?" Mike said in haste.

"Calm down and relax, playboy. When I said I had a plan, I gotta plan. Now just watch it take place."

Ten minutes later, Italia showed up with a basehead. Ed got out and talked to the head, and he took a walk with him. They strolled up on P

Double's purple Porsche, and the head went to work. The car alarm went off, but the door was open in a matter of seconds. Ed bent down, placed something under the seat, and locked the door back. They both headed back to the Hummer. Ed gave the greedy basehead a quarter of coke, and the head made a fast retreat.

Next, Ed told Mike, "Let's go back in the Waterfront."

Mike said, "Yeah, fuck it," with a quizzical look on his face.

Ed called someone and said, "This guy in a purple Porsche just shot at me at the Waterfront Club. Help me, please." And he hung up the phone. They walked in the front, and Ed pulled out a little twenty-two he had tucked into his boot and shot a couple of shots into the air. The crowd screamed, and everyone ran for the exits.

$ $ $

P Double was happy when those two faggots looked at him and bowed down. They left quickly, and P just laughed. He always knew Ed was a pussy anyway. Weak-ass niggas didn't make it in this world, and P realized that quick in the game. P grabbed his fifth of Hennessy and went to the dance floor. Andrew Tees was spinning "One More Chance" by Biggie, and P Double had two bitches freaking him. After the song was over, he snatched both chicks up and brought them back to the table. Trina and Adrian were looking at the don with lust in their eyes when he told both of them to suck his dick right then. Both dames dropped to their knees under the table and went to work.

P Double was about to bust in Adrain's mouth when the club erupted with shooting. The don dropped to the floor at once as the club went crazy. People were getting trampled on. Chicks were screaming everywhere. P grabbed Matilda in case someone was shooting at him or his team. Then they all ran out the back entrance. The two bitches followed P and jumped in the Porsche with him. As he was exiting the lot, police blocked him in and rushed his car with guns drawn. P remembered what had happened to Ben Scholfield and was scared to death. They took him out of the car, searched it, and found some coke, the gun he had on him, and a gun under the seat.

P Double said, "What the fuck? That's not mine."

Peogi smiled and said, "That's your ass, Mr. Postman."

P Double looked around and caught Ed's eye. Ed winked at him and laughed. P just bobbed his head up and down. He had underestimated Ed a great deal. Now he was paying for it.

CHAPTER 13

THE LOW

Double went to court the next day in severe pain. Tony Peogi and some of Curley's friends worked him over pretty badly. His ribs felt like they were broke, and he spit up blood twice that night. As soon as Vinny saw Judge Ford on the bench, he knew it was a wrap for his client. Sure enough, Judge Ford revoked P Double's bail and said he was a danger to society. He was mad that the young don got out on a half-million-dollar bond, so this time, he gave him a five-million-dollar bail, and on the case with Curley, there was no bail. P Double's grandmother fainted while all his chicks started going crazy. Judge Ford had Melony and Shante arrested because they started fighting in the courtroom.

The bailiff brought P downstairs and threw him in a bullpen that smelled like urine and sweat. P Double was glad he wasn't around the rest of the heads. He needed time to think and focus on how he went wrong. It didn't take a rocket scientist to know that Eddie Haul and Mike Tuitt planted the drugs and gun in his Porsche. Their facial expressions said it all when he looked their way. P Double just wanted to lay low and rest. His mind, body, and soul were burned out from running the streets. In a way, he needed this vacation. He just hoped his stay wouldn't be long. He woke to the guard opening the gate and saying his government.

"Yeah, that's me," P said in a groggy voice.

"Come on. Transport is here," the CO explained.

P walked into the hallway with sixteen other bodies, and they handcuffed him to a stinky dope fein. The Puerto Rican guy had snot coming out his nose, and he kept farting strongly. The fein's stench was kicking P in his ass big-time, but he had to roll with the punches. They all reached Hamden County House of Corrections a half hour later. P Double called his grandmother and told her everything was all good and to come up there and drop twenty-five hundred in his account. After he had been stripped and fingerprinted and gotten pictures taken, they sent him to medical and then C-4.

P Double walked in there and dropped his blue crate with all the clothing they gave him on the floor. He showed the cop his ID, and the cop told him he was in cell twenty-four. P walked upstairs and was glad the cell was empty. He made his bed and went straight to sleep. Three days later, they said he was going to A-4 in the A Tower. The building was built like a high-rise with three floors. P walked to the second floor and into a hallway that said "A-3 and A-4." They were right across from each other. He rang the buzzer for A-4, and they let him in the first set of sliding doors. When that door closed behind him, the other one opened, and he entered the unit. As soon as he walked in, he said, "Oh shit."

"Oh shit is right, fuck face," Murphy said. "Damn, Presley, I haven't seen you since I transported you to Westfield a while ago. I see you haven't changed one bit."

P looked at him and said, "I see you haven't changed one bit either, because you're still ugly as fuck."

At that moment, somebody had grabbed P Double from behind and picked him up like a rag doll. P tried to get up out of it, but whoever had him was as strong as an ox. Then he put him down as quickly as he picked him up. P Double backed up a few feet and spun to see his best friend in front of him.

"Boy, you better get your weight up fast because you're melted," Fatback said.

P Double said, "That's from all the pussy I was fucking out there."

"Shit, nigga, I heard, I heard. Yo, Murphy, throw my man in my cell," Back said.

"What about Reed?" the cop said.

"Reed is packing his shit up right now and getting the fuck out," Back stated.

P asked, "Who the fuck is Reed, yo?"

"That's your boy, Raheem."

"Damn, everybody up in this bitch," P said as he spotted his man Jujito.

Murphy finally let the boys move in together, and it was like they were never apart. They stayed up all night talking about how Back fucked Roberta to death that day and about how Eddie Haul and Mike Tuitt set him up.

Fatback said, "My trial is in a month. Don't worry. When I get out, them chumps are in trouble."

P then told him about how he'd been holding it down for them. That month flew by quickly, and Back was off to trial. Fatback came back that day with a smile on his face and told his boy that it was looking good for the home team.

A couple of days later, Mark Mastrioni beat the case, and Fatback went home. P Double was happy and sad at the same time. His man Ricky Bates copped out to a five for shooting Curley and swore P had nothing to do with anything. The judge dropped all charges he had with Bates except for the trafficking cocaine charge. Vinny got the coke thrown out on a motion though, because P didn't get caught at the scene of the crime, so it was kind of hard to prove that it was his in the first place. All he had left was the gun case and the coke case from the Waterfront. Vinny broke it down to him quick, fast, and in a hurry.

"They're asking for two and a half for the coke and the guns. Now, the car is in your grandmother's name, so unless you're saying the shit was hers, you got no choice but to cop out to the two and a half."

P Double said he'd think about it and got sent back to Ludlow. When he got back, his man E was in the block. He got snatched up for some bullshit, and they revoked his bail for sixty days as well. E came in with an ounce of Hawaiian, and it was on. The whole unit was walking around, laughing at ugly-ass Murphy. P Double opened up his own store and casino in the joint, and it was like he had never left the streets. The only thing was there was no bird. He also worked out every day, and he made sure he played ball every day for stamina. Plus, he was the best point guard in the jail hands down. It wasn't too long before P had to show his hand skills. It was a piping-hot day on the rec deck, and they were playing three on three—the blacks against the Puerto Ricans. The game was to eleven, and two thirty-five-dollar commissary sacs were on the line. The Ricans were up eight to six, and P Double's team was already tired from running six games back to back. P Double said, "Fuck that." All his life he was a winner, so why stop now? He caught his second wind and took the game in his own hands. He crossed Spanish kid Flacco over and layed it up. The next play, he broke him down off the dribble again, but instead of taking it to the cup, he jumped back and popped one for the tie. This time, he knew they were gonna be all over him, so he hit Felton with a no-look-behind-the-back pass to take the lead. The Puerto Ricans started talking in Spanish at once to each other. P didn't know what they were saying, but he could always read a man's character with no problem at all, and the vibe was wrong. P inbounded the ball to Joe Beatty, and Beatty missed the jumper.

Taz grabbed the rebound and hit his manito with a pass behind the free throw line. Flacco popped a jumper that hit straight net. The game was tied again. Taz then tried to inbound a lazy pass to Roblez, but P stole the pass. He drove to the basket and swung the ball back out to Joe Beatty. This time, he wet the shot with ease. P Double inbounded the ball and screamed, "Point," in Flacco's face. Felton caught the pass, but P called for the ball back. P Double asked for an isolation. He took Flacco off the dribble again. P crossed over and left him, but he waited for the man to recoup and play defense again. Then he crossed him so bad Flacco's knees were touching when P Double drove past him. Roblez stood under the basket, but P elevated over him and dunked on him for the game winner. When he came down, P Double screamed on the man and banged on his chest. P didn't notice Flacco come up behind him and swing. P Double took the weak blow and turned around. Flacco was bouncing in a boxer's stance, but he wasn't ready for the young don's quickness. P ran at him like he was about to scoop him and caught Flacco with an uppercut that stood the man straight up. P then followed up with a right hook and left cross that put Flacco on the ground. Jujito quickly broke it up before Murphy could see it. Flacco wanted to fight, so he and P went in a cell.

As soon as they entered, Flacco tried to rush P, but P hit the man with two sharp hard combos that backed the man into the corner of the cell. P just went to work from there, hitting the man with everything he had from crosses to hooks to uppercuts and body blows.

The way P was working the kid, it sounded like he was punching a punching bag. Jujito yelled that the man had enough. P stopped punching on the man and just let him slump down the wall. Flacco was drowning in his own blood when P Double walked out of the cell. After they saw their leader take a beating of that magnitude, the Netas respected him a lot. A couple of months went by, and P got hit with some bad news. Fatback got caught shooting at Eddie Haul, and Moe was with him. They both went down for the gun and some coke Back had stashed. Three days later, they were all united again. Moe's bail was only five grand, but he told P he just wanted to see him before he bailed out. They called Moe and told him to pack it up, but P hit the man with some wise words before his student hit the streets. Moe gave everyone dap and was out the door. P went to court the next week and copped out to the two and a half. He would be out before '98, with good time.

As soon as he got to green, his time flew by quickly. Kev, Andy Cap, E, and A-Dog wound up doing time with him. P and Kev were in the drug unit doing some program they had over there to get good time. Little did Ludlow know, that C-5, the drug program, had the most drugs in the whole damn jail. They had dope, coke, pills, weed, and acid for the crazy white boys. C-5 also had the crazy casino going. P Double had five hundred soups stashed around the unit. Nowadays, you had to keep shit on the low, or they were taking your food because you were only allowed to order twenty soups a week. P Double found himself surrounded by the best gamblers in Springfield, Massachusetts. You had Chill Will, Dink, LD, and Shawndel from the Ave. Then there was L.A. Dre, Sammy B, and Chino Weeno from Cambridge Street; Tobi from Maynard; Ray Dukes; and Laprese, a.k.a. Presie. Everybody was holding strong, but the nigga Dink's stash was crazy. He stuck niggas up and sold caine a hundred miles an hour. Dink was also known to have a couple of unproven bodies lying to rest as well. He got kind of close to P. He even showed him a couple of tricks he knew, like stacking the deck and how to read cards. P didn't know if the nigga Dink really liked him or if he was trying to get close to him so he could put him in a trunk in the near future. Nobody ever knew what Jimmy Lee, Dink, was thinking. If the story was correct, he was born in a gambling spot. His mother's water broke while she was shuffling a deck of cards. That was why he was a beast at every card game.

To P Double, C-5 was the closest thing to the streets there was. As long as nobody got worked over in the unit, the COs didn't give a fuck what you did. One day, Dink got in a crazy argument with Big Jeff. Jeff was a six-foot-tall, 250-pound monster. His arms were twenty-four inches, and he had a five-hundred-pound bench press. The cells in C-5 were real big so you could really maneuver in them. Dink had skunked Jeff for three hundred soups, and he refused to give Jeff a cop out, so Jeff wasn't trying to pay any of it.

"Jeff, you got one more time to say you ain't paying me, and I'm gonna fuck you up for real," Dink spit with a smile on his face.

Dink's man Big Dell was in the room also. At five eight, 275 pounds, Big Dell was a beast in his own right. Jeff laughed at Dink and said, "You heard what the fuck I said, little muthafucka. Matter of fact, for your smartass mouth, I don't even want the cop out. Get it like Jessie got it, chump. That means take it in blood."

Big Jeff acknowledged him. Dink smiled that shady-ass grin and struck Jeff with a lightning-quick two-piece stunner. The blows were so hard you could hear the knuckle slaps outside the cell. Big Jeff staggered back, and Dink rushed him and penned him up against the wall.

Dink said, "Now, I want my three hundred soups, big boy, or I'm gonna throw your ass off the tier. I'm tired of playing games, nigga," with the same shady-ass grin on his face.

Jeff tried to use his strength to get up out of the hold, but the little man had a crazy lock and leverage.

"Big Dell, pack my shit up for me. Grab them soups on the wall and under his bed," Dink ordered.

Dell packed both laundry bags full of soups, and Dink released his hold on the big man. "Nice doing business with you. Don't let this shit happen again though," Dink said, smiled at the man, and walked out the room sucking his thumb.

P Double was holding the door the whole time. That was when he knew Dink was a beast and a serious cat you didn't wanna cross at any point in time. P asked him how he worked the big man over.

Dink said, "We all work out heavy every day, but the key is you gotta watch everybody's work out while you doing yours. And I noticed that all he does is upper body. That's why he so strong, but he never does legs. So basically he's just top heavy, so I used his weight and my legs to hold his ass against the wall. That's all. You always gotta look for a weakness in everybody."

P Double nodded and said, "What's mine?"

Dink laughed at the young don and walked off with his thumb in his mouth. Before P Double knew it, he had six months left. They moved him to A-5, and he got a hallway job. He almost lost it fucking with this kid named June Live. June Live walked up the stairs mean mugging P like he was a bad boy or something.

P said, "What you wanna do, bitch nigga?" But June Live was already walking inside A-3's doors when he said he'd whip P's ass. The next day, P Double, Tavis, Kev, and a couple of other cats were chilling in the hallway when A-3 was coming back from breakfast.

June Live and P made eye contact when Live said, "What, bitch nigga?"

P just answered his what with a three-shot combination to the gut. When Live doubled over, P grabbed his head and started kicking the man in the face. Wu-Tang broke the fight up and said, "Y'all need to cut that shit out, man. Y'all too old for this back-in-the-day war shit."

P Double just said, "He started the shit." And he went on about his business.

Right before P Double was about to go home, he got a visit. When they called his name, he hopped into the shower, lotioned up, and put some Muslim oil on. P walked in the visiting center, and the CO said, "Do you see your visit?"

P Double scanned the floor, and he didn't see any of his bitches. Then all of a sudden, he got the shock of his life because there on the dance floor was his former probation officer waving at him, looking more extravagant than the last time he saw her.

P said, "Yeah, my visit out there." He walked onto the floor with poise and curiosity. He was happy that Jaynce had come to see him, but why was what he wanted to know. She was at a table looking radiant when P Double sat across from her.

"What's good, Jaynce?" P Double said.

"That's what I came to ask you, Presley. Please tell me you're all done with the P Double act because it's getting boring, I think."

P looked at the classy dame and smirked. "I don't think so, Miss Magill. I love my life. Not too many people can do what I do on a regular basis. To me, it's a hard job being that nigga. You need to try it sometime, baby girl."

"Please, Presley, I thought this time that you did would've made you grow up and become a well-distinguished gentleman, but I guess you can't turn little boys into men, can you?" she asked.

"Jaynce, I know one thing. You might not think I'm grown, but that seven point five million I got stashed says I'm quite grown, sweetheart. That's what separates me from a lot of dudes. I got morals and goals, and I'm not stopping anything until I can roll in a billion dollars," P said.

"Why don't you invest some of your money and get it that way, Presley?"

"See, now you're not acting grown, ma. How can a twenty-one-year-old man explain where I got anything to invest in the first place, Jaynce? Plus, the only investing I know is if you spend three, you guaranteed to make back six. And you already know how, love. So that should answer all your questions now and for the future, but forget about me. How has the world been treating you, love?"

P Double got her to talk about a lot of her dreams and aspirations, and then she shocked him by asking him if she could take him out sometime. P said yes, and they announced that his visit was over. Jaynce got up and smothered P with a strong hug that blew the young boy's mind. Then she whispered her number in his ear, and P Double made sure he wrote it down when he left.

Jones, the CO, asked, "Who the hell was that?"

P Double said, "You like that, huh?" and Jones laughed.

P Double walked out of the visiting room with the smell of Jaynce's perfume still in his nose. He was crossing the tee where all the different housing units separate when a monsterous blow caught him off guard.

P Double staggered back ten paces from the punch that had been delivered. Big Butch was being restrained by all the police in the tee. "I was waiting to catch your bitch ass, Presley. This shit ain't over, nigga," the big brute was saying as they hauled him off to the segregation unit. The other cops let P go back to his unit, since he didn't throw a punch. But not even Butch could ruin this day because for some reason or another, Jaynce had reached out to P and he was willing to accept her with open arms, for sure.

CHAPTER 14

WELCOME BACK

Double went back to the unit and told E, "Faggot-ass Butch sucker-punched me on my way back to the unit. He pulled a stunt in front of police as usual. You already know that nigga is bitch made. Yo, I'll drop ten stacks in your account if you make sure that nigga needs a lot of medical attention."

"Say no more," E answered, and the deal was sealed.

That night, P called Moe and made sure everything was in order for his guest appearance back in the streets. Moe assured P everything was straight and said, "I gotta surprise for you as well, my nigga."

P Double said, "Now, that's what's up," and he hung up.

That night, P really didn't get any sleep. All he did was contemplate move after move until his mind was an official chessboard. Truthfully, the young don just wanted his streets back. He knew everything had a price, but whether were you willing to pay the price was the answer to that question. As he finally drifted off to sleep, he was woken up by the doors popping and the announcement of breakfast time. All his people came to his door to see what was good with him, but he told everybody he was falling back and taking a shower.

Two hours later, they said, "Presley Williams, pack it up," over the loudspeaker.

P Double left all his shit to E and Andy Cap. He gave everybody dap and blew to intake like the wind. When he got there, they gave him a check for his money and ran a worldwide bop to see if he had warrants in any other states. P Double then changed into the clothing Moe had brought up to him yesterday. P was mad about the orange leather coat and Timbs. Moe also blessed him with a cream-and-orange Pepe suit.

Valika, the secretary in intake, said, "You go, boy," and wet her lips as she looked at the young don with a lustful glint in her eyes. All he needed was an escort so they could walk him to the front, and he was out of there.

Brian Murphy walked through the door and said, "Come on, fuck face, if you wanna get the fuck out of here."

P laughed and said, "Damn, every year, you get uglier and uglier," as they walked down the long hallway to freedom.

Murphy was still talking shit when they reached the exit, but P didn't pay the ugly man any mind. Moe gave him dap and threw some keys at him. "I copped you something pretty, to kick dust in. Wait till you see her. She's beautiful."

Murphy laughed and said, "How can a car be beautiful with a face like that behind the wheel. I gotta see this, Williams."

They went outside, and P Double and Murphy both said, "What the fuck?" at the same time.

At the door was an orange-sherbet 600 Benz with some twenty-inch chrome rims that sparkled. The tint was so dark the car looked like it was rocking shades.

Moe opened the door and said, "Watch this." He pushed a button, and the hard top disappeared. It was a convertible. Moe let the windows down, and the white-and-orange interior looked sweet. P Double jumped into the driver's seat without opening the doors and turned the radio on. Jay-Z blasted through the airwaves with, "If I shook you I'm brainless / if you shoot me your famous / what's a nigga to do?"

P Double left Murphy standing there with his mouth wide open as the V-12 ate the road up in style. Moe gave him a phone and told him the number. He noticed that Moe had three phones on his waist.

P had to ask him, "Moe, you rocking like that out here, baby?"

"P, shit changed out here a whole lot, daddy. If you can't adapt to the new wave, you're gonna get left behind," Moe told him. "By the way, drive to your crib in Chicopee. I got two more presents waiting for you."

"Damn, you took care of my crib too?" P asked the young boy.

"Yup, both of them," he said as he lit up some Branson.

Moe tried to pass the el to P, but P Double declined. "Nah, Moe. I need all my wind, but if we got some Hennessy out there, everything is everything."

P pulled up at the apartment in record time and put the top on the Benz. He hit the alarm button on the key chain and locked the doors up. They walked into the apartment, and Moe had redecorated the whole place. Everything was up to date. Then out of nowhere a beautiful redbone walked out of the bathroom butt-ass naked. She was thick as fuck, with firm, round breasts. P Double wondered if he could balance a cup on her ass.

Moe said, "This is Quadria, and that's Fantasy over there."

P did a 360 to see another thick redbone smiling at him. Moe gave him dap and told him to have fun. As soon as Moe left, P Double went to work. After a couple of sessions with the girls, he was back to status. He got up off the bed and poured himself a glass full of Hennessy. He drank the whole glass, and then he poured himself another drink and walked back to the bedroom. Both dames were sleeping comfortably.

"Yeah, I still got it," he said to himself as he jumped into the shower.

An hour later, Moe came through and said, "I got two point five in the trunk for you also. Where do you want it?"

P said, "Let's take a ride."

They drove to East Long Meadow, and P went and hugged his grandmother. They talked for an hour. Then she said she had to run; it was bingo night. She asked P if he still had the key, and he said, "Of course."

After she left, P and Moe unloaded the truck and brought the money to P's office with the giant portrait of himself. He told Moe to step out real quick as he opened the safe. Then he called him back in when it was wide open.

Moe said, "Now, that's what's up. This safe is big as fuck, P. I just got my money everywhere." He walked into the big safe, saw the AR-15, and said, "Now, this is what's up!"

P told him how he snatched it up from Mike Tuitt and how he got on. Moe was just glad he didn't have to go through all the shit P went through. P Double grabbed a forty-caliber from his arsenal, and they were gone.

When they got in Moe's cream Range Rover, he asked Moe what Eddie Haul and Mike were up to.

"Mike Tuitt is locked up somewhere. The alphabet boys came and snatched his ass up about a month ago. As far as Ed, he's still doing his thing out here but on the south end. He's rolling with some Puerto Rican cats down there," Moe finished.

"Oh yeah, what the fuck is he pushing out here?" P asked.

"Just a GS 400 sky blue. Ed also got a black Q 45 Infinity with the murder tint," Moe added.

"What's good with J.G. ass ?" P asked.

"That nigga is doing his thing. Him and Marlin got shit on smash. Plus, they fuck with some Indian Orchard niggas." P then asked Moe what was up with Rudy in the city. Moe informed the man that the alphabet boys snatched him up also. So he was copping from some cat named Mariano around the corner from them.

Then Moe said, "Do you wanna see Melony?"

P Double said, "Yeah, what's up with her anyways?"

"Same old shit. She was fucking with D Nice again, but you know who her heart really belongs to, P."

P told his man to call her and see what was good but not to tell her he was out. Moe called her and said he had a surprise for her and he'd be right over.

"Do she still live out in Westfield, Moe?" P asked.

"Yeah, she do," he answered. "Drop me off at my whip, and tell them bitches at the crib not to go anywhere. I'll be back for some more action."

Moe dropped P off at his car. P Double looked in the mirror to make sure everything was all good. Then he looked at the CDs Moe had bought for him. He saw his boys Mobb Deep and threw them in. Prodigy came through the fifteens he had in his trunk talking that shit. "The inventor of crime rap niggas if left stranded / shut down your operation / closed for business / leave a foul taste in your mouth like Guinness."

P Double just kept rewinding that song because that was how shit was for real, and that was how he felt. After being on the highway for twenty minutes, he pulled up at Melony's house and jumped out of the six with that jail glow. He rang the doorbell, and D Nice answered.

P said, "Where's Mel at?"

He said, "Hold on," and shut the door in the young don's face. This pissed P off dramatically, especially after listening to Mobb Deep. P didn't wait for Mel to come to the door. He pulled out the forty-caliber and made his own entrance.

Melony saw him and tried to give him a hug, but P pushed her out of the way and walked into the living room. D Nice jumped up when he saw P Double roll in with the gun.

"Yo, what's the matter, little nigga?"

P Double said, "Little nigga," and the forty-caliber echoed throughout the big house.

D Nice held his leg in pain while Melony begged P to stop the madness. P moved her out of the way and shot D Nice in his other leg. This time, the giant dropped to his knees in pain.

"Yeah, bitch nigga, that's what the fuck I'm talking about. You bow down to a don nigga."

Melony cried and grabbed P Double's legs, begging him to leave D Nice alone. This infuriated P even more.

"You're choosing this wimp over me? Bitch, you ever look at me again, and I'll kill both of y'all sorry, broke muthafukas."

P Double smacked her with the biscuit and stomped D Nice a couple of times before he left. He looked back, and Melony was leaning over her man crying. P said, "Fuck it," emptied the clip in both of them, and sped back to the field in the six. Halfway home, he had to turn back because his prints were on the door and doorbell. He wiped them clean.

He stopped at the package store and copped a pint of Hennessy. P listened to "What's Beef" by Biggie all the way home. When he got there, he was kind of bent since he hadn't drunk in two years.

As soon as he walked in, he shoved his dick into Fantasy's mouth. Any man could see why her name was Fantasy. To get his dick sucked the way she gave head was every man's fantasy for sure. Quadria came up behind him and started eating ass. This drove him over the top, and he creamed down Fantasy's throat. She made sure she deep-throated his dick because she liked the feeling of come shooting down her esophagus.

After P finished, he bent the pretty redbone over and ran up in her roughly. Fantasy let out a loud gasp as the don pumped her guts full of lead. Quadria watched with lust as P Double was blowing her girl's back out. P Double yanked his dick out of the juicy bird, so Quadria could taste the juices of her best friend. Then the girls both took turns sobbing on the young don's dick until he mounted Quadria and fucked her savagely. She was screaming with both pain and pleasure on her beautiful face. Fantasy was sucking on Quadria's firm breasts, making Quadria come even more. P Double took his dick out and threw both of Fantasy's legs on his shoulders, and he fucked her until his dick hurt. Finally, he shot up in Fantasy's hot pussy, and the girls went back to sucking while P passed out.

$ $ $

P Double woke up with Moe shaking his legs. "P, wake up, wake up!" Moe screamed.

P woke up and wiped the crust out of his eyes. "Man, what the fuck?" he whispered groggily.

"Somebody murdered Melony and D-Nice," Moe said.

P said, "Man, you woke me up for that bullshit? That's what happens when you mess with broke niggas. Now, what club is jumping tonight? I need to let the people know the champ is here."

Moe just looked at P and said, "Damn, you're heartless. Anyways, there's this club called Razzels in the north end. Jay-Z is supposed to be there tonight, doin' his one-two thing."

P Double said, "Well, why are you standing there? Go get dressed. Call the crew up, and let's turn Razzels out."

"Sounds like a plan to me!" Moe shouted over his shoulder on the way out the door.

P Double ran some bathwater. When the tub was full, he made the two ghetto dimes wash his body and suck him off too. He looked into his closet and said, "Damn, I need some new threads." He looked at the clock, and it was 8:00 p.m. "Fuck!" he shouted. Then he called his man Scallachi at Scallachi Fashions to let him know he was about to swing through there.

P Double dropped the chicks off at Quadria's crib and shot straight to Scallachi's. When he got there, the dread greeted him and told him to pick out three expensive outfits that matched with his whip, and he was gone. P shot straight to his grandmother's crib and changed into his orange-and-cream Maurice Malone outfit. He grabbed the jewels he told his grandmother to pick up from the low and a 93-R Beretta out of his weapons stash.

After Melony and D-Nice's demise, he made sure to toss the Gat in the Connecticut River and kept moving. P Double called his crew and told them to meet at Razzels. When he got there, the line outside was crazy. P pulled up front and let his system pump "Money, Power, Respect," by the Lox.

Bitches were creaming in their panties, wanting to know who drove the six. P Double saw his man Ronnie taking people's money and letting them in. So he decided to show off and make his girl take the top of her bikini off. When he dropped the top, everybody said, "Oh shit, that's a convertible?"

At first, Ronnie was blinded by the ice P had on. Then he saw it was his boy, and he told his man to take care of the line for him. "P, when did you get out, baby?"

"Today," P answered.

Ronnie asked if P was coming in, and the don replied with, "Of course, but I got my lady with me."

Ronnie said, "No problem," and P went to park the six. All the bitches went crazy when they saw some fresh meat with that jail glow. Before he even got to the door, chicks were fighting over him. "Bitch, I seen him first!" one shouted, and then hair, clothes, and nails were everywhere while P laughed and made his entrance. P went straight to the bar, copped two bottles of crystal, and popped them both.

Ten minutes later, the Bristol Street crew was Mobb Deep in that bitch. DJ Clue was on the wheels of steel doing his thing mixing it up. P Double's crew all gave him dap when the lights went out, and Jay-Z came out and rocked songs from Reasonable Doubt and Volume One. After Jay finished, the club banged for another hour and then shut down.

P Double was pissy drunk. He turned around to leave and bumped into Mike Tuitt. P Double was about to grab his hammer when Stacy spoke, and he found out it was her and not Mike. "When can I get a trip down memory lane, baby boy?" she said with lust all over her face.

P Double looked at the repulsive dame and said, "Never, you mannish bitch. Now get the fuck out my way."

Stacy just watched him and his crew leave. She uttered, "Oh, I'm gonna get some more of that. You just wait and see."

When they got outside, Moe asked P Double if he was all right because he looked kind of saucy. "Bitch nigga, are you all right?"

P Double shot at him, "'Cause I'm a grown-ass man, dog, and don't forget it."

Then he jumped in the six and skidded out. P dropped the top so he could get some air. Truthfully, he was fucked up, but when people saw you fucked up, it was a sign of weakness in your armor. He was mad at himself for getting smashed the way he was. Somehow, P had made it on the hill. He passed out on Buckingham Street with the top down and his system pumping.

$ $ $

Jaynce went crazy when she woke up to loud music thumping outside of her house. Buckingham Street was a quiet neighborhood, and she was about to give the disrespectful muthafucker a piece of her mind. She opened her front door and ranted and raved all the way to the orange convertible in front of her house when she saw Presley asleep in the car.

First, she cut the music off. Then it took her a minute to figure out how to raise the top on the car. When she did that, she tried to rouse him. He woke up just enough so that she could help him into the house. She couldn't believe it. He smelled like a liquor factory and expensive cologne. Jaynce laid him on the leather sofa and took him out of his Timberlands and the leather coat he was wearing. Then he started coughing like crazy, and she ran and grabbed the little trash can she had in the downstairs bathroom in time for him to spill the contents of his stomach in. She helped him up out of his sweater and wet a cold washcloth so she could wipe his face off.

Pretty soon, the young boy was snoring up a storm, knocked out. Jaynce took the gun out of his pants and laid it on the table. This young boy in front of her was bad business. He stood for everything that she hated, but for some reason, Jaynce found herself attracted to the young thug. She was thirty-two years old and owned her own home. She had a bachelor's degree and a great-paying job, with no kids and no social life. The men in Springfield were tired to her. Most of the men she went to high school with turned out to be crackheads or dope feins and winos.

The rest of them were dead or in jail. When Presley Williams entered her office for the first time, she knew he was special. The way he carried himself, his tone, and his demeanor were just what she craved in a man. As time passed, Jaynce found herself infatuated with him. When he wined and dined her at Chez Josef, Presley won her heart, but she was scared off by the thugs who tried to take their lives that night. Awhile later, she saw that same crazy-ass face in the obituaries and knew Presley handled his business, which turned her on even more. In the game he was in, you had to hunt or be hunted, and she knew Presley was a hunter from the start. Jaynce went to work massaging his hard body. She had to admit, the young boy was ripped. She knew exactly what he did with his jail sentence because he was straight muscle all over.

Jaynce woke up lying on his chest. It was eight o'clock in the morning. So she jumped into her usual routine of bathing and cooking breakfast. Jaynce threw on her Anita Baker CD and started making a deluxe breakfast for her and Presley.

$ $ $

P Double woke up with his head throbbing from a hangover. At first, he couldn't open his eyes because the pain was unbearable. When he opened his eyes, he looked around and wondered where the fuck he was at. Somebody was playing some Anita Baker and cooking some good-smelling food.

P saw a table in front of him and the bottle of aspirin that was sitting on the table. He popped three of them and washed them down with some ice water that was also lying there.

"Damn," he whispered. He had to piss like a racehorse.

P Double rose from the couch and found the downstairs bathroom. He washed his hands and let his nose lead the way to the kitchen. When he walked in, P saw Jaynce with her back turned, slaving over the stove. She was singing at the top of her lungs when she turned around and saw Presley looking at her.

"Damn, all this for me, Jaynce?"

"For sure, baby boy. I figured after whatever you been through last night, you deserved it because, boy, you were ripped."

P Double nodded, "True, true." Then he told her about going to Razzels and getting smashed with his crew. She told him about finding him in the convertible knocked out with his system threatening to break every window on the street. P Double quickly apologized for his behavior, and she made him a plate with scrambled eggs and cheese, toast, sweet and spicy sausages, ham, hash browns, and coffee and orange juice if he chose. P picked both and went to work on the food.

Jaynce should've been a five-star cook as well because that shit was serious, the young boy thought. When he finished, she asked him how it was, and he said, "Sweetheart, you're a drug dealer's dream, ma. My stomach is all yours." And they both laughed. Then P's phone vibrated like crazy. He dug into his pocket and pulled his phone out. "What's good?"

Moe was calling to see where he was at and trying to see what his plans were for the day.

P said, "I got your number on the phone, so I'll hit you back. One!"

Moe shouted, "One!" on the phone before he hung up.

"Jaynce, do you feel like driving, baby girl?"

"That all depends where I'm driving to, and you already know I'm not into the illegal business bullshit," she said.

"Nothing of that nature crossed my mind, ma. I swear it. I'm just a couple years behind, Jaynce; that's all. Which means I need a whole new wardrobe and some new jewelry; that's all. So how about New York for the day?" he asked, giving Jaynce his best puppy dog look.

"Presley, I don't know …"

"I promise no illegal activities, ma."

"Well, okay, when do we leave?" she asked.

"Right about now."

$ $ $

P Double gave Jaynce directions to his grandmother's house. When they arrived, she wasn't there, so he ran the story of why he bought the house and gave it to his nana. They walked into the library study / office, and Jaynce was blown back by the style and grace of the place. She knew Presley had great taste, but this place was really exquisite. Then she saw the twenty-foot portrait of Presley when he was younger and said, "Wow, who painted this?"

"Well, I had this customer who did oil paintings for a living, and the rest is history," he explained.

When she walked over to see what types of books he read, P opened the safe up and walked inside. Jaynce was admiring his taste in authors when she found out she was talking to herself. She walked over to where the twenty-foot portrait was open and screamed, "Oh my god." It was the most money she had ever seen in her whole entire life. When she went to see him the other day in Ludlow, she really thought he was joking about the $7.5 million, but obviously, this young man was on top of his game, and he wanted Jaynce to act like she knew it. He turned around and asked her what was wrong.

Jaynce cleared her throat and said, "Presley, this is crazy. I've never seen this much money in real life. And why do you have all these guns? And is that a bulletproof vest?"

"Why, yes, it is, love. Would you like to try it on and see what it feels like?" He laughed.

Jaynce said, "Hell no. Let's go."

P was stacking a duffel bag full of dough when she said, "Boy, I told you I'm not down with no illegal activities. Why are you bringing all that money?" P broke it down in grown-man terms for her.

"Jaynce, do you think any of this gold I got on with these diamonds are fake?"

"No, but—"

"Right," he said, "and the clothing I rock don't come too cheap either. Plus, I might see something I want you to have. Now let's go make the city know that a king and queen are on the way." He walked out and locked the safe up. P left his grandmother a note on the kitchen table, and they hit the highway in style.

P threw on his best of Keith Sweat CD, and Jaynce's panties got wet. She whipped the Benz with precision, and they entered Manhattan in record time. They hit up a bunch of stores—Macy's, Gucci, Dr. Jay's, Eddie Bauer, Harlem USA, and more. P Double even took her to the Disney store and bought her some Mickey Mouse slippers in twenty colors. He hit up Saks Fifth and Jacob the jeweler last. He went and spent some good money on jewelry. They copped his and her platinum watches that were iced out and a couple of bracelets to go along with it. Then he astonished Jaynce by buying her a platinum chain with an iced-out heart locket.

P got himself a chain, and they were gone. The Celtics were playing the Knicks that night so they stayed in the city to catch the game. Knicks fans were angry that the Celtics won, but P and Jaynce were happy that their team won. When they left there, Jaynce said she was hungry, so they drove to Little Italy and ate at a small Italian restaurant. They ate their food in deep conversation. Then when they were getting ready to leave, P Double did his best Scarface impression when he was drunk in the restaurant. Jaynce fell out laughing at the scene. Then they headed home.

P Double pulled in front of her house and helped her bring everything he bought her in. When he said goodbye and was about to leave, Jaynce grabbed him and tongued him down. Her whole body sparkled from that kiss.

When they split apart, she wrote his number down and told him not to get into any trouble. He laughed and was out the door. P jumped in the six. He had forgotten he had his phone off all day and night. He turned it on and got ten voice mails from Moe. P called his man up and explained he needed a day for himself to get his mind right, so he went to the city to blow a couple of stacks with his boo. Moe then gave him Frankie's number and told P that Frank had been blowing his line up all day long. P Double then told Moe he would rock with him in the a.m. P called his man Frank up as soon as he got off the line with Moe.

"What up, Frank?"

"You nigga, come over and holla at your boy for a second," Frank said.

P said, "Okay," and Frankie gave him the address.

When P got there, Frankie opened the door and invited P in.

When P walked in front of him, Frank smacked the don with a big-ass Taurus. P staggered from the blow and said, "What the fuck!"

Little Frank bust a shot in the air and told P if he moved the wrong way, he was a dead man. As P walked into the living room, he saw Shante crying with two black eyes. Her lip was split down the middle as well, and she was holding a little girl who was also crying.

P said, "Man, what the fuck is this, Shante?"

Frank ran up to P and cuffed him with the massive handgun twice before he started calling Shante "filthy whore" and "slut." "Bitch, for years, I've been trying to have a kid by you!" he cried. "But no, you wait for me to go to jail and start fucking this yellow bastard. First, I'm gonna kill him, and then I'm gonna kill you and that little yellow bitch in your hands."

Shante set the baby in the seat and crawled on her knees to Frankie, begging him not to kill Presley, but this just added more fuel to the raging inferno. Frank gun-butted her twice and split her eyelid wide open, screaming, "You nasty bitch, you're still sticking up for this piece of shit." Then he ran and put the gun to P Double's head, but Shante let out an animal cry and tackled Frankie as the gun went off. The loud sound deafened P. But he knew he had to act or be dead for real. Before Frankie could recover, P ran over and stepped on his hand. With his other foot, he kicked the Taurus out of Frankie's hand and down the hall. Then he went to work on his longtime friend, hitting him with lefts and rights and stiff kicks. Just when P thought Frankie was out of it, he grabbed P's leg and tripped him. Frank got on top of P for a second and rained his own fury of blows, but P flung the little man off him like a rag doll and hit him with everything he had in him once again. But Little Frankie's broken heart made him psychotic. He wasn't your average man with the state of mind he was in. While P stomped Frankie, he didn't notice the man digging in his back pocket until it was too late. Frankie hit the button on the switch blade and rammed the sharp blade into P's leg. P screamed in pain from the sharp jig and backed off his prey.

Frankie got up with a bloody facial mask of pure hate as he swung the knife at P Double with a hacking motion. P Double was dodging the ferocious swings until he tripped over a living room table. Frankie stood over him about to stab P when he heard five shots go off. Frank just fell. P rolled his friend off him and saw Shante in a shooter's stance. She stood there shaking with the gun in her hands. The Taurus had smoke coming out of the large barrel like it was evaporating out of its body, like Frankie's soul was climbing out of his. P walked over to the distraught woman and made her lower the gun. The next thing they knew, police were at the door. The place was a circus. Police took Shante into custody, and P snatched his newfound daughter up, as he answered a couple of questions for the boys in blue. He called Vinny at his home number and told him to defend his baby's mother to the fullest extent. Instead of going to the hospital, he drove to his grandmother's house and broke everything down for her.

Mrs. Williams didn't know whether to be angry, scared, or happy. All she knew was her grandson was the father of a beautiful baby girl. She asked Presley what the baby's name was, and he had to admit that he didn't know. He just keep calling her his little princess. His grandmother bandaged him up, and young P fell asleep with a new burden on his shoulders.

CHAPTER 15

BACK ON THE GRIND

The next day, Jaynce buzzed P Double's phone bright and early. She told him that he and Shante were all over the news and the front of the local newspaper. The page said, "Man Dies because of Love Triangle." P broke every last detail down, including the two-year-old daughter he didn't know he had. After five minutes of his confessions, they both hung up on a good note. P Double would be eating a home-cooked meal on Buckingham Street tonight. But first things first; he was tired of pussy-footing around. It was time to make his name felt in the streets again. He called Moe early and asked what the prices looked like.

Moe broke down that he was paying twenty-five a brick because prices went up. P said, "Okay, I'll holla back in a minute." As soon as he hung up, he cussed Moe out. There was no way in hell a nigga like him was paying twenty-five stacks for a brick. P drove to his grandmother's house and packed a million and a half in two large duffel bags and hit the highway early.

P arrived in the city about eleven o'clock in the morning. Hot 97 was playing "Twenty-Four Hours to Live" by Black Rob and the Lox. P pulled up at the Spanish restaurant but said, "Fuck that," and kept it moving. He drove all the way to Twenty-Seventh and Broadway and parked his car in a garage that had security. Niggas in the city were expert car thieves. He had a million five in the trunk, and all it took was sixty seconds for someone to steal his whip, so he parked at the garage. After twenty minutes, he finally got a cabdriver to stop and take him back Uptown to Harlem World. P forgot cabdrivers were scared to pick up black men in the city because of the high robbery rate in New York. With all the lights and badass city drivers, it took another twenty minutes to reach the Spanish restaurant. P paid the cab and walked in.

The place really hadn't changed that much in five years. P saw a young Dominican cat at the counter who had a crazy rock on his pinky. The don said, "Excuse me, brother, but I'm looking for an old Dominican cat by the name of Tanto that I met five years ago."

The Dominican kid said, "And your name is?"

"P Double, my man."

The Dominican pulled a phone out of his back pocket and placed a call. He talked Dominican into the jack for two minutes and passed P the phone. The old bounce on the phone said, What does P Double stand for?"

P laughed and said, "Because my first name begins with a P and I double everything, my money, my bitches, even the nuts I bust. I even send out double shots when I bust my gun."

The old man laughed and said, "That's my boy. How have you been?"

P hollered, "Good, if you can meet me on a serious level, pops."

"No sweat. My daughter, Malinda, will bring you to see me. The guy at the counter is my son, Migalito. Give him back the phone."

P passed the phone back to his son, and he spoke to his father for another two minutes and hung up. Migalito gave P a firm handshake and called his sister.

When the gorgeous beauty walked out, P's dick got hard at once. Malinda was a silver-dollar fuck a dime. Migalito spit some fast words, and they were on their way. P Double tried to holla at the beautiful damsel, but either she didn't know English, or she wasn't in the mood for his bullshit. They wound up catching a ferry to Long Island.

When thy got off the ferry, she drove for a while until they pulled up to this big, classy neighborhood. P said to himself, "Now, that's what's up." After driving a little ways, they pulled up in front of a big-ass gate with a guardhouse. The guard told P to step out of the car. He frisked him and made sure he was clean when they drove through the gate. Malinda parked in front of the big white mansion, and they got out. The butler said Malinda's father was out back in the pool, so they followed the stone path around the house.

P was amazed even more. Tanto had a giant cage with two white-and-black Siberian tigers in them. There was a basketball court, tennis court, and lake in the back. There was also some shit that looked like a giant greenhouse, but the windows were foggy. They walked in, and P saw that it was an indoor poolhouse. In the glass house, it was warm. P did think Tanto was crazy at first when the Butler said the old man was in the pool, because it was damn near Christmas. Tanto saw them, and he got out of the pool and sat in a lawn chair. He told P to have a seat and for Malinda to fetch him a towel.

"Now, what can I do for you, young blood?" Tanto asked.

P broke down everything from the gasoline coke Tanto sold him to falling out with Ed and copping off the Jamaicans to just getting out. He told him he heard prices were up to twenty-five. But he wanted to spend one point five right then if Tanto was willing to give them to him for eighteen. The old man thought about it for a second and finally agreed. P said the money was in his car.

Tanto said, "Malinda will drive your car to make the pickup and drop your car back off to you at the restaurant."

P and the old man shook hands, and Malinda and P boogied back to Manhattan to pick up the car. P got the car out of the garage and parked on twenty-seventh.

Malinda came over to the six and said, "Damn, poppy, you got great taste in cars."

"I know, ma. I also got great taste in women as well."

And P Double blinked at her. "Listen, ma. Hit this AC switch three times, and the backseat is gonna lift up like this," and he showed her that the money was there and also how he wanted the coke stacked up. She said, "Okay, papi," and grabbed his crotch while getting in the car. Malinda laughed and said, "Nice."

"Don't start nothing you can't finish, mommy," P spit. And the beautiful

Dominican dame hit the switch for the seat to go back down and chirped out. P Double pushed the van back to the restaurant and waited.

While there, he ate some pepper steak and rice until the work came through. As soon as he took his last bite of pepper steak, his car pulled up. He went outside, and Malinda said, "Everything is in order. Next time, don't be a stranger, baby boy. All work and no play makes P Double a dull boy."

Then she grabbed his crotch again and laughed, "Nice, nice," entering the restaurant. P jumped in the six and drove home. By the time he made it back, it was dark. He pulled up in his grandmother's garage and let the door close behind him before he got out. Then he hit the switch and made sure he got everything that he was supposed to. Satisfied, he started moving the work to the big safe except for ten bricks, which he left in the car. P Double then wondered where his grandmother and his daughter were. *Oh well*, he thought, *I'll just see them later*, as exited the garage, satisfied for the day.

$ $ $

Jaynce was in the kitchen doing her thing hard. She had some salmon steaks in the oven with macaroni and cheese. On the stove was corn on the cob and scallop potatoes. She thought to herself, *Damn girl, you ain't did this serious cooking in years.* Cooking was another one of her passions, but having no one to cook for but herself for the past couple of years, she only made simple things.

Jaynce couldn't even remember putting this much love and grace in her food, period. She just wanted Presley to be happy. That was all. This morning, she was real disgruntled when she turned her TV on and saw his face all over the news. But when she found out that he had a baby's mother, this really drove her up a wall. To think that he actually had a kid with someone else was repulsive. This drove her mad. She wanted to be the first one to bring him that special gift of being a father. She wanted to be the first one he ever shared that special bond with, period. Instead, this gold-digging little scuzzi had stepped on her toes by giving him the gift of a beautiful baby girl.

Jaynce didn't wish jail or death on anybody, but she wanted that bitch Shante dead or to remain in jail forever. Shit, if she thought she was gonna get anywhere near her Presley period that bitch was dead. Then she thought about it. *Girl, you're bugging. You haven't even slept with this man yet, and he already got you fucked up in the head. Matter of fact, let me call his trifling ass and get a explanation from him of why he didn't tell me this before.* That was when she called him, and he broke everything down to her. Damn, her juices were flowing from his voice alone. P made her feel young and like she was a freshman in college again. She finally broke down and invited him over for dinner. Jaynce had just shut the oven off, and the doorbell rang. She knew it was P, but he was early. When she opened the door, all she saw was a bunch of all different colors of roses. Then Presley's head popped up behind the roses. She hugged him and took the roses out of his hand so she could set them in some water.

P Double smelled some bomb-ass food and ran straight to the kitchen. As soon as he opened the oven, Jaynce said, "Nigga, if you don't sit your ass down so I can serve you, I'll kill you up in here."

P said, "You got that, love." And he moved over to the sink and washed his hands.

Jaynce lit two candles in the dining room and placed all the food on the mahogany table. P sat down patiently and waited for the older woman to romance him. She made him a plate and poured him a glass of red wine to go with his meal. As she walked into the next room, P glanced at her beautifully shaped buttocks. Jaynce definitely was packing strong luggage for real; for a woman, she had a lot of tone. DJ Envy blessed the airwaves with slow jams as Jaynce sat down and looked at her prize and asked him how his day was. P explained to her that he was trying to get back in the hang of things and reintegrate back into society like a man of his stature was supposed to. He took a couple bites of everything and complimented her on her great skill of throwing down. "Damn, Jaynce, I can't lie, ma. When I first sized you up, I said to myself, 'She looks too good to know how to cook a meal.'"

Jaynce said, "Nigga, please, you should know that sisters know how to throw down."

"Not the new-wave sisters, ma. Ever since they invented the microwave, women haven't been on they dean in them kitchens."

"Well, I don't know about the new-wave hotties out there. I just know Jaynce do her thing, and now you know," she finished.

P nodded and answered, "True, true."

After he finished, they went into the living room and cuddled up on the couch so they could watch a movie. Jaynce put in *Boomerang* and said, "Presley reminded her of Eddie Murphy in the movie, but just a ghetto version."

By the time Robin Givens was getting her rocks off, Jaynce was ready for rock too. She started kissing on P's neck to find out the young boy fell asleep. She unlaced his Gortex and fell asleep lying on her king's chest.

$ $ $

The next day, Jaynce had to go to work so she left a note and a spare key on the table and left. P Double woke up with Jaynce's beautiful fragrance still in the air and found the note on the table. He drained the cobra in the bathroom and walked into the kitchen. He opened the oven and found a plate with pancakes, sausage, bacon, hash browns, and eggs on it that she had left for the young don. He ate, walked over to C-Town grocery store, and copped some fresh baking soda and a bunch of baggies. He brought two cakes in the crib and said, "Man, fuck it."

P ran out, got the other eight, and stashed them in Jaynce's basement. This was his first time in a long time cheffing up some coke, but the shit was like riding a bike; once you learned, you always know how to ride it. P broke the package open, and the raw coke smell filled the kitchen. P Double loved that smell. To him, it smelled like money, which was the sweetest smell in the world besides Jaynce. P rocked up both keys and made twenty-five hundred grams. He already had the plan. He was gonna sell his shit for seven hundred an ounce and fuck the streets up. Everybody else wanted a dollar twenty five a ball, when he only wanted ninety. That day, he went around his block, sold some caine, and passed his number out. He hit Worthington, the north end, the south end, Forest Park, Hilltop, Locust Street, Rifle Street, and Cannon Circle. He saved the Ave for last. Christmas was in a week, and he knew he was gonna spend some good money, so he was making sure everything was gravy by the New Year.

P Double pulled up on the curb at the Ave store and walked in. Wheat Lox was playing *Mortal Combat 3* when P walked in.

"What's up, Wheatie? You seen Jimmy Lee out here?"

Lox said, "Nah, that nigga be low out here."

P said, "Yo, how much you paying for caine out here, my nigga?"

Lox said, "About thousand an ounce. Why? What's good?"

"Man, that's too much. Wheatie, you know that. I got some fire for seven an ounce right now."

Wheatie said, "Fuck this game. What's good?" as they walked outside.

Lox saw the six and said, "Oh shit, this you right here?"

P said, "Yeah."

"Yo, let me drive this shit."

P Double threw him the keys and said, "Let's ride."

They drove around for a couple of hours, and Lox pulled up in front of his crib on Ashley Street. He was about to get out, and P said, "Hold up." He hit the switch on the stash.

The seat popped up, and Lox said, "What the fuck?"

P Double threw a brick of eggshell white on his lap and said, "Bring me back twenty-eight stacks."

Wheat Lox said, "Are you serious?"

"Yeah, nigga, we been beefing for years out here on these streets, Lox, for nothing. Now, let's see if we can get some money together and make it something the streets will really remember forever."

They exchanged numbers, and P had a new member on his team.

$ $ $

Big Butch did ten days in the box for the bullshit with P Double. He was at himself for lack of discipline. He could've caught this nigga in the hallway and really worked him instead of pussy-footing around. When they told him he was going to A-5, he jumped with joy, because that was the same unit P Double moved to after he completed the drug program in C-5. He walked out the door ready to come straight back to the box, but it took him a second to realize that when you and a nigga got into a beef, they didn't send you to the same unit with that person. He knew then that the only way he was gonna catch P or Fatback was on the streets. He walked up the six flights of stairs and was huffing and puffing when he got to the unit and rang the buzzer. He put his bag on the floor, and they told him he was in cell seventeen. He liked it up there in the penthouse suite because the cells were nice for fighting. His only regret was not moving to this unit in the first place.

Damn, he thought, if only he could've caught P Double in one of these cells here. Fuck it. He only had two weeks to wrap up anyway. His ass was all done when the monster stepped on the scene. He walked out of the cell and looked around the unit. He spotted faggot-ass Andy Cap, and he already knew where his food was coming from that night. Andy Cap would have to pay taxes if he wanted to walk around A-5. Butch also saw A-Dog and E. He walked over and hollered at E on a positive note. Then they called gym, and the unit lined up. Butch and E signed up for the gym along with the rest of the unit.

E said, "Hold up. Let me grab something real quick." E went to his cell and came back just as the sally port opened to let them out. When they got to the top of the stairs, E looked at Butch and said, "P Double said to hold this." E pulled out a sock with a water faucet fixture in it and smacked Butch in his dome.

Butch grunted as he tried to block the next blow, the sock caught him again, splitting his forehead wide open. Butch lost his balance and fell down the stairs. This time, Andy Cap, A-Dog, and E started working the big guy over with socks. Butch passed out a bloody wreck as the boys just left the socks on him and walked to the gym.

Anne Calley walked out of A-5 to go meet Major Weldon at the staff cafeteria. She'd been fucking the major for a year on the low. Anne was old, and her husband had stopped paying her attention, but the convicts in jail hadn't forgotten about her beauty. Then she just decided to get freaky as black people called it, and she seduced the major. She was on her way to get a quickie in the staff bathroom when she saw a bloody man lying on the floor. She let out a bunch of earth-shattering screams before her mature side showed, and she radioed it in. "We gotta code red, blue, or whatever the hell you call it on the stairs of A Tower."

While her fellow officers came, she was letting up coffee and the rest of her breakfast. Medical came, put Butch on a stretcher, and got him up out of there.

$ $ $

Christmastime was the shit that year for P Double, because he got to spend it with his three favorite girls: Jaynce, his grandmother, and his daughter. P went all out this year. He almost bought the whole damn Toys R Us out. His daughter had a bunch of Barbies and dollhouses. He bought his grandmother a mink coat and an all-expenses-paid trip to the Madi Gras in New Orleans. She was heavily into jazz music, so he blessed her with that. He copped Jaynce a pink Range Rover and himself a platinum one. He also had another half-million-dollar surprise waiting. His grandmother was making a special dinner, and the whole family was there to celebrate. Of course, P Double and Jaynce were the main attraction at granny's right then. Even his mother was hating on Jaynce's beauty. Jaynce was dressed up in an all-white Dolce and Gabana pantsuit; that was tough. Her hair was in the usual Halle Berry do. And she had a see-through purse with the open-toe sandals to match. The only ones who expressed their happiness were his daughter and his grandmother. They both were in love with P Double's newfound interest. P Double's father even made a guest appearance at P's grandmother's. He had just wrapped up a five-year bid upstate on the twenty-fourth. P really didn't care for the man too much. As far as he was concerned, the streets were his father because they raised him up to be the man he was. His grandmother was his mother, and that was that. The two parading around acting like they were his parents were strangers to him.

Finally, five o'clock came, and it was time to open presents. P Double's daughter had so many presents to open the adults started helping her. His grandmother damn near passed out when she saw the mink coat and the first-class ticket to New Orleans. She kissed him and thanked her grandbaby. P gave his sister five grand and told her to do her. P Double announced that he had a big surprise for Jaynce, and he tied a hanky around her eyes and guided her through the house as the rest of the family followed. He stepped into the garage, and everybody said, "Oh shit." She took the blindfold off herself, and in front of her was a pink Range Rover. She started screaming and jumping up and down, going crazy. P opened the door for her, and on the pink-and-white suede seats was a pink mink coat. She got into the luxury ride and noticed it was fully loaded. It had two TVs in the headrests and a drop-top flat screen in the front. It also came with navigation and a crazy Pioneer sound system. P even had her favorite CDs on display. Jaynce shed a tear, but the young don said he wasn't done yet. He told her to start the Range and turn the TV on. She did and young P came on the screen and asked Jaynce to marry him.

When she turned around to ask him if he was serious, there was a 2.5-carat pink diamond that blinked at her. His grandmother said, "Oh my goodness." When she saw the luster on the pink gemstone. Everybody else said, "Damn! Diamonds come in pink too?" Jaynce started full-fledged crying and sealed the marriage proposal with a kiss. She said yes. One of P Double's aunts ruined the affair by asking P what he got his mother and father.

P said, "Oh yeah, I almost forgot." And he went over and embraced them both with a powerful hug. "Merry Christmas."

His aunt said, "Wow, that's it? You lucky I didn't birth your little ass."

P said, "Yeah, because I would've been ugly as fuck like you." And she walked into the house with that "Well I never" look, grabbed her jacket, and stormed out of there before they ate dinner.

The whole family walked into the house and washed their hands before they sat at the table. Since Jaynce was the newest member of the family, everybody asked her to bless the food and say grace. They all held hands and bowed their heads while P Double's future wife baptized their food.

P Double's grandmother carved the turkey and ham. The other food was just passed around the table. P Double made his daughter a plate and watched her try to eat. Jaynce got mad at him for not teaching her the right way and started feeding her.

His mother got up, snatched the fork out of Jaynce's hand, and said, "Excuse me. I think I can feed my grandbaby from here. Thank you." And she started feeding P Double's daughter.

P jumped up, snatched the fork out of her hand, and told her to get the fuck away from his baby girl. She slapped P with an open palm and left a handprint on his face. P laughed at her, and she tried to slap him again, but he caught her hand and gave her a rough shove. P's father jumped up and pushed him.

"Nigga, shove me, boy."

P walked up to him and spit a lewy in his face. His father then threw a wild punch, but P Double sidestepped it and caught his father with a three-piece combination that staggered him. Big Presley let out an animal cry as he charged his son full speed. P Double just got low, picked his father up, and ran with him a few feet before he slammed him. P got on top of his pops and started giving him the business when his two uncles snatched him up off of him. His father got up and gave him a couple hit shots before P Double's grandmother put her foot down.

"Now, that's enough ruckus in this house for one day."

P Double's uncles let him go, and he said, "Y'all wanna jump me, huh?" And he ran to the study. His grandmother was getting everyone calmed down when P Double came back with the AR-15 assault rifle out.

"What's up now, muthafuckers?"

People started running everywhere. Jaynce jumped in front of P and said, "Baby, no, please put the gun down."

P Double's grandmother ran up to him and gorilla palmed him twice. "Boy, don't you ever disrespect my house with no bullshit. You hear me, Tinco? Answer me, boy. You leave that street shit in the streets. Now get that shit the fuck out of my house, and you can go with it until you know how to act."

P turned and ran up out of there with Jaynce calling him. His daughter was crying so Jaynce picked her up and calmed the little girl down. Mrs. Williams was still rambling on about the nerve of P disrespecting her house like this. The rest of the family came out of hiding, and the rest of the night went swell.

$ $ $

Shante was going through the motions right now. This was her first time in Ludlow, Hamden County House of Corrections, and she hated it.

She had only been down twelve days, and she had fifty letters from horny-ass jail niggas. She opened and read one letter and never bothered to open another one. At night, she stayed up stressing, wondering why this shit had to happen to her. At least P got her the best lawyer in Springfield, but even he couldn't get her bail, so she could celebrate Christmas with her daughter. In her mind, her daughter was in good hands with her father. She just wished they could be one happy family together. Instead, Shante found herself locked up with a bunch of feins and hookers. When she stayed up late night, all she heard was grown women moaning from carpet munching. It took a couple days for the swelling of her eyes to go down, but the bruising still looked crazy when she looked in the mirror at herself. Her cell mate was a white crack addict / hooker named Roxy, who was locked up for ten counts of common nightwalking, which is hooking. Roxy schooled her on the dos and don'ts of the joint and who was who. This black dike bitch named Weenie was running the unit. She was the queen of the baseheads, and all the other crackheads were scared of her. She and Shante brushed shoulders her second day in the joint. Everybody wanted to suck Shante's pussy because she actually bodied a nigga. Weenie didn't like the fact that the little young bitch was stealing her shine so she bumped her and made a scene. Weenie called her a couple of names and kept it moving. But for the last past twelve days, Weenie was watching all the fan mail the young bitch was getting. Pretty soon, everybody in the unit was gonna roll with the young girl. So she had to make a move to let Shante know that she was the queen bee up in this joint. And if she didn't play by her rules, her little ass would get stung. Christmas Day came, and they all filed out and walked to the chow hall. When they got there, Weenie noticed that a bunch of her girls sat at the table with Shante so she decided to invite herself to the luncheon.

When she sat down, her homegirl asked her how it felt to have a baby by a kingpin. Shante started to explain when weenie shouted, "Boring. Nobody really wanna hear that bullshit around these parts."

Shante said, "Where was I at before this little no-dick-getting bull dagger interrupted me?"

Weenie jumped up like, "Bitch, you got one more time to get smart up in this piece, and that's your little ass girl."

Shante laughed at the dike bitch and told her to suck her pussy. That was when Weenie jumped over the table with catlike reflexes, but Shante moved like a cheetah and slapped the older woman with her tray twice. Weenie took the two blows and landed a couple of wild punches of her own when Shante snatched her orange shirt over her face and went to work. When the COs broke up the fight, the older woman didn't know if she was coming or going. The chicks in the chow hall started slamming their trays on the table chanting, "Shante, Shante!" until they dragged the two women up out of there.

Weenie finally recovered from the beating she got and yelled, "This ain't over, bitch. One of us gots to die."

Shante said, "So it sure won't be me, you old bitch," and they put them in two different units.

$ $ $

The first couple of days Jaynce went to work she had a new glow to her. All her fellow coworkers were happy about her engagement. But then a couple of weeks went by where she hadn't heard from Presley at all. She tried calling his cell phone only to get his answering machine. She even stopped by his grandmother's house to see if he had stopped by there to see his daughter. To no avail, he hadn't even done that. Jaynce was ready to call the boys in blue, but his grandmother said, "No, Tinco just needs to do him right now. He'll come back soon. Trust me."

Jaynce just went back home and cried to herself. But every time she went home, she knew he had been there after a while because she started noticing little things like the toilet seat up or an extra dish in the sink. It got to the point where she left notes for P, but for some reason, he wouldn't respond. She loved him, and she really needed to tell him that they could work through the hard times together, because that was what couples did. On her extra time, she would ride around to see if she could spot the Range Rover or the 600, but she hadn't one time. Finally, she just decided to pray and let nature take its course.

$ $ $

Eddie Haul was laid back on his recliner, getting his issue. Christina had been bobbing up and down on his dick for twenty minutes when he finally exploded in her mouth. His phone chirped why she was still extracting his goods.

"Speak!" he yelled into the phone.

"Yo, Ed, It's Edguardo. I need to talk to you, papa. Shit is serious be." Ed told his captain to come over.

When his man got there, Ed told him to come in. Christina's thick Spanish body was bouncing up and down on Ed's dick like she was bouncing on a trampoline when Edguardo walked in. Edguardo already knew Ed was a freak. He just sat down and broke shit down to his general. "Yo, the moranos are all getting their coke from some new guy named P Double."

Ed threw the little bitch on the floor and said, "what?"

"Raheem and the rest of his crew all work for P Double. His crack is better than ours, and the price is much cheaper."

"So that little nigga is back out here on the streets, huh? Well, fuck that. If niggas ain't buying our coke, then they can't pump down here, and that's that. I want Heem's mother's house shot the fuck up right now and all the cats that rock with them. If we can't eat, papa, then nobody eats," Ed said.

"Si, papi, say no more," and Edguardo called the rest of the clique.

$ $ $

P Double was on the grind full-time. He was hitting the streets like there was no tomorrow. After his family spazzed out on him, he just said fuck the world. The only thing that never turned their backs on him were his money and the streets. Of course, he loved Jaynce, but she couldn't understand things right then. She was still his queen, and he didn't wanna really turn her on to the lifestyle he was living. She was a good girl. And once a good girl went bad, she was gone forever. He went through every day and cooked up. Right then though, he was trying to get back on his dean and make shit happen. Just when he thought he had his mojo back. Shit got crazy. The Spanish niggas were taking his people to war, and he was losing the battle. Ed's boy snatched up Raheem and took twenty birds of P's work.

Then they had cats like Duncan and Da'vey scared to pump on the block because they were straight up clapping niggas.

P said, "Fuck it." He called his man Wheat Lox up and told him it was time to ride. Lox was always ready for rock. He thought he was the black Wesley Snipes of the streets because he favored the man. Wheatie rented an '83 caddy off one of his feins and picked up P in Forest Park. Both men were dressed in all black. They even painted their faces black. P Double snatched up the AR-15 and three ninety-round clips of pure punishment. Lox had two Tech 22s and full body armor. It was time to ride.

$ $ $

The Latin Kings were partying hard. They managed to chase all the blacks out of the neighborhood, and they were doing their thing. Ed and Edguardo put their heads together and managed to downsize the odds by taking Raheem out of commission. They even got lucky. The little punk had twenty birds. Ed didn't like the fact that they were planning to move that much work in their streets, period, so they did what they did.

Edguardo and twenty members of his team were chilling on Oswego Street, kicking it with a bunch of bitches. They were too fucked up to notice the black old school Caddy pull up slowly. P Double rolled down the window and said, "Who gotta fifty?"

Five dudes ran up to the window and got mowed down. Lox hopped out of the driver's side and let both Tech 22s empty. P jumped out, emptied a clip, and reloaded. He walked up to some cat who was crawling and said, "Tell Eddie Haul that P Double said the boy is back." And he gave the kid a ten-round burst in the legs. P Double and Lox chirped to Wendell Street a couple of blocks up, stashed the guns in the six, and drove off.

$ $ $

They made it to Forest Park, and P Double and Lox planned out their next step while enjoying a bottle of Hennessy. P Double was ready to take Eddie Haul up off of there. For years, Eddie Haul couldn't let go of destiny. So what P Double stole his dame and blew up? It was his time to blow. Ed couldn't just step down and crown him king. So P Double had to make him know shit was real. Lox just wanted to shoot shit up every night, but that wasn't the way. P wanted Ed to feel helpless and defenseless. Plus, he wanted his twenty bricks back. He thought about snatching up Italia to see how much she was really worth to Ed. Plus, he could torture the bitch and find out about Ed's operation. Lox told him that Italia came to his crib once in a while. Wheatie lived in a duplex, and right next door was where Pooh and the rest of the play girls took up residence. Also, Lox was fucking this chick named Angel and her sister Candy. Italia also rolled with them. That was when the plan was formed. P Double laughed out loud. "Yeah, Ed, the boy is back."

$ $ $

Ed was chilling in the south end, running money through his money counter. With prices being up in all, P Double's twenty bricks came in nice and handy. Who the fuck did the little bastard think he was around here? He learned everything he knew from Ed. Bristol Street was his. Now, the little fuck wanted to get greedy and try to stake his claim on the south end as well. P Double's mistake was thinking Eddie Haul was a pussy, so Ed fucked him with no Vaseline.

Ed bundled up 250 stacks, and his phone chirped with some bad news. P Double and some other cat killed nineteen of his men, including his captain. They also killed seven chicks as well. Ed screamed and flipped the table. "So the punk wants war? I'll show his bitch ass war. Eddie Haul bows down to no man."

Italia ran into the living room, trying to calm her man down, but he was out of control, throwing shit everywhere. She ran up to him and grabbed him. "Baby, please stop. Tell mama what's wrong."

"Bitch, if you ever say that name again, I'll kill you." Ed didn't notice he was choking his girl until she had turned purple. He released his grip, and Italia fell to the floor, gasping for air. As soon as she recovered, she grabbed her keys and ran out of there. Eddie had blown a head gasket somewhere, and he needed time alone, so she was gonna give it to him.

CHAPTER 16

THE DRAMA KING

The war between Bristol Street and the Latin Kings got serious. Half of Bristol Street didn't even know how the war had transpired. They were just ready for war. Little Lee got out of the joint and was in the hospital the same night nursing gunshot wounds in his legs and chest. A-Dog caught a couple slugs as well. They were both watching from the sidelines.

Lox came through for P Double in a big way one day. He was at Angel's house, and Italia was staying over there because she was scared of Ed. P Double told Lox to take her for a ride and bring her to the Forest Park apartment. Lox did as he was told, and P Double started turning the charm on heavy. She was down and out, and Italia really needed a shoulder to lean on, so P Double provided the arm. He took her out to Enfield to dinner and a movie.

P Double gave the bitch a fake name though, because he was very sure Ed had cursed his name plenty of times, so he didn't want to scare the lady. On her way back from dinner, Italia broke down and told all. P was always a good listener, and he soaked every last drop of information in, as he maneuvered the platinum Range Rover on the highway. Italia leaned on his arm for comfort. P asked her where she wanted to get dropped off at. Italia started shedding tears at once when P Double asked.

"I don't know. I have nowhere to go," she cried.

P said, "Don't worry. I have everything under control."

He drove to the Forest Park apartment and jumped out of the Range. He opened Italia's door and grabbed her hand. She stepped out of the Range with tears in her eyes, and P walked her into the apartment building. They walked up to the third floor in silence, and P opened the door. He told her to make herself comfortable, while he went to the bathroom. P had to piss as bad as fuck. The whole time he was taking a leak, he was about how things were going. Stupid-ass Ed left the door wide open with this stupid bitch of his. He was gonna fuck Ed in two ways. First, he was gonna fuck his dame. Then he was gonna take the chump for his worth. He finished draining the cobra, and then he decided to go out there and pump Italia full of stiff muscle and then pump her for information.

Before he walked out of the bathroom. He heard Mary J Blige flow through the airwaves. He walked into the living room, but there was no sign of Italia at all. P thought the bitch had bounced, but he saw that his door was still locked, so he walked into Fatback's bedroom and there she was, butt-ass naked, with her legs wide open, ready to get conquered. P started undressing, but he couldn't stop looking Italia over. Her body was sheer perfection. Her chest was a firm D cup, but her nipples were the size of doorknobs. P kept looking at the size of her bush. If she didn't have a rain forest down there, he didn't know what it was. Italia looked at the young don, and she licked her fingers seductively and started rubbing her mound. Then she stuck two fingers into herself and moaned lightly.

P Double just watched as her fingers disappeared inside her rain forest. P Double crawled onto the bed and sucked one of her giant nipples while playing with the other one. Italia arched her back up in the air with a loud sigh of pleasure. When she pulled her fingers out of her snatch, they were dripping with her juices. P said, "Fuck that," and entered her roughly. Italia let out a loud yelp as P shoved his cobra in her. All P could think about was *Damn, this bitch pussy is bomb.* She had a snapping turtle between her legs. The way her snatch gripped the young don's manhood and refused to let go.

At first, P was long dicking the bitch with slow, practiced strokes. Then he gutted her with long, quick strokes. Italia was holding on to P for dear life as her pussy gushed like a hot spring. P came when she did, but he just kept on pumping away. His man refused to get knocked out in the first round of this bout. Italia's screams and moans were filled with the utmost pleasure and pain. Eddie Haul had never fucked her with this much intensity and lust before. This young nigga was definitely giving her the business as she gushed again. P snatched his dick out of the tropical rainforest of Italia's snatch, and he instructed her to assume the position and bend over on all fours. She did as she was told, and P had to admire her apple bottom. He looked at her bird and swore the shit was talking to him, saying, "P Double, fuck me." His cobra was already dripping wet with venom when he bit the pussy again.

This time, he pounded Italia and made her ass clap with applause as he banged out her inner core for a half hour, until he roared like a lion when his cobra spit. They were both drenched in sweat and juices when P, laid her down. But Italia wasn't finished yet. She decided to talk to the young boy's manhood verbally as she took him in her mouth. P had to salute this bitch because she was truly a brain surgeon the way she operated on his dick. Instead of him pumping her, she was pumping him, but this wasn't gonna be a third-round knockout either. Italia spit his dick out with a popping noise and mounted him. This bitch was a desperado, fuck a rider. She rode his dick like she used to ride horses with Jesse James back in the stagecoach days. The more she rode the tighter and wetter her pussy got. Finally, Italia's eyes rolled up into the back of her head as she started nutting everywhere. P Double was drenched in her juices when he finally sprang a leak. She fell asleep on top of him, with his dick still in her.

$ $ $

Eddie Haul was pacing back and forth, going crazy. Who the fuck did this bitch Italia think she was? For two weeks now, the bitch had been on the lam. If she thought that little choking was something, wait until he got his hands on her this trip. Ed needed his dick sucked badly. All his other chicks could suck a dick, but Italia made your toes curl up the way she attacked a penis. For days now, he called up all her friends trying to find his boo, with no such luck. Her friends weren't shit anyway. As soon as he went to Angel's house, he fucked her little ass to death. Angel thought she was that bitch too, with her dry-ass pussy. If it weren't for the lube on the condom, his dick would've looked like he was fucking a package of razors.

Everything else was going fucked up as well. P Double had half of his crew scared to go outside; the other half had warrants and were on the run from police. Damn, why did he teach the little fucker the game? He wouldn't be going through any of this shit now if he didn't. But right then, he couldn't think. He needed his dick sucked so he called Christina to handle the job.

$ $ $

Ever since Lox was fucking with the nigga P, he was coming up for sure. He copped two CRXs all kitted up with the works. He even had a hundred pairs of sneakers and Timberlands. But he felt a bad vibe coming from his people, because everybody knew he was one of Bristol Street's protégés.

P Double had the best and cheapest coke in town, so his boys had no choice but to cop off him. "Fuck them broke niggas." He laughed to himself. He was the black Wesley Snipes, and as long as his pockets stayed fat, the haters could keep hating and the chicken could keep clucking. That night, he was going across the street to the Wishing Well bar to have a good time. They were having one of their little parties, so he decided to make a guest appearance.

Lox threw on a pair of blue-and-cream Gortex with the spikes in them. He had a cream-and-blue Willie Esco suit to match and a cream-and-blue shearling with the fur hood. Lox threw his vest on underneath and grabbed his twin forty-fives. Now, he was ready for rock. Since the well was only across the street from his crib, the young thug walked over there. When he swaggered in there, shit was jumping out of control. The whole Eastern Ave crew was up in there chilling and bouncing. Wheat Lox went straight to the bar and gave the bartender a hundred bucks for a fifth of Hennessy. As soon as he took the first couple of sips, he took his leather off and started hollering at an outlet of dimes. They were feeling him, of course, because it was his world. Lox was straight stunting right then. He had his two white-gold chains on with some iced-out doorknockers in his ears.

Charmaine was trying to get his number when he saw his man D.A. throw on his jacket. He ran up to the nigga quick, like "What's good?"

D.A. was drunk and said, "Everything is good now, my nigga. I was kind of cold."

Lox looked at the older cat and said, "Man, what's good with my jacket and the couple stacks you owe me?"

D.A. was a skinny Jim Jones-looking nigga. He always kept mad bitches. D.A. looked at the nigga and said, "I know you ain't trying to stunt in front of everybody. Matter of fact, good looking on the handout. We don't fuck with Bristol Street niggas on this side." And he turned his back on Lox.

Wheat Lox grabbed an empty beer bottle off the bar and smacked D.A. on the back of the head and went to work on the older nigga. He was hitting D.A. with right hooks and uppercuts, when he got smacked with two bottles. At first, Lox couldn't believe his own people were jumping him, but then he realized that Eastern Ave was made up of a bunch of niggas who hated everything and everybody. His man Pudge, whom he grew up with all his life, was now stomping him out like he was from another set for real.

Pac was also giving him a little footwork along with D.A. He couldn't reach for his guns because he had to protect his face with his hands. Lox was rendered unconscious in a matter of seconds.

$ $ $

P Double had been fucking Italia for weeks now. He made her a part of his stable and finally broke everything down to her. Italia soaked up everything. She was so fucked up over P that she thought Eddie Haul was just a figment of her imagination. P then went on and broke the plan down to her officially. At first, she was scared and timid, but with a quick fuck from P Double, she was ready for rock as usual. P left on that note and went to Jaynce's house to rock up some work. He really missed his ghetto princess, but until this war was over, he wasn't going near her. How could he explain that to her? He couldn't. That was why he had chosen to stay away from the beauty. P went down to the basement and grabbed six birds.

He cut his phone off and got in his zone at once. P threw in his Jay-Z tape and turned the stove on. It was time to make it snow.

$ $ $

Jaynce was a mess. For weeks, she couldn't sleep or eat right. Her life was full of shattered dreams and broken promises. How could Presley do this to her after she gave her heart to him? She was ready to make love to him for the first time when he walked out of her life a month and a half ago. Every single day, she called his grandmother's house, asking Mrs. Williams if she had seen her grandson. But every day she got the same reply—no. P hadn't even bothered to check on his own daughter. At first, she thought something had happened to him. But then she started noticing little things misplaced in her house, so she knew he had been there.

On a few occasions, she had noticed that her kitchen had a strong, funny odor to it. She always wound up cleaning with Pine Sol and making the smell go away. That day, she was at work, burned out and exhausted. Her boss saw the stress on her beautiful face and bags under her eyes, and he gave her a two-week vacation.

At first, Jaynce tried to say nothing was wrong and that she didn't need the break, but Mr. Bennett wasn't having it. So Jaynce wound up stopping at Dunkin' Donuts and ordering a large caramel-flavored coffee with two blueberry muffins. Whom was she fooling? She really did need this time off to get her life back in order. As she pulled the pink Range Rover in front of her house, she noticed that there was a rental Maxima from Enterprise in her driveway. She got out, crept onto the porch, unlocked the door, and entered the house quietly. Jaynce heard loud music coming from the kitchen. She kicked her shoes off, grabbed a candleholder, and walked slowly to the kitchen.

$ $ $

P Double was in the kitchen bouncing to his theme music, *The Streets Is Watching*. Because that was what the streets did at all times—watch. He was cooking his third bird over the stove. The caine melted down smoothly. It was time to hit it with the arm and hammer. P had a giant box of baking soda. He'd been cooking coke so long that he didn't even have to weigh the amount of soda to put in. He could just do it by eye. He was pouring the soda in slowly, watching the shit bubble when his music shut off and he heard a familiar voice flow through the airwaves.

"You dirty muthafucker, is this what you decided to use my house for? A cocaine-manufacturing plant."

As he turned around, most of the box of baking soda flew into the pot. P swore under his breath and said, "Baby, what are you doing here?"

"Muthafucker, I live here. Is this all you wanted me for? You walk out on me a month and a half ago, and now I come home to witness you manufacturing cocaine!"

"Baby, listen, I can explain everything. Just give me a minute."

"You got two minutes and two seconds to make a love connection Presley." P turned back to the stove and started whipping the caine, while explaining everything to Jaynce except for Italia.

Jaynce broke down and shed tears. "Presley, I love you. You're supposed to come to me with anything. I thought I was your earth?"

"Jaynce, you are a sweetheart, but I lost Mama over some bullshit like this, and I'll be damned if I lose you to some bullshit as well." P rocked up what looked like two thousand grams from all the baking soda that went into the pot.

As soon as he dumped the pot on some paper towels, Jaynce said, "I don't think I can take this shit. Being a drug dealer's wife might be a little too complicated for this old-school girl." And she turned to walk away.

P Double knew he couldn't afford to lose his queen in this chess match, and he ran up to her and spun her around with a kiss. At first, Jaynce didn't respond, but with a little more lighter fluid, P Double lit a flame that couldn't be put out. At once, he ripped her shirt open, while she in turn pulled his shirt over his head. For five long years, Jaynce hadn't experienced sexual bliss. P Double hiked her skirt up and ripped her panties off. Then he pulled his pants down and entered her roughly.

At first, he couldn't squeeze his head in until he rammed the rest of his

manhood in with a violent thrust. Jaynce cried out and raked his back. P
then lifted her up against the wall and pumped her slowly and dramatically.
Tears were rolling out of Jaynce's eyes a mile a minute, while moans escaped
her mouth. She wasn't crying because of pain. Jaynce was crying because
she hadn't experienced this kind of bliss it seemed like in an eternity. P
started pumping faster as Jaynce came harder and harder. Finally, he shot
a well one deep in her, and he let out a moan of his own.

They both slid to the floor of the kitchen with P on top. "I love you,
Jaynce."

"I love you too, Presley," she whispered out of breath, as he began
pumping away.

$ $ $

Lox hit up P that night with news of how his own people had jumped
him. P Double went and scooped up his young capo at once, and Lox
broke the whole ordeal down to his mentor. That night, they got dressed in
all black and went hunting only to come up empty-handed. Wheat Lox's
people already knew he was crazy, so they were probably held up in a motel
somewhere getting right.

Lox and P Double cut through the Wishing Well and waited to see if any
of the goons had showed up. While they were nursing a couple of drinks,
Lox's cousin scrambled through the door. Joe Joe was a five-seven, brown-
skinned money getter. He wasn't stacked up in the looks department, but he
wasn't an ugly cat either. Joe Driver fucked a lot of bitches because he was
a certified hustler, and he had a lot of game. As soon as he came to holla at
Lox and P, Wheat Lox pulled out one of his forty-fifths and rammed the
big pistol under the man's chin.

"Nigga, you're supposed to be my family, and you let these bitch-ass
niggas jump me." Lox was going crazy with tears running down his eyes.
"I should shatter your brains all up in this bitch!" he screamed.

Joe Driver saw the devil in his cousin's eyes and begged for his life real
quick. "Come on, Lox. We all fam. I didn't know what to do."

Lox smacked Joe Driver with the giant pistol twice. The whole bar was in an uproar as Joe Driver fell unconscious to the floor. The white bartender was on the phone, trying to call the police when Lox put a couple of well-placed rounds in the phone, exploding it. Bitches and niggas were ducking under the pool table, scared for their lives. If any of y'all see Dallas, Pudge, or Pac, tell them the Lox is coming." And both the men left the bar in a leisurely manner.

$ $ $

Shante got into the rhythm of being locked down after the first couple of months. She wasn't stressed out anymore. Her baby's father's lawyer told her not to sweat it. The trial was in June, and she would be home by July, in time to make it to the July Fourth celebration. Also, P Double's grandmother made sure she brought her daughter up every week. She made commissary every week also, thanks to his grandmother as well. Right then, Shante was the queen bitch in the joint after she fucked up Weenie. All the other chicks in the joint were waiting on her hand and foot. Shante was hand-washing her laundry and cooking her commissary for her. If she even raised her voice, bitches locked in. Weenie was still sending threatening messages, but Shante laughed it off. As far as she was concerned, Weenie was no more of a threat than a preschool toddler. Saturday morning came around, and Shante was headed to the programs building to get her hair done at the beauty shop / barbershop. Her daughter was coming up that day, and she had to look right. As soon as she got there, this light-skinned chick named Maggie gave her a note. She read it and her friend Detrick told her to meet him in the bathroom.

Detrick was a six foot hunk she had met in the joint. He was also awaiting trial on a shooting charge. Every week, he managed to dick Shante down in the bathroom for a good five minutes. Shit, if they thought they were gonna stop her from getting a nut in the joint. They were high and out of their minds. Her pussy got wet thinking about the last time Detrick fucked her. They almost got caught because of her moaning. He put his shirt in her mouth and gave her a five-minute pounding that was out of this world. As Shante stepped through the other side of the doors, Big Paula, a fat, 350-pound ball of blubber, was about to enter the bathroom. Shante told her fat ass to take a hike. Big Paula mumbled something under her breath as she let the young girl enter.

As soon as Shante walked into the dark bathroom, she was blindsided by a sock that was stuffed with batteries. Big Paula then entered the bathroom and cut the light on. She grabbed the younger woman from behind as Weenie continued to work her over and over with the loaded sock, while talking to her. "I told you this is my joint, bitch! Didn't I tell you I was gonna get your little ass? Huh, huh!"

Each time the sock full of batteries hit Shante, it made a sickening thud.

After a minute, Paula let the girl go, and she dropped to the floor. Weenie stripped her and shoved a banana into her pussy and another one in her ass. Then Weenie pulled her own pants down and urinated all over Shante's face. "Consider yourself fucked, bitch." Weenie laughed and strolled out of the bathroom.

$ $ $

Big Butch was happy to be out of the low. His little brother Pudge and his man D.A. came and snatched him up from the bing in a rental Expedition with an ounce of nose candy and three sluts in tow. D.A. was driving while some redbone shorty was sucking him off on the highway. Angel was sniffing coke off Pudge's dick while pudge was Scarfacing out of a hundred-dollar bill. Big Butch took a one on one out of the hundred-dollar bill, and his dick was rock hard. Michelle was a chocolate bunny of a chick who was stacked in all the right places. She wasn't the cutest chick, but her body made her the baddest bitch. She took a powerful blast and lifted up her skirt to show Big Butch she wasn't wearing panties. Big Butch sprinkled some coke on her bird and sniffed and licked it off. After the pussy was moist and numb, Butch got on top of her and pumped away a hundred miles an hour while Michelle was still sniffing coke. While Butch was pumping away, Pudge was telling him how they worked Lox over last night at the well and how he was fucking with them Bristol Street faggots. Butch managed to work up a sweat and grunted, "What is Presley doing out here?"

"Man, that's who Lox rocking with right now, D.A.?"

"Yeah," D.A. answered in a low moan as the girl was working him and sped up her pace.

"Butch, Butch, this is his caine we're sniffing right now," Pudge laughed.

Michelle was still powdering her nose when Butch finally came up in her. Butch snatched the bill out of her hand. "Greedy bitch," he said and snatched her by her hair and made the coke whore buff him off why he filled both his nostrils with fish scale.

"Damn," butch snorted, "that nigga got some good shit. We gotta get some more of this shit."

Pudge laughed again. "How, Butch? How? Your Boy D.A. already set it off, man."

"I'll figure something out. Believe that, little bro." And he took another powerful snort.

$ $ $

P Double made Italia go back home to Ed for a week. She tried to argue with him, but it was either that or have Ed think the bitch robbed him and have him come after her. P didn't want that because he had future plans for Italia. The bitch had some platinum pussy, and P was gonna put it on the market in the near future. Besides, she told him everything—Ed's daily routine, where his money and Caine was located, how often he copped, and how he transported his product. P went and got dressed in all black while he waited for his phone to ring. As soon as Italia called him, he was gonna pack up all Ed was worth in his range. She called him five minutes later and told him to go ahead. Most likely, Italia was sucking him off to hold him down.

P drove down to the south end and parked in front of a two-family house on Lawrence Street. All the lights were off, but P still took out the 93R Beretta and slapped a silencer on the muzzle. He approached the house with caution. P then shot up the locks on the door and pushed it open. As he started to walk up the stairs, a big-ass dog growled and leaped in the air. All P Double saw was a shadow and some white teeth leaping through the air at him. The young thug emptied the clip at the shadow and moved to the side. The dog landed at the end of the stairs with a crunch. P dropped in a fresh clip and cocked it back as he proceeded with caution. He got to the top of the stairs and stepped in a pile of dog shit. He swore under his breath and kept it moving. P walked into a bunch of empty rooms until he got to one where the door was closed and locked.

P put his ear to the door and didn't hear a sound. He then wheel-kicked the door and jumped back as it flew open. A big two 250-pound massive dog came at him. P shot it eight times and the beast still grabbed his arm. P pumped two more rounds into the beast, and it dropped. The young thug was running off some adrenaline. He didn't even feel the pain. P walked into the room and pulled out the little penlight he had in his pocket.

As soon as he flashed it, he said, "Wow." Ed had a bunch of money stacked up against the wall and a bunch of bricks on the other wall. P Double already came prepared with a box of trash bags on him. Packing up all this shit and bringing it to the Range was gonna take some time.

$ $ $

Ed was on the phone trying to get his dick sucked by this new bitch he met named Lacresha when Italia walked through the door. Ed hung up the phone on Lacresha quick when he saw his ghetto princess walk through the door. At first, he was happy that she had made a guest appearance back in his life, but just that quick, it receded and his anger arose. Who the fuck did this dame think she was leaving the great Eddie Haul for two and a half weeks? He ran up to her and slapped her silly twice.

"Bitch, where the fuck have you been?"

She started crying at once from the sting of the slaps.

"Bitch, you got two seconds to explain yourself, or it's gonna be a funeral around here, and it won't be mine."

Italia said she was at Angel's house, but he knew that wasn't true since he had fucked her ass a little while ago. Ed cuffed her again. This time, her knees buckled out from under her, and she was kneeling in front of him.

"Where the fuck do you get off lying to me, bitch?" he said with spit flying everywhere.

Italia knew Ed was a sick puppy so she said the first thing that came to mind. "But, daddy, I was until I called Dorchester and found out my mother was in the hospital. She got cancer, Eddie." And she grabbed his legs and started to cry. This whole new situation broke Ed down. He felt like a real piece of shit for doing what he had done to her. Ed bent down and lifted Italia's head up to meet his gaze. He apologized to her in every way. Then Ed sealed his apology with a kiss.

At first, Italia didn't respond, but then she saw her chance to keep Ed busy. She kissed Ed with passion, and then she unzipped his pants and popped his dick into her mouth. She milked him for a minute, and then she told him she had to go to the bathroom. Italia ran inside and cut the water on. Then she called her real man P Double and told the young don everything was under control and hung up. Italia then flushed the toilet and went back to sucking Ed's dick. She hated sucking this weak nigga's dick. He couldn't even fuck her for longer than two minutes without coming and deflating. The only time his dick stayed hard was when she was sucking it.

P Double was certified grade-A prime beef. He fucked like he was a pit bull. Italia tried to make him tap out every time only to find herself locked in a submission hold, fucked to death. Right then, she wasn't sucking Ed's dick. In her mind, she was sucking P Double's dick. Twice, he let out an animal cry, busting in her mouth, but she kept sucking like a vacuum cleaner that couldn't be unplugged.

Ed's phone rang, and he answered it with a low moan. His little man Marcus Early needed ten bricks right then. The only thing that was better than a dick suck was Ed's paper, so he pushed Italia off of him, pulled his pants up, and raced for the stash house.

$ $ $

P Double was sweating like crazy. This shit was a work out. He packed up twelve trash bags. He was on the last run to grab the other two, when his phone vibrated. Shit, it was Italia's number. She told him Ed was on his way down there. He told her, "Good looking," and blew a kiss into the phone. P Double ran up the stairs and opened the back door. When he grabbed the other two trash bags, he heard Ed saying, "What the fuck?" and knew Ed had found the dead pit bull downstairs. P quietly closed the back door behind him and descended the stairs as quietly as he could.

§ § §

Ed jumped into his GS 400 and quickly maneuvered over to the stash spot a couple of blocks over from his crib. Marcus Early always spent good money with Ed. He was one of the only cats from his block who spent money with him. The rest copped off Double or Moe, which was still P Double. Ed turned down Lawrence Street and saw a gray Range Rover that he'd never seen before on the street.

Ed jumped out and walked up to the stash spot. He knew something was wrong because the door was slightly open. Ed pulled out the big fifty-caliber Desert at once. He tried to open the door all the way, but there was something behind it not allowing him to open it all the way. He stuck the gun back there just in case there was somebody back there. But the only one back there was Tyson, his dead dog. He said, "Fuck," as he walked up the stairs. Then he thought about it. He knew he had to call for backup because there might be more than one nigga up in there. He called a couple of his crew while he walked upstairs. Ed started cutting on every light in the house only to find no one. When got to the back hallway, he saw his big Italian mastiff dead. He shed a tear for Brutus as he walked into the back room to find it empty.

Ed let out an animal cry in a note that Mariah Carey couldn't hit as he saw the room empty. Then he heard a car door slam, and he ran to the front of the house and out of the top porch, just in time to see the platinum Range Rover speed down the street.

§ § §

P Double left the back door open downstairs and ran as fast as he could with the two heavy bags. He didn't have time to pack them right, so he threw one of the bags on the floor in the front and the other bag on the seat. He slammed the door, started his truck, and sped down the street. P

Double hit the highway and drove straight to East Long Meadow to count up his jux money. When he pulled up in the three-car garage, he was happy his grandmother's Caddy wasn't in the port. He brought all twelve bags to the safe and counted up two hundred bricks of raw, uncut coke and $5.5 million. P laughed and said Ed wasn't doing too bad for himself.

$ $ $

Meanwhile, Ed was going crazy in the south end. All his hard-earned money was gone in the wind. He knew he shouldn't have had all his eggs in one basket any fucking way. There were only two people who knew where he kept everything, and that was his bitch and his dead captain. At once, he put the word out about the platinum Range Rover he saw speeding away. As soon as he went home, Italia was trying to suck his dick. Ed slapped the bitch three times and called her every name in the book as she cried and cried. "Nobody got time to be getting their dick sucked around here, you stupid bitch. That's all you wanna do is fuck and suck!" he shouted, and he kicked Italia until she passed out. Then he put the word around town about the platinum Range. An hour later, Marcus called him with some news he didn't wanna hear. Only one cat had a platinum Range Rover, and his name was P Double.

$ $ $

Lox was happy when P dropped him fifty birds and told him to do his thing. P even blessed Lox with his phone and told him to do him as well. The thug was happy that P trusted him with that much work, but he had other things on his mind, and that was bringing it to D.A. and his little cocaine cowboy crew. All them niggas were junkies. All sniffing coke was gonna do was turn them into future crackheads. Lox couldn't wait for that day so he could serve them like the rest of his feins. He threw on his vest and parked across the street from the wishing well in P Double's black Maxima rental waiting on his pray.

$ $ $

Shug and Greg Harris were on their way to the wishing well. Sal already told his brother Greg and his nephew Shug how they jumped their little cousin Lox in the well the other night. Shug was five ten with a stocky build. His baby face made him look like he was in his early teens, when in fact he was in his midtwenties. All his life, he lived on the Ave, and all his life he had to fight to survive on the Ave. That night, he just so happened to be throwing back a fifth of VSOP with his uncle Greg when Sal gave them the war report. Shug marched to tell on a mission.

As soon as Greg and Shug walked in, the air thickened with trouble. Shug ordered himself and Greg two Budweisers and took them down within a matter of minutes. The duo had been getting drunk all day long.

Shug said, "Man, I gotta piss."

Greg laughed and said, "Me too."

They both walked into the bathroom and found D.A., Butch, Pudge, and Stimey powdering their noses. Shug approached D.A. and said, "What's up with that bullshit between you and Lox, nigga?"

D.A. looked at the thug repulsed and said, "You need to stay out of grown folks' business and take your punk ass back to James Street."

The whole bathroom laughed except for Shug and Greg. D.A. lowered his nose in his bill, and Shug caught him with a two-piece that broke D.A.'s nose. Shug continued to swing wildly, and D.A. pulled out a switch blade and jigged him a couple of good times.

The others in the bathroom broke up the fight, and the men started arguing in the bar. Shug was running on so much adrenaline that he didn't even know D.A. had stabbed him at all. Shug took two steps toward D.A., and his eyes rolled into the back of his head. The thug collapsed on the floor. D.A. and his crew ran up out of the bar quickly.

Meanwhile, another fight broke out. Butter and Keith Eddington were beating the shit out of a nickel-and-dime hustler name Tyair because he had socked Butter with some brass knuckles earlier that night, knocking the older man out. Tyair was knocked out and damn near butt-ass naked before somebody stopped them from damn near beating the man to death. By the time the ambulance came, the whole Harris clan was at the wishing well thirsty for blood. Sal was screaming at Lox, saying it was his fault.

But a couple of cats said Lox had chased them niggas down the street and emptied both clips trying to kill them. The paramedics told Greg that Shug might not make it, and the crowd went nuts. That night was one to remember.

CHAPTER 17

WELCOME BACK

When P Double counted all the bread, he called Jaynce up and made her take a whole month off so they could do some serious traveling. He gave Lox and Raheem fifty bricks each, and he hit Moe with a hundred and told them he'd see them in a month's time. First, P and Jaynce took a trip to Miami. Then, they hit Jamaica, Tahiti, Africa, China, South America, and Mexico. Their last stop was Las Vegas to get married. They both decided that neither one of them were into the big wedding thing at all. From there, they flew to the city of love, Paris, to celebrate their honeymoon in the right way. P wondered what was going on in the streets of Springfield, Massachusetts. If he only knew.

$ $ $

Springtime was upon the city of Springfield. It was good, but it was also bad because with the warm weather came more drama and frustrations. Shug made it after being in critical condition for almost a month. The first day he got out of the hospital, they sent him to Ludlow to serve two years, mandatory, for possession with intent in a school zone. D.A. was locked up as well, serving his parole time upstate. He was happy that Shug didn't die, but he was still fucked, because he had six years to wrap his parole.

Eddie Haul was taking out his vengeance on any and everything moving. Somebody had to pay for what P Double did to him. Every day, he rode by and shot Moe's mother's house up. He even shot up the block until those niggas tried to wig him one day at J&J's. If it wasn't for his driving skills, he would've been another addition to the Oak Grove Cemetery. Ed thought everybody was scared of him, so he met Marcus Early at J&J's early morning to kick the shit. Ed was breaking down prices when he saw Little Lee, Kev, and Andy Cap jump out of a Honda and let off. Ed heard Marcus grit as he fell from a gunshot. Ed quickly hit reverse and backed up out of the package store parking lot. A car was coming from the other direction, so Ed hit the gas harder and backed up into the gas station's parking lot across the street. Andy Cap and Lee were still filling his GS with holes as Ed spun a doughnut and drove into oncoming traffic on State Street. He punched the GS down a side street and thought he got away until his whole back window shattered from a couple of well-placed rounds. Ed cursed himself for even being on the hill in the first place, and he pulled out into oncoming traffic. He barely made it across the street, and when he looked back, the white Honda was still on his ass, the occupants firing shots randomly. Ed knew his only chance to live was to make it to a busy intersection and lose them that way. He pushed the GS down Middlesex Street until he hit King Street.

Ed then drove down near Water Shop's Pond. There was a four-way intersection, and the side Ed was on was stopped at a red light. There were cars still coming down the other way, but Ed timed the shit just right and jumped into the oncoming traffic lane and spun a quick left, right in front of an oncoming car. As Ed hit the sharp left, he heard the Honda smack into the oncoming car that he had barely missed. He wiped the sweat off his brow and drove to Fred's sneaker store, where he called a cab and reported his whip stolen. He copped Italia a couple pairs of Timberland boots because he still felt sorry for the ass-kicking he gave her. Italia had been there through thick and thin with him. He didn't know why he treated the dame like she was a piece of shit. It was just hard trying to find another Mama, but he had to admit, Miss Italia was the next best thing by far. As soon as he got his financial situation back in order, he was gonna ask her for her hand in marriage.

$ $ $

Mike Tuitt stepped out of the federal courthouse and took in a breath of fresh air. They had had him locked down for six and a half months. Finally, Judge Ponser decided to give him bail. Luckily for Tuitt, he decided to flip his money in real estate in addition to coke, or he would've been a done deal. Tuitt still couldn't believe how he got snatched up. The Feds had been watching Rudy for a couple of months when he had gone to cop. Usually, when he went to the city, he would always rent a car or a Jeep. This time, he made the mistake of going in his own Acura Legend, and they traced his plates. Ever since they had been trying to make it all stick like glue. When they came for him, he had two hundred and fifty thousand dollars in a safe in the basement. Besides that, they got him on a wiretap ordering some food from Rudy. He always made sure not to talk on phones period. So all he had to do was beat a conspiracy charge, and he was off the hook. He hated the Feds with a passion. They even snatched up his girl Kadejia and charged her as well, trying to break her. But she was stronger than a rock and could not be broken. After a month of hard time, they decided to give her bail and watch her carefully, but Mike had schooled his first lady to the game if some shit like this were to happen. Tuitt had stash spots all over the city inside of a lot of his renter's cribs. So every time he went there, they couldn't tell if it was for a purpose or not. Since the Feds took him out of commission, he let his cousin Ed peddle off a lot of his work. He also had a million dollars stashed in his baby mother's house that she didn't even know about.

Mike hugged his first lady and asked her what was up with their status out there. Kadejia didn't wanna break the bad news to her man, but somebody had to. She told him how Ed had only given her $1.2 million from all the bricks he had left. But the real bad news was he got robbed for two hundred bricks and $5.5 million.

Tuitt thought he was about to pass out for a second. He had left Ed with a hundred keys strong, and the stupid fuck must have kept everything together. If it wasn't one thing, it was another. The Feds had him on some kind of federal bracelet watch. So he couldn't even go a hundred feet from his house without them coming for him. As soon as Mike walked into the crib, his girl stripped him and threw his dick in her mouth. He thought to himself, *It really feels good to be back.*

$ $ $

Mike wasn't the only one making a guest appearance back into society. Fatback hopped off the Peter Pan ready for rock. Nobody knew he was coming home that day except for him and the Department of Corrections. Fatback didn't even tell his best friend he was coming home. He always liked that element of surprise. Fatback got out with that glow. He looked like he belonged on the cover of *Flex* magazine. There wasn't an ounce of fat on the big dog. He just wrapped up three years and one day, and he made sure every last one of those days was accounted for. Back took a cab to the Forest Park apartment to see if he could surprise his road dawg.

When he got there, he heard Davina pumping in the airwaves. The first thing he said to himself was, "I know my man ain't went soft on me." He put his key in the lock and said, "What the fuck?" There was this badass bitch dancing in his living room in a thong. She looked at him like, "Who the fuck are you?"

Back looked her up and down and said, "Bitch, I live here. Where the fuck is P Double at?"

$ $ $

Italia was fed up with Eddie Haul's bullshit. He worked her over for trying to do what he always wanted done, and that was getting his dick sucked. She stayed there a month without hearing from P Double, but then she just got fed up, said, "Fuck it," and packed her shit. She at least left Ed a note saying why she couldn't fuck with him anymore. And she admitted that she had fallen in love with P Double. He couldn't get mad. At least she held him down slightly for a while. She could've been a mean bitch and told him he couldn't fuck at all. Italia was stressed. What she needed was a good old-fashioned dickin', and she needed it now. She called P Double's phone for the millionth time and got Wheatie again. This time, she managed to get Lox to open up the Forest Park apartment for her. Where the fuck was her man at when she needed him? Italia was hot and horny. She popped in baby, got back two, and pulled her vibrator out. Italia worked herself over for a good hour, and then she decided to listen to some music. She was making her ass clap to Davina when some short-cock diesel muthafucker walked in talking some gibberish. He said he was P Double's best friend.

For some strange reason, the thug just radiated power. She thought to herself he wasn't a half bad-looking dude. Of course, her P Double was that nigga, but Italia could tell Fatback had just come home from the bing, because his body was filled with jailhouse muscles all over. She started thinking to herself about seeing what it would be like fucking this gorilla-ass nigga. Why not? What P Double didn't know wouldn't hurt him.

$ $ $

Fatback smacked Italia on her ass to bring her up out of the daydream she was in.

"Where's P Double at, ma?"

She told him she didn't know and that he'd been MIA for about a month now. Back sized the sexy dame up and asked her what P Double's number was. Italia gave him the number and said, "Every time I call, Wheatie answers his phone."

Back started going crazy, talking about "If them Ave niggas kidnapped my man—" but Italia cut him off real quick and explained to him that Wheat Lox and P got money together.

Fatback called the phone at once and said, "Who this, Wheatie?"

"Yeah, this the Lox man. Who this?"

Fatback heard some old az in the background mixed with the sounds of the street, and he knew Lox was driving around. "Yo, where the fuck is this nigga P at, my nigga?"

Lox told him his man took his girl on vacation for a month. So Fatback already knew the chick in front of him was just another one of P's groupies. Maybe if he played his cards right, he might have a shot at the title with the beautiful damsel in front of him. Lox agreed to pick back up later on in the day and take him shopping. Fatback agreed and asked him if he knew Moe's number. Lox shot it at him, and he dialed the seven digits.

Moe answered on the second ring and thought he was talking to P Double until Fatback said, "Slow down, stranger." At once, Moe questioned who was on the other end of the line.

Back said, "A cat goes away for three years, and already he's forgotten."

Moe said, "Oh shit, daddy, when did you come home?"

Back told him, "A hour ago."

Moe was still on the phone when he told Back he was in front of the house and to come outside. Back walked outside and jumped in the red Expedition with the murder tint. As soon as he opened the door, a cloud of Branson engulfed him. Back gave Moe a hug that almost crushed the young cat and snatched the el from his hand. Fatback inhaled a strong toke of Branson and went into a coughing fit immediately.

"Damn, Moe, this is some strong shit," he said as his eyes began to water.

Moe drove off laughing, and he went around the corner and copped back thirty pairs of the latest boots and kicks with thirty hats to match. Then he stopped at the wreck shop and copped Back fifteen outfits, and they hit Scallachi's up for fifteen more. Back just threw on one of the outfits he got from Scallachi's and was ready for rock. Young Moe then gave him the whole breakdown of the field and all he had missed when he was gone. Moe then drove to Sixteen Acres to one of his cribs, and he threw Fatback the keys to his platinum M-5 BMW. Back jumped behind the wheel of the luxury sports car and found that Moe had laced all the numbers in the speedometer along with the gauges in diamonds. Moe gave Back thirty grand for his pocket and told the man to holla if he needed anything else from him at all.

Back gave the young don dap and promised not to be a stranger. He then took all the clothes out of the Expo and threw them in the back of the M-5. His next stop was Bristol Street. When he pulled up, Andy Cap,

Kev, and Jarell were all posted up at the building on the end of Bristol. He jumped out, and his people all thought they had seen a ghost by their facial expressions. Back was kicking it for twenty minutes when a black Blazer pulled up with the murder tint. The windows on the driver's side and rear rolled down. Somebody said, "Take this, you bitch-ass niggas." And two Techs started spitting instant death.

Back jumped through the open first-floor window and stayed low. Crazy-ass Jarell backed out a .357 and put a couple of holes in the rear door. Kev jumped over the porch and started busting his Taurus while Andy Cap ran into the hallway and picked up the shotgun. He let a round go from the cannon, and the cats in the Blazer knew he meant business when the buckshot laced the door up. They sped off quick as Jarell ran down the street still trying to pump rounds in the SUV. Back found himself in Catalina's sister's bedroom. Paula was a gorgeous redbone with mass appeal. At the time, she was surprised when a body came flying headfirst through her open window, but then she heard the shots and got low her damn self.

Fatback dusted himself off and said, "What the fuck was that about?"

Andy Cap looked at his man and said, "That was some of Ed's manitos that just swung through. It's like that every day out here on these streets. You better get you a Gat, because if you get caught slipping out here nowadays, you'll be taking a very long dirt nap," Cap finished.

Kev said, "Yeah, niggas are playing for keeps out here right now. You best believe ain't no half stepping."

Back said, "Damn, shit is crazy on the streets, huh? I'm ghost. I done seen too much action for one day already, daddy." They all gave their man dap and said peace.

Back opened the door to jump in the M-5, and Kev said, "Yo, Back!" Back said, "What's good?"

"Welcome back." And Kev laughed as his man started the M-5 up. Fatback stopped at Jim Dandy's and copped himself and Italia some chicken. He drove back to the Forest Park apartment and grabbed a bunch of bags out of the M-5. When he walked up to the third floor, he heard a lot of moaning. Back turned the lock slowly and put his bags on the floor. He heard bed springs creaking and a man and two women moaning in his bedroom.

Fatback opened the door slowly and saw Italia in his bed watching a porno flick. She was working herself over with a vibrator. Back's dick bulged out of his jeans at once. He stepped into the room and stepped out of his pants. Italia still had her eyes closed, moving the vibrator in and out of her pussy slowly. She didn't open her eyes until Fatback grabbed her hand and said, "Baby, I got something meaty for that snatch."

Italia grabbed his muscle and spit on it. Then she threw it in her mouth and power-sucked him. Back grabbed Italia by her hair and started fucking her face until he shot a mean load down her throat. Italia started gagging because when he shot his load, he rammed his dick into her mouth to make sure it went way down her throat. Fatback pulled his still stiff muscle out of the nympho's mouth and put her legs on his shoulders. He entered the already juicy snatch and jackhammered it like he was trying to drill new holes in the pussy.

Italia was screaming out of control for him to wait a minute, but Back was already in rhythm when he started chanting his song. "One, two, three, four, poke that pussy; she wants more. One, two, three, four, poke that pussy till it's sore. Needle dick, needle dick." Italia was trying to wiggle out of the young boy's embrace while screaming at the top of her lungs. Fatback took it as she was having a good time and long dicked her even more. Italia had tears in her eyes, screaming for help. What the fuck did she get herself into?

$ $ $

P Double and Jaynce reached Bradley airport early that morning. They went back to Jaynce's house, and P Double fucked her to sleep. He had to admit he was in serious love with this one. Jaynce was a bad bitch all the way around the board. Right then, he was on cloud nine, but he came back to earth quickly. It was time to holla at his first love, the streets.

First, he called up Raheem, and Heem brought his money to Westminster Street, a street over from Jaynce's crib. Then he told Moe and Lox to meet him at the Forest Park apartment with his paper. P Double sat outside the apartment in Jaynce's pink Range Rover until both men showed up.

Moe said, "Your boy is out."

P looked at him and said, "Who?"

"Fatback, boy," Moe spit.

P Double said, "Where the fuck he at?"

Moe looked around, saw his M-5 parked on the side of the building in the driveway, and said, "He must be upstairs because I let him use the M-5, and it's right there."

The trio rushed the stairs, and they all looked at each other and said, "What the fuck?" They heard a broad getting fucked to death inside the apartment.

P took the key from Lox and opened the door. They entered and started rolling because the chick was screaming, "Okay, stop please! Oh fuck, it hurts! Stop!" and she was crying.

P Double opened the door and saw his man jackhammering Italia. Back was still chanting "One, two, three, four, poke that pussy; she wants more. Needle dick, needle dick." Fatback was dripping in sweat as he was throwing every last ounce of dick into the bitch.

His back was bleeding like crazy from where Italia had been clawing him. Lox started laughing more and said, "Yeah, Back, fuck that whore. I'm next."

Two minutes later, Back nutted up in Italia and got up drenched in sweat. He wrapped a towel around himself and said, "What's good, my niggas?"

P gave him dap, and he said, "I'm going to wash my hands real quick."

Italia lay there crying. She couldn't move. Wheat Lox said, "Good, bitch, because I told you I was next." Lox had already put his dick in a condom when she was screaming, "Please, I can't take no more." But the young thug already mounted her and went to work. Italia was screaming for P to help her, when he looked at Moe and said, "Do you wanna go first because I'm gonna finish her," and they all fucked Italia until she passed out.

CHAPTER18

UNFINISHED BUSINESS

Eddie Haul hadn't slept in days. His eyes were blood red, but his heart had stopped beating a day before. He couldn't believe how the day had turned out. First, the little niggas from his original hood tried to kill him. Then he went home to find out his bitch had left him for P Double. The young punk kept winning in every way possible. Ed cried to himself because he had no one to blame but himself. He had created this monster they called P Double. Every time he tried to finish what he started, Young P was always ten steps ahead of him in every way. When he found the note left by Italia, he immediately went into a rage. First, he grabbed both his nines and whipped over to Angel's house on a solo mission.

Ed kicked the door wide open and found Angel's sister Candy sucking some little nigga's dick. He let kid have it, to let them know he wasn't in the mood to play games. Little Candy started screaming out of control. Ed slapped her with one of the nines.

"Shut the fuck up, you stupid bitch. Where the fuck is your slutty-ass sister, bitch?"

Candy started sobbing saying she didn't know where Angel had gone.

"One of her boyfriends came and snatched her this morning, and she didn't come home yet."

Ed tucked one of the nines in his waist and walked over to the phone.

He ripped the cord out of the wall and walked over to Candy. "Where the fuck is Italia at?" he asked, foaming at the mouth.

"I swear I haven't seen her, Ed," she pleaded.

Ed shook his head. "You're good for nothing," he said and smacked Candy with the burner, rendering her unconscious. Ed tied the young dame up and waited on her older sister. "Now, I'll wait for your stanking-ass sister."

$ $ $

Shante was a quick healer in many ways. All the so-called friends she met in the joint sided back with Weenie, except her cellmate Roxy. Roxy hated what Weenie and Big Paula did to her friend, and she vowed to help her road dawg seek revenge. At night sometimes, Shante cried into her pillow. She often prayed and asked God why the world was so cold. First and foremost, she found herself in jail for murdering her boyfriend in self-defense. Frankie had done nothing wrong; all he did was love her unconditionally. And what did she do? She went and broke his heart by sleeping with his friend and getting pregnant. She knew Presley was the devil in the flesh, but who wouldn't fall in love with him? He looked good, and his whole aura spoke money, power, and respect. Frankie had a little bit of paper, but next to P Double's, his money was childish. P Double's cake was quite grown. But then she found herself trying to mend a broken heart. The man she loved went and married some old-ass lady. While she was behind bars, some old hag had moved in on her man. Shante stopped sweating it though, because she had an ace in the hole as her trump card. They shared a daughter together, so she would always be in his life one way or another. Plus, she figured on making the old chick have an accident. She might just take a drastic spill or her brakes might just go out. Shante hadn't figured it out yet, but by the time they decided to let her out, she would have it all covered.

Shante and Roxy went to bed late one night with a plan to evacuate in the morning. That morning, they got up and ate breakfast with the rest of the crew. When breakfast was over, Weenie and her crew acted like everything was normal. When breakfast was over, Weenie and her crew walked by Shante and laughed on their way out of the chow hall. The girls' unit was located all the way at the top of C-tower, which was up about six flights of stairs. Big Paula had an elevator pass because she really couldn't walk up all those flights of stairs without having an asthma attack. But for two days now, the elevator had been out of order, so Big Paula had to walk up the six flights of stairs. It took her like twenty-five minutes to climb all those stairs because she had to rest in between. So Weenie and the rest of the crew usually left her behind so they could go crawl back in their beds. Shante walked past Paula on the fourth flight and waited for her on the fifth, while Roxy lagged behind. Big Paula walked up the fifth flight, tired and sweating. When she got to the top, Shante was bent over tying her shoe. All of a sudden, Shante sprang up with a sock stuffed full of Lisa soaps saying, "It's time to pay for your sins, fat girl."

Big Paula tried to scream for help, but she was out of breath, so it came out as a whisper. She started backing up as Shante came at her, twirling the sock. Big Paula backpedaled, but she stepped on something that wasn't a stair and fell backward, breaking both her arms and a leg. Roxy was ducked down on the stair when Shante came at her. That was why Big Paula tripped. Roxy pulled out a package of cupcakes and shoved them in the obese woman's mouth. She then pulled out a sock of her own, and both women went to work until Big Paula was damn near dead. Then Shante and Roxy both shit on her face and laughed.

Shante said, "You can't have your cake and eat it too, you fat bitch."

And both women laughed as they walked up the stairs.

$ $ $

Italia woke up sore as hell. P Double and his crew had been bouncing up and down on her for a couple of days now. She cried on her way to the bathroom because it hurt so much. It even hurt when she pissed most of the time. At least they hadn't sodomized her. Italia ran some bathwater and let herself soak in the tub. How the fuck did she manage to get herself into this situation? When she was younger, her mother always told her that good dick would get you caught up every time. Now she wished she would've taken heed.

Eddie Haul loved her, and she did him wrong. Italia knew she could never go back to Ed. He would kill her most definitely for this. So she had no choice but to stay where she was at. She had already made her bed; now she had to lie in it. Just when she tried to relax and dry off, Fatback came into the bathroom to take a leak. He flushed the toilet just as Italia was bending over to dry the bottom half of her legs. The next thing she knew Fatback had rammed his dick into her, and she thought, *Not again*, as the young boy gave her a serious pounding.

$ $ $

P Double bounced to the city in the six hundred. It was time to sit down with Tanto and have a serious talk. He made it to Long Island three and a half hours later. P Double rang the doorbell to the big house and waited. The door was opened a couple of seconds later by a beautiful brown-skinned lady dressed in a maid getup.

She said, "Yes, may I help you?" in broken English.

"Yes, I'm here to see Tanto."

The pretty woman asked his name and then pulled out a little walkie-talkie and spoke Spanish. P Double then heard a man speak back in rapid-fire Spanish. The maid said, "Si," into the walkie-talkie. Then she told P to follow her.

P took in the sights as they cut through a beautiful red-and-gray living room. The carpet was red while the seven-piece sectional sofa was red and gray. The living room also had red and gray wallpaper as well. Tanto also had a bunch of shelves stacked with leather-bound books. P Double also noticed Tanto had a big cherrywood piano on the side with two grandfather clocks next to a huge fireplace that looked like the shit came from the medieval era.

As they exited the living room, P looked up and saw three crystal chandeliers. The maid then led him down a long hallway that had a bunch of giant portraits on the walls. P could actually see his reflection in the marble waxed floors. She led him to two large doors. The maid pulled out the walkie-talkie and spoke in Spanish once again. A large security camera zoomed in on them. Then the doors opened outward to let them in. P was amazed at the sight of the big room. Inside was a big state-of-the-art pool table. He also had a Jacuzzi and a giant movie theater screen with three rows of seats. There were pictures of great Latinos all over the walls. P saw Carlos Santana and Tanto and Julio Iglesias and Tanto. Tanto even had a picture of him and Al Pacino from the *Scarface* era. But he had a giant pic of Pablo Escobar. The back of the room was lit up by two giant crystal chandeliers. Tanto was in the Jacuzzi watching P Double's favorite movie, *Scarface*. The whole room had surround sound.

Tony Montana said, "I told you I don't kill kids," after he blew Sosa's enforcer away. Tanto was puffing on a Cuban cigar when P Double and the maid approached. Tanto spit something in Spanish, and the maid walked over to a closet and came back with some shorts about P Double's size. P stripped, put the shorts on, and joined the old man in the Jacuzzi. Tanto then introduced Estel, his maid, the proper way. P kissed her hand, and she asked Tanto if he needed anything. The old man requested a Long Island iced tea and asked P Double what he needed. P requested a double shot of Hennessy. The maid walked over to a large bar in the corner and mixed the drinks. She came back, handed both men their drinks, and left. Tanto shut the doors with the remote control and asked P how he was doing. P answered, "Not as good as you, daddy, but I'm trying to get there."

The old man laughed and said, "All in due time."

P Double said, "I got seven million for you right now, but you gotta drop the prices. And I need it delivered."

Tanto laughed at the young don's request. "Young blood, do you know how hard it is to get this coco into America? The coast guard is on every ship moving. The DEA is at every airport terminal with dozens of dogs. They're even busting underground smuggling lines from Mexico to Texas. So you're lucky to be getting it for eighteen, young blood. I charge your boy Eddie twenty-two."

P looked at the old man and said, "First of all, me and Ed have been at war for years now, over a piece of pussy he never owned. Two, Ed is a pussy who can't even hold a chick, never mind, trying to run an operation. I bet he didn't even look you in the eye and try to even get a deal like this."

Tanto said, "So you got big balls, huh?"

"The biggest balls you ever seen in your life, papa." P laughed.

All of a sudden, Tanto's hand came from underwater, brandishing a chrome 454 Casual revolver. Tanto placed the gun under P's chin and said, "What if I end your life now and take your money, huh, big balls?"

P said, "Well, that will just be your loss, old man, but I doubt you'll kill me though."

"And why is that, young blood?" Tanto stayed nuzzling the big cannon further underneath the young don's chin.

"Because one, seven million dollars is only a smooth smack in the face for you. And I know you know that I will bring you way more than seven million dollars next time. And two, it's not God's plan to kill me off yet, or he would have been ended my reign, papa. Fuck around old man, and in two to three years, I'll be supplying you. And three, you won't kill me because you like my style. Now put that cannon back in the underground compartment you got it from, and let's get down to business here."

P moved the gun from up under his chin without any struggle at all from Tanto. The old man saw a lot of himself in the young boy, and for a split second, he had to admire the young man's poise. He could tell that the young boy had seen the world through his eyes. They were the same eyes the great Pablo Escobar possessed as well. He knew the young boy in front of him was way ahead of his time and would soon become a vintage don. Tanto laughed, put the gun back in his underwater chamber, and passed P Double a Cuban cigar out of the heated box he had near the hot tub. He then said, "P, I like you a lot because you remind me a lot of myself back in the days of old. But if you ever try to fuck me, in any kind of way, I'll kill you. Now I'm gonna bless you like you need to be blessed, but you have to grant me three wishes."

P Double said, "Speak, and they shall be granted."

"One, you must promise to stay loyal to this family and this family only."

P Double said, "Si.

Tanto said, "Two, you must agree to sell some work for me as well, at the price that I want charged."

P Double said, "Si," again.

"And finally, number three, sometimes I might need you to speak to a couple of people who forgot who made them, at any time."

P said, "Man, that's a small thing to a giant," and they shook hands.

Tanto said, "How does ten thousand a key sound to you?"

P Double said, "Man, that sounds like music to my ears."

And they toasted a long friendship.

P said, "Now, start this shit over; it's my favorite movie."

$ $ $

That night, Tanto gave P his own room in the big mansion. As soon as Estel showed P Double the bed, he was in love. Inside was a king-size canopy bed and wall-to-wall carpeting of the finest kind. To the left, P Double had a personal bar and a door that led to a deluxe bathroom with the tub and Jacuzzi in one. There was also a shower stall with an overgrown sink, with a giant mirror in front of it. The bathroom had marble floors and walls. Hanging over the tub was a large crystal chandelier of the finest vintage. Even the toilet was made out of marble. P Double picked up a remote control and wondered what it was for. The young thug hit the buttons, and the wall behind the Jacuzzi opened up, revealing a sixty-inch screen. "Now, that's what's up," the young don said to himself, hitting the off switch and walking out of the bathroom.

P walked back into the bedroom. On the right side of the large bedroom was a baby living room with cream leather couches and a recliner. P also had a large marble fireplace. There were two remotes on the table in front of the sofa. P hit the button of the largest one, and a large, sixty-inch TV appeared over the fireplace. He hit the on switch on the little remote, and it showed a TV camera shot of the front of his door. P looked again, and Malinda, Tanto's daughter, was standing in front of his door. He hit the open door switch on the remote, and the young princess entered. She had on a cream catsuit that hugged every curve of her beautiful young body.

Malinda was a beast in her own right. She swaggered up to the young don and slid her tongue into his mouth. Her lips and mouth tasted like cotton candy to P.

After exploring the young don's mouth, she pulled back and said, "Welcome to the family, papi."

P blushed and said, "Do you always greet people who get welcomed to the family like this?"

She laughed an energetic laugh and said, "No, only when they spark a keen interest in me; that's all." And she grabbed his manhood again and said, "Nice, nice. I think I'll have to try this out later on tonight."

P grabbed a handful of the Dominican princess's ass and tongued her down again. Then he slid his other hand between her legs to feel her camel toe, and this time, he was the one saying, "Nice, nice."

She turned around and walked away, saying, "I'll see you at dinner, papi. I gotta couple runs to make." And she turned around and blew a kiss at him. She left the smell of Camay soap and expensive perfume in the room.

P Double said, "Yeah, it's gonna be a long night," to himself.

$ $ $

Back in the field, Eddie Haul was sitting next to Candy's dead boyfriend. Angel and her boyfriend John Doe walked through the back door. Ed shot John Doe in the head immediately. Angel screamed, and Ed socked her, knocking her off her feet.

"Shut the fuck up! Now, I wanna know where the fuck Italia is, and I wanna know now," he said, foaming at the mouth.

Angel said, "Please, Eddie, calm down. What's wrong?" in a pleading voice.

"Bitch, I'll show you what's wrong." And he grabbed her by the back of her hair and cuffed her with the gun twice, splitting her eye and lip.

Angel spit two teeth out in between tears and said, "Please, Eddie, I haven't seen her."

Ed snatched her by her hair and dragged the lightweight freak over to the gas stove.

Angel was wondering how to save herself from this madman when he turned on the eye of her gas stove.

"Bitch, I'm gonna ask your slutty ass one more time, where the fuck is Italia?" Ed's eyes were glazed over, and he looked like he had aged ten years in a couple days.

Angel said, "I don't know."

"Bitch, you think this a game?" and he pushed her face over the hot gas flame on the stove. Burnt flesh filled the air in the kitchen along with burnt hair follicles. Angel let out a scream that sounded like death.

She stopped screaming and said, "I swear, Eddie, if I knew I would tell you."

"Wrong answer, bitch," and Ed placed her face back over the flame to cook.

$ $ $

P Double asked Tanto if he could use one of his cars to go cop some gear since Malinda had taken his six hundred to grab the money out of it. The old man said, "Take whatever car you like, but if you crash it, you buy it."

The butler led him outside to the thirty-car garage. P walked in and was blown back by the powerful machines that were in his presence. Tanto had old Porsches, up-to-date Porsches, Ferraris, Aston Martins, motorcycles, Jeeps, and two Lamborghinis. P Double snatched the keys to an eggshell-white Lamborghini Diablo. He jumped in it and fired up the powerful V-12 engine. P put it in first, and the shit chirped off like a rocket.

After a couple of blocks, P was handling the powerful car like it was just a regular Honda Accord or something. A little while later, P pulled up at Doctor Jay's and hopped out of the expensive toy. Chicken heads started clucking from every angle. After ten minutes in the store, P didn't see anything special to celebrate his newfound donhood. P jumped in the V-12 and hit the Versace store. He copped a twenty-five-thousand-dollar eggshell-white Versace suit with some matching loafers. P copped a red hanky and a red-and-white vest. P Double also bought some diamond cuff links. After a heavy day of driving, P Double pulled up at the mansion around six o'clock. Dinner was to be served at seven sharp.

The god took a hot shower and threw on some good-smelling lotion and baby powder for the big dinner. At exactly 6:58, P made a guest appearance in a big, lavish dining room. The dining room had a big mahogany table in the center of it. The table sat thirty people. On top of the table was the finest of crystal glasses and plates. The silverware was made out of solid gold. Tanto had two giant chandeliers that lit the whole entire room. After two minutes, Tanto, Malinda, and her brother came downstairs. They were sitting and drinking some champagne when a beautiful golden-skinned woman entered the room. She had emerald-green eyes and fire-red hair. She wore a white-and-blue gown that enhanced her eyes. She apologized in broken English for being late and took her seat on the side of her husband. Tanto sat at one end of the table while his son occupied the other end. Malinda sat across from him.

"Forgive me for being rude, P Double. This is my wife, Maria. And no, this is not my children's mother either."

P Double walked over, took Maria's delicate hand in his, and kissed it. He walked back to his seat and tasted her elegance on his lips. The gorgeous creature smelled and tasted like fresh strawberries. After a little bit of small talk, Estel brought in the main dishes. She had cooked smoked salmon in lemon sauce with baked seven-cheese ziti. There were also sides of corn and Dominican salad. Tanto said a short prayer before everyone dug into the food.

P Double took down a couple of spoonfuls and said, "Now, this is what's up right here. Tanto, you're my kind of man. Your taste is what white people would call superb."

After dinner, Tanto excused the family while he and his new protégé talked. "P Double, do you have any of this good money you spend invested in any businesses?"

The young boy shook his head no as he and Tanto walked in the garden outside.

"I suggest you step your game up a little bit more 'cause when the Feds come, baby boy, that's it. Seriously, son, I own part of a multimillion-dollar oil and asphalt company along with a couple restaurants, a couple of barbershops, and a nightclub. But that one little restaurant where you met me at got me all of this."

P Double said, "Thank you for the valuable advice. I will make sure I do the right thing at once, sir."

Tanto patted him on the shoulder and said, "Good, good. I can tell you're a smart boy. Now, one more thing: stay away from my wife, and me and you are me and you." The old man laughed after he said this, but P could tell that he meant exactly what he said.

Tanto said, "I'm going out for a while. Enjoy yourself."

$ $ $

P Double went to the room and turned the TV on. He had just made the most important deal of his life, but his mind was on other things. He wanted his own big playboy mansion in a secluded area. Right then, his cake was chump change to a nigga like Tanto, but to a lot of cats, he was that nigga. He was lucky in a way because a lot of hustlers stayed nickel-and-dime hustling until they ended up with a life bid. Other cats gotta lot of bread but went to jail broke because they didn't know how to stack that paper right. God gave him game, and P always vowed to do something with it. Faggot-ass Ed should have been rich. He could've done the same thing he'd done, but of course, the great Eddie Haul didn't have the balls to do it. P was lying back daydreaming about the big mansion he would one day own when his door opened, and Malinda swaggered in with a pink Victoria's Secret lace robe on. He was about to say something when she walked up to him and shut him up with a kiss. His dick sprang up immediately from the fruity flavor of her scent. Malinda cupped his sausage and said, "Done already." And she undid the white silk pants, so his member could breathe. Malinda grabbed his dick tightly like she was choking a chicken. She wrapped her beautiful lips around P's cobra and charmed his snake with the beautiful vocals of her mouth.

First, she looked him in his eyes while she sucked slowly and powerfully. Then she started power sucking him fast and hard. If she bobbed for apples in any race, P already knew the Dominican thoroughbred in front of him would win. As soon as he was about to explode in her mouth, she gripped his dick tighter, and then she spit it out and slapped his dick a couple of times saying, "Bad dicky, bad dicky. Malinda didn't say come yet." And the Dominican tart laughed. Malinda stood straight up, unlaced her robe, and let it melt off her onto the floor.

P said, "Damn," out loud because her body was dope.

Malinda had the crazy six pack and her size C titties were perfectly round and breathtaking. The bitch even had the nerve to have a pretty-ass pussy. Whoever said pussy ain't have no face lied because Malinda's cunt was gorgeous. It was shaved and meaty. She grabbed P's head and moved it to her snatch. P smelled her essence and went crazy over the peaches-and-cream flavor of her love box. Young P ate the bitch while she stood up. Malinda moaned, and for a minute, her knees buckled while P ate the forbidden fruit. After a minute, Malinda pushed P's head back roughly, and the young princess mounted him. Her pussy was tighter than her hand was as P felt every crevice of her Dominican walls. Malinda started going crazy as she was riding. She started saying all types of swear words in Dominican and throwing her head from side to side. P threw a couple of pumps from the bottom, and the bitch started drooling as she rode him on a mission. Malinda came, and her pussy gripped his dick tighter than a baby grabs an adult's finger. Her pussy erupted and soaked P as if she had peed on herself. That was when P launched his own atomic bomb in her. They both moaned and throbbed together. P then flipped her and got on top. He didn't care anymore if Tanto heard their cries of passion or not. He was gonna show this young bitch how a Springfield baller rocked.

P pumped away on the Dominican princess with intensity. Malinda was screaming and clawing as the don left his mark. P found himself quoting his best friend's song. "One, two, three, four poke that pussy till it's sore. Needle dick, needle dick." P shot off another one, but he pushed his dick all the way up in her stomach so much she was trying to inch away from the dick. They were halfway on the bed and halfway on the floor, sweating and huffing and puffing. P recovered first, and he walked over to the bar, poured himself a double shot of yak, and lit a Cuban cigar. Malinda crawled over to the bar on her hands and knees. She looked at the god with animal eyes and popped his dick into her mouth. All P thought was, *Damn, another Catalina.* "Round three, fight."

$ $ $

He woke up that morning feeling like a sticky bun. It took him awhile to focus, but it didn't take him long to notice that he was alone. P hopped into the shower to wash Malinda's juices off his person. He thought about the Dominican bombshell, and his dick started to salute him with the thoughts of her. Then he thought about it, fuck. He should've never mixed business with pleasure. He didn't think too kindly about what Malinda would do if she found out he was married. Pussy wasn't anything but trouble, but P loved trouble. That was why it always followed him. P dried off and threw on some jeans he had on the other day. He was applying lotion to the upper parts of his body when a soft knock came from the door. P checked the camera and saw that it was Estel outside. He buzzed her in, and she told him breakfast was waiting. She couldn't help looking at P's body, and he saw lust in her eyes.

"I guess the walls do have ears," he said to himself. P finished grinning and went downstairs. When he walked in, the only two people who were at the table were Migalito and Malinda. P Double greeted the pair and said, "Good morning."

Malinda yawned and said, "Is it ever?" And she smiled at P.

Migalito looked at his sister and shook his head. "My, my, my, are you falling in love with the help again, sis?" he said vulgarly.

P sipped the orange juice in front of him and said, "Listen, playboy, I got my own bread. I'm my own boss. Don't ever forget that."

Migalito laughed at the comment and said, "We own your nigger-ass, boy."

P got up ready to smack fire out of the Dominican prince, but Malinda jumped in between the two and grabbed P.

"Please, P Double, don't," she said.

"Yeah, please, P Double, don't be in a hurry to get your shit split, nigga boy," Migalito said in a tone mocking his sister.

P Double said, "It's always the spoiled silver-spoon-fed muthafuckas that always wanna get their teeth knocked out. Fuck you, Dominican pussy." And P tried to spit in the man's face.

Migalito was throwing a quick punch, when his father stepped into the room.

P quickly sidestepped the blow and was ready to answer back with one of his own when the old man said, "You two will not fight in my home. Migalito, get the fuck over here."

Tanto slapped the man and said, "You wanna fight? Go to the gym and throw the gloves on the right way."

"But, Father, this American pussy wouldn't dare fight me in a squared circle!" Migalito screamed.

P Double said, "For one, I'm half-Jamaican, rude boy, and two, my heart pumps no fear for no man, especially a flyweight-ass nigga like Flacco—I mean Migalito."

Migalito looked at P and said, "Follow me, bad boy." He walked ahead of P Double on the way to the gym.

Malinda grabbed the don's arm and said, "Please, P, don't. He's a Golden Glove boxer and kickboxer."

P laughed at the high-maintenance tart. "Well, I guess that makes me a platinum-fisted streetfighter then." And he removed the girl's hand from his arm.

They walked down some stairs and into another hallway. They walked all the way to the end and entered a mini gym. Inside was a regulation boxing ring, weights, punching bags, and a baby jogging track. Migalito striped down to his boxer shorts and started wrapping his hands. P followed the other man's lead, doing the same. Migalito pulled out some foot pads as well, and he tossed P a pair. P was almost ready when Migalito said, "I hope you fight as well as you fuck."

P said, "Fighting was my first love; slinging cock came after. Maybe I'll teach you how to do both one day after I beat the shit out of you."

Migalito stepped into the ring, and P stepped in after. They stood in the middle of the ring and tapped gloves. The two men backed away from each other and got in their respective fighting stances. The first thing P noticed was that Migalito was a southpaw. Each man took a couple of jabs at the other, trying to feel one another out. P noticed Migalito had fast hands and fast feet. P got tired of playing games, and he threw a jab that was followed by a powerful right and left cross. Migalito got up under the punches and countered a left hook to the body and a right cross to the head followed by a jaw-rattling upper cut that sent P backpedaling. P knew the man had speed; now he had to respect the man's power as well. Migalito took P's backpedal as a sign to go for the kill. P Double backpedaled all the way to the ropes.

As Migalito came at him, P bounced off the ropes and connected with a lightning-quick left hook and right cross. That shocked Migalito. The prince staggered back a couple of paces and shook the two heavy blows off. Migalito laughed it off, but now he also had to respect P Double's punching power as well. Both men were bouncing around the ring for a second, trying to figure out the other man's next move. P got tired of playing games and caught the prince with two swift jabs. When P tried to follow the jabs with a right hook, he made a fatal mistake because he put all his power behind it. Migalito ducked and caught P with an uppercut and a jump kick that made the don see stars. Migalito threw all types of combinations backing P into the corner. All the don could do was block and hope the prince would tire soon. P got tired of trying to fight the prince's way, so he got low, picked Migalito up, and earth-slammed the man. P got on top of Migalito and went to work.

First Migalito's nose broke, and then P split the man's eye all while talking to him. P got up and started football kicking the man. After four field-goal kicks, Tanto and Malinda jumped in the ring and broke the fight up. P apologized to Tanto, but Tanto shook his head and told P he was not in the wrong. He actually thanked him, because Migalito had been getting real cocky lately. Tanto called his driver, Vincent, and had him drop his son off at the emergency room. Then he turned around to P and asked him when he wanted the order.

P said, "Give me a couple of days to get straight back home, and I'll let you know what's good."

Tanto agreed and said, "To celebrate our new alliance, you can have the car of your choice in my garage."

P Double shook the older man's hand, and they all walked to the garage. On the way there, Tanto whispered, "I think Malinda has her eye on you."

P looked at the beauty, and sure enough, she was looking like Cupid had shot her in the ass with an arrow. When they stepped into the garage, P walked over to the Lamborghinis. He had already driven the Diablo, so he picked out the baby-blue Murcielago.

Tanto said, "You have marvelous taste. It's yours."

They shook hands, and P Double said, "I gotta get back home and make some arrangements for shipment."

Tanto said, "Just call me, and always remember, my home is your home," as he walked away.

Malinda couldn't wait for her old man to leave. She kissed P, grabbed his dick, and said, "Nice, nice."

P told her to make sure somebody drove his car home when the shipment came. Malinda agreed for another kiss. P hopped into the Murcielago and fishtailed the muscle car up out of there.

$ $ $

Meanwhile, the governor of Massachusetts was going haywire. "Somebody better explain why Springfield is ranked eighth as the most dangerous city to live in. Shit, Compton, California, is ranked seventh in the nation, so that means Springfield is getting out of control. I'm not taking the heat on this shit either," he said, pacing back and forth in his office. "Stewart, get me the mayor of Springfield, the chief of police, and the FBI. We're gonna put a stop to this madness right now."

"Yes, sir," the male security said as he went to work at once.

$ $ $

Eddie Haul started drinking like crazy. He had to kill Angel and her sister. Those bitches knew where his beloved Italia was but wanted to play games so he just took his anger out on them. After a couple of days of soaking his life in a bottle, he decided it was time to replace the bitch.

Fuck it. Razzels was the shit on Sunday night, and it was time to make a guest appearance. One thing he did know was if any of those Bristol Street cowards were there, it was a wrap for them. At one time in his life, he was MSP, but since they wanted to ride with P Double, that just made them his enemies more. Ed called up his crew and told them that night they were gonna get Mobb Deep and party hard. Then he called up his barber and told him to make a house call. He was about to get back in the swing of things.

$ $ $

Italia was a pro with a dick now. For days, they had been fucking her to death. Now, she was fucking them to death. Italia was bouncing up and down on Fatback's dick like she was a jackhammer. She hoped his balls hurt, as she rode harder and faster every time he moaned. She came for the third time and soaked his dick with her nectar. When she started to slow up, Fatback lifted her up off his dick. He then threw her nicely shaped legs on his shoulders ready to pound her, when she said, "Yeah, baby, pound that pussy like you always do."

Fatback ain't like that. She was used to getting fucked hard so he smiled and rammed his dick into her ass.

Italia said, "Uggh, wait, wrong spot, uggh, fuck, wait!" But that was all Back wanted to hear, and he started quoting his song, as he ripped her virgin asshole to shreds.

$ $ $

As P got off the highway, all he was thinking about was where he was gonna keep all that coke. When he got off on the Forest Park exit, he decided that they should just cop a couple of houses, maybe open up a real estate company where he would buy cheap houses and fix them up and sell them or rent them out. He pulled up at the building and was gonna explain the plan to his partner in crime. As soon as he entered the hallway, he just shook his head because he heard Italia screaming at the top of her lungs. When P walked in, Fatback had Italia's legs on his shoulders pounding her asshole. She looked at P for help, but all he did was put Back's T-shirt in her mouth so he could shut her the fuck up, and he said, "I got next."

$ $ $

Detective Tony Peogi was going crazy. He punched a hole in the wall and started foaming out of the mouth like a mad dog. "Larry, I told you to let me take that little fucker out, but no, everything had to be by the fucking book. Fuck the book! I'm killing the little bastard on sight."

Larry got tired of his partner's bullshit and said, "Why do you just got a hard-on for one guy? He can't be to blame for the whole city in chaos."

"Larry, are you blind or fucking stupid?" Larry stood up, grabbed his long-time partner by his shirt, and rammed his back into the wall. Peogi chopped at Larry's arms so he could loosen his grip, then he shoved him back and followed up with a hard shot to the jaw. Larry rolled with the punch and countered with two blows to the white cop's weak midsection, doubling him over. Then Acres caught him off guard with a stiff uppercut, dropping the man. Peogi lay on the floor mending his busted lip as Larry stood over him in a boxing stance. After a minute, Larry Acres snapped out of it and helped his partner up. They both brushed themselves off when Tony broke the silence.

"Look, us fighting ain't gonna change the fact that the crime rate and death rate skyrocketed as soon as Presley Williams stepped foot on the streets. Now you can act like you're blind, but I can see clearly for both of us."

Just when Acres was about to respond, there was a sharp knock on the door. Peogi opened it to see a six-foot-eight giant and another man who had to be at least six five.

"Sorry to interrupt, but I'm looking for Mr. Larry Acres," the shorter giant said.

"That's me, and may I ask who you are?" Larry Acres asked.

"Of course," the shorter man said. "I'm Agent Gamble, and that's Agent Claiborne. We're from the FBI, and we need all your files as far as gang members, unsolved murders, and the major drug pushers. Then we'll be on our way."

Peogi and Acres looked at each other and said, "Sure, right this way."

$ $ $

P Double got out of the shower and changed clothes. After he broke down the plan for Fatback, they both agreed that it was time to invest in something besides the drug trade anyway. They were kicking it about bigger things than real estate when P Double's phone buzzed. "What's good?"

He answered, "What up, my nigga? When are we gonna get up?" the voice on the other end said.

P knew he recognized the voice, but he couldn't place the face to it right then.

"Yo, who this?" he asked.

"Damn, you forgot my voice already, playboy? It's Jujito, baby."

P Double said, "Oh shit, when did you get out?"

"Today, as a matter of fact. We need to holla," Ju said.

"No doubt, my nigga. How about I scoop you tonight and we hit Razzels up?" P said.

"Sounds like a plan, baby. One," and they hung up.

P had to call the number back and ask Ju where he was staying. Once he got the info, he was ready for rock.

$ $ $

Razzels' parking lot looked like a car show. It was kind of early to go inside, so all the ballers were stunting hard out. Ed was chilling in his 420 CLK. He had to show niggas he was still the man regardless. Even though P Double had put a giant dent in his pockets, he wasn't gonna act like it at all. Ed's whole Puerto Rican crew was out there stunting in the flyest rides, chilling. All the chicks were riding their dicks until a baby-blue Lamborghini pulled in, followed by a couple of Expeditions, Range Rovers, and Escalades. Everybody wanted to know who was in the Lamborghini.

The doors went up, and P stepped out in a baby-blue Micheal Kors suit with the baby-blue loafers to match.

Eddie Haul grabbed his gun, and so did the rest of his crew as they ran up on the Bristol Street don. P didn't even see it coming as Ed ran up on him and slapped him with the forty cal. The rest of P's crew jumped out with guns as well, ready for war until Jujito hopped out of the Lamborghini.

"Alex, Juan, Felix, let me find out your rolling with this bitch-ass nigga," Ju said.

They all looked scared to death as Jujito, their real leader, stood in front of them. "Me and my brother Vito go to jail, and you start rolling with this weak-ass chump?" Jujito ran up on them and smacked the shit out of all three goons. The rest of the crew backed up. They had all heard about the legendary Jujito. He was the craziest Spanish cat of all time. Crossing him was gonna get your family laid in a ditch somewhere. All three of the goons got on their knees and begged for mercy. "Please, Jujito, we didn't know he was *familia*," meaning that P Double was family.

This drove Ed mad as he saw his crew on their knees, bowing down to some Spanish chump he didn't know. "Felix, get the fuck up now. What the fuck are you bowing down to this bitch nigga for?"

That was all Jujito was waiting for. Ed had the forty pointed at the ground when Ju moved with lightning-quick speed, grabbing the gun out of Ed's hand. Ju then caught Ed with a right cross that dropped him. Jujito threw the forty cal to P Double and screamed on Ed, "Get up, *puta*. We ain't done yet."

"Felix, Juan, shoot this faggot!" Ed ordered.

But Jujito already had their hearts in the palm of his hand.

"Fuck y'all bilingual bitches then. I got this shit all by myself."

Ed got up and rushed Ju, but Ju ran at him, got low, and power slammed Ed. As Ed hit the ground, all the wind was knocked out of him, and he lay there gasping for air. Ju got up and caught Ed in the face and stomach with a couple of well-placed kicks, all the while talking to Felix and the rest of the Puerto Rican cats who were rolling with Ed. "This is the pussy y'all chose to be your leader while Vito and I were gone. Get the fuck up, pussy-ass nigga. He can't even fight," Ju said, kicking him until Ed started spitting out blood and crying, "Okay, okay, okay."

Ju looked at P and said, "Why the fuck is this restarted-ass nigga fucking with you?" and he kicked Ed in the balls this time, making him howl like a bitch. P broke down the killing and kidnapping of Mama and told Ed how his own cousin had laid her to rest. Ed started screaming at P, calling him a liar, forgetting about the pain that Jujito had just inflicted on him. Ju looked at Ed and kicked him again, this time rendering him unconscious.

"Now, let's do what we came here to do—party," Ju said as he walked to the door of the club. Ju turned around and only saw P Double's crew. "Felix, Juan, and the rest of y'all, what the fuck are you waiting for?"

All the Latinos walked up to P Double and his team and the two crews gave each other dap. It was time to rock.

CHAPTER 19

WHEN YOU'RE UP, IT ALL FALLS DOWN

P made Jaynce buy two beautiful homes, one in Wilbraham and the other in Chicopee. All of them had to be in very discreet places where no one would watch them coming and going, and they had to be secluded so they wouldn't stand out. A couple of days later, he called Tanto and requested shipment along with his Benz. Malinda shocked him by coming through herself, driving his car. P Double gave her the protein she craved by fucking her to death and sending her on her way. He was sorry to find out that her brother had suffered from a broken nose, jaw, and eye socket, but again, Tanto said the boy needed that very valuable lesson. Tanto made it even easier for P by telling him to call ahead of time for the product, and it would get delivered to him. All he had to do was send the money back when the coco got there.

The summer was lovely. Jujito and his team were moving units like there was no tomorrow. Raheem was on smash mode also. Worthington Street was a gold mine in itself, along with the south end. Wheatie had the Ave on lock, and Rubin had Indian Orchard screaming. The only part of the field P didn't have was Bay Street, Robinson Gardens, and Rifle Street. Also, he didn't have Maynard, but that was a small thing to a giant like him.

Shit was moving like clockwork until Lox spazzed out on Maynard Street one day. That was when the streets got sour.

$ $ $

Lox was on Marlin's back porch, playing blackjack, giving it to the Maynard Street don. Bank was twenty-five thousand, and it was Marlin's bread. Marlin kept stopping the bank losing. Lox had the hot hand and was just laughing at Marlin every time he raked in his dough. Marlin ran into the house and came back out with twenty-five thousand. He threw the twenty-five on top of the other twenty-five and said, "Down," meaning run the twenty-five back.

Ol Dirty said, "Damn, this nigga lox got Baby Willie chasing."

J.G. bigged his man up, saying, "That's small change to a fucking giant, nigga."

Lox laughed like, "Yeah, listen to that bullshit if you want to. Pretty soon, Maynard Street is gonna be experiencing a drought if this keeps up." Lox shuffled the deck three times and then set it down. Marlin cut and lox dealt. Marlin had an ace showing, talking shit, while Lox only had a king of spades showing.

Marlin said, "Blackjack," and smacked up a queen of hearts to go along with the ace of diamonds. "Give me my shit back," he said, reaching for the fifty stacks.

As soon as he had his hands on the money, Lox smacked the king of spades and the ace of spades on his hands screaming, "This is the real blackjack, bitch."

Everybody on the porch said, "Oh shit."

Baby Willie couldn't believe the shit himself. Lox had a horseshoe in his ass. Lox started stuffing all Marlin's money in every pocket, laughing. "Yo, Ol Dirty!" he shouted.

"What's good, Lox?" he answered back.

"I got zero's for six and half's for three. Holla at a real nigga when you need some of that eggshell white." Lox laughed.

Marlin said, "Man, that chump is broke, trying to act like he got it. The shit I got on my neck cost more than he got in his stash." He laughed. "As a matter of fact, don't you work for Bristol Street niggas and you're supposed to be from the Ave? Now that's crazy." Marlin's whole crew started laughing at Lox. Then Lox hit Marlin with a two-piece that dropped the Maynard Street capo.

Lox was screaming, "Talk that shit now," while stomping the shit out of Marlin until J.G. hit Lox with the fifth of Hennessy he was sipping on. Ol Dirty then caught lox with a two-piece that staggered him. Lox jumped off the porch and ran to the front, but Mongo came from around the front of the house and caught Lox with a right cross that rendered him unconscious.

An hour later, Lox woke up in his boxer shorts in an abandoned backyard on Maynard Street. When he tried to move, his muscles hurt so bad he felt like he was an NFL football player after a big game. Lox felt his face, and he knew they did a number on him from all the blood that was on his hand. He got up and searched around the yard he was left helpless in. A few feet away, he spotted his pants. Lox groaned when got up to reach for his pants. He walked over and retrieved his Enyce jeans and was happy when he found his keys to his candy apple red CRX. At least they didn't snatch his car, but they did manage to strip him for all his jewelry and cash. Lox threw the Enyce jeans on and found his Air Force Ones a few feet away. After he jumped into those, he looked both ways, up and down Maynard Street, but the coast was clear. He jumped in the CRX and drove straight to his crib. It was time to call the wolves and hunt for food.

$ $ $

Lox called P Double and Fatback at once. Of course, Fatback was ready to go over to Maynard Street and let them clowns have it, but P Double had to scream on his man. "Nigga, listen, we gotta multimillion-dollar operation going on. We can't just go to war with these broke-ass niggas without a plan, daddy. You already know we're gonna handle our BI, but we gotta make them feel it on the low," P explained. But his whole team was a bunch of goonie goo goos, meaning that all that planning shit went over their heads, in one ear and out the other. Fatback, Wheat Lox, and Jujito wanted blood so bad they could taste it. So while P Double said, "Give me a day or two to get a plan in order," they agreed, but as soon as the don left, they packed up an arsenal and waited for it to get dark out.

$ $ $

Eddie Haul was stressed out. He couldn't believe how much of a snake Mike was. His own cousin had murdered his girl in cold blood and acted like it was nothing at all. The whole time he was chilling with the snake-ass nigga. He paid for his lawyer and even took care of Mike's girl when Mike got snatched up by the Feds. Eddie Haul had been drinking all day long when he staggered to his closet and grabbed two Glock 9s. He made sure they were fully loaded, and he threw on a deep-dish Champion hoodie. He jumped in his CLK. He wanted answers, and he wanted them now.

$ $ $

The Feds had been outside Mike Tuitt's house for months, trying to learn something new so they could put the street scum away for life. But so far, after having taps on his phones and all throughout the house, he was clean as a whistle. All he did was listen to loud-ass rap music all day long and fuck the shit out of his girl Kadejia all day long. Agent Callahan was in love with the pretty little Kadejia. He loved the way she screamed and moaned while she was getting fucked. He wondered if she would make the same erotic sounds if he was the captain of the ship. They were listening to Mike fuck the little dame to death when a 420 CLK pulled up, and a guy wearing a black hoodie shirt ran out and kicked Tuitt's door in. Callahan was about to get out, but his partner, Agent Brown, grabbed his arm and said, "Hold up a minute. Let's listen. This might be the break we've been waiting for."

$ $ $

Ed drove over to Mike's crib listening to Mackavelli. He had the juice right now, and he was gonna show Mike that he wasn't a man to be played with at all. The whole time he was in a trance chanting, "Run quick. See, Hail Mary. Come get me. What do we have here now? Do you wanna ride or die, ridddddaaa." Ed quoted Tupac. He pulled up in front of Mike's crib and didn't bother to shut his car off as he threw the CLK in park and jumped out. Ed ran up the stairs and kicked the door in with a strong kick.

Kadejia was on top of Mike, taking it to him when Ed came in unannounced and on a mission. She was coming all over Mike's dick when they both heard the loud crash.

Ed said, "Yeah, muthafucka, I caught you with your pants down, huh?"

Mike threw Kadejia off of him and stood up with a rock-hard boner. "What the fuck kind of drugs are you using that you dare kick in my door and pull a gun on me?"

Ed didn't see a simple way to say it, so he said, "What the fuck happened to Mama, Mike?"

"Nigga, you came over here and kicked my door in behind some bum-ass bitch that was fucking a little nigga. You should be glad. I did your bitch ass a favor," Mike said with malice all over his tongue.

Ed went crazy and let the whole clip empty at once. Mike couldn't believe what the fuck had just happened as he ran over and tried to keep Kadejia alive. Ed had emptied a whole clip into the exotic beauty.

Mike cried, "She didn't have nothing to do with shit."

"Yeah, and neither did Mama. Now you know how I feel!" Ed screamed with tears in his eyes before he emptied the other clip in Mike Tuitt.

Ed ran out of the crib with both guns in his hands. But he was surprised when he was met by two Feds outside.

"Drop the fucking guns now, muthafucker!" Agent Brown screamed. But Ed already knew he wasn't built to do life behind bars so he pointed both empty guns at the Feds and went out in a warrior's dance as they riddled his body full of holes.

$ $ $

Meanwhile, on the other side of town, the Feds were getting ready to make a buy from Baby Willie again. He had been serving them for two months. In total, they bought seven hundred grams of crack cocaine from him. They were waiting for him to come out with the three hundred grams they needed to make their quota. Then they were gonna come back and take everybody down in the house and see who would be the first one to give up and turn state's. They wanted the connect and also an informant. Baby Willie came out of the house and was about to run across the street and serve them when a black Honda pulled up and said, "Yo, Marlin, who's the bitch now?" And they gave him a twenty-one-gun salute before they drove off."

Agent Riggs and Agent Gentry were shocked at what had just happened. All they could do was call it in and give the plate number up and description of the vehicle. They called an ambulance and prayed that Marlin survived so they could catch whoever did this to him.

$ $ $

Jujito, Lox, and Fatback drove over to Oak Grove Ave and parked in the back of Lox Man Ron's nice old house. They hopped into an all-black MPV and drove over to Marion Street. J.G.'s sister lived there in the building on the corner in a second-floor apartment. They all put their ski masks on, ran up to the second floor, and kicked in the door. J.G.'s sister said, "What the fuck?" as Fatback folded her with the Desert Eagle he had in his hand. She folded like a broomstick as she leaked from a wound on her forehead. At the sound of all the commotion in the living room, J.G.'s sisters friend ran out of a back bedroom to see what all the noise was about. She saw three thugs standing over her friend, and she grabbed a butcher knife out of the kitchen.

Vanessa ran at Jujito full speed. The thug let her get close, and then he caught her with an overhand right that left the cutie snoring. They tied both women up and drove straight to Wilbraham. It was time to get paid and have some fun at the same time.

$ $ $

P Double was worried all night long. For some strange reason, Ju, Lox, and Back didn't answer their phones at all. He hit Raheem up and asked him if he knew where anyone of those crazy-ass niggas were. Heem said he hadn't seen or heard from any of those niggas and asked P if he had heard what happened to Baby Willie.

"What the fuck are you talking about, Heem?" P asked the Worthington Street general.

"Man, somebody shot that nigga up badly. And when I say bad, I mean he's in critical condition type bad. They say he might not make it. Then I know you heard about J.G.'s sister and best friend disappearing, right?"

P said, "Nah."

"Well, somebody snatched both of them, police claim. The streets are real sour right now, my nigga. Be safe out here," Heem said.

P said, "No doubt, daddy. You ain't got to worry about that." And P hung up on that note. Damn, he already knew they weren't gonna listen to him and would go do some stupid shit. That was the problem with messing with a bunch of livewires. They always wanted to do shit their way or no way at all. P just hoped his team was safe. He had his own problems, like going to court for his baby's mother in two days. He needed Shante on the streets to be a mother to his child, not doing life behind bars. P Double went home and jumped in Jaynce's arms. Damn, he hoped his team didn't get caught up.

$ $ $

Shante was on her knees in the staff bathroom sucking a correctional officer named Freeze off. She had been fucking him for the last month and a half now. He was the reason she had fifteen thousand dollars in her inmate account. After she sucked his dick for the first time, she had him wrapped around her pussy. Freeze started bringing in grams of dope and crack for Shante to get rich off of. It was all planned out lovely. Every time Shante went to work in prison industries, she would bring a banana and suck on it. Then, she would eat it in front of Freeze until he bit and said, "So you really can suck the hell out of a banana. What would you do with the real thing?"

She said, "First of all, it would have to be long and thick for me to wrap my lips around it."

Freeze then slipped her a note, and it had been on and popping since. That day, he was supposed to bring in some brass knuckles so she could do a job on Weenie before she went to trial. Shante cupped Freeze's balls as she sucked him to almost climax. Then she got up, bent over the sink, and said, "Pound this pussy like a steak, baby."

Freeze put Shante's shirt in her mouth and tenderized that pussy. They came together and kissed, all out of breath. He gave her the Ex Lax she had asked for and the brass knuckles.

"Baby, just use them and throw them in the trash can at the desk, and I'll handle the rest."

She got dressed and slid out undetected. Now it was time to put her plan together. After she and Roxy beat the shit out of Paula, they cornered Shauna and made the bitch do their dirty work and inform them of everything Weenie had planned. Now they gave her the Ex Lax and told her to put it in Weenie's favorite chow hall snack: chocolate pudding. At lunchtime, Shauna worked her magic. It was time to go back to work and wait for the Ex Lax to take effect. Fifteen minutes later, Weenie started farting like crazy and excused herself as she crept to the bathroom. She almost didn't have time to lace the toilet before shit started pouring out her rectum.

Next thing you know, the stall door was kicked in, and in front of her stood Shante with a pair of brass knuckles. "Bitch, get ready to meet your maker," Shante said right before she beat Weenie's face into hamburger meat. A half hour later, they found Weenie lying in a pile of her own shit, worked over.

$ $ $

J.G. didn't know what to do. He didn't know these niggas were that crazy. Of course, Lox and his team would come after him, but he never thought they would snatch his sister and her friend. Now that was crazy. They wanted a quarter million dollars to release his people. J.G. didn't have any choice but to pay in order to get his family back. J.G. packed up the bread and drove to Dugan Junior High School to drop the payment off.

When he got there, Lox pulled up in the MPV and said, "Where the fuck is the dough at? J.G. pulled out a Mac and said, "Release my family, or I'm just gonna air your ass out."

Lox laughed and opened the door to the empty back seats. "You stupid muthafucker, you think I'm gonna bring them along with me? Nah, shit don't work like that. First, you pay; then you get them back safely. That's the way things work nowadays, baby boy. Now put that toy gun down, gunsmoke, and cough up the bread."

J.G. saw that he had no wins, so he just threw the Mac-11 in his Infinity and handed over the money. Lox dumped the money on the front seat and threw the bag out the window. All that FBI tracking device shit wouldn't work. But he saw that everything was clean, and he called J.G. before he hopped in his whip. "Yo, don't you wanna know where I dropped them off at?"

"Yeah, where they at?" he asked on his way back to the MPV.

"They're in hell, the same place you're going." Lox let J.G. have it with the forty-four Desert Eagle he carried. Just to make sure J.G. met his maker, Lox hopped out and placed two rounds in his dome, splitting it like a watermelon. He grabbed the chain off of J.G.'s neck along with J.G.'s iced-out baking soda box pendant chain. "Bitch nigga, and I fucked the shit out of your sister to," Lox said to the corpse before he jumped in the MPV and drove off.

$ $ $

Shante was glowing when she saw her baby's father in court. Every time P Double made eye contact from the stand, he sent chills up her spine. Her trial had been a success so far because clearly it was self-defense. It didn't take a rocket scientist or a neurosurgeon to figure out their lives were in danger. That was why she had to do what she had to do. Since she had been in the joint, Shante had gained a good twenty-five pounds, but of course, it went to all the right places, like her ass, thighs, and breasts. Plus, she just had that jail glow to her that made her look yummy. Shante was five five and a 145 pounds of grade-A prime beef, and she wanted her number one spot back with her baby's father, P Double. He was the king of Springfield, and if she wasn't the queen, then she was damn sure the first lady. She knew he had gone off and married some old-ass bitch, but it was gonna be just like that commercial if she made it up out of this. Move over, bacon, because I got something meatier.

When Vinny finished cross-examination of her baby's father, he called her to the stand, and she poured her heart out. She made the judge and jury feel all the pain she felt and went through. The way Shante was breaking it down on the stand, you would think she was an award-winning actress the way she performed on that bitch. Finally, it was time for the jury to deliberate.

To Shante, this was the longest hour of her crazy life. The five-woman, seven-man jury finally came back with a not guilty verdict, and she jumped for joy. P's grandmother had brought her daughter, and they ran and embraced each other with hugs and kisses. She gave P a long-awaited hug that made her cream in her panties. Then the bullshit began.

This beautiful cocoa-complexioned model-looking chick stuck her hand out and introduced herself as Presley's wife. Shante grabbed her hand in a death grip, but Jaynce's handshake was firm as well. From the eye contact they made both women knew there was gonna be a battle for supremacy, but who would be the victor?

$ $ $

Baby Willie was a fighter. Somehow, he managed to survive fifteen slugs, four operations, and a weeklong coma. He awoke to his two beautiful sisters and his aunt crying over him. His body felt like he had been hit by a tank or a SCUD missile. Marlin tried to reach out to hug his sister, but he found out one of his arms was handcuffed to the bed. Brandy hugged her older brother and cried, telling him that J.G. and Ol Dirty both got murdered. She told him they also believed J.G.'s sister and friend were brutally murdered as well. J.G. had gotten shot at the back of Dugan Junior High School, but Ol Dirty had died at Roscoe's trying to defend his chain.

As the family shed tears together for the dearly departed, two men walked in in business suits, looking sharp. Marlin said, "What's good, Tango and Killa? Why the fuck are y'all wearing suits? I ain't dead, baby." Baby Willie laughed in pain.

Then Agent Riggs and Gentry showed Marlin their FBI credentials, and he wished he was dead. "You got two choices," Agent Riggs told him. "You can come work for the winning team, which is us, or you could play for the losing team, which is the streets, Marlin. Right now, this could be the last days your family sees you. We already know you got two sisters you look out for, but who's gonna look out for them if you're gone?"

Brandy, Tyra, and his aunt all started crying together. Marlin couldn't stand to see his kinfolks cry. His mother was taken from him at an early age, and he couldn't just leave his sisters out there to fend for themselves, so he told them everything he knew and made them believers.

$ $ $

Jaynce snatched P Double to the side and said, "I don't think your bitch is too fond of our relationship together."

P looked at his beautiful wife and said, "First of all, she's not my bitch. Second, she has no choice but to respect you. We're married Jaynce."

"Well, don't say I didn't warn you when shit hits the fan, baby boy. Just because I look like a good girl don't mean Jaynce can't get down for hers. I'll be damned if another bitch is gonna come in and lay her hat in my home, and that's for real," Jaynce said, rolling her eyes and getting real ghetto.

P Double smacked her on that beautiful ass of hers and said, "I only have eyes for you, Jaynce. You know that. Chill, I told you I got this. Now, let me take her shopping and to show her the apartment we got for her, and I'll be back in a flash."

Jaynce said, "Okay," and P tongued her down until somebody said, "Excuse me," and started clearing her throat really loudly. Shante said, "The freak show can start later. Right now, my daughter and I need someplace to rest our necks, Presley." All the while, she was looking at Jaynce with hate in her blood.

P spun around and said, "Let's go, Tay," as he walked ahead.

Shante looked at Jaynce and whispered, "You're one dead old bitch, ho. I'm back, and I'm gonna get my man back."

Jaynce whispered, "My heart is big, and my bite is even bigger. Looks can be very deceiving, so don't write a check your little ass can't cash, because it's sure to bounce, bitch."

Shante said, "Yeah, I got your bitch for you," and she grabbed her pussy like she had a pair of balls down there before she walked out and caught up to P.

Jaynce couldn't believe the nerve of that mannish bitch, but she knew one thing: the war was on.

$ $ $

The Feds raided Lox's mother's house with a warrant for his arrest in the attempted murder of Marlin and the death of J.G. They also charged him with kidnapping and the disappearance of J.G.'s sister and her friend. When they raided Lox's crib, they found a couple of guns and a brick of powder cocaine. They also found close to five hundred thousand dollars. They read Lox, his mother, and his stepfather their rights before they took them to Pearl Street.

When they pulled up in the garage, they took Lox upstairs to the interrogation room and tried to run the good cop, bad cop routine on him. Agent Riggs smacked the fuck out of him and said, "Where the fuck are the ladies at?"

Lox spit out blood and said, "Man, what ladies? I don't know what the fuck y'all pigs are talking about."

Riggs smacked the thug out of his chair this time and delivered two sharp blows to his midsection. The young thug coughed up blood and laughed. "Y'all might as well kill me because I'm not saying shit until Dan Bergan, my lawyer, gets here."

Riggs kicked him in the balls, making Lox roll over in a world of pain.

Agent Gentry grabbed Riggs and said, "That's enough. We're not getting anywhere using this method at all."

"Wheatie, where is P Double? We know you didn't mastermind this operation. We also know you're a worker, so tell us why he made you do it and tell where his stash spots are, and we'll let you and your family go home."

Lox sat there, thinking for a minute. The Feds thought he was contemplating turning state's, but Lox was really thinking about how he had gotten his man tied up in some bullshit he didn't have anything to do with at all. Once again, Lox asked to speak to his lawyer. This time, both Feds worked him over until he passed out.

$ $ $

P Double and Shante were arguing to the mall and from the mall. P must have told her he would kill her if she touched one hair on Jaynce's head at least thirty times. Jail had made Shante one crazy bitch, but she had better realize who the fuck that nigga was out there quick, fast, and in a hurry. One thing P had to admit was jail made Shante one badass bitch, and that was for real. She was thick in all the right places. Plus, the summer sun had turned her skin a golden tan color. Yeah, Shante was a badass bitch.

P Double was daydreaming about fucking the shit out of his baby mother when his cell phone rang. He answered it, and his lawyer let him have it. "Jesus Christ Presley, what the fuck have you gotten yourself into this time! Attempted murder, murder, kidnapping, and trafficking! To top it off, they're even throwing in tax evasion with all that."

P turned pale when he heard all of this. "Vinny, I swear to god, I don't know what the fuck this is all about. I didn't kidnap or murder no one for that matter."

"Well, they got you tied in with some guy named Ivory Downing, a.k.a. Wheat Lox. They raided his crib and found a kilo of powder along with close to a half million dollars in cash. From what I hear, the Feds have some kind of CRI that's saying you two are crime partners. The Feds are looking for you with an arrest warrant as we speak."

P didn't know what the fuck to say. He had told those crazy muthafuckers to plan some shit out first. Now his ass found himself cooking slowly over the fire. All he could say was, "Vinny, I'm innocent. You gotta help me, please, and money is no problem either."

Vinny said, "I might not be able to get you out of this one here. Let me see what they got, and I'll get back to you."

P said, "Thanks," and hung up. He looked at Shante and said, "Baby, do you have your ID on you?"

"Of course, I do, P. Why?"

"Get on the highway, and don't ask no more questions."

They drove all the way to Hartford and left the Range Rover parked at the bus station. P Double and Shante took a cab to Bridgeport, Connecticut, and she rented a room at a Motel 6. P was N.O.R.E.

CHAPTER 20

NOW I'M ON THE RUN EATING

The Feds kicked in Jaynce's crib, looking for her husband, only to come up short. They also raided the house in East Long Meadow, coming up short. Jaynce was interrogated thoroughly and let go. So far, they had no leads on Springfield's most wanted, but they were determined to get him at all costs whatsoever. The Feds ran his face in newspapers and the news in Massachusetts, Vermont, New Hampshire, Maine, Connecticut, New York, and New Jersey. They labeled him as armed and dangerous. Fatback saw his man's face all over everything, and a chill ran up his spine. His man needed him at all costs, and he was gonna be there for him. The temperature was rising. Back had to run things for a while, which he had no problem doing at all. Luckily for him, his name wasn't mentioned in the four-alarm blaze that Lox started. He swore to himself, "Fuck, them Ave niggas are the hottest niggas on the planet. Now, Lox got my man jammed up."

Fatback moved all the work in about a month and a half. He didn't know what that nigga Moe was doing, but he was moving bricks like they were twenties of crack. Back copped a big excursion with the crazy stash spot to put all the money in. He met P Double in Bridgeport, and they drove all the way to Long Island safely.

$ $ $

P Double hopped out of the Excursion dressed like a woman. Fatback said, "Damn, P, you a little cute bitch." And he squeezed P's ass and laughed. P punched his man in the chest and told him to cut the bullshit.

Tanto saw P dressed up like a chick, and he couldn't stop laughing. P took the curly wig off and threw it at him. "Both of y'all think this shit funny, huh? Get your laughs now, muthafuckers."

Tanto told his new son to calm down and to explain everything in detail to him at once. P broke down how the Feds had a hard-on for him because of his best friend and two members of his team. Then he introduced Fatback as his best friend and explained how he was gonna run things up north for a while for him while P went to North Carolina and tried to become the king of the South. Tanto shook Fatback's hand and said, "Any friend of my son's is a friend of mine."

Fatback said, "That's what's up, daddy. I got your bread outside in the truck. When the food gets dropped off, I'll send our money back with your people."

Tanto said, "I like Mr. Back already. I see you're a take-charge kind of guy."

"That I am, Tanto. By the way, pack a hundred pounds of food in the truck so P can get moving down south and do his thing."

P said, "They got your boy N.O.R.E., Tanto."

Tanto laughed and said, "What the fuck is that?"

"Now. I'm. On. The. Run. Eating," P explained.

"Jesus Christ, where do you boys come up with this shit!" Tanto laughed. He then picked up his walkie-talkie and called Malinda. She said she'd be down in five minutes, and that was that.

For five minutes, the three men were shooting the shit until Malinda made a grand entrance, looking ravishing as ever. She ran over and hugged P Double. Then she said, "What the fuck do you got on?"

Then he broke shit down to her, and she laughed and said he made a cute chick.

P said, "By the way, this is my road dawg, Fatback. He's gonna handle things up north for me while I'm down south."

Malinda shook Fatback's hand and asked her father what he wanted.

Tanto told her to take the truck outside, empty it, and load it. Malinda pouted like a spoiled brat when Fatback handed her the keys and told her about the stash spot. An hour later, the beautiful princess was back with the order. P Double walked upstairs with Malinda as Fatback and Tanto started talking about past books they had read. As soon as they stepped into her room, they were all over each other. She lifted up the dress P had on and stroked his dick through his boxers. P took the dress all the way off while Malinda came out of her tight-fitting jeans. He didn't even wait for her to take her thong off. P Double just pushed her on the bed, pushed her thong to the side, and entered her roughly. She cried out in both pain and pleasure as her eager cunt soaked his dick in a matter of seconds. He had to admit he was in love with this young chick. The sex was on point at all times. Malinda wrapped her legs around P's waist and flipped him so she could ride the dick and pleasure him.

"Who's dick is this?" she screamed as she bounced up and down faster and faster until they both jerked releasing fluids in and on each other. Malinda whispered she loved him, and P admitted he loved her too. Then he asked her to go down south with him, and sure enough, she said, "When are we leaving?"

"How about right now?"

They got dressed, and she told her father that she was gonna drive him down south. Tanto didn't want to agree at first, but after she buttered him up, everything was a go.

$ $ $

Six months later …

P Double was living it up to the extreme. Even he couldn't believe how well he had adapted to the dirty South. P and Malinda made the trip down to Kinston, North Carolina, safely. His grandmother almost ruined things for him by asking him if this was the woman that he had devoted his heart to and married. Luckily, Malinda thought the old woman was talking about her when he said yes. From there, P made his grandmother cop him two trailers right next to each other, one to warehouse the coke and one to live in. P Double then got up with his cousin who was a small-time hustler and told him he had it for twenty a gram all day long. Within a month and a half, P Double was that nigga. He had cats coming from Tennessee, Atlanta, South Carolina, DC, and both Virginias with the price he put out there. Now six months later, Malinda was having a baby, and he was building a house from the ground up in Maxton, North Carolina. Malinda was seven and a half months pregnant, and Tanto was pissed at first, but gradually, he let them be as long as his princess was happy. He vowed that if P Double did anything to hurt his little girl, he might as well count his days. Tanto would never forgive him for stealing his daughter away from him, but he knew a father's love was no match for a good dickin', so he left it alone. Plus, P Double and Fatback were two money-getting muthafuckas. They made him a thousand times richer than he was. P Double had his money invested in all types of shit. His grandmother's name and Malinda's name were on everything. He missed his wife and baby mother, but all he could do was send them money every month to show his love.

Jaynce must have shed a thousand tears, but he promised himself and her that one day he would make it all up to her. P Double kissed Malinda and told her he'd be back in a few days. He had business to handle and money to make. She never questioned his comings and goings like the average chick did. That was why he loved her. Right then, they lived in a penthouse in downtown Charlotte until the house was ready. P jumped in his cranberry GS 400 and whipped to the new strip club he had just copped. It used to be called The Jaw Drop, but he renamed it Thong Island. P had rappers and celebrities from across the globe checking the action. He believed in housing nothing but the baddest bitches in the world. Thong Island was much more than a strip club. P Double made it into a regular club, comedy club, and bar and grill all in one. Shit, if things went right, he was gonna turn Thong Island into a franchise. P Double had a whole new identity down there. To the southerners, P Double meant Preston Wilson. Only a few people knew his real name, and they were immediate family.

He pulled up, parked in his usual spot, and greeted his bouncers. P walked in and told a beautiful waitress named Candy Apples to bring him a fifth of Hennessy in his office. Two minutes later, the beautiful redbone walked in and brought the don his order. "Is there anything else you want, boss?" she asked.

P Double just stood up and unbuckled his Rocawear jeans. Candy Apples dropped to her knees as P sat back down behind his desk. Her head game was second to none. P lit a Cuban cigar and tipped the bottle of yak to his lips as Candy Apples went to work. Just when he was starting to relax and reap the benefits of being P Double, there was a sharp knock at the door. P looked at the camera and saw that it was his man Jack Tripper, standing outside the door. Jack was a straight money-getting nigga who helped P run the club. Jack was six five and 250 pounds of solid beef. He had a baby face and always smiled, but if you took his kindness for weakness, you were a dead man. P Double knew Jack was a perfect candidate to help him manage the club, so he gave him the job. Another reason was because Jack was his cousin's best friend, and he came highly recommended.

P buzzed him in, and as usual, he was happy to see his man.

"What's good, blood?" Jack said as he reached out to give the don dap. "Damn, I see I caught you at a bad time." Candy was slurping and making moaning noises like P was fucking her.

P laughed, "Yeah, give me a minute. I'll holla at you in a moment."

As soon as Jack walked out, P opened the desk drawer and pulled out a Magnum. Candy Apples opened the condom and put it in her mouth. P was amazed as he watched her slide the condom on with her mouth. She rolled the rest of the Magnum down with her hands and stepped out of her thong. P picked her up and placed her on the desk. Candy guided his manhood into her juicy snatch. P fucked her slowly, making her feel every inch of his dick. Candy creamed on his pole from the first couple of strokes and moaned, "Daddy, I've been a very bad girl. Please punish this pussy."

P grabbed both of her legs and went to work, pounding hard and fast. All you could hear was moans of pleasure and meat smacking together.

"Oh, yes, daddy, ughh fuck me!" Candy Apples screamed as P pounded the pussy harder.

The deeper his dick went, the juicier her pussy got. After fifteen minutes of raw poundage, P came in the beautiful nympho. They came together, lost in each other's eyes for a moment. He left his throbbing muscle in her for a minute, and then he pulled out slowly, making Candy cream even more. When he was all the way out of her, she took the condom off and drank the come like she was a semen vampire. Then she sucked his dick with a pop to get the rest of the kids out. Candy Apples giggled when she was done and said, "Now, that was yummy," like she had had the best snack on earth. P smacked her on her well-defined ass and told her to get back to work. She threw on her thong and acted like it was a regular day in the neighborhood. P hopped into the shower he had in the office and changed his clothes. It was time to greet his customers and talk business with his boy Jack Tripper.

P walked out into a jampacked club. Chicks were dancing on three stages to "All I wanna do is zooma zoom zoom and a boom boom. Just shake your rump." And all his best rump shakers were on stage shaking it. P found his man at the bar nursing a couple of drinks and said, "What's good, my nigga?"

"Shit nothing much. I see you're still trying out the help, to see if it's top of the line." Jack laughed.

P said, "You already know I gotta make sure we got the best product in this bitch."

"Well, wait until you see this new bitch I found. Man, she's gotta be the baddest bitch in the world. I mean this bitch is a steak, rib tip, shrimp, lobster dinner, all in one,"

P said, "Jack, I had a lot of bad bitches in my life, but you make this bitch sound like she is it."

"Man this bitch five seven, a hundred and sixty pounds of prime beef, and get this, she ain't got no stomach. As a matter of fact, the bitch got the nerve to have a six-pack. I asked her for her dimensions, and she said she's a thirty-four/twenty-seven/forty-five. And she's a chocolate beauty," Jack expressed with a wild glare in his eyes.

"Did you try out the merchandise, baby boy?" P asked.

"Man, I threw all types of game at this chocolate bunny, but she let me know real quick and easy that it wasn't that type of party at all. I did audition her, and, man, I'll just let you see for yourself."

P said, "That's what's up, but what's good with the food?"

"We only got fifty pounds of food left; then we're done. All the money is in the usual spot."

"Yeah, I guess it's about that time again," P hollered when all the lights went off.

Jack had hired Bill Belamey for the night to announce the acts. "Coming to center stage is the baddest bitch on the continent. Her measurements are thirty-four, twenty-seven, and forty-five, and she's definitely a chocolate bunny worth tasting. She's so sweet her mama named her Sweetness. For the ladies on stage two, here to perform his new hit single live, called 'Back that Ass Up,' is Juvenile and the Cash Money Click."

The lights came on, and Sweetness came out dressed as a sexy nurse.

P said, "Damn, that bitch look mad familiar." He tried to go through his mental Rolodex but kept coming up blank. Sweetness had the whole stage covered in hard-earned cash. Fuck dollar bills. Cats were throwing fifties and hundreds up there with their phone numbers on them, hoping that Sweetness would give them a shot at the title.

Jack tapped P like "Watch the grand finale."

Sweetness had to have the biggest ass in the world. The music went off, and you could hear Lil Wayne's voice a cappella. "Cmb, drop, drop it like it's hot now."

And Sweetness did the splits, bounced her beautiful ass on the floor, and rose up. Then nothing in the world could've prepared anybody in the club for this. Lil Wayne said, "Now, wobbly, wobbly, wobbly, drop, drop it like it's hot." And Sweetness clapped her ass cheeks together so hard niggas thought somebody was shooting in the club, so everybody started ducking until they saw that it was Sweetness. That was when the money really flew on stage. The whole club gave Sweetness a standing ovation. There was so much money on stage Sweetness came back with a big vacuum cleaner and sucked up all the bills, and then she made her ass clap again leaving the stage. "Bang, bang." And niggas ducked again.

Everyone clapped when she left the stage again, even the ladies. Sweetness had Thong Island in an uproar. All P Double was thinking about was where he knew that beautiful face from. But he couldn't because any man would've remembered an ass that big for real.

"Yo, Jack, I gotta have that bitch, my nigga," P expressed with lust written eyes.

Jack looked at his boy and said, "Man, everybody wanna cut that shawty there. But the attitude she gave yesterday proved she was nothing to fuck with!"

"Just bring that bitch to my office and let me holla," P said.

"Boss, man, remember I told ya!" Jack shouted as he walked off to go to the dressing rooms.

Ten minutes went by before there was a sharp knock on the door. P checked himself in the full-length mirror behind him of course, and he liked what he saw. He buzzed the door for Miss Sweetness to enter. Sweetness looked at P and threw a scornful look at him.

"So you own your own club now, you no good lying son of a bitch," Sweetness said, shedding tears at once.

P looked at the beauty and still didn't recognize her. All he could say was, "Excuse me?"

"Oh, and now your dumb ass can't even remember your ex-girlfriend, Presley. What happened to two weeks? Matter of fact, I'm out of this bitch. Fuck you, bitch-ass nigga."

As soon as she grabbed the door handle, P remembered that sweet, beautiful face. It was Akasha, his chocolate princess. "Akasha, wait a ..."

She turned around and said, "I waited six long years to tell you this. Fuck you, Presley Williams, and stay the fuck away from me." And she slammed his door hard on her way out.

P couldn't really say shit. He was in the wrong for breaking her heart so long ago, but somehow, some way, he was gonna get her back, and that was his word.

CHAPTER 21

A PLAYER NAMED FROSTY

Double hired a private investigator to tell him everything about Akasha, a.k.a. Sweetness. Ever since she found out he owned the club, she never bothered to come back to work. For days, all P could do was reminisce about the love they shared together so long ago, and he wanted that back. So he hired a private investigator in North Carolina, a dude named Max Hammersmith, who came highly recommended. Max sat down and handed P Double the report he wrote along with a couple of pictures of some chocolate Mac-looking nigga who was mad icey. Sweetness dropped out of college when P left and suffered through different stages of depression until a year later when she met this New York nigga named Derrick Jackson, a.k.a. Frosty. According to the report, they called him Frosty because he had a cold heart that was made of pure ice, and he had no problem putting muthafuckers in a freezer or a morgue. Plus, he wore so much ice you thought it was hailing outside when you saw him.

Frosty was six one and weighed a 185 pounds. He was born and raised in Harlem World, USA. Derrick ran with Mase, Stephon Marbury, and Killa Camron back then. Word was he was the top point guard in the nation at the time. Duke wanted him, along with North Carolina, UCLA, and Kansas, but one day, on his way home from school, some Queens Bridge niggas approached him about a one-on-one game with a member of their crew. Derrick was one of those who never turned down a challenge, so he played kid named Dribble from Queens Bridge. Dribble seemed nice with the rock. Then Derrick discovered that he wasn't so nice when you made him drive to the left. Derrick wound up stripping him five times and beat him eleven to six. Dribble didn't take losing nicely, and he shot young Derrick in both his hands and his feet. Last but not least, they shot him in his knee. They had to operate on him four times to get his knee straight. After that, Derrick Jackson wasn't considered a basketball prodigy anymore. He was a liability no one wanted. His man Marbury became the top point guard out of New York and went to Georgia Tech. Derrick became known as Frosty. He started slangin' dope a hundred miles an hour.

One day, he found out where Dribble lived, and he shot him, his mother, Dribble's girl, and his one-year-old daughter. Police arrested him because some lady said she saw him come out of the apartment. Derrick was the top prospect in New York, so of course his name was always on the news for basketball until he got shot up, so he was a face that everyone knew. Derrick went to Rikers Island for a year, where he earned mad respect in the Five Percent Nation.

Trial time came around, and the state of New York had to dismiss the case against Derrick Jackson because the prosecution's star witness was found on the bottom of the George Washington Bridge with a bullet in both hands, her feet, and her head. The newspapers named Derrick Frosty for the cold-blooded murders he got away with. Young Derrick just took the name and ran with it. He knew that if he committed any crime in the state of New York, they were gonna hang him, so Frosty migrated south where he blew up off the dope game. Every Friday, he would go to Duke and run ball with the students. Word was that was how he met Sweetness because she used to always be there watching basketball games. The rest is history. They shared a penthouse right next to the Duke campus. Frosty let Sweetness dance because that was what she was doing before she met him, and whatever made her happy made him happy. Plus, she played so hard to get that he knew she wouldn't dare holla at another nigga.

P Double finished reading the report on his competition, and he handed Max ten grand for his services. Max said, "Anytime," as he walked out the door.

P said, "Damn," to himself. "Kid must have some serious gwawk moving that boy."

When P asked an old-timer who had sold dope all his life why all the Spanish cats sold it, the ol' G replied, "Because coke will make you rich, but dope will make you a millionaire."

P sat back and started thinking of ways to win his grand prize back, and what P wanted, P always got.

$ $ $

Frosty jumped out of his Aston Martin on shine as usual. The rest of his crew pulled up at Thong Island in big Suburbans and Escalades. Frosty's team gave new meaning to doing it. They defined it. Frosty and Akasha had a serious relationship going, so they swore to tell each other everything, even the little things. Sweetness drove back home that night, shedding tears, and she told her man everything. Frosty uttered a couple of words she wanted to hear, and they made passionate love all night long. But after that, Frosty started getting curious about the competition. This cat who called himself P Double had only messed around with Akasha for a couple of months, but somehow, he had her all fucked up that she was ready to hang it up behind this nigga. A couple of weeks went by, and Frosty couldn't take it anymore, so he called his team up and told them they were going to Charlotte to a banging new club called Thong Island. That was how they ended up there. Frosty told the bouncer he wanted his team seated in the VIP section. Frosty's entourage consisted of himself; Glock, a young killer from the Bronx; his man Cobra; and Big Chaos, the six foot seven giant.

As soon as they sat at their table, a beautiful chocolate bunny named Stephine Melons came and took their order. When she came back to the table, bringing their four bottles of crystal and half gallon of Hennessy, Frosty said, "Come here, shorty. Where's the owner of this fine establishment?" He smiled, damn near blinding her with his iced-out grill.

She replied, "He's probably in his office. Why?"

"Tell him Frosty wanted to compliment him on this fine establishment personally."

Stephine said, "Whatever." And she went to his office.

She knocked on the door and waited for P to open it. P was fucking the shit out of this little black chick they called Dynamite. And he could see why, because her pussy was serious. P heard the knock, looked at the monitor, and saw Stephine outside. He had fucked her a couple of nights before, but he wanted her to see how he was fucking the shit out of her homegirl. P buzzed her in and kept drilling the fuck out of Dynamite. The four-eleven bombshell was nutting up a storm when Stephine walked in.

"Boss, some cat named Frosty wanna holla at you. He said he wanted to compliment you on this here fine establishment," Stephine said with a mad look on her face.

P stopped in midstroke and said, "What?" And she repeated the message again.

P took his dick out of little Dynamite and said, "We'll finish this later," as a million things ran through his mind. "You tell him I'll be out in a minute."

P sat back and wondered what the man wanted. For one, he must have come in peace because the bouncers at the door didn't let anybody in the club with a strap except him and Jack. P grabbed his P-89 automatic out of his cherrywood desk, tucked it into the back of his pants, and walked out. He had the upper hand on Frosty, so he decided to see what the clown-ass nigga wanted.

P figured that he could find Frosty in the VIP section, and sure enough, he was there, blinding muthafuckers with all his ice and popping bottles with his goons. Frosty didn't notice P until he was right up on them. He was shocked because the waitress wasn't anywhere around, so how did the nigga even know what he looked like? He thought to himself, *Homeboy, must've been doing his homework, and he walked up by hisself. Yeah, I gotta watch this nigga. He's dangerous.* Frosty extended his hand out to the don, and P shook it, all the while keeping eye contact with his man and keeping one hand behind his back in case things started to get ugly. Frosty smiled and said, "This is a nice club you got here, pa, but this champagne taste a little bit flat." And his team all laughed at the little joke.

P stopped a waitress and told her to bring five bottles of crystal. When they arrived, he said, "Everything y'all want is on the house, daddy, and by the way, tell Akasha—oops, I mean, Sweetness—I said what's good. Any friend of hers is a friend of mine." And he spun off on them before Frosty could even reply. By all means, P was gonna get his bitch back, and he meant that.

Frosty wanted to kill that nigga for the remark, but he would handle the matter delicately. He understood the true meaning of "Bad boys move in silence," and that was how he was gonna move. Frosty was awakened from his daydream of killing the nigga when Cobra said, "Yo, Frost, how that cat know your woman, yo?"

Frosty hated when niggas asked questions, so he gave his goon one of those leave-that-shit-alone looks, and they popped the fresh bottles of crystal. Frosty and the crew were living it up when the lights blacked out and the announcer said, "Coming to the stage from Queens Bridge, New York, is Prodigy and Havoc of Mobb Deep to drop their new smash single, 'Quiet Storm.'" Then he said, "Big shout out to Frosty from P Double. This song is from P to you, playa."

Prodigy said, "I been through it all, man—blood, sweat, and tears." Then the beat dropped, and Prodigy said, "I put my lifetime in between the paper lines / I'm the quiet storm nigga who fight rhymes / P, yeah, you heard of him."

Frosty was nodding his head until he realized that P was sending him a message through Mobb Deep. In Frosty's mind, P was as good as dead. Who the fuck did he think he was sending subliminal messages at him? No one disrespected Frosty and got away with it—no one. His band of goons were stupid as fuck. They were two-stepping to a diss song meant for him. That just pissed him off even more. Frosty scanned the club and saw P Double mouthing the words of the song to him. Frosty pointed two fingers at P and acted like he pulled the trigger and then blew on his fingers, acting like the pistol was smoking. Frosty laughed at the clown-ass nigga and left his dumb-ass crew there, bouncing to the diss song. He hopped into his Aston Martin and maneuvered back to Durham, North Carolina. P Double was a dead fucking man. He just didn't know it yet.

<blockquote>
CHAPTER 22
</blockquote>

PAIN IS LOVE, AND LOVE IS ABOUT PAIN

It was P Double's birthday, and Mrs. Williams rented out the Waterfront Club in Springfield to keep her grandson's memory strong. It had been ten long months now since her grandson went on the run and fled Springfield. She missed him so she had to do something to honor him. Fatback paid for the whole affair while Jaynce and Mrs. Williams cooked all the food. The party was live. Fatback hired DJ Clue to be the DJ at the event. Clue even brought Memphis Bleak with him. Everyone was having a good time until P Double's daughter ran up to Jaynce and gave her a hug.

Shante ran over there and snatched the little girl out of Jaynce's arms with quickness. "Bitch, don't you ever touch what's mine," Shante hissed.

"Bitch, you still mad he chose me and left your slutty ass with nothing. I know you see my brand-new pink X-5 outside. Yeah, bitch, don't hate. Step your pussy game up!" Jaynce screamed.

Shante laughed and said, "I already whipped it on him, bitch. Remember the day I got out? I made sure I bounced on that dick. You're the one with a cheating husband, not me. You're the one that needs to step your old-ass game up, not me."

"P would never cheat on me with a grotesque-looking bitch like you," Jaynce said.

But that was enough for Shante. She jumped on Jaynce, and both of them started throwing wild punches, but Jaynce was getting the best of Shante until Roberta jumped in. Both ladies were working Jaynce over, until she grabbed two beer bottles off the countertop and bashed both girls in the head. Once they backed off of her, Jaynce reached into her back pocket and pulled out a box cutter. "Y'all nasty bitches wanna play! Well, let's rock then," she said, wiping her mouth with her left hand.

Fatback came and jumped in front of Shante and Berta. "Please, Jay, put the box cutter down," he begged.

"Hell no! These bitches wanna jump somebody. What's up now?" she yelled.

Fatback talked his way close to the wild lady and made his move. Back snatched the box cutter out of her hand and said, "Now, y'all cut this shit the fuck out."

But Berta wasn't having it. She ran at Jaynce full throttle. Fatback saw her coming and punched the fuck out of Berta. Before she hit the ground, she was in a deep snore. "Somebody carry this stupid bitch up out of here, and you go with her, Shante!" Fatback hollered, standing over Berta.

Shante said, "I'm not going no-muthafucking-where. You must got me fucked up with the next bitch. I'm the baby momma!" she screamed.

Before Fatback could say anything else, he heard, "Freeze, FBI. We gotta body warrant for Presley Williams, and nobody's going anywhere until we see some ID from everyone in here."

$ $ $

Down in the dirty South, Malinda was waiting to have the baby any day now. Since her pregnancy, P noticed she had started bitching about every single thing. So he stayed at his flat most of the time. This day was a beautiful Friday. It was also P Double's birthday. P called up Jack Tripper to see how things were moving with his work. Since he found out about Frosty, P Double had expanded his hustle. He copped a bunch of e pills and a bunch of exotic weeds. He had everything, from Poppi to Branson to regular. P even invested in some crystal meth. Fuck that dope money; he was killing them in every other market. P told Jack to come scoop him up. They were going to snatch his cousin and play a good, old-fashioned game called basketball.

$ $ $

Tommy was happy to be chilling with his cousin on P's birthday. Candice was going crazy because he was going out with P. She didn't like him because of the way he dogged Akasha and the simple fact that P fucked everything moving. If it wasn't for his little cousin, he would still be nickel-and-dime hustling on a corner somewhere. P was also the reason he was with Candice. When they left the club that night, he took Candice to the Waffle House and then charmed her with some of that Southern hospitality of his and ended up at a motel; the rest was history. He thought P had something major mapped out for his birthday, but Tommy was shocked when his cousin said he just wanted to play ball. When they got to the Duke campus, P asked if Jack and Tommy had their ladies with them, meaning guns. Both men nodded, "Yeah, of course."

P always knew that both men never left home without them, but still, he had to ask.

"Just watch my back while I ball," P said, changing into the throwback Grant Hill Duke jersey he just had made for himself. Both men looked at him with a curious expression on their faces, but they didn't ask questions. They walked to the gym, and P shook hands with the security guard.

"Hey, Charlie, what's been up?" P said.

"Man, I ain't seen you in a long time. What's up, P Double? You still nice with the rock?" Charlie asked him.

P laughed and said, "Come watch me on your break, my man."

Charlie said, "Now, that's the young boy I know. By the way, your ex-girlfriend is in there with her boyfriend. He's kind of good too, but he ain't no P Double." Charlie laughed.

P said, "I'll holla later on. It's time to ball," and P and his crew walked into the gymnasium.

Tommy looked at his cousin with that "I knew you were up to something" look. P winked at him and kept it moving. When P and his crew walked in, Frosty and a couple of cats were engaged in a full-court five-on-five game.

P walked in and said, "Who got next?"

If looks could kill, P would've needed nine lives because Frosty looked highly upset. But Frosty kept his composure and said, "You do." P then walked over to near where Akasha was sitting, and he winked at the beauty. Frosty noticed all of this and accidentally threw the ball away.

P Double blew a kiss at her, but she turned her nose up at him and kept watching the game.

Tommy walked up to her and gave her the hug of the century. They kicked it for a minute, and he said, "Wow, I see you still got my cousin head over heels for you, huh?"

"No, I don't. All them other chickens he got clucking do," she said distastefully.

Tommy said, "I can't tell. Today is his birthday, and out of everything or anything, he could've did in the world, he chose to play basketball. Now, that's crazy. I think he knew you were gonna be here; that's why he came."

"Well, tell him I said, 'Happy birthday,' but he's wasting his time as far as this goes. Akasha don't believe in second chances."

Out of the corner of his eye, Frosty was watching Sweetness talk to Tommy, and he was going crazy inside. Since they were talking, he had gone zero for three and now had two turnovers. Frosty's team was up ten to nine when young Elton Brand banged on this big white boy Frosty and his team had for a center. Now, it was game point for both teams. Jason Williams brought the ball up court and passed it to Corey Maggette. Corey dished the ball to Frosty on the wing.

Sweetness yelled, "You can do it, baby!"

That was all the motivation that he needed to build his confidence back up. Frosty got low and was pivoting with one foot, trying to take the freshmen Chris Duhon off the dribble. Frosty put the ball on the floor and stutter-stepped the youngster. Then he crossed him and went baseline. Frosty jumped the same time Elton Brand jumped, but Frosty got the best of him and dunked on the Duke center. He landed and screamed in Brand's face. Then he looked at P with pure hate and said, "Game."

P smiled at the man and said, "Let's ball." He picked up Duhon, Brand, Boozer, and Dunleavy. P said, "I got him," pointing to Frosty.

"Boy, you couldn't stick me if Gary Payton lent you his skills." Frosty laughed.

P said, "I guess little miss Sweetness never told you I'm from the home of the basketball hall of fame, and we ball for real, on and off the court, daddy." P spoke while still stretching.

Brand and the big white boy did the jump ball. Brand tapped the ball to P Double. P crossed Frosty but stopped. He crossed him again and blew by him. He drove to the basket, but Maggette picked him up, so he kicked the ball out to Dunleavy for the open jay, and it dropped. P jogged up the court and smiled at the beautiful Akasha. Even when she pouted, she was gorgeous. Jason Williams brought the ball up and kicked it to Frosty.

Frosty called for the isolation, and he crossed P over, but he stepped back and shot the jumper, hitting nothing but the bottom of the net. Frosty banged on his chest and ran up the court. Duhon brought the ball up the court and set it up. He swung the ball to Boozer, who swung it to P Double. P quickly posted Frosty up.

Frosty wasn't expecting this, as P backed him down low and hit him with a quick spin that lost Frosty for an easy lay-up. P then banged on his chest and ran up the court. Both teams were playing hard for a good twenty minutes when P Double called for a time-out. The score was tied at ten to ten. P and his team had the ball. Charlie came to watch the last couple of shots in the game. P said, "Man, just give me the rock. He can't stick me."

Boozer inbounded the ball. He kicked it to Brand, who kicked it to P.

P said, "Yeah, nigga, this is it, playboy." P crossed him, but Frosty didn't bite, so he put him in the post again. This time, he backed Frosty down, but instead of spinning around him, P spun away from him and splashed a fade away in Frosty's face. Then P blew a kiss at Akasha and said, "Game."

Charlie said, "Damn, boy, you still got it."

As P was walking away, Frosty ran up behind him and tackled him. Both men rolled on the ground, swinging wildly until they both stood up.

P acted like he was gonna hit Frosty with a right. When Frosty ducked, P scooped him and power-slammed the man hard, knocking the wind out of him. Frosty's team jumped to help their captain, but Jack Tripper and Tommy pulled out their hammers and stopped traffic. P got on top of Frosty and started giving him the business when Akasha came up and said, "Please, Presley, no more."

P saw the tears in her eyes, and he knew he couldn't hurt her again, so he got up, spit on the nigga, and walked away. He was finally happy now. He got to play ball on his birthday and beat up a nigga he didn't like. This was a hell of a birthday. Frosty got up with a busted nose and lip, yelling all types of obscenities as P Double and his crew left the court. P grabbed his dick and told Frosty to suck it on his way out the door.

Jack Tripper laughed and said, "Wow, that's crazy. He got beat up in front of his chick. I couldn't even look a muthafucker in their face after some shit like that."

P said, "The bad guy always wins in real life while the good guys lay on their ass and get beat the fuck up."

$ $ $

Frosty was steaming when he went home. Never in a million years had he lost in anything except those years ago when Dribble shot him all up and made him feel helpless. He lost his basketball career, which was his life back then. Now some punk-ass nigga embarrassed him in front of his girl and his crew, not once but twice. First the kid called P Double had taken it to him on the court. He had to admit the boy had skills, but when he blew that kiss at Akasha, he also blew a head gasket in Frosty, and Frosty attacked him out of anger. Even though he sneaked P Double, P still managed to come out on top. It took Akasha to stop the beating he was taking, which further infuriated him. He took a loss in front of a crew who looked up to him for leadership and guidance. P Double had to die for this, and he had to die soon. Frosty was running around talking about how he was gonna kill P and his boys when Akasha said, "Please, Frosty, let it go, baby."

Frosty stopped pacing and said, "What the fuck did you just say to me,

Akasha? Let it go! Are you fucking crazy? That punk muthafucker had the nerve to put his hands on me! He must die!"

"But, baby, you hit him first. Please just leave it alone. I can't stand to see somebody die over stupidness."

"So what the fuck you telling me, Akasha? That that muthafucker is gonna kill me too? No, I get it now. You still got feelings for that muthafucker. Yeah, that's exactly what's going on. I seen you talking to that other chump a long time. What? Where you setting up a meeting for later, huh?" he screamed at her.

Akasha shed a tear at his words. "How could you say something like that to me, Frosty. You know I love you. I just don't want no bloodshed." She cried.

"Well, it's gonna be a lot of that and crying going on because that nigga just signed a check he can't cash!" Frosty screamed.

Akasha dropped to her knees in front of Frosty and begged for P Double's life. "Please, daddy, don't do it," she begged, holding on to Frosty's leg.

But this drove him off the handle, and he punched her over and over again. "Bitch, you still love that punk-ass nigga! Well, die with him then!" Frosty pulled out his Glock 9 and put it to Sweetness's head.

"Please, daddy, I'm sorry," she begged through bloody lips and swollen eyes.

Frosty snapped out of the trance he was in and started crying. "See, what the fuck you made me do to you, Akasha? All I did was love you, but you couldn't just love me, could you? Baby, that nigga is dead, and that's all there is to it."

Even though Akasha was beat up, she still pleaded with him not to take P Double's life. This enraged him once again until he beat her unconscious.

$ $ $

Frosty hopped in his Aston Martin and drove to his mistress's house. He got there and pulled out a couple of bags of heroin, and he took a couple of snorts. The H was stamped good pussy, because when you sniffed or shot it, you felt like you were in some good pussy. Frosty couldn't remember how he got hooked on his own shit, but he did. He kept his secret away from Akasha and his crew though. The only person who knew he had a habit was Ebony, his mistress. Ebony was cute, but she was the complete opposite of Sweetness. Ebony was a high-yellow beauty with no education whatsoever. She dropped out of high school in the ninth grade because she fell in love with a pimp named Slick Rick, who turned her out to two things: selling pussy and sniffing dope. Ebony got tired of Rick beating the shit out of her, so she laced his dope with some rat poison and laid him to rest. She met Frosty at a strip club she worked at, and he gave her that dope dick that turned her out. He made her leave the strip club scene alone, paid all her bills, and the whole nine. Anything he told Ebony to do she did at will, unlike Sweetness, who had a mind of her own and did whatever she wanted to. Ebony had a fifteen-bag-a-day habit, but she didn't look like it at all.

Frosty kept her refrigerator stocked up so she could stay thick and healthy. That night, when he walked in, she knew something was wrong with her baby. Frosty broke down all the drama that he went through that day with P Double and Akasha. Ebony wanted to smile so bad because this was the chance she had dreamed about for so long now. She was tired of riding the bench when Akasha was in the starting lineup.

Ebony said, "Don't worry about a thing, baby. Ebony will always be here for you, through thick and thin!" as she unbuckled his Maurice Malone jeans. She threw Frosty's dick in her mouth. A dick suck would always soothe the savage beast, and Frosty was a straight sucker for head.

$ $ $

Akasha woke up and looked in the mirror to see somebody else staring back at her. Frosty had worked her over so bad she didn't even recognize herself. She cried while she was packing her shit. Never in a million years had Frosty ever laid a hand on her, but he did that night. In Akasha's book, that was a straight up and down violation, and she wasn't gonna be one of those dumbass chicks who stayed in an abusive relationship so long that the man wound up killing her. Hell no, she was straight. Akasha packed up all she could in her trunk and the backseat of her purple 740 BMW and drove to Candice's house in Kinston. They stayed up all night together crying in each other's arms. If it weren't for her best friend, Akasha would be lost in her own pain and anguish. They fell asleep hugging each other.

$ $ $

Frosty went home in the morning after fucking Ebony and snorting that good pussy all night long. He realized he flew the coop by putting his hands on his first lady. Frosty walked into the house with toilet paper all in his nose from all that snorting. He had two dozen orchids and pink roses in his hands. He went into the bedroom only to find that all of Akasha's clothes were gone or thrown around the bedroom. Frosty threw the roses down and went into a crazy rage, destroying everything in his path. Who the fuck did that bitch think she was leaving him? He screamed, "When you were fighting depression, ready to kill yourself, who the fuck romanced you and brought you up out of that shit, bitch? Frosty, that's who! Yeah, they think they gonna play me, huh? Fuck that. When you become Frosty's girl, it's a lifetime commitment. Now I gotta lay both of y'all to rest," Frosty said as he ripped open another bag of good pussy and inhaled the poison into his nostrils. It was time to play the game the only way he knew how and that was rough.

CHAPTER23

I GUESS THE GOOD DIE YOUNG

Tommy let P Double know that Akasha was staying at his place back home. P Double sent her a hundred dozen purple orchids and a brand-new 1999 purple Escalade, fully equipped with TVs, a deluxe sound system, and twenty-two-inch chrome rims. He also bought a mannequin and dressed it up with a purple mink coat and mink scarf and hat to match. Akasha screamed when she opened the door and found the purple-and-white ostrich seats with "Sweetness" engraved in the floor mats and seats. Tommy said she was happy with the gift, but she still didn't want anything to do with P Double whatsoever. So the next week, P Double sent her a purple Range Rover fully equipped with purple chinchilla fur inside. This time, he sent two hundred dozen orchids with a written apology of why things happened the way they did. Akasha agreed to see him, and it was on and popping again.

$ $ $

Frosty was losing his mind now that his baby girl was gone. He was sniffing three bundles of dope a day and shoveling coke into his nose at a hundred miles an hour. Frosty got word back that Sweetness had been seen all over North Carolina with a new purple Escalade and a purple Range Rover. He flew the coop. He called up the Four Horsemen, and they drove to Kinston in the all-black 1500s they used for missions. Frosty bought Tommy's address from a couple of small-time local hustlers who hated that Tommy was that nigga now. Chaos kicked the door in, and they ran up in the crib.

Unfortunately, Tommy got caught with his pants down for real. He was pumping away on Candice when the goons came in. Candice screamed for dear life until Big Chaos punched her in her mouth, knocking out four teeth. "Shut the fuck up, you stupid bitch," he said, demanding respect.

Frosty stood over the couple, smiling his usual award-winning smile. "Where the fuck is Sweetness and that nigga P Double at?" he asked, still grinning from ear to ear.

They both said, "Not here."

Frosty smacked Tommy in the head with his Glock twice and screamed, "Do I fucking look stupid to you? I know they ain't here. Where the fuck do that nigga live at?"

Tommy said, "I swear I don't know."

Frosty said, "So you wanna play rough? Cobra and Glock, tie this muthafucker up while I have some fun." Frosty started folding his clothes up nice and neat.

He put on a condom, and Tommy screamed, "No, please don't!" with tears in his eyes.

"Glock, shut him the fuck up. I gave him a chance to make amends, but he wanted to play."

Candice started screaming, "No!" trying to fight, but Frosty smacked her with the pistol and said, "The next step is death." He entered her and started pumping away as Tommy cried. Frosty had the bitch in all types of positions before he finally came. Then he got dressed and said, "Garbage-ass pussy." And he smacked the fuck out of her.

"Chaos, try that trash out while I talk to ol' boy here. You might like it."

Twenty seconds later, Big Chaos was grunting as he fucked Candice.

"Tommy boy, what's good, baby? You wanna talk now?"

Tommy said, "Okay, okay, he lives in a penthouse in downtown Charlotte. That's all I know, I swear. Now, let us go!" he pleaded.

Frosty laughed and said, "Where the fuck do that other nigga live?"

And Tommy gave him Jack Tripper's address as well, along with the three hundred thousand he had in his safe.

Frosty said, "Good looking out, son, but one thing us New York muthafuckers hate is a rat bastard." And he squeezed two shots off in his dome.

Candice didn't even know her boyfriend was dead. She was in another planet somewhere while Chaos was fucking the shit out of her. The giant finally busted his load and got up.

"Yeah, Frosty, you were right. Her pussy is straight trash."

Frosty said, "Say good night," and he put the Glock 9 in her pussy and let his gun bust two nuts in the bitch as well. Then he laughed and said, "Did y'all hear that?"

All the guys looked at him like, "Hear what?"

"Even the gun said that bitch had some straight trash." Frosty then went to the fridge and grabbed a block of cheese they had in there. He stuffed it into Tommy's mouth and yelled, "Rat bastard!" as they exited the crib.

$ $ $

Jack Tripper was in the crib rocking the new Donell Jones CD. "Where I Wanna Be" was pumping loud out of the sound system. He was chilling with this bad bitch he had just met named Zoe. Zoe was an Indian and Spanish chick he had met at the club one night. They had been feeling each other and going on little dates here and there for a minute now. That night, he was on the same level as Biggie and R. Kelly because in his head, he was saying, *Bitch, you must be used to me spending and all that sweet wining and dining. Well, I'm fucking you tonight.* They were on his burgundy-and-white leather sofa getting to know each other a little bit better, meaning exploring each other's bodies.

Jack was stroking her like a finely tuned instrument when Frosty and his crew kicked in the door with their guns out.

"Man, what the fuck y'all niggas want, man?" Jack screamed knowing this was his last day on earth.

Frosty laughed and said, "Your life, playboy." And he emptied a clip in Jack.

Zoe started screaming and begging for her life. Glock ran up to the beauty and put her to sleep with three well-placed head shots. It was time to pay P Double a visit. Frosty was in town, and things were gonna get real chilly around here.

$ $ $

Malinda was lying back watching *Oprah* when the buzzer in the penthouse rang. Their maid, Esmeralda, answered the door intercom, and Henry, the door man, said there was a fresh delivery of two dozen pink roses downstairs. Henry let them know that he was on his way up. He wanted them to push the button so that he could catch the elevator upstairs to the penthouse on the fifty-fifth floor. Esmeralda waited for the delivery, but when it got there, she got the surprise of her life.

$ $ $

Frosty shot straight to the building P Double lived in and was met by a doorman who looked Israeli. Frosty looked around the lobby and saw no one in sight, so he pulled out the nine he had tucked into his waistband and placed it to the doorman's head.

The doorman said, "Please don't kill me," in an Israeli accent and started praying to Allah.

Chaos and the rest of the Horsemen laughed when Frosty smacked the dude in the head with the burner and said, "Allah ain't got shit to do with this shit. Call the penthouse suite and tell them there's a delivery of roses down here for the missus."

Henry did as requested, and all five men hopped on the elevator. When he put his key in the elevator and hit the fifty-fifth floor, Frosty put the muzzle of the gun to the back of Henry's skull and pulled the trigger. "Your services are no longer needed." He laughed as the bell rang, letting them know they were on the fifty-fifth floor.

As soon as the door opened, they saw a Spanish chick dressed in a maid's uniform. Big Chaos ran at her full speed and slapped her with the pistol, making her fold like an ironing board. Big Chaos caught her before she hit the ground. She was knocked out, so he laid her down slowly. They crept into the living room and saw another Spanish chick; this one was pregnant. Frosty thought Tommy had given them the wrong address until he saw a picture of her and P Double hugged up on the wall. Frosty snatched her up and said, "Where the fuck is P Double at?"

Malinda screamed, "Oh my god, papi! I don't know, I swear!"

Chaos and the crew searched the rest of the penthouse and reported back to Frosty that everything was free and clear. Frosty told the crew to grab the doorman off the elevator and wipe it down. It was time to have some real fun. He figured since P Double was fucking his chick, he might as well return the favor. Frosty ripped Malinda's gown and went to work. Malinda fought hard, but Frosty punched her in the face at least twenty times breaking her jaw, nose, and eye socket. Frosty entered her and pumped away until he came. Then the other Horsemen did the same.

When they all had finished, Frosty grabbed a butcher knife from the kitchen and said, "Hold that bitch down while Dr. Frosty operates." The Horsemen grabbed her arms and legs.

Malinda tried to fight, but the men were too strong. All she could do was curse P Double and God for putting her in this situation. Frosty slit her stomach open and cut the sack open that was holding the baby. He snatched the baby up by his leg and cut the umbilical cord. Then he looked at the bloody baby and said, "How cute."

Then he repeatedly flung the unborn fetus into the sixty-inch TV screen over and over again. "Chaos, put that bitch out of her misery!" Frosty ordered, and Chaos shot Malinda twice. Frosty put the baby in her arms and put a note on top of her chest. The note read, "I guess the good die young."

CHAPTER 24

SAY HELLO TO THE BAD GUY

P Double woke up at the Ritz Carlton with a lovely piece of eye candy next to him. Finally, he was able to taste the beautiful Akasha. Sweetness was definitely the best name for her because everything about her was really sweet. P smiled at himself because he had really outdone himself this time. You could say his bird game was on a whole different level. P Double got out of the king-size bed and stretched it out. His body felt like he had run four quarters of NBA basketball. You really had to fuck Sweetness. If you came half-ass, you couldn't make the cut, and you were sent to the locker room to pack your shit early. P hopped into the deluxe shower and washed the sweet essence of lovemaking off him. As he was toweling off, he walked back into the bedroom and noticed Sweetness had just woken up. Damn, even in the morning, the chocolate beauty looked like a vintage dime. She walked up to P and swapped spit on her way to the shower. All P could think was *Damn, even the bitch's morning breath is sweet.*

P Double threw on his Iceberg sweatsuit and walked over to the bar to fix himself a shot of Hennessy. Then he lit a Cuban cigar and turned the TV on to watch Sports Center on ESPN. P cut both of his phones on, and they both started ringing off the meat rack. The first call was from Mitch, his contractor, telling him his crib in Maxton was complete. The next couple of calls sent the don into a rage like no other. P Double started smashing everything in the room.

When Sweetness walked out of the bathroom, she screamed, "Baby, what's the matter?" running over to P and grabbing him. P turned around and explained that Candice, Tommy, and Jack Tripper were all murdered yesterday. Sweetness just collapsed in his arms, and he carried her over to the king-size bed, where he shed a single tear himself. He left out how they had murdered Malinda and his junior. P flipped his phone open and called his man.

P Double and Fatback hadn't spoken in months, but as soon as he told Fatback what had gone down, Back asked for the address down there and told P that he was bringing the fam. P Double gave him the address for the crib in Maxton, and they broke the connection. It was time to play the game the only way young P Double knew how to play it, and that was for keeps.

$ $ $

Frosty sniffed a bag in each nostril and started laughing to himself. "You think Frosty's a joke, nigga? Hardy ha, muthafuckers," he said to himself as he loaded both the chrome Tech nines with thirty-two rounds of instant death a piece. Frosty sniffed two more bags of good pussy to get his swagger back. He was popping bags like they were Skittles. Even his mistress tried to slow him down, but he wound up slapping the shit out of her and made her suck the barrel of his forty cal for an hour while he inhaled the exotic poison. After the hour, he kicked her in the chest and said, "Your head game is trash, bitch. Riffraff can't even bust." Then he let out a sick laugh.

Ebony knew this nigga was out of his fucking mind, but like her mother told her a long time ago, you get what you ask for. Now she found herself with a full-fledged madman and dope fiend. Frosty sniffed so much dope one day that he fucked her for five hours straight and couldn't bust. He just pulled out and smacked her a couple of times. Frosty told her she had some garbage that was about to get thrown out unless she stepped her game up.

"Sweetness pussy stayed tight and sweet. If I wanted to fuck a dry pussy, I would've jerked off."

Ebony ran out of the room and locked herself in the bathroom. She slid to her usual spot on the floor and cried her eyes out. This had all happened a couple of days ago. Today, Frosty was treating her like a queen. For some strange reason, he was in a good mood. She wondered why he was loading the two guns when Frosty said, "I'll be back in a couple of hours. When I get back, have my dinner ready and your pussy greased up."

All she could do was say, "Yes, daddy."

Frosty walked out the door and jumped into his Aston Martin, and Ebony shed tears. She was knee-deep in a relationship she couldn't get out of. Meanwhile, Frosty was on his way to Kinston to say hello to Sweetness's parents.

$ $ $

Back in Springfield, Massachusetts, Fatback was on his thug dizzel. His paper was longer than the Panama Canal. Nowadays, all he did was count paper, stack his chips accordingly, and fuck strictly vintage dime pieces. Lately, he was fucking the shit out of J.G.'s ex Brandy. Brandy had Fatback fucked up in every way. Her head game was extravagant while her sex game was better than winning any gold medal, Super Bowl, or NBA championship.

One day, after she finished riding the Bristol Street don, he found himself asking her what the fuck she had in there. In all his days, he had never had a woman who came with the two deadliest components in the world. Not only was Brandy beautiful as hell, but she had the necessary brains to go along with it. Brandy was in her second year at Springfield Technical Community College, where she majored in criminology and held down a 4.0 GPA. Brandy was also an all-American point guard, leading her team in points and assists. Her team was undefeated as well. So when she asked Fatback to sell her brother a couple of keys of coke, he grunted and thought nothing else of it. Then his best friend called him and told him he needed his help to take out a couple of clowns. He called up Kev, Darris, A-Dog, and P Double's big cousin Flowie. The team of hardheads jumped in Kev's money-green Excursion and broke south. It was time to make Bristol Street ring bells down south.

$ $ $

Jaynce missed her husband badly, but she had other things on her mind that kept her busy on a regular basis, such as running the real estate company her husband made her establish. At first, it was a bogus operation for his stash houses, but Jaynce took a couple of late-night real estate courses, and she became a real estate mogul overnight. She found herself buying and selling properties every day of the week. Real estate ran her life so much that she resigned from the head of juvenile probation spot she had held down for so long. Now, she saw why P Double loved hustling so much. The power of the hustle had taken over her life. Shit, real estate was on the same level as selling drugs, except it was legal. Jaynce had just come from East Long Meadow scouting a couple of houses when she decided to treat herself to a French vanilla coffee from Dunkin' Donuts. She had the AC turned up full blast in the X-5, bumping Jon B. "Don't listen to what people say. They don't know about this here."

She was rocking to a steady rhythm, mouthing the words and reminiscing about her husband when a platinum Jetta with dark tint pulled up next to her. Jaynce didn't notice Shante roll the tinted window down until her window shattered from a .380 round. Jaynce peeled off, ramming the side of the Jetta, trying to get away from sudden death. The X-5 sped off in traffic with the Jetta hot on its tail. Shante fired twice more, and the X-5's back windshield collapsed like a lung. Jaynce let out an earth-shattering scream that only she could hear. Jaynce knew Shante wanted nothing more than to end her life, so she made the 4.6 show its worth.

As she put the pedal to the floor, she heard two more quick shots and screamed once again. She said a silent prayer with tears running down her eyes, and she saw her chance to escape the wrath of Shante. She banged a sharp left right in front of an eighteen-wheeler and kept it moving down a side street. She banged a couple of rights and lefts and saw that she was clear. Jaynce pushed the X-5 to a nearby auto shop that was closed and called herself a cab home. Shante was a pest that had to be exterminated. She sat down and put a plan together before she went to the gun store. If Shante wanted to tango, she was ready to dance.

$ $ $

For two days now, Tanto had had butterflies in his stomach, but he wasn't able to put his foot on it. Business was at an all-time high, and all his legal ventures were running smoothly as well. Tanto lay back and lit a Cuban cigar. He had just poured himself a double shot of Remy when Esmeralda came to his study and told him police wanted to talk to him.

"What the fuck do they want?" he questioned, but all Esmeralda said was, "They wouldn't say. They told me that it was urgent and they had to see you at once."

Tanto grunted and told the maid to tell them to give him a minute. As soon as his maid left the study, he called up his attorney, Maxwell Jerrenski. He was the best Jewish attorney in New York State. He was on his way over so that made Tanto feel a little at ease. He radioed his maid to bring them to the study. The two plainclothes detectives walked in and introduced themselves as Officers Manning and Kent. Tanto shook their hands and offered them both cigars. Both Manning and Kent turned the offer down.

"Sir, there's no easy way to say this, but do you have a daughter named Malinda?"

Tanto said, "Oh my God," and grabbed his heart at once. The officers didn't even have to finish the statement. Tanto already knew his beautiful daughter, Malinda, was gone. He clutched at his heart and started turning beet red. Officer Kent called for an ambulance while Officer Manning attended to the old man. They managed to rush him to the hospital, where the doctors said Tanto had had a mild stroke.

$ $ $

Frosty pulled up in the driveway and sniffed two more bags of good pussy. He grabbed both Techs and knocked on the door politely. Mr. Jackson answered the door at once. Sweetness's father was in his early fifties. He was six foot six and still had an athletic build with salt-and-pepper hair. He opened the door and said, "How may I help you, son?"

Frosty laughed and said, "Nigga, I'm beyond help, muthafucka. You need help."

And he brandished both Tech nines from behind his back. Frosty shot Mr. Jackson in the foot, making the old man jump around. Frosty then buried his shoulder in the older man's midsection, making him fall into the hallway. He then closed the door and yelled, "Mama, I'm home."

Mrs. Jackson heard all the commotion and rushed right into harm's way. She started screaming when she saw her husband lying on the floor grabbing his foot in pain. Mrs. Jackson was in her early fifties as well, but she looked like she was in her early thirties. She and Sweetness could pass as twin sisters. Frosty was so far gone in his mind he started calling Akasha's mother "Sweetness." He ran over and tried to kiss her, but she started swinging wildly. That was when Frosty took control and smacked her with the Tech.

"Bitch, you want that nigga P Double over me? Well, you're gonna have to kill this thoroughbred first, sweetheart."

Mr. Jackson screamed, "I'm gonna kill you, nigga." And he ran full speed at Frosty.

Frosty smiled and emptied both clips inside of Sweetness's pops. Then he looked at what he thought was Sweetness and said, "Baby, that's how you kill a muthafucker." Mrs. Jackson ran at Frosty punching, scratching, and yelling, "Why? Why? Why?" as she fought like a savage.

Frosty picked her up and power-slammed her, screaming, "Bitch, you were fucking him too?" He then jumped on her, wrapped his hands around her neck, and squeezed the life out of her.

"All I ever did was love you, and this is how you gonna treat me!" he yelled in her face time and time again, but he was talking to himself because her soul had already exited her body. Frosty started saying he was sorry and kissing the lifeless body of Mrs. Jackson. He then ripped off the Victoria's Secret negligee she had on and entered her roughly. He pumped away on Mrs. Jackson and vowed his undying love for Sweetness. Awhile later, Frosty grunted and exploded in the lifeless body. He sniffed two more bags of dope and got himself, along with Mrs. Jackson, dressed. Frosty carried her to the passenger side of his Aston Martin and strapped her seat belt on. He jumped in and called Ebony.

"Baby, I'm on the way right now, but we have company. So please set another place at the table." Frosty hung up and slapped in "Where I Wanna Be" by Donell Jones. In his mind, this was where he wanted to be.

$ $ $

P Double gave Akasha his Black Card and took her to their new 12,500-square-foot palace. The big front gate had "P.D." for P Double on it. The mansion was on a hundred acres of land, with a nice man-made lake P had them build. He had to stock it with fresh fish of all kinds so he could fish. The inside of his home had marble floors and pillars. P had giant chandeliers hanging everywhere. He told her to decorate every single room in the house. Sweetness hugged her soul mate and went to work.

By the next day, their kingdom was sizably furnished the right way. P Double was in their home movie theater when Sweetness buzzed him and told him that a money-green Excursion was at the front gate with a couple of rough-looking types in it. P Double hit the security camera on the big theater screen, and then he zoomed in and saw his man Kev driving and Fatback in the passenger seat. He buzzed the gate, and the band of thugs followed the red-brick road until they ended up at the main house. P Double ran outside and hugged his road dawgs at once.

Fatback said, "Man, what the fuck? Who the fuck do you think you are living like this?"

Kev said, "This shit is crazy, my nigga, word up."

Fatback said, "You still didn't answer my question, homeboy. Who the fuck do you think you are living like this?"

P Double said, "I'm that fucking nigga, that's who. You act like you don't know, nigga!" And the men hugged again. P Double jumped into the passenger seat of the Excursion and said, "Get in. Let's go!" He told Kev to drive around the lake.

Five minutes later, they pulled up to a mini version of his crib. "This is the guesthouse, where y'all can stay anytime y'all in town." They walked into the 4,500-square-foot home and were blown back by the extreme luxury of the dwelling. All the hallways had the shiniest black marble floors. Every room was huge and blessed with the finest wall-to-wall carpeting, while all six bedrooms had walk-in closets and their own deluxe private bathrooms. On the second floor of the guest home was another giant movie theater, and in the basement was a two-lane bowling alley.

Big Flowie walked into the living room and said, "What the fuck?"

P Double had a big gargoyle water fountain in the middle of the floor. The shit was spitting water out of its mouth.

Flowie said, "Man, this spot is too much, man. I gotta take the load off my feet." He sat down in the cranberry love seat only to discover that the shit was made out of pure suede.

P gave them all the security code to the playpen.

Fatback was like, "I can just imagine the inside of your home, because this shit is off the hook."

Just then, Sweetness ran into the crib, calling for P Double, crying.

"Baby, I'm here," P said.

Sweetness ran into the room, grabbed P, and started mumbling gibberish with more and more tears.

One of P Double's crew said, "Jesus Christ."

And they all started singing, "She's a brick house."

P gave his crew one of those this-ain't-the-time-for-this looks and said, "Baby, what's wrong?"

Sweetness said, "My father got shot sixty-four times last night, Presley, and my mother is missing. He has my fucking mother, Presley!"

Everybody said, "Who the hell is she talking about?"

"She talking about these fake-ass New York chumps, ran by a punk named Frosty. I beat the shit out of the kid, and he feeling some type of way. By the way, this is my earth. Her name is Akasha, but everyone calls her Sweetness."

Fatback said, "Don't worry, ma, because that chump won't breathe too much longer fucking with my fam, and that's one check that will never bounce."

She cried and thanked Fatback for caring. P Double told her to call and order two party-size pizzas with no pork toppings. Then he said, "I'll be home in a minute, baby girl."

Sweetness kissed him and drove back to the main house.

A-Dog said, "You just convinced me that they have steroids just for the ass muscle because baby got back."

Kev said, "Please tell me she's got a sister, my nigga."

Fatback said, "Nigga, I got first dibs if she do. Fuck that."

P Double got angry and said, "Man, cut the shit. Fatback, they killed Malinda."

Fatback looked at his man and said, "Oh shit."

"Yeah, my nigga, shit just got realer than you think, partner."

Flowie, Kev, Darris, and A-Dog said, "Who the fuck is Malinda?"

"That was our connect's daughter, which was also P's baby mother," Fatback announced.

Everybody looked at the don and said, "Oh shit."

P Double said, "Sweetness doesn't know I have a baby's mother or had one for instance, so we're gonna leave it that way also."

Everyone nodded to that effect.

"Back, what's good with my wife?" P asked.

"Jaynce is a stone-cold hustler, daddy." Back laughed.

"Man, what the fuck you mean my wife is hustling?" P said in mock anger.

"Just as I said, she's a stone-cold hustler, P. Jaynce is buying and selling more real estate than Donald Trump, baby boy, and that's real."

After Fatback finished, P let out a sharp breath of air. He thought he had turned Jaynce on to selling drugs or something. He was happy when Fatback told him she was hustling in a different way, which was legal.

Flowie stood up and said, "I'm ready to fuck some shit up. Where these bitch-ass niggas at?"

"Well, all I want y'all to do is take his clique out. They call theirselves the Four Horsemen, and from what I know, they're stone-cold killers," P Double said.

Fatback jumped up and said, "Wait a minute here. What about this cat named Frosty or whatever the fuck they call him?"

"Don't worry about him, son. He's mine, daddy. You see, Frosty thinks he's a bad boy, so I want him to say hello to the bad guy personally."

"Man, it ain't no fun if Fatback can't have none. Shit, the rest of y'all get the Horsemen. You already know, P, we ride together or we don't ride at all," Fatback stated.

"Good looking out, my nigga. You're right though. Matter of fact, I couldn't agree more," P said.

Then they put their heads together and formed a plan of attack.

$ $ $

Flowie and A-Dog parked the rental MPV down the block and watched the building complex. Neither one of the goons knew anything about Raleigh, North Carolina, but they weren't there for sightseeing at all. P Double wanted them to take out Big Chaos, the biggest member of Frosty's team. The private eye P Double had hired before had given him a picture of Chaos along with the kind of car he drove, his apartment number— the whole nine yards. He even had Chaos's favorite food on the report. They were sitting in the MPV for two hours when A-Dog started getting impatient.

"Man, where the fuck is this jolly-green-giant-ass nigga at? I gotta fucking drain the weasel." A-Dog was reaching for the door handle when Big Flow snatched him up by his shirt with one hand.

"Muthafucka, you better hold that shit. Now we came here on a mission, and neither one of us is doing anything until this shit is done. So man up, little nigga," Big Flow spit. Flowie was six two and 290 pounds of pure animal in his own right. He really didn't play with guns too much, because his hands were lethal weapons in their own right. Flowie was what you would call a knockout artist.

As soon as he let go of A-Dog, A-Dog said, "Yeah, I think Polly's gotta a fucking cracker." And he pointed at a candy-apple-red Expedition, with some big-ass tires on it.

Flow saw the truck pull into the underground garage, and he started the MPV up and drove straight into the garage. "Yo, follow my lead, playboy. Fuck killing this nigga just yet. I wanna get his worth first. Then we're gonna dump his ass someplace."

They pulled into the underground garage and hopped out right next to the Expedition. Chaos got out and sized both men up at once. He had never seen these two men a day in his life, so his red alert sensor was ringing bells like crazy.

Chaos started reaching for his heat when Flowie said, "Man, this ride is it right here. Where the fuck did you cop those big-ass tires?"

Chaos let his hand drop off his waist and smiled. His one weakness was his ride. He could talk about all its features for days on end. "This baby is sitting on some custom-made twenty-fours with the chrome-and-gold Davocci rims. I paid twenty grand for these babies. Everybody knows there's no such thing as twenty-four-inch rims," Flowie said.

"Damn, daddy, you killing 'em! What's on the inside of this piece?" As he asked this question, he inched up close to the giant.

Chaos opened up the trunk, showing them the custom-made Gucci leather seats and the matching flooring. Dick riders made his day all the time. And these two cornballs were making him shine. Chaos explained all the fine features he put on his truck, and then he asked the men, "Where y'all from? I know y'all not from down here."

Big Flow laughed and said, "You're damn sure right. I'm from Springfield, Massachusetts, nigga."

And Flowie hit the giant with a powerful right hook. That rang the giant's noggin. Chaos staggered back when Flowie charged him, this time catching him with a left cross and another right hook, but the giant didn't drop because he staggered back into the open door, catching his balance. Chaos put Big Flowie into a bear hug and tried to squeeze the life out of him. Flowie knew he had made a terrible mistake trying to go blow for blow with the giant. Chaos was utterly strong. Flow was a beast in his own right, but he couldn't break the giant's embrace for the life of him. A-Dog saw the situation get out of control real quick and fast; he wanted to laugh, but shit was serious business. A-Dog pulled out the Calico he had in his waist and slapped the giant in the dome five times before the big man went limp. A-Dog pulled out the rope and bound and gagged the big Goliath.

Flowie and A-Dog struggled picking the big man up. They threw him into the MPV and splashed him with a bunch of cold water. Chaos woke up struggling against his bonds.

A-Dog said, "Flow, your boy's up. You're lucky I was there because ole boy was about to beat that ass." A-Dog laughed.

"You better be lucky I'm kind of out of breath, or I would beat your ass for making me struggle. Now shut your muthafuckin' trap, or I will show you that Big Flow is not a myth. I'm a legend, nigga. Now let's get back to the matter at hand."

They both turned around and looked at the struggling Chaos. Flowie put some platinum brass knuckles on and punched Chaos twice, breaking the big man's nose at once. Chaos howled like a bitch in heat behind the gag.

"Yeah, big boy, that was for making me sweat tussling with your big ass. Now, all we wanna know is where's the dough and the work you got? Oh, and we wanna know where your boss is at. You answer these questions, and you're very free to go." Flowie snatched the gag out of the man's mouth just to catch a fat lewy in the face. Flow punched the man in the mouth four times, knocking out his front and bottom teeth.

Chaos started gagging and spitting up teeth. A-Dog laughed and said, "That's how you make a muthafucka swallow his teeth."

A-Dog screwed a silencer on the muzzle of the Calico. "Now, big baby, I'm not the beat-on-you-until-you-squeal type. I just want the location and combination to the safe, or you could say good night, plain and simple."

Chaos knew the smaller man wasn't playing games, so he told them what they wanted to hear. Flow punched him in the temple, rendering the giant unconscious again. They searched his pockets and found ten stacks and the keys to the Expedition and the crib. Both men went upstairs and cleaned the safe out. Big Chaos had $750,000 in the safe along with three keys of raw, uncut dope. The two men smiled at each other and said, "We hit the jackpot."

They went back downstairs, and A-Dog pumped two slugs into the sleeping giant. They drove to the nearest dope block, tossed his body out of the van, and kept it moving. The first part of their plan went well. Flow and A-Dog just hoped everyone else was golden.

$ $ $

Cobra was at Gold's Gym getting his swole on. He was an even six feet tall and 225 pounds of solid beef. He stretched out his massive wings in front of the mirror, admiring his bulk. Cobra had crazy cuts all over his body. When he went to the beach and took his shirt off, other muthafuckers put their shirts back on. Cobra never had a problem bagging a chick. He just had a problem with keeping one. Once they found out he had a crazy attitude problem, not to mention he was overly possessive about his women, they ran and never looked back. Cobra had 405 pounds on the bar. He bent over, snatched it up, and stretched his back out. Cobra was doing deadlifts. On his last one, he stretched out and screamed as he let the massive weight hit the floor. He was looking at the sweat glistening on his body when a short, cocky muthafucka appeared in the mirror next to him. The kid was about five eight and 210 pounds solid.

"Yo, Money, do you mind if I get that money with you, son?" Little Kev asked.

Cobra said, "Yeah, if you can hang, no problem. If not, I'm dropping you back off. As a matter of fact, it's your set."

Kev went over to the bar, squatted down, and wrapped his hands around it. Cobra was about to tell him that he was on his third set and that he had only started off with 225 when the kid picked it up, repped it ten times, and put the bar back down quietly. Cobra was impressed with the kid's show of strength. Cobra said, "What's your name, pa?"

"Kev, daddy. What's yours?" Kev answered back.

"My peoples call me Cobra, pa."

Kev looked at him and said, "Your set, my nigga."

Cobra got down, about to squat the weight up, when Kev said, "Hold up, daddy," and he slapped two forty-five plates on each side, increasing the weight to 495. Cobra knew he could lift the weight, but he didn't wanna burn himself out before he could finish his whole workout. Cobra's pride was on the line so he got down and deadlifted the weight up eight times before he let the weight drop to the floor. Kev came up, threw the weight back with no problem, and put it back down silently. Cobra was out of breath when Kev said, "Your set," and slapped two more forty-five plates on the bar, increasing the weight to 585.

Cobra got down and almost gave himself a hernia trying to lift that much weight. Cobra blew his back out and fell. "Help me, Kev. I can't move, my nigga."

Kev already knew where his car was at, but he asked him anyway to make it look good. They got to the black Escalade, and Kev said, "My boy told me to tell you that that was fucked up."

Cobra asked him who his man was.

"P Double, you fucking punk." And he power-slammed the helpless Cobra and then hit him with two strong right hands that rendered Cobra unconscious. Kev put him in his truck and suffocated him. Job two was done. He hoped everyone else did their thing to.

$ $ $

Glock was at the gun range firing off his favorite weapons, two beautiful nickel-plated Glock 9. His father taught him how to shoot a gun when he was ten years old. His first weapon was a little chrome twenty-five. His father, Henry Watkins Senior, gave it to him and told him to keep it on him at all times. The South Bronx streets were filled with murderers and robbers of the worst creed.

One day, he saved his father's life and caught his first body at the same time. Young Henry was walking home from school one muggy afternoon. He was eleven years old, and he already had three girlfriends. Henry took the elevator to the tenth floor of his project. When he walked off the elevator, he passed the stairway and heard commotion. Young Henry heard a familiar voice say, "Please, I didn't mean nothing by it." Then he heard a couple of knuckle slaps and a man who sounded like his father grunt in pain. Henry opened the stairway door and saw his father lying on the ground getting worked over by two hoods who sold crack in front of his building. His father looked at him when he walked through the door and begged the hoods not to beat him up in front of his son.

K-Swiss and Pretty Tony both looked at the young boy, and one said, "Your father is a disrespectful muthafucka. He likes to disrespect people's females, so I'm putting his old ass on punishment."

Then both men turned their backs on the young boy and continued beating on his old man. Henry pulled the twenty-five from his back pocket, shot K-Swiss four times, and put two slugs in Pretty Tony before he ran down the stairs. K-Swiss was shaking on the ground begging for his life now. Little Henry walked up to him and said, "I'm a disrespectful muthafucka too, bitch nigga." And he put the last two slugs in his brain and spit on him.

Henry Watkins Junior looked at his father and lost all respect for him from that day on. His parents sent him to Harlem to live with his grandparents to keep him safe. That was where he got turned out to the streets and became a hustler. That was also where he met Frosty. Every time Glock fired a weapon, he remembered that day. Glock ran through four boxes of ammunition before he decided to call it a night. He jumped into his CLK 420 and was on his way home when some cat rear-ended him from behind. Glock jumped out on fire with two guns out, going crazy until he saw that there was no real damage. He put his guns away, and Darris jumped out of the rental 4Runner with one hand behind his back.

"My bag daddy, this dro got me seeing shit," Darris said.

Glock said, "Yeah, it almost had you seeing your last days, punk muthafucka."

Darris replied, "Well, P Double said today is yours."

Glock's eyes got big as he tried to reach for his guns, but Darris had the drop on him. Darris hit him up thirty times with the Uzi he pulled from behind his back. Then he ran his pockets, leaving them empty, and he grabbed the two nickel-plated nines. He said, "Now, let's go to your house and see what a playa named Henry got for me."

$ $ $

Ebony was in the bathroom throwing up once again. If she hadn't been convinced that Frosty had lost his mind, she was made a true-life believer. Frosty's idea of company was a dead body he dragged in. He kept calling the corpse Sweetness, when in fact, she could tell that the lady had to be the girl's mother or older sister. When she told Frosty the lady was dead, he knocked her tooth out and made her fix the dead body a plate. Then the stupid muthafucka tried to feed it. When he saw that the body wasn't swallowing the food, he ran up on Ebony and hit her with two ear-ringing open-palm slaps that made her head spin.

"Bitch, Sweetness said this shit is nasty and bland. The next time I come home to some shit like this, you know where you're gonna be swimming, bitch." The next words he spoke made her sick to her stomach. "Sweetness said she wants to have a threesome with your fine ass."

Ebony looked at Frosty with tears in her eyes and begged, "Baby, please don't do this to me."

"Bitch, give Sweetness a bubblebath and lotion her up." Frosty took all of Akasha's mother's clothes off and sat her in the tub.

Ebony turned the water on and added the bubbles. She scrubbed the dead body to death because Frosty was making her sleep with the thing. Ebony called Frosty when she was done, and he picked the lifeless body up and dried it off. She threw some apple-cucumber-melon lotion on the body while Frosty watched. Next, Frosty went over to the entertainment center and slipped in R. Kelly's *Twelve Play*. She couldn't believe this sick muthafucka had the nerve to play "Bump 'N' Grind."

Frosty stripped and made her suck his dick. After a while, he told Ebony to crawl on the bed and eat Sweetness's pussy. She hesitated for a minute until Frosty gave her that I-will-kill-your-ass look, and she started licking the corpse's pussy. Even though she had bathed the body and lotioned it up, the shit was starting to stink, and she almost threw up then. Frosty sneaked up behind her and started pounding the pussy. All the while, he made sure Ebony continued to eat the corpse out. Frosty pulled out of Ebony's hot, wet pussy, and he told her to move over. He threw the dead woman's legs on his shoulders, and he fucked her savagely. After twenty minutes of pounding away on the dead woman, Frosty came with a loud shout. Just when Ebony thought the worst of it was over, Frosty made her suck his dick. Ebony gagged as she tasted and smelled the dead woman on Frosty's still-hard penis.

While she was blowing his socks off, Frosty was eating out the corpse. Ebony thought white people were some sick psycho pathetic muthafuckas. Apparently, the world didn't know Frosty. Frosty made her ride his dick for twenty minutes, and then he pushed her off him and went another round with the body. It appeared to Ebony that Frosty was fucking the body with more raw intensity than he had fucked her. At the thought, she cried even more because she couldn't even outfuck a corpse. Frosty came again with another cry, and he made her suck his dick again. This time, she couldn't take it, and she threw up her dinner all over Frosty's dick. He smacked her with both hands twice, grabbed her by her ears, and started ramming his dick down her throat at a rapid pace. Ebony was choking and gagging from the harsh treatment. After fifteen minutes of this, he came down her throat. Ebony got up, ran to the bathroom, and locked the door. She curled up and cried herself to sleep for the next five hours until Frosty kicked in the door and started the whole process over again. When he finished, Frosty handcuffed Ebony to the body and slept between them. Ebony woke up that morning and started throwing up at once. The whole room smelled like a morgue. The stink was unbearable. Frosty was fucking the corpse again when she woke up. He let her sniff two bags, and then he uncuffed her and let her use the bathroom. Ebony ran to the toilet and threw her guts up.

$ $ $

P Double and Fatback pulled up outside the biggest house in Durham. One thing P could say about the punk was he had a nice house and good taste. He even liked the kid's style somewhat, until kid acted like a little kid in a candy store, out of line. Now, P Double had to act like an adult, spank the little nigga, and put him on punishment for the rest of his life. P reached into the backseat of his Suburban and grabbed a large duffel bag. He opened it up and pulled out a platinum AK-47 with a solid-gold clip. P even had gold bullets with the iced-out tips.

Fatback looked at his man like "That's just fucking ridiculous, P."

Back really went crazy when P said, "Every bullet cost a hundred and ten bucks."

Then P had the nerve to have an extended clip that carried a hundred and fifty rounds. He slapped the extended clip in, and he handed Fatback the duffel bag. Inside was its identical twin. Fatback smiled like a little kid going to Disney World for the first time.

"You know we gotta ride the same, daddy," P Double said, "or not at all."

Both men strapped on their bulletproof vests and got ready to exterminate a big rodent. Back walked up to the front door and said, "The only way to enter the door is the hard way."

They looked at each other and stepped back before they kicked it at the same time. Both men slid in, ready to drop everything moving.

Back said, "I'll take the top, my nigga. You take the legs, meaning the bottom."

P Double crept around the bottom floor, exploring every room, only to find no one. As soon as he put one foot on the stairs, he heard a number of gunshots.

$ $ $

Fatback eased up the stairs very quietly and opened the first door he saw. Nothing was inside but a spare bedroom. Back checked three more rooms, and he started to gag. Something smelled terrible up there. Fatback opened another door and caught eight nine-millimeter rounds in his chest and stomach. The impact knocked the man unconscious as Frosty laughed at the bogus attack.

Ebony let out an earth-shattering scream when she saw the man fall down and die. Frosty smacked her with one of the Tech 9s in his hand to silence the dumb dame. Ebony dropped right next to the very deceased Mrs. Jackson in an unconscious state. Frosty got smart, because he figured he dropped one cat and he didn't know how many men P Double brought along for the ride. Frosty opened the window and dropped the twin Techs. He climbed down the oak tree and picked his weapons up. As he ran the fifty yards to his big ten-car garage, he looked up at the second-floor window, and the killas' eyes met in a battle for supremacy. P Double stuck the AK-47 out the window, and he let the weapon jump in his hands as it spit rounds of death near Frosty's feet. Frosty ducked into the garage and jumped into his white Hummer. The Hummer ripped out of the garage, catching a barrage of slugs that shattered its windshield. Frosty laughed as he got the fuck out of Dodge.

$ $ $

When P Double heard the shots, he ran upstairs ready for action. When he got to the top, he almost died from the crazy stench that floated through the second-floor area. P Double looked down the hall and saw his man laid out. He felt his pulse and knew that he was just knocked out. P saw the window open, crept over to it, and saw Frosty trying to enter a garage. P let off half a clip, but Frosty ducked into the garage and bounced out of it in a white Hummer at a rapid pace. P Double let the windshield of the vehicle have it. He knew he missed though, because the powerful SUV kept moving. P Double walked over and felt both women's pulses.

Sweetness's mother was gone while the other lady was still alive. P Double woke back up first. Fatback screamed getting up. He knew his man had cracked ribs. P woke the lady up next, and he told her to get dressed. She had a lot of questions to answer.

CHAPTER 25

THE HUNTED

When P Double, Fatback, and Ebony left the house, they found the Suburban shot up and useless. Ebony said she knew where all the keys were kept. She and P Double jogged to the garage and hopped into Frosty's blue Escalade. P Double picked Fatback up in front of the house. The trio drove straight to Maxton and had everyone meet up at the guesthouse. P gave Ebony her own room in the guesthouse. He told her to take a long, hot bath and a nap. P also got clothing measurements and had Sweetness grab the lady twenty outfits and some boots, shoes, and sneakers to match.

Ebony took a hot bath and reviewed her pitiful life in her head. For some strange reason or another, she was attracted to the wrong kind of nigga. All her life, she got used and abused for all the wrong reasons. Since the man in black who called himself P Double saved her life, she had been given a second chance to cherish life and live it to the fullest extent possible. She found herself wondering about the man who had rescued her from the hell-bent Frosty and wondered if he had the potential to be the same type of animal he was. P Double seemed like he was a born leader, unlike Frosty, who was pushed into this way of life. Ebony found her pussy getting wet just thinking about P Double, the bad boy. She snapped out of her daydream and wondered how she was gonna be able to face Akasha after she had been fucking her man for years now.

$ $ $

Back in Springfield, Massachusetts, Jaynce managed to cop herself a woman's forty-five automatic. She had no problem getting a gun license since she had no record at all. Jaynce got her FID card and went back to the gun store. The first time the owner told her to go get those two items and come back. Now she was the proud owner of a nickel-plated forty-five with a rubber grip. Jaynce called P Double's grandmother to ask her if she needed anything. Mrs. Williams told her to bring some cookies and ice cream from Friendly's for P Double's daughter. Jaynce agreed, but her mind went into overdrive at once when she found out the baby wasn't with Shante.

Jaynce jumped into her pink Range Rover and drove all the way to Colonial Estates, where Shante lived. When she got there, she noticed Shante's car was there. "Yeah, bitch, you wanna act grown? Now I'm gonna show you how a real bitch gets down for hers," she said to herself as she exited the Range Rover. Jaynce pulled out the forty-five and opened the screen door. Before knocking, she tried the door handle and was surprised it was open. She rushed in with the gun, swinging it around wildly, but the living room was empty. Jaynce heard the bed upstairs squeaking and some loud moans. Queen Shante was getting her freak on. Jaynce said, "Yeah, you nasty bitch, the party is over," as she walked up the stairs quietly.

$ $ $

Shante was happy for Mrs. Williams to take little Emani for the weekend. That would give her enough time to get a good dickin'. Lord only knew the last time she had some good dick. She missed her baby's father dearly, but she didn't have time to think about him right then. Shante had one thing and one thing only on her mind, and that was busting a good nut. Damn, this town was a fucking disgrace. So many niggas littered the town, and only a handful could fuck. She flipped through her phone book and found a bunch of disappointments. Just when she was about to give up the hunt, Shante remembered this cat who slid his number to her at Club Escape the other week. She ran to her hamper and dug through it to find the Baby Phat jeans she had had on that night. Sure enough, she found the matchbook cover with the name "Johnny Steel" written on it. She laughed to herself because she asked him why they called him Johnny Steel, and he replied, "I got twelve inches of raw steel to give out."

She laughed and took his number. Shante knew that most cats who bragged about their dick size wound up with a baby dick between their legs. She called Steel and kicked it about some bullshit when she finally said, "Look, nigga. I need some dick. Are you coming or what?"

Of course, Steel said, "Hell, yeah."

Then Shante gave him the address and changed into something more comfortable, which was a pair of thongs and a nightie she had copped from Victoria's Secret. Mr. Steel was there in fifteen minutes flat. He was six feet four inches and remarkably cut. To Shante, he wasn't no fine-ass nigga. He just had a piece of meat that she wanted. She snatched him by his hand and said, "Follow me, big boy." And they maneuvered up to the second-floor bedroom.

Steel undressed while Shante was acting like a USDA beef inspector waiting to inspect the beef sirloin Johnny claimed he was packing. Johnny whipped his member out, and sure enough, Shante licked her sexy lips and mumbled, "Approved."

She lay back on the bed and said, "Taste it first, big boy."

Steel got on all fours and sopped Shante up with a biscuit. Shante moaned with delight as her cupcake creamed in his mouth multiple times. Steel strapped up his big submarine and got ready to sink a battleship. He entered her slowly to see how much dick Shante could take before the damsel tapped out. Surprisingly, she took a good amount. At first, they moved to the same rhythm, looking into each other's eyes with sheer, raw intensity. Then Steel said, "Fuck this shit," and he started drilling for oil. Shante's pussy gushed hot fudge as the twelve-inch submarine attacked. Steel pulled out and said, "Fuck this. Assume the position, ma."

Shante got on all fours, and Steel got behind her and pounded away. From the way he was fucking her, you could've sworn someone was being tortured from all the screaming she was doing. Both of them were drenched in sweat.

$ $ $

When Jaynce crept up on the porn session, Steel let out an inhuman moan as his steel rod turned out some hot steel. Jaynce ran into the bedroom and smacked Shante in the head twice with the forty-five. Steel pulled out and said, "Oh shit," still filling the condom with the pleasure of his conquest. He was about to try to grab Jaynce, but she pointed the barrel of the big forty-five at his member, and he begged her, "Please don't shoot it."

Jaynce let off a warning shot, and Steel grabbed his clothes and screamed like a bitch on his way out the door. Shante's head was split from the damage of the two smacks from the large cannon. As soon as she tried to recover, Jaynce was on her, beating her savagely. "You wanna try and kill a bitch, huh? You nasty bitch. What's up now?" she said as she hit the younger woman ten more times with the gun.

Shante's whole face was bloody as she lay there facedown and ass up, unconscious. Jaynce spit on her and left, exhausted from the beating she had given the other woman. She jumped into the Range Rover and drove straight past flashing police lights. She laughed because she knew the bitch-ass nigga who had been fucking the shit out of Shante had called the police. Jaynce didn't drive home. She went to Friendly's and took her bloody jacket off. Then she went to visit Grandma like nothing had ever happened.

$ $ $

Back in North Carolina, things got real crazy when Sweetness came back from shopping for Ebony. Sweetness started flying the coop.

"P, you better not be trying to fuck that skank bitch because it will be two dead muthafuckas up in here, and I mean that shit."

P Double just laughed at the beauty and said, "Never that, ma. Calm down, baby girl."

"Take me for a fucking joke if you want to. Damn it. I just lost the only two people I ever loved on this earth, and I'll be damned if I lose you to some fucking scalleywag. You ain't leaving me this time unless you're dead or in jail, and I still ain't going for either one of those ultimatums, ya heard."

Sweetness started shedding tears a hundred miles a minute. P Double hugged his superwoman and said, "Baby, we're gonna be together forever.

I promise, love." And they kissed. Now go and give that shorty that gear so I can get the heads-up on Frosty. While you go do that real quick, I'll make the funeral arrangements for your mother so the services can happen the same day as your father's."

Sweetness wiped her eyes and hugged her man. She jumped in the purple Escalade and brought Miss Ebony her items at the guesthouse. She walked into the foyer, and most of P Double's boys were smoking some dro and bumping some Jay-Z while a couple of them were shooting pool in the living room.

"Which room is that skank ho in?" Sweetness asked.

"All the way down the hall on your right. Second floor," Fatback said.

Sweetness closed the door and lugged five bags upstairs. There were still twenty more in the truck. She got there, knocked on the door, and entered. Ebony was trying to put herself back together again when Akasha walked into the bedroom.

"So you're the dame Frosty was fucking while he was with me, huh? The stupid muthafucka should've chose better."

Ebony admired the other woman's beauty and brains, but there was no way she was gonna let the next bitch disrespect her gangsta in any kind of way whatsoever.

"In a way, he did, Miss Thang. If you were treating your man like he wanted to be treated in the first place, he wouldn't of been sucking my pussy. Now would he?"

Ebony rolled her eyes at Sweetness and went back to work on herself. "Bitch, Frosty wouldn't eat your skank ass if you scrubbed yourself with all the Bath and Body Works in the world, skank ho," Sweetness said, snapping her fingers.

"Shit, I'm sure Frosty or P Double ain't eating that big ass. Ill, it look like it stink."

That was when Akasha flew the coop and snatched Ebony up, and they started banging. Fatback slowly walked upstairs when Sweetness made that skank ho comment downstairs. He already knew there was animosity between the two. So when he saw the room torn up and them banging, it was no surprise to him at all. He watched Sweetness give it to the older woman a little bit more before he broke the fight up.

Fatback snatched Akasha up off of Ebony. And he dragged her downstairs kicking and screaming. P walked through the door and said, "What the fuck? I thought I told you not to start no bullshit."

Sweetness said, "Man, that bitch wanna play games? Well, I ain't the fucking one." And she started shedding tears.

Everybody came out of the living room, wondering what was going on. P told Sweetness to go to the crib and chill out. He would update her on a later note. She agreed, but she said, "If you go near that bitch, Presley, I'll kill both of you."

They kissed, and Kev helped get the rest of Ebony's bags out of the SUV. Fatback laughed and said, "Akasha was giving that bitch the business when I went up there." He grabbed his ribs and added, "She worked me over too."

P Double and Fatback took the rest of the bags upstairs and sat down on the disheveled bed. Ebony had all kinds of tissues in her nose when they went up there.

"You need to control that crazy maniac bitch of yours because she's out of control."

P laughed and replied, "Sweetness just had a lot of pent-up frustration in her. I'm sorry about that, but you got my word that, that shit won't happen again. Now I'm gonna give you a job and take care of you, but you gotta tell us everything and where you think Frosty could be hiding."

Ebony let out a deep breath like she had been waiting to exhale for a minute now. She ran down her whole life story from how she met Frosty to how she made him start abusing his own product with her. She ran everything down until Frosty came home with the dead body. Ebony burst into tears recalling the sick memory of what the love of her life had made her do. After a little bit of pampering, she finally let it all out.

Fatback said, "Man, that's some sick, twisted shit."

P said, "Okay, Ebony, where do you think we can find Mr. Frost?"

Ebony broke down the two trailers he took her to one time and how he had keys to her house and made her move in with him.

Fatback looked at P and Ebony and said, "Let's ride. We're wasting valuable time as we speak."

$ $ $

Frosty went crazy when he called up the rest of the Horsemen only to come up empty-handed. He laughed to himself because he knew it was a wrap for his crew. He had underestimated P Double by far, and now he was paying the price for it. Frosty reached into his pocket to grab some dope to sniff only to find out he had no more bags. Fuck it. He still had fifty kilos of China white left. Frosty opened Ebony's closet and grabbed a fresh brick of product. He threw the kilo on the table and tried to rip the shit open. Frustrated because the package wouldn't rip, he pulled out his trusty Glock 40, Riffraff, and shot the kilo twice. Raw dope flew everywhere on the table. Frosty walked into a dust cloud and inhaled the fumes. The fumes alone had him doing the Micheal Jackson lean like in "Smooth Criminal." Of course, that was what Frosty was anyway, a smooth criminal.

Frosty finally came out of the nod and ripped the rest of the package open. He knew the poison was too powerful to just sniff straight up raw, but he didn't give a fuck. Who the hell had time to actually sit down and cut some pure dope? Frosty did a Tony Montana move, put his nose to the desk, and inhaled like a vacuum. He dropped to one knee and jumped up, only to fall back into the luxury recliner. He flew into an immediate nod at once. Frosty saw all the way back to when he came out of his mother's womb to the present. Dope was his livelihood. Frosty opened his eyes only to hear an old-school song in his head. "I'm your momma, I'm your daddy, I'm that nigga in the attic, I'm your brother when you need, have some coke." Frosty found himself bopping to the imaginary tune. He knew these were his last days, but he vowed to go out with a bang, and he didn't mean a little one either.

$ $ $

P Double loaded the clip to his platinum AK-47, and he slapped on his bulletproof vest. Frosty had caused him a lot of pain and suffering, not to mention the money. P already knew after he finished with Frosty, he was gonna have to fight a bigger war, and that was with Tanto.

"Back, I think you should stay here and rest up, my nigga." P spoke, already knowing the answer to that statement.

"Are you fucking crazy? That clown-ass nigga tried to take me up off of here. I'll be damned if I let y'all ride without the kid," Fatback stated, meaning every single word.

P Double said, "This is what's going down. Flowie and A-dog, y'all hit the first trailer while Kev and Darris hit the other one. Fatback and I are gonna hit the house up. We'll all meet back here and discuss profit sharing. Everyone agree to this?"

They all nodded and went back to Durham to wreak havoc.

$ $ $

Flowie and A-Dog noticed there were no cars around the trailer. Even though they didn't see any cars, the duo proceeded with sheer caution. Flowie crept up the stairs and put his ear to the door to see if he could hear anything. Neither one of them saw or heard anything, so A-Dog shot the door locks up with the silenced Calico. Flowie opened the door and was about to walk in when a big-ass pit leaped at him out of the blue. Big Flow met the dog with a solid punch to its nose rendering it unconscious. Flowie wasn't prepared for the other two beasts that jumped on both of his forearms. Flow tried to swing both of the sixty-five pound females off him. But they both had their jaws locked on the big man's arms, shaking their massive heads back and forth. A-dog put two slugs in the white-and-black pit attached to Flowie's right arm, but the animal seemed to take the slugs and smile. Neither man knew Frosty had the animals on a dope diet. Every time he fed them, he would lace their food with some dope. A-Dog gave the beast two head shots and the other animal three. Neither one released their hold even after death. A-Dog had to pry their mouths open with both hands.

Flow said, "Kill that other muthafucka before it wakes up. Damn ole boy must have these shits on steroids."

A-Dog pumped the other beast with a three-round burst, stopping its snoring. Both men entered the trailer covering their noses. There was dog shit everywhere. The trailer was empty besides three cardboard boxes with money stuffed in them. "Bingo! We hit the jackpot once again," A-Dog said.

"Remind me to kiss my cousin for making this a rich experience," Flowie added. Flow ripped a sheet and tied it around each arm. Both men hoped the rest of the crew came up as well.

$ $ $

Darris chambered a round in the silenced submachine gun. Like his older brother, he had a fetish for beautiful women and guns that spit rapidly and held a lot of slugs.

Kev said, "I think it's empty, my nigga, but this bitch-ass nigga might be the quiet type."

Darris said, "So are these slugs he's gonna catch if he's up in this bitch."

Kev said. "On three, I'm gonna shoot the locks," and he opened the door and got the fuck out of the way. Kev put five slugs in the door, and then he pulled it back. Three wild and vicious pit bulls jumped through the door, trying to get their powerful jaws on anything. Darris let the Uzi rattle in his palms. He dropped two of the beasts, but the other one locked on his arm. Darris dropped the weapon and started punching the fuck out of the dog. But the shit still wouldn't release its hold. Kev pumped five fifty-caliber slugs in the brute. Darris pulled the beast off him, and then he picked up his gun and emptied the rest of the clip in the hound from hell. Darris slapped another magazine in the gun, and then he pulled the bolt back, chambering another round in the death machine.

"I know that muthafucka better not be in there because I'm gonna kill his ass very slowly," Darris said before entering the trailer. All they found was dog shit and three cardboard boxes stuffed with cash.

$ $ $

P Double told Fatback to take the back while he took the front. Each of the thugs waited one minute before they kicked in the door with guns ready to blaze. P entered the living room not seeing a soul, while Fatback came through the kitchen. The men met in the hallway, and one said, "We stick together this trip."

Fatback kicked in the doors. P was ready to clear shit out. Fatback opened the basement door, and three massive pit bulls rushed both men. P Double and Fatback opened up on the dogs with both AK-47s blowing brains and guts all over the place. It was time to check the last room before they hit the basement.

$ $ $

Frosty woke up out of his nod to hear machine guns rattle. He knew the thugs came for his life, but he wasn't ready to give it to them without a fight. Frosty snatched up both Techs and ducked behind the recliner just as Fatback kicked the door. Frosty let the twins rip. P Double caught a couple of slugs in the vest, but he let the AK show his anger for him as they went through the recliner and found their mark, exiting Frosty as well. Fatback moved P out of the way and let his machine rip. Frosty dove and let the twins spit again, hitting Fatback in the chestplate and knocking the thug back against the wall.

P Double emptied the rest of the clip into the desk, and he reloaded.

Frosty yelled, "You stole my bitch. Now you wanna steal my life? Well, let's do this muthafucka 'cause Frosty plays rough." He let his weapon spit in the hallway.

Fatback and P heard his bolt click, and they knew this was their chance. They riddled Frosty's body with at least thirty shots, and he still managed to grab his forty cal and fire two shots that laced P Double in the leg. P Double and Back left their fingers on the triggers as Frosty did his dance of death. Frosty fell on the desk and took a powerful sniff of his dope one last time. He looked up and smiled, showing his million-dollar dental job, when P sent two 7.62-millimeter rounds that split Frosty's head in half like a grapefruit. P limped into the room and emptied the rest of the clip in Frosty, making sure the toughest foe he had ever faced was gone.

P and Fatback searched the closet in the room and found forty-nine bricks of China white. They searched the basement and found ten cardboard boxes all filled with big faces.

"At least there was some kind of reward for taking this nigga out." Fatback laughed in pain from taking more slugs in his vest.

P Double tied a cloth around his leg to stop the bleeding. They drove back to Maxton on eggshells. There was enough dope in the car to send them to jail for eight life sentences.

CHAPTER 26

CAN'T ESCAPE TRAGEDY

When they got back to the crib, Fatback and P told the men to split what they had found among themselves. The four men were so greedy they didn't realize that Fatback and P Double didn't want a share of their earnings for a reason. They had found the motherload while the pups found scraps.

"Anytime you need me, cuz, for any legwork, just holla, my nigga," Kev said. "I'm going to Baltimore to set up shop. Anytime you need to holla, you got my one-eight-hundred-piece holla."

Fatback and Darris both agreed they were going back home together. Back told P Double to hold his share and that he'd be down again in a short while. The two men were hugging each other when Fatback's Nextel chirped. He answered it and looked at the don with a sad look in his eyes. He asked if she had made bail yet. The whole time P wanted to know what the deal was. Fatback hung up and told his man that his wife got locked up for pistol-whipping his baby's mother. Fatback told P Double not to worry about a thing. He would straighten everything out as soon as he touched down. Meanwhile, they had to find a new coke connect, because both men knew Tanto was out of the equation.

"Don't I always come through in the clutch, my nigga?" P Double smiled.

"You wouldn't be that nigga if you didn't, big boy," Fatback acknowledged, giving his man dap once again. "Just tell my wife I love her and make sure you get her up out of that bullshit. Tell Shante she better cut the shit, and tell her I love her too."

Fatback laughed and said, "You and these chicks are a real live mess."

A-Dog walked in and was like, "I guess it's just you and me playa. Fuck the field. North Carolina's got some good money and some thick women. I'll be back later. I'm going to explore the South more."

P Double's whole team left on that note, leaving him to do some serious thinking.

$ $ $

A week went by before Fatback hit P Double back. Jaynce told him to tell P that she was sorry for getting out of control, but the little bitch had it coming anyways. Back then broke down the story of how Shante had tried to kill her a couple of days before she took action into her own hands. P got kind of angry when Fatback told him Shante had twelve inches in her when Jaynce walked in and pistol-whipped the younger woman. Jaynce said the only reason she went to the crib like that was because his daughter was at his grandmother's house. Fatback told him that at four o'clock sharp, Jaynce was gonna go to the Springfield Library and get on the internet.

"She wants you to go to the nearest Kinko's so she can holla at you over the internet. Just log on to '4-everyour. com,' and holla at Shayla. Use the name Peter Diamond, and she'll know it's you."

Fatback said, "By the way, Shante said she'll let your old lady ride for a cool million dollars and a good dickin' down, and that's the extent of it."

"Tell that stupid bitch she better stop playing fucking games with me," P Double said with straight malice in his voice.

"Yo, I'm down to ten blocks, my nigga. What's good with a wholesale connect, daddy?" Fatback expressed with concern.

"I told you I'm on it already. Just relax, and let me work my magic. Meanwhile, I gotta couple sales for this shit. At a hundred stacks, we can't go wrong."

P expressed, "Yeah, but I don't wanna lose my edge, period. Just stay safe, and don't be a stranger."

They both said, "One love," and broke the connection.

P Double phoned the guesthouse and told Miss Ebony he needed to see her at once. They met outside by the lake on the docks. "Listen, Ebony, I already know about the dope habit and all. But I need you to kick that bogus habit so you can manage my club, sweetheart. I'm trying to turn Thong Island into a franchise, love. I want one in every major city of the world. Now, if you don't wanna go into rehab and handle that order, I can always give you a quarter of a million dollars and let you do you. But, of course, I think you'll make out better in the long run if you do things the other way. But, love, it's up to you."

Ebony let the tears roll down her face as she looked her savior in the face and asked him, "Why are you doing all of this for me? I mean, why do you even care?"

P Double looked at the beautiful damsel and said, "Because a lot of other cats would look at your beauty and would want you as an exotic piece of ass. Me, I see growth and potential for a beautiful woman who is strong and smart and should've been on top of her game. All I'm doing is giving you a little boost; that's all."

She hugged the don and said, "Thank you for the job and trusting in me."

P said, "Now you know this is a lifetime commitment."

She smiled and said, "I wouldn't want it no other way."

Next, P Double called around and found a private rehab called Sunshine House. It was a ninety-day program. He sent Ebony on her way the same day. He was all alone now. Sweetness left a week before to go mourn with her family. Plus, P Double couldn't attend the funeral anyway, because when people got brutally murdered like that, police attended the funeral to see if the killers or killer or anybody out of place would attend.

P Double drowned himself in a bottle of Hennessy and a Cuban cigar. He inserted the movie *Hoodlum* and jumped into his hot tub to think. Jack Tripper and his cousin Tommy were very valuable assets in his hustle game. With them gone, he either had to handle a lot of the work himself or draft a couple of hungry niggas who had hustle to his team. To P Double, that was a very important ingredient you had to have in order to rock with him.

Nowadays, there were so many fake Willy niggas that it was crazy. Some people got hit with weight and sold weight all their life. That wasn't a hustler in his book. A hustler was a cat who stood on the corner, all year round, breaking down twenties, dimes, and fifties to reach his goal. That was the way he started. All of those other cats were spoon-fed muthafuckas he didn't respect at all. P was watching Bumpy Johnson fight for his set when he passed out in the Jacuzzi. P Double was dreaming he was Bumpy Johnson and that he had to protect his set from Dutch Shultz, when he felt someone tapping him. P woke up with ten infrared beams on his face and body.

At first, he thought Tanto had called in the goon squad until a sharply dressed Colombian cat came out of the shadows. "So this is the man that they call P Double, who cost me millions." The Colombian spoke in a heavy accent.

P said, "You know who the fuck I am, but I don't know who the fuck you are."

"That is so, so correct, Mr. Williams. Allow me to introduce myself. I'm Don Omar Fabian Ochoa from the Ochoa family."

P Double laughed and said, "Nah, I never heard of you."

One of the armed men gun-butted P Double and said, "You never disrespect the don, you fucking peasant."

P jumped out of the tub, ready to swing on the man until he saw the five beams drop to his private parts while five stayed on his face.

Don Omar threw P one of his custom-made towels that had "P Double" inscribed on the fabric. "Please get dressed, Presley; then we can continue this conversation further. By the way, please don't try to run or escape because I have men covering every secret passageway you had built in this house. I also know you like to kill, but don't think about that either, because my guerrillas are trained to do the same except they're highly skilled," he said, puffing on his Cuban cigar.

P Double had never felt so helpless in his life. Whoever this cat was, he smelled like serious money. All P could do was get dressed and listen.

P put on a Rocawear sweatsuit and poured himself a glass of Hennessy. He offered the don a drink, but the man declined saying he didn't believe in drinking cheap liquor. "Now, my boy, Mr. Frosty was a little pawn in my organization, but he made me ten million dollars a month. That's four hundred kilos of pure China white he used to move for me and my brother every month."

P said, "That's it. And I thought Frosty had some serious cake." P laughed.

"Well, Mr. Williams, I'm glad you think it is so easy to move more because you have the job now," Don Omar said. "You fucking muranos got so much fucking pride that it gets your nigger asses killed every fucking time. You have no fucking choice in the matter whatsoever. You see, Presley, if you thought Frosty was heartless, you haven't met a pissed off Colombian who will kill your whole family—your wife, Jaynce; your girlfriend, Sweetness; your pretty little daughter; even your grandmother. Do I need to say more? Now, since you think you can handle more than Frosty. There's gonna be eight hundred kilos of pure China white dropped off here in two days. I want my money a month from then. Is there anything else I can help you with, Presley?"

P said, "Fuck," to himself. He took out a problem, and then he took on another one, but then a light bulb went off in his head. This cat sitting in front of him might be the answer to his prayers. P just had to play his cards right. They were already dealt; he just had to play them correctly. P said, "You know what, Mr. Ochoa? P Double doesn't bow down to no mortal being. So all that 'I'll kill your family' and all that other bullshit, it really means nothing to me because that already been tried and done. The only thing I bow down to is the almighty American dollar bill. That's what I live every day for. My blood is made up of money, Mr. Ochoa. My fucking heart is a big face, and it pumps the little faces around my body. But since I'm a hustler before being a businessman, I'm gonna accept your offer, but on certain conditions," P said.

"And what are those, Mr. Williams?"

"Well, I need some pure cocaine as well. Since you know everything about me, you should know my connect for coco is kind of distraught and angry right now. And I wanna be the distributor for all the cats you got in this country," P said lying back.

"Well, that's a small order, Presley. I thought you wanted me to give you the world." Don Omar laughed. "But, seriously, I've been watching you very closely ever since you started copping from Tanto. I guess you have put two and two together by now, and you know that you've been moving my work already. I've noticed that you cop more and more coco every time and that you'll do anything to retain your riches. Your heart is the size of the universe and as cold as nitro glycerin. You're a born leader, P Double, and I see a lot of you in myself. But if you ever try to fuck me, I'll fuck you even slower and harder than you can imagine. By the way, your wish is granted. In two days, I'll drop you three tons of China white and six tons of coco. Make sure you have somewhere to store it by the way. I will also send you a list of people all over the country, like you asked. All shorts are on you. The ball is in your court, P Double. Make sure you bring the championship home. Now, Frosty also owed me ten million dollars. Please have that ready for me on delivery. By the way, I'll tell Tanto to charge it to the game, but watch your back anyways. I hope you can handle him because you're gonna be supplying him. I'll be in touch."

Don Omar got up to leave, and P said, "Hold up. Thank you, sir."

Then P punched the fuck out of the man who gun-butted him. The man dropped, and P took out a two-shot Dillinger and pumped both shots into the man.

"Nobody puts their hands on Don P and lives, nigga. Och, grab your man on the way out," P said.

Don Omar laughed and said, "That's why I like you." Then he shouted something in Spanish and the rest of the guerrillas carried the man out.

$ $ $

P Double called Fatback and hit him with the news. Both men laughed and cried at the same time. It was hard for them to realize how far they had come. It seemed like yesterday. They were both on Bristol Street with the same dream they were about to live. Fatback told his man he was going to Dunmoreland Street to gamble with the Jamaicans. He would meet P in a couple of days, so they could celebrate their newfound wealth. That night, Sweetness came home, and he told her he was about to really become a vintage don. He told her to open her hand and hold it out. P Double put a platinum chain in her hand with an iced-out spinning globe. Each continent had diamonds of a different color.

"Baby, now we got the whole world in our fucking hands. Next, it will be the universe."

Sweetness hugged P Double and shed tears. "I love you so much, baby. I'd give you the universe if I could, daddy."

Young P wiped his queen's face and said, "You and the world are enough for right now, baby girl."

Sweetness looked at P and said, "Baby, make love to me."

P laughed and said, "I thought you would never ask."

$ $ $

The next morning in Madrid, Don Omar met his twin brother, Angel, out on their sundeck for breakfast. Don Omar had newspapers from around the world in front of him. He had just taken a bite out of his poached salmon when his brother said, "Omar, are you sure you trust this peasant of a man, or should I say, kid, to run all of our affairs over in North America?"

Omar laughed at his brother's insecurity in his decision. "Of course I trust him. I've been watching this kid for a long time now. He takes no bullshit always, and his mind is on the most important thing in the world."

"And what's that, Omar?"

"Money, of course. You see, all the other people we supply don't have the drive this young man has. Not none of them whatsoever. He's a fucking stallion, Angel. Trust me."

Angel took a sip of his coffee and said, "Well, whatever you say, bro, but I'm telling you now. Muranos tend to get out of line when they hit the limelight."

Omar shook his head and said, "Not this one here. Trust me. He's gonna be our meal ticket for a long time to come. But if he does become a health hazard, I'll take care of him personally. But for the time being, Angel, I need you to contact that mole you have at FBI headquarters and tell them to lose whatever evidence they have on Presley Williams and his codefendant Ivory Downing. That way, our boy can have a fresh start. The evidence they have on P Double is bogus, but they have his codefendant by the balls. So in order to keep—"

Angel finished off the rest of the sentence for his twin. "The ball rolling we need to skip the intermission."

Omar smiled and said, "Exactly. Oh and call Tanto and tell him we don't want no problems with our racehorse."

Angel laughed. "He has a problem with Tanto?"

"So it seems our horse was fucking the old man's daughter until Mr. Frosty killed her, and P got rid of him. Now, of course, the old man wants retribution but not this time."

Angel said, "Your man seems to be more problems than he is finance."

"Well, brother, looks are deceiving," Omar said after another bite of his salmon.

"Okay, brother, I'll get on it right after we eat," Angel replied. And the rest of their meal was spent talking about the stock market.

$ $ $

P Double walked out of Kinko's happy and sad at the same time. He was happy because he finally got to talk to his wife, even though it was over the internet. A void in his heart was filled with that alone, but it was time he had a one-on-one with his whole family back home, but he didn't know how he was gonna make that happen and duck the alphabet boys at the same time. P Double just drove around town stressed until he found himself at the package store. He bought a half gallon of Hennessy to soak his problems into. By the time the platinum Porsche turned into his driveway, half the bottle was gone. P raced up the driveway with a need for speed. He crashed into his rose garden, but what the fuck? It could be replaced. P Double rolled out of the car, falling and staggering until he made it into the house. As soon as he walked in, he fell, and the half gallon of yak hit the floor with a loud crash.

Akasha heard the noise and ran downstairs. "What the fuck are you doing, Presley? Okay, hell no, I know you ain't been out all day and walk up in this bitch drunk?" She held her man up and walked him to the elevator since he was too drunk to take the stairs.

As soon as she got him to the bedroom, she took his jeans off and saw that he was rock hard. "I know your bitch ass better not had been fucking, Presley Williams, or I'm gonna kill your stupid ass, I swear." She pulled his boxer briefs down and smelled his dick. Satisfied that he wasn't out fucking, Akasha threw his dick into her mouth and went to work. As soon as she gave P's dick CPR, the don responded to the mouth to mouth by taking his shirt off. Sweetness stopped and took her purple-silk Victoria's Secret negligee off with her thong, and she jumped on the hard muscle and rode her wave to nutting. P grabbed her massive ass and fucked back, letting Akasha know that he was brought back to life. P grabbed her waist and rolled her over. He pounded the beautiful sirloin steak under him like he was a human meat tenderizer. Sweetness loved when P fucked her with raw intensity that showed his animal attraction for the goddess. They both grunted and moaned as they went at it like two animals in heat. P pulled out and told her to bend over. When she bent over and arched her ass up in the air, P had to admire the work of art. Her ass looked like Mount Everest and Mount Rushmore. P Double grabbed the monstrous ass and spread it apart like Christ did the sea, and he slapped every inch he had in the chocolate bunny. Sweetness screamed and tried to jerk forward, but P acted like an angry pit bull and had her lovely ass in lockjaw. The don pumped and pumped until he struck oil. Akasha's sweet pussy gushed like a Texas oil field while P filled her with super unleaded. Akasha fell on the bed and said, "Thank you, daddy," and she passed out while P Double grabbed both of his phones and hit the showers.

P said, "Fuck a shower," turned the Jacuzzi on, and filled it with bubbles. He put *Belly* in the VCR and lit a cigar. Just when he was trying to relax, his phone buzzed, and Moe hit him with the news that Fatback had died on a motorcycle coming from Dunmoreland Street. He took the dreads for a quarter million dollars playing blackjack. The young thug went to go pick Brandy up when a car backed out of their driveway fast, not looking, and hit him. P didn't even wake Sweetness. He jumped in the Lamborghini and ate the road up. P went to his wife's house and cried. Then he got his mind right, hopped into her Range Rover, and sped to Forest Park. He cleaned the safe there out and then the safe in Chicopee. He went to the stash house and grabbed all the money there. P then went to his grandmother's house, threw everything in his giant safe, and sat on it crying. He told Omar that he didn't have any weaknesses, but truthfully, his right-hand man and his grandmother were his weaknesses. P Double would die for his right-hand man any day and then to let him die. Fatback was a true friend. When he died, a part of P died with him. P and Moe put their heads together and planned the best funeral money could buy.

$ $ $

While P was planning the funeral, the Feds were going crazy. They kicked in the Forest Park apartment and found an empty safe there. The same time the Forest Park apartment was being hit, they were hitting up Chicopee and the stash houses. All they found were empty safes. They ran up in Fatback's grandmother's house only to come up empty-handed, as well. The Feds wanted their sixty thousand dollars back, and they weren't gonna stop tearing the town up until they got what they were looking for. They even snatched Brandy up and grilled her for twenty-four hours straight, but she had already told them everything she knew. Next, they brought Agent Marlin, her brother, in and asked him what Fatback did after he copped the bricks off him. Marlin was grilled for hours before they let him go. Agents Willis and Burgen took Marlin to Agawam and told him to get out. Marlin questioned the agent why, but all he got was a busted lip from Willis slapping him in the mouth with the pistol. Marlin opened the door and jumped out quick.

Agents Willis and Burgen hopped out and said, "This is from P Double to you, rat bastard."

And each man placed rounds in the snitch's head. Willis threw his partner an envelope with a hundred thousand dollars in it.

"You get great benefits when you work for the cartel, Mr. Burgen," Agent Willis said, and both men laughed on the way back to Springfield.

$ $ $

Shante heard Presley was in town, and she tried to catch him at his grandmother's house, but she came up short, as usual. He had left not too long before. She let her daughter stay with P Double's grandmother while she drove home. She looked at her face in the mirror and got angry quick. Most of the bruises had gone down, but she still had some scarring. She hated that old bitch Jaynce with a passion. Why the fuck she couldn't find somebody her own age? The ho had to tamper with her bread and butter. Well, not for long. Shante had Jaynce charged with home invasion, assault and battery, assault and battery with a dangerous weapon, and mayhem. She was gonna make sure nobody wanted the bitch by the time she got out of Framingham prison for women. All Presley had to do was kick up a million dollars and some dick, and he could have the old buzzard if he wanted her. Shit, one thing she knew for sure was that Jaynce wasn't gonna be styling and profiling in X-5s and Range Rovers while she was pushing a Jetta. Hell, she was the baby momma and only got the short end of the stick but not this time around. She would make sure of that.

Shante pulled up and went ballistic when she saw the pink Range Rover sitting in front of her crib. She pulled the .380 out of her purse and approached the truck, but nobody was in it. "I know this bitch ain't break in my fucking house?" she said as she opened the door.

She walked in and saw Presley sitting on a bunch of mini sandbag-looking things.

"How the fuck did you get in my house, and where's your bitch?"

P jumped up and said, "Close the door, and shut the fuck up. And she's at home, by the way."

Shante started ranting and raving about how Jaynce was going to jail when P grabbed her and in one swift motion bent her over the couch. P then ripped her panties off and pulled his sweatpants down.

"Get off me, nigga. I ain't fucking your dirty dick ass!" she cried before P Double entered her roughly and pounded away.

"Is this what you want, bitch, huh?" he said as he pulled her hair and fucked her savagely.

"Yes, P, fuck, yes," she moaned, taking the well-deserved pounding. The way P was making her ass clap, you would think she was giving somebody applause.

All you heard was meat smacking together as his body slammed into hers hard and fast. Shante was coming so hard it looked like she was going through convulsions. P snatched his dick out of her and threw Shante on the couch. Shante could barely breathe because she was nutting. P hiked her skirt back up, threw her legs in the air, and went to work. Shante was acting like she was drunk off the dick, because she was shaking her head from side to side, speaking in tongues. P grabbed her face and said, "Look at me!"

Shante opened her eyes and looked at the man she had been in love with for years. P Double acted like he was Count Dracula the way he was trying to fuck the blood out of the dame. Their eyes met in the battle for supremacy, and of course, P Double won because Shante was nutting out of control again. Finally, P Double came with a holla as well, and he made the nympho suck her juices off his muscle. She was sucking his dick with need and hunger when he ripped his dick out of her mouth and pulled his sweats up. Shante looked like a newborn baby who just had her bottle taken from her the way she pouted.

P said, "Your million dollars is right there on the floor. I hope I don't have to hear about you going to court again because you know snitches wind up in ditches."

Shante cried and screamed, "How could you threaten me like this, Presley? I'm your baby's mother."

P looked at the woman like she was common trash and said, "You lost that right when you became a snitch."

She threw one of the sandbags she thought was filled with money at him. P ducked, and the package hit the wall and burst open, spreading white powder everywhere. Shante screamed, "What the fuck is this?"

"It's over a million dollars in cocaine, baby girl. I suggest you sweep that up," he said about to walk out the door.

Shante cried, "But what the fuck am I supposed to do with all this shit?"

"You'll figure it out, love. You're a smart dame." And he left her crying with a hundred kilos of pure cocaine.

$ $ $

The funeral was filled with all types of street dons and divas. Every block in Springfield knew the streets just lost a real nigga. Hancock Street was filled with cars from all over. Everybody showed love to him, even crackheads. The other feins who didn't show up were angry because every crack dealer in Springfield, Massachusetts, was at the funeral, paying homage to a fallen don. P hired the Lox, which was Fatback's favorite rap group to rap at the funeral along with Mary J Blige. P was dipped up in a black Armani suit with a white-and-burgundy tie. He had some white-and-burgundy gators to match. P dressed Fatback up in an all-white Armani suit with a black-and-cream tie and black-and-cream gators to match. Fatback also had his platinum chain on with the iced-out B on it for Bristol Street. He also had his bracelets and earrings on sparkling everywhere. P Double's and Fatback's mother and grandmother were all greeting everyone until the Feds came in screaming, "Freeze! We gotta warrant for Presley Williams."

The crowd of hard heads started going crazy until P grabbed the mic from Jadakiss and told everybody to calm down. "Let these boys do their job, and you pay my man his respect; that's all." He gave Jada back the mic while the Feds read him his rights and brought him in.

$ $ $

They brought him to Ludlow and put him in A-1 with Wheat Lox. Lox told his man how sorry he was for getting him caught in his bullshit. P told his man to relax, and he started kicking it to him about all the shit he had been through in the past year. Then he told him about the new connect.

Lox said, "What good is that gonna do us in here?"

He told his man to relax and be patient. A week later, they went in front of Judge Ponser at US District Court. Ponser dropped the charges on both men due to the fact that the Feds found their key witness slain, so they didn't have any evidence against the men. Even the kilo of coke and the money they found in Lox's house disappeared.

Peogi stood up and said, "This is fucking bullshit," and he ran out of the courtroom.

P whispered to his man, "I told you, my nigga."

Both men walked out of the courtroom with smiles on their faces. Jaynce was in the hallway waiting when they came out. She handed P Double his new chain. It was a platinum link with an iced-out snowflake.

Lox said, "That shit is it right there, baby."

P said, "Yeah, we're about to make it snow out in this bitch."

Jaynce said, "I'm sorry to ruin this celebration, but when were you gonna tell us about this?"

P looked confused and said, "Tell you about what?"

That was when Akasha came from out of the cut and said, "This."

P Double looked at Lox and said, "Oh shit." For the first time in his life, he was at a loss for words.

$ $ $

Tanto had buried his daughter two weeks earlier. Since then, he was just thinking about how to avenge his daughter's brutal death. Then he got a call from Don Angel that almost sent him back to the hospital. He told his son that P Double was their new supplier and that he was guarded by the cartel. The prince went on a monster rage at once, shouting and swearing in Dominican. "Pop, we can't fucking cop from that piece of shit. We'll just have to get shit elsewhere."

Tanto just laughed at the thought. "If we cross the Ochoas in any way, we're dead, Son. Nobody crosses them and lives, nobody. We'll just have to find another way to terminate the problem; that's all. Don't worry, Son. I will have my vengeance."

And both men started forming a plan of action at once.

$ $ $

THE END

CPSIA information can be obtained
at www.ICGtesting.com
Printed in the USA
LVHW020337030221
678219LV00003B/144

9 781480 897403